OWEN

THE BOYS OF CASTLEVIEW COVE - BOOK 3

VH NICOLSON

To Donna,
"I like you just the way you are."

Copyright © 2023 by VH Nicolson

All rights reserved.

Published by: Kristina Fair Publishing Ltd

Owen is a work of fiction. Characters, names, organizations, places, events and incidents are the product of the author's imagination and any resemblance to actual person, living or dead, is entirely coincidental.

No part of this book may be reproduced in any form or by any electronic or mechanical means, including information storage and retrieval systems, without written permission from the author, except for the use of brief quotations in a book review.

Editing by Sarah Baker, The Word Emporium.

Cover image: © Photographer: Ren Saliba

For my Forces friends who became family

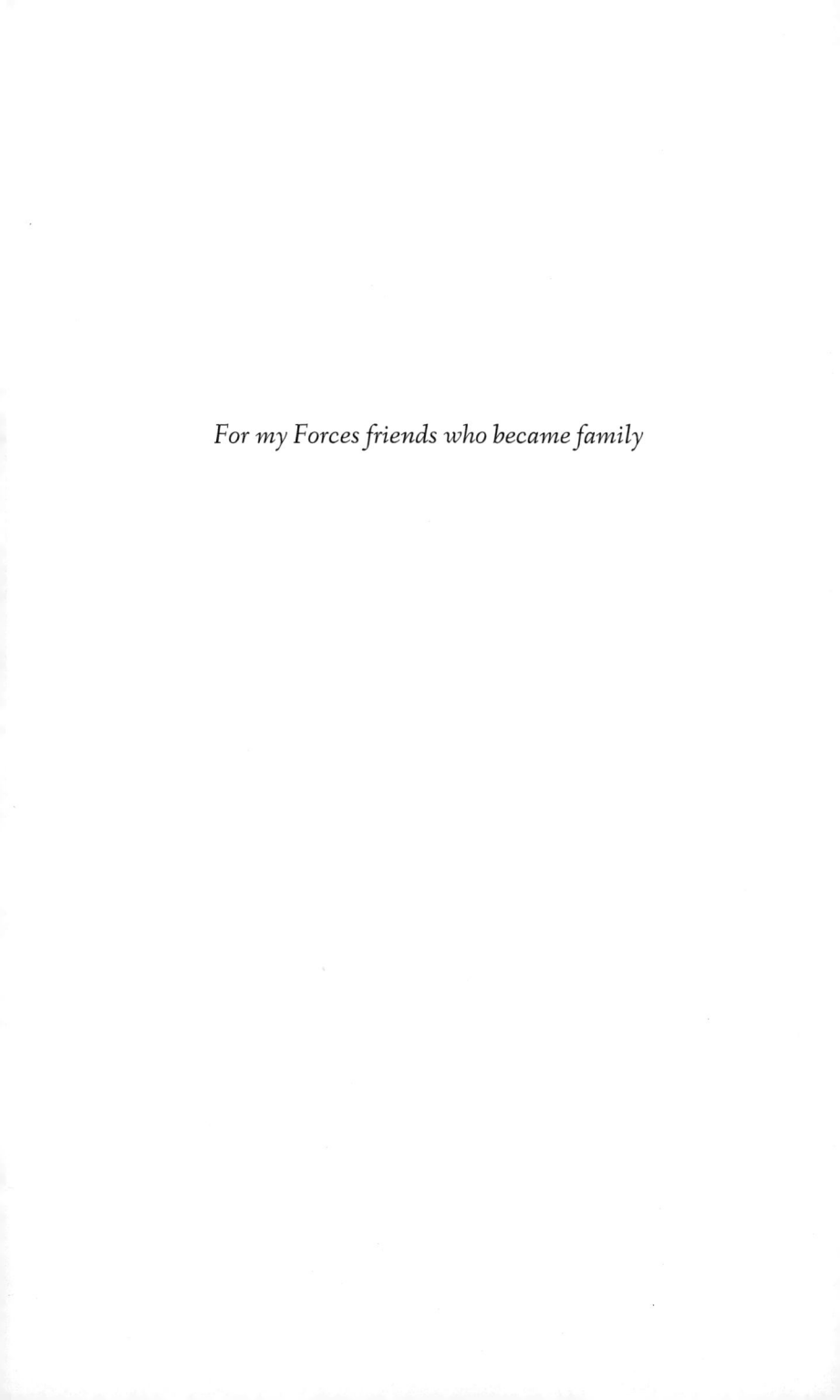

AUTHOR'S NOTES

Please note this book comes with a content warning. This book is intended for over 18s.

My books all come with the guarantee of a happily ever after but sometimes the journey to get there can be a hard fought one. The main focus of my books is love, romance and happiness.

Also, there is lots of humor too. Please keep that in mind.

However, just in case you aren't sure, and if you are a sensitive reader then please proceed with caution, here's a content warning list.

Triggers: Car accident (fatal - happens off the page and not described in detail), plane crash, emotional childhood abuse, runaway groomsman, jilted bride, blackmail, gambling, absent parent, sexual harassment in the workplace.

For Content Warnings & Tropes of All My

AUTHOR'S NOTES

Books, Please Scan the QR Code at the Top of The Author's Note Page.

Please can I ask if any little typos or errors have slipped through the rigorous editing process, to please contact me directly so I can fix these immediately. I pick up every email personally: hello@vhnicolsonauthor.com

Happy reading... let's go...

CHAPTER ONE

Owen

"You've turned a funny color. Are you okay?" My lifelong friend and best man, Lincoln, straightens my pink silk tie.

"It's too tight." I'm almost wheezing as I hook my finger inside the neckline of my baby blue dress shirt and arch my neck in an attempt to loosen it. I'm pretty sure it's self-tightening and trying to strangle me to death. I can't seem to catch my breath since I put the stupid fucking thing on.

Today is my wedding day.

Wedding day. Pfft.

It's supposed to be the happiest day of my life, but all I can think about is ripping off this stupid outfit I've been forced to wear by my future wife, Evangeline, and my mother, and tell them both where to shove it.

They didn't even let me wear a kilt. I'm a Scotsman. By right, on my wedding day, that's exactly what I should be wearing.

But oh no, a kilt wasn't good enough for Evangeline. I had to wear a blue and pink embroidered floral suit, made by some designer prick, specially commissioned for daddy's little princess.

Whatever Evangeline wants, Evangeline gets.

She never wants me to touch her, so I don't.

She never wants me to kiss her, so I don't.

She flinches when I so much as brush against her by mistake, making everything we do together awkward.

If I try to make conversation with her, she chastises me. Mocking me every chance she gets, telling me how stupid I am.

Considering I've put up with my mother's verbal attacks since I was a child, you'd think I would be used to them by now, only I'm not and never will be. Each vicious word out of Evangeline's mouth is like another lash of a whip, opening old emotional wounds, each one cutting deeper than the last.

Playing the *good boy* just as my mother instructed, I've put in all the effort, with Evangeline's family, her friends, even her stupid Persian cat, Angel.

Believe me, that cat is no angel. It may be all white fur and innocent faced but once I move into the new house, it is going to claw me to death in my sleep. I bet it's made a *How to Kill Owen Plan.* I just know it has. It's already had me at the doctors after it bit me, giving me an infection.

Angel is going to kill me off, limb by fucking limb. Just wait and see.

But the killer cat is the least of my problems.

I've tried to make this ridiculous farce of a relationship work for our families. God, have I tried hard.

I even grew my hair longer for her because she said I would look better. Although that's not what she said, her exact words were, *"It'll distract people from your enormous nose."* What the fuck is wrong with my nose? Oh, I know, absolutely nothing. It's my entire face she can't stand looking at.

Knowing how much I messed up with Skye, my girlfriend since high school, I don't want to do that again. I was completely unaware of what a shitty boyfriend I was until Skye *informed* me. Apparently, I let her down time and time again throughout our fourteen-year, on again, off again relationship. Once I knew though, I made a vow to myself to try harder, do better, and be the man I should be for my soon to be wife.

I may have lost Skye and not been the man she needed me to be, but my other best friend, Jacob, knew exactly how to be that man. He stepped up and loves Skye with every bone in his body.

I'm not jealous of them. We were never meant to be. But I am envious of what they have together.

I want love like that.

Love that runs so deep through your veins that you can't think or see straight without it.

Lincoln has that with Violet, and now Jacob with Skye.

Then there is me.

I'm the fuck up in our trifecta. I never seem to do, say, or get anything right.

So, at the age of thirty-one, I'm standing in a floral wedding suit, looking like a prize prick, as if waiting to be summoned to the gallows for execution, to marry someone who can't even bear to look at me. My heart is breaking for a love I'm never going to find and a life that I don't want; *death by an unhappy marriage.*

Yet, through it all, I must put on a show. I will not let anyone see how destroyed I feel.

On the outside, I'm good old jokey Owen, while on the inside, I'm fucking dying.

My body may give out from all the stress that led up to today, because of all the effort I've put into making this relationship work; asking Evangeline out on dates, taking her to fancy restaurants, shopping trips, cocktails on my father's new yacht with her fancy pants, stuck up friends. She's insufferable, moody, and, trust me, I know that at only twenty-one, and ten years my junior, she's still a child, but she's truly a brat. And not in the submissive kind of way I might enjoy. Oh no, she's a full-on immature kid who is every inch the spoiled little princess her parents allowed her to be.

Nothing I've done for her, and I mean none of it, has been or ever will be, good enough.

I'm not good enough.

Something my mother has told me every day since the day I was born.

So, it must be true, right?

My heart feels like it's being eviscerated by the devil's claw as sharp shooting pains rip through my chest, forcing me to bend at the waist while I suck in ragged breaths to ease the discomfort.

I feel Lincoln and Jacob on either side of me, patting my back while telling me that I'm going to be okay.

Only, I'm not okay.

I don't know how the hell I am going to get through today, or the rest of my life for that matter.

Being around Evangeline is deeply unpleasant and tomorrow we move into a house her father bought for us.

How can I live with someone who hates me?

Without knowing a single thing about me?

Because she's never taken the time to ask.

We're simply doing as we're told. Our whole lives are being dictated.

And our parents are the ultimate puppet masters.

What the fuck am I doing?

Every millisecond leading up to this day has made my heart beat slower and, with each decision taken on my behalf, *for the good of the family*, a little more of my soul dies. Marrying Evangeline is simply the icing on the shit-cake that comes from being born a Brodie.

I've always wanted to marry for love, and we *definitely* don't love each other.

This wedding is a complete sham.

A façade.

We are being *forced* to marry one another to 'strengthen and unite our families'... apparently.

Build an empire, bring more Brodie children into the world to carry on the screwed-up legacy. Although I'm not sure how that will happen when she won't even let me hold her hand. Something I'm sure our parents haven't thought about in their grand plan.

Evangeline's family are millionaires, mine are billionaires. Joined through our marriage, our fathers will work together, strike deals, and become the largest printing house in the United Kingdom, printing every newspaper, magazine, and comic strip. My dad has plans to go international and add an indie author publishing arm to the business, and, he informs me, the only way we can do that is through Evangeline's father's contacts. He's well connected, and has already started negotiations, but doesn't have the funds to make it happen. That's where we come in. *He scratches our back; we scratch his.*

So, for today... for the rest of my life... and for my family's sake, I've to fake smile, make small talk with assholes who are only here so they can say that they attended a Brodie wedding, and push my heartbreak so far down it'll rot me from the inside out.

She doesn't love me.

I don't love her.

But we'll pretend we are so deeply in love… for the sake of the family, because I was raised to fulfill their expectations without question.

God, I feel sick.

Within the side room of the church, my two best men, Lincoln and Jacob, help me regain my composure and then try to distract me by laughing and joking around, but I'm lost in my own thoughts remembering a conversation with my mother earlier as we neared the church.

"She's from great stock," she informed me, with her bitter tone and filler-filled face, reminding me, yet again, of the terms of my marriage. She made Evangeline sound like a fucking piece of meat.

Is this what Evangeline wants? To be sold to the highest bidder like a fine painting at an art auction?

I know I certainly never wanted this life.

I feel more nauseous every minute the hand on the clock gets closer to the ceremony.

To be the perfect fiancé, I've been faithful to Evangeline since they announced our engagement, and for the last year, I've thrown myself into work while my bride-to-be planned the *wedding of the year*.

One whole year and no pussy.

This wedding won't break my dry spell either.

I shudder at the thought of consummating our marriage. Don't get me wrong, she's beautiful. Long dark hair and killer legs, with deep hazel eyes that are so dark, they are like a black hole, sucking your soul. Except her beauty is all superficial. Skin deep, that girl is fucking miserable to the core.

Black heart, black soul, and not an ounce of compassion or love for anyone other than herself.

She'll probably tell me I'm shit in bed and to hurry up. She's a bossy bitch, with more emphasis on the bitch part.

My mind wanders down a dark path as I think about my future with her... imagining what our life together will look like.

They'll be no date nights, laughter-filled holidays, or even hand in hand walks along the beach.

She looks at me like I spoiled her whole day by simply breathing the same air she does, and I can't see that changing when we're married.

My best friends, Lincoln and Jacob, see it too and have nicknamed her the ice queen.

They're not wrong.

She radiates 'fuck off and leave me alone' vibes. Even more so than my mother does, and she is the most emotionally detached person I know.

My heart plunges a little deeper into my chest when the enormity of what's about to happen here today sinks in.

My life is heading in the same direction as my parents. Two people who tolerate each other, only having sex to breed heirs. Two people who otherwise have separate lives, separate bedrooms, holidays, and even meals.

They hate each other.

A mirror image of their lives is not something I want.

I can't do this.

"Yes, you can," Lincoln reassures me.

Shit, I didn't mean to say that out loud. I push my shoulders back, pulling fresh air into my lungs.

7

Facing me, he brushes the fabric across my shoulders, then grabs my upper arms in a firm grip. "You've been telling us this is what you want for the last year and it's all going to be okay." A deep *V* forms between his brows, now doubting my words. "I'm sure you'll be fine once you're at the altar saying your vows." Lincoln tries to bolster me, but it doesn't work.

I might vomit or have a heart attack. Either option would be good right now as a way to save me from this horror.

Lincoln stands back, using his pointer finger to motion up and down my outfit. "One thing's for sure. We can have a good laugh at the wedding photos afterward. Your suit is fucking hideous."

Jacob stands shoulder to shoulder with Lincoln, chuckling as they both eye me. "We should hang you up on a wall in your parent's castle. You'll look right at home beside the tapestries in the foyer."

"Oh, fuck off." I roll my eyes and shove my hands into my trouser pockets.

Lincoln punches my shoulder. "It's just as well you're a handsome fucker."

"You look like a human Ken doll. Model material." Jacob throws me a wink.

I let out a heavy sigh. "You two are really fucking enjoying this, aren't you?"

"You don't have to go through with this, Owen." Jacob's face drops, his deep frown letting me know how concerned he is for me, too. "I told you a year ago to cut all ties and find someone who loves you and who you love back. You should have put a stop to this months ago."

Lincoln folds his arms across his body and stands wide. "I know you said it's what you wanted, and we support you. We really do, but it all seems so archaic. Who the fuck marries out of convenience these days? It's barbaric, Owen. They shouldn't be making you do this."

And yet, they are.

Usually the one to be told to shut up, today I'm at a loss for words. I don't know how to respond.

"Well, at least I don't look like pink blancmange," I joke, taking the piss out of their equally dreadful outfits, ignoring the fact my blood is racing through my veins at supersonic speed, making my heart race even faster in my chest.

"I'd like to think of us as two oversized pink cotton candies. We look cute," Lincoln replies sarcastically.

"You look like a pair of dildos," I mutter deadpan.

Jacob looks down at his outfit, then Lincoln's. "We fucking do. But neither of us is getting fucked up the ass. You, on the other hand, are getting fucked up the ass by this farce of a marriage. So, is this it? Live unhappily with the ice queen forever?" The timbre in his voice takes on a serious tone.

On more than several occasions, Jacob and Lincoln have tried to talk me out of marrying Evangeline.

I know they are only trying to protect me because they love me, but they don't understand the implications if I don't marry her.

I remember how my stomach turned when my mother made the terms of our marriage more than clear. I'll lose my inheritance, my home, my car, my job... everything.

As if reading my thoughts, Lincoln says, "It's all materialistic shit. You know that, right? Cars and houses are replaceable. Love and happiness, no amount of money can buy those. You only get one life and you're choosing to live yours in a miserable, loveless marriage."

"I know," I whisper.

"It's not too late to pull out of this, Owen." Lincoln

plonks himself down in the wooden chair behind him. "You're braver than I am. I couldn't do what you're doing today."

I don't feel the least bit brave, Lincoln.

"Do you have savings? Stashed away somewhere your parents can't find it?" Jacob questions, biting his lower lip.

I nod my head slowly. I have the trust money I received when I turned twenty-one, so I have at least five million in savings. I made sure I put that somewhere my mother and father would never find it... in an overseas account.

"So, what the fuck are you doing here, then?"

Not wanting to reply, I shake my head.

"Owen?" Jacob pushes me for an answer.

I pace back and forth as my friends finally ask the questions that need to be answered.

"Because I've never been good enough," I blurt out. "In the eyes of my family, I am not worthy of anyone's time. I'm the fool. The spoiled boy who gets what he wants, regardless." I poke myself in the chest. "All I ever wanted to do was to make my mother happy. But not even the first-class degree I got at university, the contracts I win at work, or that I work longer hours than anyone else at my father's business wins her affection. For once, I thought, just maybe, this..." I point to the door, referencing the wedding ceremony about to take place and the hundreds of guests waiting, all seated in the wooden pews of the giant church. "... would make her love me. Do what she asks of me. Help to strengthen the business. Maybe then I'll be worthy of her love. Just maybe if... if... if I do this... carry on the Brodie empire, do as I'm told..." I pant, gasping for breath like a fish out of water.

My friends look at me like I've grown two heads, then Lincoln says, "Owen, believe me when I say this, and I know this from experience. No matter what I did in my past, or do in my future, it will never change the way my mother feels about me. She abandoned me when I was a baby, and there was nothing me or my father could have done to change the way she felt about me. Instead, I learned to accept her decision, knowing her issues are not a reflection of me. I feel so much better for it." Lincoln pulls himself to his feet and steps in my direction slowly. "You can't do this just because you think this will make her love you. Her shit is her shit. Let her deal with that."

Fuck, I might cry, and I never cry.

Jacob steps forward. "Lincoln is right. Your mother married your father as part of an agreement. You told us they are miserable together, Owen. So are your sister and her husband. Is that what you want? To be unhappy and stuck in a loveless marriage?"

As I go to reply, the wooden door flies open, creaking as it does, and a chirpy, smiling wedding organizer informs us it's time to make our way to the altar.

Ignoring my friends, I storm past them, hoping they get the message to follow me.

I can't face this conversation. It's too late to walk away now, anyway.

It's time to seal my future.

Face to face, I stare at my future wife.

Her stern, almost impassive features show no emotion.

Lincoln and Jacob's words swim around my head, and I realize they're right.

I'm going to spend every day and every night fighting, wrestling, and arguing with my wife; what night we should consummate the marriage, how many times a week we should have sex, how many kids we should have to satisfy our parents, and then we'll end up living in separate wings of that fucking ridiculously oversized house her father bought for us. I don't want to live like that and I sure as hell don't want to bring kids into a life like that... a life I've endured for thirty-one years.

A sharp ringing in my ears deafens me. As if I'm wearing noise-canceling headphones, the minister's voice becomes muffled as the onset of what I am pretty sure is a panic attack takes hold.

Evangeline's mouth moves, but I can't hear what she's saying.

She stiffly holds her hand out. On autopilot I take it, noticing my touch makes her nostrils flare.

She hates me.

I glance over my shoulder at my two best men. They both catch my eye and look at me with concern and sympathy.

Where is all the happiness and laughter? The all-consuming feeling of love and joy?

I want *the one*. The one you simply can't survive without.

I fucking want that.

Looking back at Evangeline. I know she's not happy.

I'm not happy.

My boys are right; no matter what I do, I will never make my mother happy either.

It's a lose-lose situation.

"I can't do this." I release her hand and step back as a look of utter horror washes over Evangeline's face.

Like someone turns off the noise-canceling switch in my ears, I hear the gasps of shock and the murmur of low voices throughout the five hundred guests.

I take another step back, straighten my hideous suit jacket, and turn to face the crowded church.

Eyeing Lincoln, then Jacob, who are both standing taller and prouder, looking at me with admiration on their faces, when Jacob mouths, *'run'*, man do I run.

Past the unbelieving crowd.

Past my mother shouting at me.

Past my father, whose roaring echoes of disappointment follow me out of the church.

I flag down a cab and jump into it, heading to the hotel to pick up my suitcases; the hotel we were supposed to be staying in tonight.

Within minutes, I'm back in the waiting cab with enough clothes to last me a couple of weeks, along with my passport, wallet, and phone.

"Where to now, big man?" asks the broad-accented Scottish taxi driver.

"Airport," I answer with no idea where I will end up and no plan for my future.

All I do know is that I feel better than I have in months.

As if I've been carrying a ten-ton truck around on my shoulders, and now I feel lighter, happier, and able to breathe again.

Then it hits me.

The life I'm walking away from.

The billions I was due to inherit.

Fuck.

I begin to sweat buckets.

Oh Christ, what have I done?

CHAPTER TWO

Owen

A faint scent of chlorine wafts in my direction as the gentle breeze causes the water to slap against the sides of the private pool I'm seated next to.

Squinting under the glaring sun, I look down at the phone in my hand. My gaze landing on the voice messages icon, notifying me of how many I've yet to listen to.

Seven days of ignorance, not knowing or facing the mess I left behind. Seven days of reflecting. Seven days of uncertainty, worrying about what I should do with my life now; the one I ran from. The one I left behind.

The only thing I know is that I will stay here for the next few weeks, or maybe even longer, while I figure out what to do next. *Travel?* Maybe. *Start my own business?* Nah. *Go home to Castleview Cove?* I shudder at the thought; my body's reaction confirming that's a firm *no*.

Like a lighthouse on a foggy night, the red notification icon dot on my phone warns me to stay clear of the voice messages; avoid the shitstorm that I created a week ago.

Although it feels like a lifetime since I called my cousin,

Gregor, from the airport to see where he was currently based. Because of the rift between our families, he was the only one, along with his parents, who didn't get invited to the wedding. He wouldn't have been able to make it anyway due to work commitments.

So, within five hours, I'd landed in Cyprus, two thousand miles away from anyone finding me.

Voice mail after voice mail filled my inbox until it was full.

Choosing not to listen to any, I deleted them as they hit my phone. However, it didn't prevent it filling up again, with what I can only imagine are irate messages from mine and Evangeline's family, so I stopped deleting them. I let it fill up to capacity, so no one can leave any more, and I hit that *block caller* button on my parents' contact details. Not permanently. Just until I decide what my next action will be.

I'm not ready to speak to them. Not yet.

If ever.

Like a strategic move on a chessboard, I'm no longer the pawn, but the ruler of my own destiny, and this time I'm playing to win. To find my queen and be the king of my own goddamn castle—on my terms. Whether my parents like it or not.

Let's hope I can withstand the wrath of my mother, because when she finds me, she'll kill me with her own perfectly manicured claws. I'm certain if my father gave her the nod, she would sink them into my heart first.

Although my mother was never physical with me growing up, choosing verbal abuse as her preferred choice of attack, I may have pushed her too far this time. Even at thirty-one years old, she still talks to me and treats me as if I am a child.

I can't imagine she will ever forgive me for the shame I have cast over the family name.

Do I care? A little.

Do I care about my sanity more than the family business? Right now, absolutely.

Making me flinch, my phone vibrates in my hand. It's a welcome sight to see Lincoln's name on the screen.

Knowing he was going to call, I hit the accept button, uncross my legs, and lay back on the sun lounger, taking refuge from the blazing heat of the sun under the parasol.

"Hey, stranger." Lincoln's familiar dark features and toothy grin come into view.

Cheerily, Violet, Lincoln's American fiancée, appears next to him. "Nice, bronzed abs." She winks cheekily at me, making me chuckle. She likes nothing better than winding Lincoln up and commenting on my body will do just that.

Lincoln teasingly tickles her side, making her squeal, as she hops onto a high seat around their kitchen breakfast island, laying her arms against the dove gray marble worktop as she leans forward.

"You'll pay for that later." Lincoln smacks a kiss on her cheek.

"Hope so." Violet side eyes him as she flicks her dark brown hair over her shoulder.

Jacob appears next, stuffing what looks like Lincoln's grandma's delicious, syrupy baklava into his mouth as he takes a seat, too. Last, Skye, my ex-girlfriend, now Jacob's wife, stands in between Jacob and Violet. It's such a heart-warming sight; to know that regardless, and with no judgment, my four friends love me unconditionally.

Violet looks at me and says, "We've missed you, Owen."

"What, this ugly face with the enormous nose?" I point

to my face, feigning confidence, secretly hoping they don't notice how completely broken I feel inside.

Thinking I'm doing a great job of masking the lack of sleep I've had and exhaustion from working out too much, Jacob declares, "You look like shit."

I sigh and slide my sunglasses that are resting on top of my head downward, pushing them up my nose to hide the deep circles under my eyes. "Can't sleep. It's too hot." My voice deflated, I lie. It's got nothing to do with the heat and they already know that. They can read me like a book, even when I try to hide how I'm feeling. You think I'd be better at it, I've been doing it my whole life.

Skye pulls a gentle smile, looping her arm round Jacob's shoulders. "You can be honest with us, Owen. It's okay to admit you're struggling."

Behind the dark lenses of my sunglasses, I watch Jacob rest his reassuring hand on Skye's swollen, pregnant belly.

While I am over the moon for them, I can't help but feel a small tug of jealousy pull at my heart as I watch Jacob and Skye's love for one another because all it does is highlight the lack of love in my own life.

Will I ever find *the one*?

Waiting for my response, my friends stay silent before I finally admit, "It's my heart and head that are at odds with one another." My chest feels heavy when I say, "Did I do the right thing?"

United, they confirm I did with firm *yeses*, sealing their approval with confident head nods.

"I heard Evangeline was screwing Adam Blumenthal the whole time you were together." I knew Lincoln was desperate to tell me something. I could sense it.

Why does that news not surprise me?

That prick hung around like a foul smell. Thank fuck, I never slept with her.

"Linc," Violet exclaims in shock, slapping the worktop with the palm of her hand. "We talked about this. We agreed to wait and tell Owen later."

His eyes widen, palm up with an open hand in my direction. "He should know now. He has no reason to feel bad about his decision. She wasn't right for Owen, and we all know that." He looks to his left and right.

"I agree," Skye chimes in. "She never wanted the marriage either, Owen, and we all witnessed how much you tried to make it work while you were engaged. We watched you give it your best shot, but she was constantly rude and mean to you. I can't figure out how you lasted as long as you did. We stood by your decision to get married because we care about you, but we could see she wasn't right for you."

"I could *feel* it." Way down in my gut, every time I looked into her empty eyes. I felt her disapproval, despair, and hopelessness; it's how I feel every time I look in the mirror. A duel of sorts, an inner battle of doing your duty to implement the family strategy while sacrificing the things you want the most; approval from your parents, love, and happiness. *A hug.*

I was raised being told those things don't matter because my worth is based on wealth. What I have is more important than the qualities I have as a man.

Skye is right. Evangeline was in the same position, but at least I had the balls to walk away and be faithful to her like the good little pedigree puppy dog my mother trained me to be.

I clear my throat, rubbing my hand over the scruff on my chin. "Anyway, Evangeline, the wedding, none of it matters anymore." The weight on my shoulders instantly feels lighter. "I hope she finds happiness with Adam." If that's what she wants, I genuinely do. I'm just happy knowing she's no longer my responsibility.

The five of us pause for a moment, letting the honesty of what I have said settle between us.

"I'm proud of you," Lincoln says. "You've taken the higher ground."

Jacob leans forward expectantly, as if wanting to ask me something. His body language is obvious. He's worried about me, he wants me home, where he knows I am safe, and he and Lincoln can look after me if I should fall into a downward spiral. Which, for the record, I will not do. Not again. I did it once when I first learned about the deal my father made with Evangeline's father. Turning to liquor for too many nights... who am I kidding, weeks. Searching for a solution to my problems at the bottom of the bottle didn't work. I couldn't drink them away. Knowing how pointless it is, I refuse to do it again.

Confirmation of Evangeline's relationship with Adam is a reassurance of sorts. I know I did the right thing; she would never have been mine and extra-marital affairs make me want to vomit.

"How long are you planning on staying in Cyprus?" Jacob finally asks.

"Gregor is here training for a month, and he's staying in this pretty sweet villa." I thumb over my shoulder in the direction of my large, white temporary home. "The Officer's Mess on the air base is being remodeled, otherwise I wouldn't be able to stay with him, so I may as well take advantage." It's not as if I have anything to go back for. I'm certain I've lost my job with the family business and my gate house home, within the grounds of my parent's estate.

"Gregor has such a cool job." Lincoln looks starry eyed as if imagining himself being a fast jet pilot.

"Epic job," Jacob agrees with Lincoln. "He does that every year, right? Goes out to Cyprus to train?"

"Usually for four weeks, yeah, but he's been here a week longer than everyone else. It was his turn to ensure the accommodation was suitable and organize the hire cars for the team's arrival. Everyone arrives today." Gregor told me that they either come to Cyprus or Greece for their Springhawk training every year because the blue skies and sunshine allow them to practice over and over again. "This is Gregor's last year. He's only assigned to the aerobatic squadron for three years, then he has to return to his permanent fast jet squadron." He was sharing stories with me earlier about all the countries he traveled to, the famous people he's met, and the things he's seen. It makes my life in Castleview Cove look excruciatingly dull.

"What does he do?" Violet scrunches her face up, trying to recall if she already knows the answer.

Much hotter than I expected for this time of year, I wipe the beads of sweat that have formed off my brow and push my sunglasses back up my nose as I reply, "Gregor is an aerobatic pilot in the Royal Air Force." I grab my uncapped bottled water off the side table next to me and take a huge mouthful.

Violet's face lights up. "Does he do all that cool acrobatic stuff for the Royal Family, like the show from the Jubilee celebrations at the palace? With the red, white, and blue smoke?"

"The very one." I lick the cool water off my lips, smirking at how excited Violet gets about all things British. She may be a California girl through and through, but she's embraced Scottish living like a duck to water. Although, she has struggled with the harsh winter temperatures, and I'm certain her love for haggis is still up for debate.

"Wow, I bet he has to fight the women off. What a job." She sighs in awe.

I've witnessed it with my own eyes. It's the best conversation starter to break the ice and the women love his thrill-seeking career.

"Will we see you in four weeks when Gregor returns? Do you reckon you'll come back?" Skye raises her eyebrows inquisitively, and I nod hesitantly, not sure if I will be back. "Or will you stay in Cyprus?" she continues. "Your longer hair does make you look like a beach bum." She pulls a soft smile, lightening the mood. "You'll fit right in."

I rake my fingers through my hair and tuck a strand behind my ear, finally getting used to its new length. The newfound rebel in me may even let it get longer and grow a longer beard, too.

If it's time for a new life and career, then it's time for a new me.

Doing what? Who the hell knows?

Lincoln jumps into the conversation. "Promise us you won't make plans yet. Or make any rash decisions. Wait and see how you feel over the next few weeks and *then* decide, yeah?" The hopeful faces of my four friends look back at me down the camera.

"I promise. If you promise to continue keeping my whereabouts a secret from everyone. I'm not ready to face the firing squad." The heavy sensation that keeps raising its ugly head reappears in my chest. It's as if someone is trying to drag me into the depths of the earth. I don't like it.

Running hasn't helped. Working out hasn't helped. Swimming hundreds of lengths hasn't helped. Nothing does.

"We swear we won't," Lincoln replies firmly.

Unaware of my situation when I arrived in Cyprus, I brought Gregor up to date immediately. He was mad at my father for trying to shackle me to a loveless marriage.

I also saw the gratitude in his eyes. He's grateful that our mothers, who are sisters, don't speak to each other anymore. Relieved that our family businesses don't overlap, or the same fate may have been sealed for him, too.

Following a takeover bid between his father and mine over a decade ago, where they went after the same company, my father severed all ties with Gregor's side of the family. However, against my father's instruction, I secretly chose to keep in touch with them all, specifically Gregor.

I was gutted that my parents didn't let me invite any of my mother's side of the family to the wedding because Gregor is about the closest thing to someone I can call family, and I'm a little envious that, unlike me, he drew the good parent straw.

The opposite of my mother, my Aunt Flora is a kind, warm and caring woman, as is Uncle David. He's a genteel man and Gregor is just like him. It's obvious where he gets his friendly and generous nature from. After all, he's taken me under his wing without question or pressure, making a promise to keep my parents in the dark about my location.

And I doubt my mother would think to contact him, assuming that I no longer speak to him.

Following his obsession with all things flying, at fourteen Gregor began studying for his pilot's license, and by sixteen he was making solo flights.

When his father spotted his natural talent, Gregor joined the Royal Air Force as a training officer, then continued his specialist flying training after that.

Having been gone from Castleview Cove for over

seventeen years, I'm certain my mother has forgotten all about him. She never mentions her family, not ever.

A loud *ding* from the front door alerts me to visitors.

I swivel myself around on the sun lounger then push myself to my feet. "I need to get that." The rest of Gregor's team is arriving today and moving into the surrounding villas within the private compound. "Gregor is out for a run." He's a crazy son of a bitch running in this heat. Running at night or first thing in the morning is way better.

Protecting the soles of my feet from the scorching poolside, I slip them into my navy slides.

"Cool. Keep in touch though, yeah?" Skye calls out as I walk quickly around the pool, into the enormous, air-conditioned white living space, to answer the door.

Almost running now, my slides slap against the marble floor of the hallway, echoing off the sparse Mediterranean style villa, as I exaggerate a loud sigh. "Yes, Mrs. Baxter, I'll stay in touch." A year in, I'm only just getting used to calling Skye by her married name. "Look after my girl, Mr. Baxter." I throw Jacob a cheeky wink.

"Stop saying that. I keep telling you, she's not your girl anymore," Jacob retorts, scowling at me, making everyone around him laugh. I sure do like fucking with him.

"Love you guys." I blow a playful kiss to them all. "Especially you, Skye."

"Mother fuck—" Laughing out loud, I cut the call, then place my phone on top of the cream and gold marble top of the console table.

Still chuckling to myself, I turn the catch on the lock and twist the brass handle, pulling open the heavy walnut door. My laughter instantly dies in my throat, as the glowing sun shines behind a beautiful lion's mane of fiery red hair that's blowing around in the gentle breeze.

I push my sunglasses on top of my head as the silhouette takes one step, and then another toward me. The red halo fades away as the most beautiful woman, with the bluest eyes, comes into clear view. I'm hit hard with an invisible force field; like all the air is punched out of my lungs with a high g-force, making me feel light-headed.

Thinking I must be hallucinating, as this Pre-Raphaelite deity stands before me, I blink twice before I realize she's talking to me.

"Hello." She's waving a hand in front of my face. "Are you okay?"

I shake my head as the words, "So beautiful," run out of my mouth, the skin of my arms now goose bumped, and for a beat, everything else loses its importance.

"I beg your pardon?" her eloquent English accent questions, as she swings a wiggling baby girl around the front of her, then replaces her on top of her other hip.

Pulling my head back, shaking it to wake me up from my daydream, I try to disguise my thinking out loud moment. "Eh, the baby is beautiful." Although she is super cute, it's not what I meant at all. It's the dawn of something new. I feel the shift, as if a veil has been removed, something has changed that I can't quite put my finger on.

Gawd, what the hell is that?

The beautiful woman smiles, lovingly looking down at the baby. "Yes, she is, but she's also a monster." She pinches the baby's cheek playfully, making her babble unformed words, then she turns her attention back to me. Her natural beauty takes my breath away.

"The guy at the security gate said Gregor has our keys. Is he here?" She looks over my shoulder, into the villa, searching for him.

She waits patiently as my brain fails to connect with my mouth.

"Are you okay?" A deep *V* of worry forms between her clear blue gems.

C'mon, man, get it together.

As if jolted back to life, I take a large audible gulp and finally say, "He's out for a run. I have everyone's keys." I turn to pick up several bunches from the sideboard, inwardly cringing that I must look like a buffoon.

I ramble on, "The red set is for villa one. It's the biggest villa, with three bedrooms, and is allocated to his Squadron Leader." I separate that set.

Curious, I ask, "Are you a nanny for one of the team members?" I feel compelled to find out everything about her, secretly hoping she's here for the entirety of Gregor's training.

"Nanny? Eh, no." Rolling her eyes, she looks as if she's pissed off with me.

Shit.

"Oh, sorry. Are you one of the wives? Is your husband a pilot too, like Gregor?" My eyes drop to her hand, searching for a wedding band. However, I can't see properly while she clutches the baby that's now pulling at the neckline of her sundress.

"Negative to that, too." She mumbles something else under her breath that sounds distinctly like *"male chauvinist idiot."*

Ouch.

"Sorry if I offended you." The keys jingle when I hold my hands up in surrender and quickly apologize. The last thing I want to do is antagonize any of Gregor's team. They are extremely tight and travel all over the world together.

They aren't just workmates; they class themselves as a family.

She does not explain who she is as she accepts my apology with reluctance.

I hold out the selection of keys for her to take as she shimmies the restless matching red-haired baby up the side of her body, then takes the red bunch for the largest villa from me.

If she's not the nanny or one of the wives, who is she?

"Poppy, baby." I hear Gregor calling out as the steady beat of loud footsteps runs in our direction, making the baby in the woman's arms squeal and clap her chubby hands together.

As the red-haired woman turns to greet Gregor, he reaches out for the baby, who willingly climbs into his arms as if she's done it plenty of times before.

The penny drops. "Are you Gregor's boss's girlfriend?" If she's not a wife or the nanny, she must be. I don't know why I feel disappointed. *Or why I am even fucking asking.*

Gregor splutters. "No, Owen, try *boss*. Squadron Leader Sommers is my boss." He acknowledges her. "Ma'am." He mock salutes her.

For a heartbeat, my mouth snaps open, then closes again.

She's his boss, and me? I'm an idiot.

She slaps his hand away from his forehead, stopping him from saluting her. "We are outside of work. I've told you hundreds of times to stop doing that and to call me Jade."

Gregor winks at me. I think he enjoys winding her up.

"Squadron Leader Jade Sommers, this is my cousin, Owen Brodie. Jade meet Owen. Owen meet Jade."

"Ah, so you're the cousin who caused the scar above

Gregor's eyebrow trying to teach him to do BMX stunts when he was teenager?"

"It was an accident." I defend myself, then mutter under my breath, "Squadron Leader?"

My eyes are glued to hers; she looks younger than Gregor's thirty-five years and she's beautiful, and I always imagined Squadron Leaders to be older. Apparently, this is not the case.

"Yes, I'm the Squadron Leader." She smirks, hearing my indiscreet musings.

"Wow," I gasp, in complete awe.

Ignoring us, Gregor admires Poppy's white cotton dress, telling her she looks pretty. Then he says, "Isn't your mommy clever? She is *wow*." He smirks, then lifts his head to address me. "Jade is the world's first female pilot to join the aerobatic display team. She's a *'badass'*." He mouths the last word, conscious of crass language around tiny ears. "Jade's flying call sign is Red 1. She's number one, isn't she, Poppy?" He tickles the skin under the baby's chin, making her giggle.

I'm speechless. That's incredible.

"What do you do?" She folds her arms around herself, lifting her eyebrows high in expectation. "Pump weights at the gym, spend your days surfing, work on your tan, take dozens of selfies, and post them all over social media?" she teases back, knowing I made an assumption about her and what she does for a living.

I don't get a chance to respond when Gregor says, "Good one." He chuckles. "Better question, *why* is he staying with me?" He looks smug as hell. "When he should be on his honeymoon."

"Oh gosh," she gasps, glancing down at my ring finger

and then back up, mouth agape, obviously confused why I am here, alone, and not wearing a wedding ring.

The opportunity to defend myself disappears when Gregor replies for me. "Owen is a runaway groomsman." He pulls his lips into his mouth and takes a step back, cowering away from me like the dumbass he is. If he didn't have Poppy in his arms, I would have him in a headlock within seconds, exactly like we used to do to each other when we were younger.

Jade exclaims, "You stood her up?"

My cousin laughs out loud while I cringe and die a little more inside.

"No." I clear up what he means. "I kind of, well, sort of..." I can't get my words out.

"He left his wife-to-be at the altar. He did the decent thing and told her he couldn't go through with it," Gregor snitches on me, and I get an overwhelming urge to slap him upside the head.

Jade's mouth falls open.

I get the chance to defend myself. "I was being forced to marry her."

Jade's voice rises a couple of octaves. "What? Is that even a thing?"

"It's a long story," I mutter, embarrassed.

"Welcome to our messed-up family, Jade." Gregor laughs, then hands Poppy back to Jade before pushing his way through the front door. "I need a shower. See you later, gorgeous." He waves at Poppy.

"You're right. You stink and keep your archaic family traditions away from my daughter." Jade tries to sound serious, but her mouth twitches at the edges, giving her away.

"Oh, our families don't talk. Again, another long story. Your daughter is safe," he laughs.

Poppy straddles her legs around her mother's waist as if she's a baby orangutan. Automatically, Jade rubs her hand up and down her little back, giving me the answer I was looking for earlier; no engagement ring or wedding band on her finger means she's not married.

Jade turns to leave. "I need to go. My mom is waiting for me. The other guys should be here in half an hour to pick up their keys."

"I'll pop round later to make sure your villa has everything you need," Gregor calls back over his shoulder.

"Thanks, Gregor." Jade turns on her heels, not giving me a second glance. "I hope an angry stab-happy jilted bride doesn't turn up on our doorstep," she mutters to herself on a laugh.

"That's never going to happen. It's more likely to be my stab-happy mother." I shudder. "It's just as well we're in a secure compound."

Jade chuckles to herself. "Hide the knives."

Poppy grants me a gigantic gummy smile, showing me her two bottom front teeth, and I can't help but smile back and wave at her.

Walking away, the knee-length hem of Jade's apple-green summer dress flutters in the breeze. She pivots on the balls of her gold gladiator-style sandal-covered feet to face me again. "See you soon, Owen."

I hope so.

She turns and continues in the direction she was headed in, her hair bouncing as she walks, shining like spun copper in the sunshine before she disappears out of sight.

Well, the next few weeks just got a lot more interesting.

CHAPTER THREE

JADE

"I should stay in." I bite my lip nervously, looking down into Poppy's crib, where she's fast asleep.

"Stop being silly, Jade." My mother pats my hand that's resting on the side of the white wooden crib. "She won't even know you've gone."

"Are you sure you'll be okay? We're in a strange country and it's our first night here. I wasn't planning on going out this evening and..."

My mom chuckles. "Will you stop rambling? This is what I signed up for; being the babysitter and live-in nanny is simply wonderful, Jade. I'm here for her, and you. Traveling around the world with my two favorite girls. I wouldn't have offered to do this if I didn't want to, and you know that."

I do.

When Mom saw how uneasy I was about hiring an au pair, she suggested making my life easier and *she* became Poppy's au pair of sorts.

She made the choice simple for me and it was a solid yes.

So, for the next two years, which is the time I have left with the aerobatic display team, my wonderful mom, alongside Poppy, will travel with me to as many tour dates as they can.

It's reassuring that Poppy is in safe, capable hands, especially knowing how unreliable Poppy's father, Michael, is. He wasn't that concerned that he wouldn't see Poppy while we're in Cyprus. When I handed him my yearly schedule and training plan, he said he'd see her on our return to England for a couple of days between display shows, which made me want to hit him in the nuts with a heavy blunt object. *Asshole.*

It's just as well I have enough love for Poppy to launch a thousand ships because Michael doesn't even have enough to float a rubber dinghy.

Mom and I both stare down at my sleeping daughter.

Who knew that such a tiny bundle of unplanned chaos —all giggles and red curls—could bring so much happiness into my life? And of course, I can't forget the mountain of plastic rainbow-colored toys we seem to have accumulated, too; we needed an entire suitcase just for those alone while we're here.

"It's just..." I begin.

"We've only arrived... I know, you've mentioned that several times while getting ready." She waves off my concerns, gesturing to the surrounding space. "However, she's in safe hands with me. We are in a secure compound." She checks the time. "It's time to go. Your team is waiting, and you know how much they've missed you while you've been on maternity leave. It's the first night out with them since you went back to work last month. It'll be good fun."

OWEN

My mom loosens my tightly curled fingers, peeling them away from the crib side.

"I know." She always talks so much sense.

She continues. "And they love you, you love them, and you deserve a night out."

I turn to face her, instantly greeted by her warm smile. "Jade." She cups my cheek. "Go out. Laugh. Let your hair down."

"It's down."

"Well, you're all set then, aren't you?" She waits a beat. "Your father would be so proud of you, and he would dote on Poppy."

He would.

"She looks just like you, Jade." Her thumb brushes against my cheek.

"Let's hope she doesn't have my fiery temperament." I sure gave my parents a hard time growing up, always thinking I knew best. *Strong-willed and stubborn.* The traits my father said he loved most about me.

"I'm hoping she gives you a run for your money." Smirking, my mom's eyes crinkle around the edges, dancing with humor. "Karma. Oh, I am looking forward to watching her grow into the same fiercely independent woman you've become. If she does, she may even become the second female pilot to make the flying team. Or she might outshine you and become an astronaut."

I snort. "I think she just might." She runs circles around us all.

"I'm willing to place a bet with you. But for now—" My mom grabs the tops of my shoulders, spins me around, and ushers me out of the bedroom door. I twist my neck back to steal a last glance at my sleeping cherub.

"—it's time to have a few drinks, reconnect with your

team, and enjoy some adult conversation." She points, silently ordering me to get down the stairs and leave.

I submit. "Okay, okay. I get the message." I grab the handrail and run down the marble staircase, which is not baby friendly, not even in the slightest. I need to nip out and buy safety gates after morning training tomorrow.

I jump down the last step and look back up at Mom. "I have to be up super early tomorrow for our first training session, so I won't be back late."

She stands at the top of the stairs, smiling down at me. "Just enjoy yourself. And do not watch your phone or study the choreography you've been working on for the last month. Save that for tomorrow, because tonight is about having fun."

My hand rests on my stomach. Although I am nervous about the routine I designed, it's not nerves I feel when Mom mentions the training program and aerobatic display I've spent hours refining, it's actually rumbling from hunger. I'm looking forward to a meal out, some me time, and maybe even a glass of wine… or two… only two.

"I love you. Thank you for being here." I blow a kiss in my mom's direction, and she pretends to catch it. "I couldn't do this without you." A bone deep calm settles within me.

"I wouldn't want to be anywhere else. I won't wait up. Now go." She shoos me, encouraging me again to leave. "You look beautiful. I'm sure he'll love your dress." She winks.

I wave back at her flippantly, now regretting telling her how handsome Gregor's cousin, Owen, is.

"I don't care if he likes it. He's not my type." Every one of my words is a lie. He was hot, like sizzling molten lava.

However, I have made bad choices in the past with

men, specifically Michael, and I will never go down that route again. Hot and handsome do not always equal nice.

I let out a sigh as I think about Poppy, who was the best thing to come out of that relationship. She was our happy accident, and it's a sin Poppy's father can't see that.

"I agree, *handsome blonde Scotsman with piercing blue eyes* doesn't sound like your type at all," she mocks me sarcastically with my own words that I used to describe him earlier. "And look at you. You are beautiful. You look like a goddess tonight in that dress. Green really is your color."

I look down at my new fine lace dress and flat gold sandals. At five foot eight, I don't need heels.

"Like I said, I don't care what he thinks." I place my hand on my hip. "And who will be interested in a single mom with a busy career schedule and a grouchy ex, anyway? Also, I'm too old for him." Well, I think I am. He looks much younger than me.

"You're thirty-nine. Not dead." She sighs at my self-doubt. "And who wouldn't love Poppy? She's adorable." Holding on to the handrail, Mom makes her way down the stairs.

While I was getting ready to go out earlier, I realized that Gregor's cousin is the first man to make my heart flutter in a very long time. I can't deny he's mesmerizing, and I felt so drawn to him in a weird way that I couldn't explain.

When Gregor spilled his secret about his marriage, Owen looked embarrassed, as if he didn't want me to know; almost as if someone had punched all the air out of him, and he was blushing. Which I found oddly endearing.

But I don't need or want a man. I'm currently focusing on my career. Between my pregnancy and maternity leave, I've been itching to get back in the cockpit of my fast jet.

Not just a few hours here and there, like I have done for

the last four weeks to get me back into the swing of things. No, I'm ready for several hours in the sky, in formation, synchronized looping and twisting through the air. I love the fluttering feeling in my stomach when I roll a plane in the sky at five hundred miles an hour. There is no better feeling. And flying simulators don't do it justice.

That feeling was exactly how Owen made me feel earlier. My stomach danced with butterflies like I'd performed a loop the loop and barrel roll.

What the hell?

I continue with more reasons to justify why I should stay away from Owen. "He has way too much baggage. He dumped his future wife at the altar. Who does that?" I'm genuinely intrigued and need all the details immediately.

While fixing her hair in the wall mirror at the bottom of the stairs, Mom answers, "Someone who isn't happy, Jade. That's who does *that*. You should find out, though. I want to hear everything." With excitement, my mom's voice speeds up. She loves a good gossip.

"I can't ask him." It would be rude. He's a stranger, after all.

"I agree, but you can ask Gregor." She rubs her hands together. "Get me all the juicy details."

A low laugh hums in my chest. "Okay, Mrs. Blabbermouth, I'll do my best." I'm instantly hit by a wall of heat as I pull open the thick wooden door.

Enjoying the blanket of warmth, my cool air-conditioned skin relishes in the contrasting, sultry evening air.

I love this climate, although my pale, freckly skin would never appreciate the scorching temperature of August. I might turn into one giant freckle.

I inhale the orange blossom of the perimeter trees. "See

you later. I need to go, or I will miss the coach we've hired to take us to the restaurant." My excited voice bounces off the marble staircase. It won't make a blind bit of difference how loud I am, Poppy can sleep through a thunderstorm.

"Have fun." My mom gives me a finger wave.

I plan to.

My ribs are sore from laughing. "Wow, I have missed you guys." I struggle to catch a breath as my team continues to tell me all the stupid pranks they have pulled on each other in my absence. Although hilarious, I'm relieved they leave me out of their childish nonsense.

"You all need to grow up." My throat dry from giggling, I pick up my glass to take a sip of water.

My team disagrees with me.

Never.

Not in this decade.

Let's not be too hasty.

In unison, they chime, except Gregor's cousin, Owen.

He's been sitting quietly all night at the opposite end of the dining table. Just observing, half-heartedly laughing when everyone else does, although I'm not sure he's really listening.

It's as if he's found the map he was searching for, but he's unsure which route to take; he looks lost.

Every single time I've looked his way, he's been staring at me. Only when our eyes connect, he snaps his gaze away faster than a bolt of lightning. *Is it because I'm the only woman here tonight?*

I cast my eyes around the table at the talented pilots and support team I get to call my friends; my family for another two flying seasons.

I can breathe a little easier tonight knowing Cobra, my Wing Commander, couldn't make it. Like flipping a coin into a wishing well, I wish for him to stay as far away from me as possible, preferably at the bottom of the well where he can't get to me because he is forever acting inappropriately around me, and his sleazy behavior makes me feel weird. Despite him, I can't imagine being anywhere else; I love the rest of my team and I know that I need to make the most of every minute we're together.

I'm all too aware that all too soon, I will be on the move again, because once my assignment with the display team is over, I will rejoin my fast jet squadron based in the heart of England, and will be back in the cockpit of what I usually fly; a Typhoon. That thought makes my stomach spin with excitement, remembering the aircraft's power and agility. Although more and more of late, and since I've had Poppy, I've been considering a change in career, possibly something safer, like a flying instructor perhaps.

We'll see.

Usually only a three-year fixed term posting with the aerobatic team to give other pilots a chance to experience this exhilarating position, mine was extended to accommodate my pregnancy and maternity leave which means, like everyone else I will still do three display seasons, and I am desperate to kick start our training.

Becoming an instructor sounds great and all, but it certainly doesn't sound as exciting as my current role or hold the same appeal.

Shaking off any unnecessary thoughts, because I have a few years to consider my options, I remove my white cloth napkin from my lap and place it on the table. "Excuse me, I need to nip to the ladies." Pushing my chair back, I loop the strap of my gold cross-body bag over my head and remove myself from the table.

Our twenty-five man table makes it sound like a full restaurant of patrons. However, now I'm up on my feet, I'm aware of the emptiness of the place, realizing we are the last ones still here. Even the waiters are sitting around their own table chatting in their fast-paced mother tongue while eating their supper.

I slide my credit card across the table of the feasting waiters, wink and hold my pointer finger up to my mouth, instructing them to keep quiet about treating the guys tonight. One of them discreetly grabs the card machine and I punch in my security pin, then place a hefty tip on the table. *"Efharisto,"* I thank them.

The four white-shirted waiters smile gratefully, and chorus, *"Parakalo,"* thanking me and telling me *you're welcome*.

When they point me in the direction of the restrooms, I use them, then wash my hands.

I stop for a moment as I catch sight of myself in the mirror and stare at my reflection. I may look confident on the outside, but inside I am equal amounts of excited and petrified.

When I returned from maternity leave four weeks ago, asides from a handful of flying hours, plus a few sessions in the flying simulators, it's been almost eighteen months since I flew with the guys as a unified team and performed a full display sequence, because I discovered I was pregnant after our first display year came to a close.

I grasp the sides of the washbasin, feeling every heavy ounce of expectation on my shoulders. The expectation to succeed. The expectation of being the first woman to be selected to join the elite team of pilots. I suddenly feel the same pressure I did the first year I joined. Only this time, the weight feels heavier; the expectation of being a mom while making this extraordinary job work around my daughter.

I know the Air Force has done everything in their power to make it work for me, and I couldn't do it without their support, but making it a success, that's all on me.

Having to pinch myself when I made the team, every minute of every display was a dream come true, and once I had proved myself as a capable pilot who could lead a team, my ultimate dream came true when they made me Red 1, just before I found out I was pregnant. Flying was incredible before but now I am the leader it's even more thrilling.

Although that's what is causing me to feel the pressure I do. I want to succeed. I want us all to succeed.

This year, we also have a couple of new pilots. Having studied everyone's techniques for hours, I'm praying we gel and that my choreography suits each team member.

Not only do I have my team mate's lives in my hands, but people are watching because I am a woman. They are waiting for the ball to drop.

In a way, that sort of happened because falling pregnant after joining the aerobatic team wasn't part of the marketing and public relationships strategy the Air Force planned to implement.

Knowing what I wanted to do with my life since I was ten years old; become a pilot within the Air Force—becoming a mom, or rather, having Poppy, was not part of my life plan nor had I ever given a thought to starting a family.

Only here I am, approaching forty, at the height of my career, with my adorable eleven-month-old baby, trying desperately to be, do, and have it all, while, masking the internal freak out I have at least several times a day.

Can I have it all?

Can I do this?

Can I have my first full day back in the cockpit of my beloved aircraft without second guessing if this is what I want anymore?

I'll be away for weeks at a time. Will Poppy forget me as I continue to pursue my career?

And recently I've started to weigh up the risky nature of my job. Something that never crossed my mind before I had Poppy.

And how will I manage a deployment away from her? Sometimes being gone for up to six months. It's fine now while she's a baby and can come with me, but as she gets older and has school, it won't be as easy.

Like a piece of paper, my heart crumples in my chest as I think about leaving her for half a year. She changes daily; how will I cope with that? And will she remember who I am when I return?

I can't imagine ever being okay with that.

I'm not now and never will be ready for that. The sad reality is that I'm more than certain, as soon as my time with the aerobatic team is up, I'll be at the top of the deployment list and not a single ounce of me wants to be away from Poppy. I can't leave her knowing Michael doesn't care about her and while my mom has offered, she is older now and should be enjoying her golden years. Not looking after a baby. My baby.

I'm so torn, my priorities have completely changed; I've changed.

My mommy-guilt has taken on new heights, much higher than my acrobatic plane will ever allow me to fly.

I stare at myself, hard, in the mirror, then push my shoulders back.

Breathe Jade, you've got this.

I tug the zipper of my bag and locate the gift my father gave me. He said it was my good luck charm; the one that would get me selected to join the aerobatic team.

Holding the glazed white stone in the palm of my hand, I flip it over and give the bright red poppy painted on the top a rub with my fingertips.

I remember those selection days as if they were yesterday. I've carried this stone with me through every assessment, interview, training, and flight I've ever taken.

So much has happened since my father's charmed gift worked its magic, and it's been a whirlwind ever since.

Sailing through selection, I then relocated to the aerobatic team's permanent base. Toward the end of the first display season, Michael and I broke up, and a few weeks later, I discovered I was pregnant. I then moved out of my single room at the Officer's Mess and into a house in the Officer's Quarters. Unable to fly for the rest of my pregnancy, I was reassigned to desk duties, then when my morning sickness kicked in, I could barely function or carry out simple administrative tasks forcing me to take months off work... so yeah, whirlwind... more like a tornado.

The morning sickness, which seemed to last all day, combined with splitting up with Poppy's father, all hit me like a bullet train; the enormity and realization that my daughter would never get to experience the concrete love my mom and dad gave me. To this day, I still don't understand Michael and his lack of concern or love for our daughter.

She's the greatest thing to happen to me; and him.

I'm hoping he'll wake up one day and realize what he's missing out on.

When Poppy arrived safely in the world, she wasn't kicking and screaming like I imagined. She was so calm and peaceful, barely a whimper left her little lungs as the midwife announced it was a girl. She's still the same to this very day; such a happy, easy-going child. I have so much to be grateful for; she simply goes with the flow.

Three days after Poppy was born, the unspeakable happened and nothing could have prepared us for it; my lovely dad had a heart attack and died, leaving a massive hole in our lives.

"I'm doing this for you, Dad," I whisper to myself and then look back at myself in the mirror, my glassy eyes full of my sadness.

Desperate not to ruin my mascara, I grab a hand towel, dabbing the corners of my eyes to catch any tears before they fall. Dropping my lucky stone back into my bag, I straighten myself up and attempt to calm my humidity-ridden hair. Gone are the glossy locks I left the villa with.

"Pointless," I mutter to myself and use the elasticated hairband around my wrist to pile it on top of my head in a messy bun. "That'll have to do." I pull down a few strands from the front to frame my face.

I smile at my reflection. "I *can* do this. Failure is not an option."

If there's one thing I am eternally grateful for, it's the mindfulness practices and the positive affirmations my mom taught me to do.

I close my eyes and repeat silently to myself, *I can do this. I am enough. I am worthy. I am strong. I am unique.*

Tomorrow will be a success. I am a great mom. I can have a career and be a fantastic mom.

I fill my cheeks with air and blow it out, feeling a sense of calm wrap around me, grounding me again.

My phone rings loudly in my purse, making me jump. Pulling it from my bag, I roll my eyes at the name on the screen, knowing what comes next.

I press the accept button. "Hey, Gregor."

"Boss." He pauses.

I make him squirm. "Just say it."

"Eh, so, we are off to a club."

"Don't tell me. A gentleman's one?" I smirk to myself, already knowing the answer. No matter where we go, those men always seem to know where the nearest strip club is located.

"No." His voice goes up a few octaves, and I know he's lying. "We didn't think you would want to come with us and stay out late, you know, with having Poppy and your mom here and everything."

I exaggerate a sigh. "Tell them all that when we return to base in four weeks, I will inform their partners about their vile extracurricular activities."

"No, you won't," he says cheekily.

"Yes, I will." He knows I'm not lying. "I'm a girl's girl. I like your partners and spouses. They deserve better than you bunch of scoundrels." Those women are like an extension of my family, including Oliver, who is Arlo's boyfriend.

"It's one night. We are not scoundrels," he argues.

I rest my phone between my shoulder and ear as I tighten the thin gold belt around my waist. "Be good."

"We will. Stop stressing." He chuckles as the guys in

the background fool around. "And thank you for dinner. We'll pay you back."

"Just get to bed before midnight, go easy on the alcohol, and promise me to be exceptional in training. There's no flying tomorrow, but I need you all to have clear heads."

"Yes, ma'am." Gregor is always so polite to me. "Oh, my cousin is waiting for you. He's called a taxi to take you both home."

My body is instantly rigid, and I stand poker straight, holding my phone tight to my ear. "He's not going with you?" I can't be left alone with him. I don't trust myself. He's too pretty for his own good.

"No. Have you seen his face? It's like a slapped ass. He's miserable."

I've seen his face, and it's handsome as hell.

Square jaw, gray moonstone eyes, a body obviously sculpted by hours at the gym, tall, super tall. Yup, I didn't just see his face. I saw *every* part of him.

Only he looks like he needs a hug.

Gregor interjects my thoughts. "Maybe you could cheer him up?" Snorting, he knows he's winding me up.

"Shut up, Gregor," I drawl as if bored with this conversation. "I'm not interested in getting involved with anyone. Especially not run-away grooms."

Only, I want to be honest with Gregor and tell him that something strange happened to me when I met Owen earlier; goose bumps, actual goose bumps erupted across my skin when he smiled at me, but I keep that bit of information to myself.

I mean, it was just a smile. Scratch that, it was a smile that awakened something within me that's been lying dormant since, well, since time began.

Out of all the billions of stars in the sky, Owen's smile

shines the brightest. It makes me feel like he sees me. That I know him. That I've met him before somehow.

Have I?

"Have you what?" Gregor asks, breaking my hopeless romantic musings.

"Nothing." I smooth the fabric of my dress over my hips. "See you tomorrow, yeah? Six a.m. sharp."

"Yes, ma'am."

"Will you st——"

Gregor interrupts me when he laughs. "Oh, I know, we're not at work, no use of the word *ma'am*. See you tomorrow, *Jade*."

I pinch my nose. "And so it begins." I pretend to be annoyed when I secretly love the banter and fooling around.

"It's great to have you back, Jade." Gregor drops his voice. "I can't wait to fly with you again. It'll be an honor."

A heavy lump forms in my throat. "Thanks, Gregor." I barely get the words out. When Gregor joined the team, we instantly hit it off and he's become a good friend. This is Gregor's last flying season on the team, and I'm going to miss him when he leaves.

"Night, ma'am." He hangs up before I can complain about him calling me that again.

It's great to be back, but it's time to get home and maybe study my choreography before I get some well-needed shut eye.

Leaving the restrooms, I'm greeted by complete silence asides from the clatter of dishes from the kitchen.

On the other side of the restaurant, Owen is looking out the window across the darkened salt lake that was covered in a blanket of pale pink flamingos before the sun went down.

Alerted by my footsteps, he turns to face me. He drags

his gaze down and then up my body, finally landing on my lips.

"I'm taking you home." His Scottish voice is gruff. "The cab is waiting for us outside."

"You should have gone with them," I say, following him as he walks to the entrance, and every bit a gentleman, he opens the door for me.

"Not my thing," he answers quickly, sounding honest.

I call back to the staff, wishing them a good night.

Nodding my head in thanks, I walk past Owen and I'm hit with a cocktail of his fresh dewy cologne and orange blossom from the surrounding trees that seem to be everywhere on this beautiful island.

No longer a light breeze, the now blustery wind catches me off guard, hiking the floaty skirt of my dress up, almost exposing me. Two things happen at once. I squeal at the unexpectedness and Owen appears directly in front of me to protect me from the worst of the strong wind.

With both hands, I reach out to grab hold of the uncooperative hem of my dress, trying to prevent an accidental panty flash bunching the fabric into my hand against my thigh.

I look up to find his wide, muscular frame towering over me by at least five inches.

For a split second, I swear time stands still, not caring when the strands of my hair free themselves from my bun and whip against the skin on my cheeks.

"Sorted?" he asks, capturing an unruly lock of my red hair, wrapping it around his thick pointer finger.

I nod jerkily, feeling suddenly nervous.

Dipping his head, he leans closer, inhaling deeply, then says, "You smell like—"

"Good Girl," I stutter, not feeling like my usual confident self.

A massive smile slowly spreads across his lips. "A good girl?" Humored, he lifts one eyebrow.

Justifying what I mean, I blurt out, "No, my perfume, it's called Good Girl. I didn't mean I'm a good girl, although I am because I'm not a bad girl. I can be but—" I kill my reel of rambling words, realizing what I am saying.

Just shut up, Jade.

He licks his lips before they make their way to my ear. "I quite like the thought of you being a bad girl." I love how his Scottish accent rolls the R on the word girl. "Do you know you're the most perfect woman I've ever seen?" His voice is low and husky, making me want to be a bad girl for him. "You're beautiful."

As if I'm hit by an earthquake, I shiver. The effect ripples from the skin behind my ear and down my spine.

Holy shit. What is happening?

"Are you cold?" he asks, concerned, leaning back to find me staring at him.

I shake my head once, if not twice. Okay, maybe three times, mesmerized by his incredible, blue-gray-colored eyes, lined by golden lashes. Barely managing a whisper, I say, "I'm okay." Only, I'm not. My brain has gone into some sort of nuclear-powered meltdown.

Lost in our mini cyclone as the wind whistles all around, our eyes transfixed on each other, I try to figure out what the hell is going on between us.

We both jolt when the sound of an angry horn blasts from behind us.

"Time to go." Owen unravels my hair from around his finger, accidentally brushing my flushed cheek. "Hold on to your dress, Ms. Sommers."

I frown. I love my first name, only in work they never call me anything other than my surname, boss or ma'am.

"Jade," he corrects himself as if reading my mind.

"Right," is all I can manage.

Before I do something I regret, I sidestep, weaving my body around his, and walk to the impatient cab driver.

I almost skip, my heart has a sudden cheerfulness about it as it basks with new information he just shared; *I'm the most perfect woman he's ever seen.*

CHAPTER FOUR

Jade

We barely uttered a word between us in the cab. I swear I imagined him telling me I was beautiful.

In the blink of an eye, we're out of the taxi, back within the confines of the compound walls, waving curt, slightly awkward goodbyes, and walking separately toward our villas when Owen shouts, "Fancy a nightcap?"

I turn to look at his bronzed by the sun, face. Examining his muscular frame wrapped in his crisp white shirt that struggles to contain his broad shoulders.

He's freakishly handsome, making my pulse quicken, and I secretly want to fling my legs around his waist and climb his laddered abs that I noticed earlier today.

Bugger. Those thoughts will not *do.*

"It's getting late. I have an early start," my sensible mouth justifies my reasons.

He jerks his head in acknowledgment, pushing one hand into the pocket of his navy dress shorts, and the other through his wavy, dirty blond hair, then disappears in the pool's direction.

Follow him, Jade.

I tilt my head back and look up into the scattered star-filled night sky. "Aw, screw it."

I take a step gingerly in his direction, then another, and another, increasing my speed, as I go after him.

Rounding the corner, he's behind the bar to the side of our shared private pool, pouring *two* drinks.

He knew I'd change my mind.

Suddenly wanting to be anywhere he is, I knew I would change my mind, too.

Placing the wine bottle down, never taking his eyes off me, he watches me walk to the bar and pull myself onto one of the high stools. With only the sound of the soft rustle of the trees, no words are exchanged between us as he slides my drink across the glass bar top.

I swirl the chilled liquid in my fishbowl sized glass for a few minutes until I can't bear the silence stretching between us any longer. "How did you know I would come back? Are you always this confident?" I ask, then take a sip of the crisp, citrusy wine.

His lips twist into a warm, knowing grin, dropping ice into his glass to keep it cool from the still-warm air. I expect him to answer me, or at least say something, anything, except he doesn't. He simply pops two ice cubes into my glass. They softly *plop*, then clatter against the glass as they submerge into the pale-straw colored liquid.

"Why did you *have* to marry?" I blurt out. A forced marriage sounds like hell. I have so many questions—for my mother, of course.

Lies all lies. I'm a nosy bitch who can't help herself. I need to know everything about him. N*ow*.

The high-pitched buzz of cicadas sing loudly through

the heated air as he continues to give me the silent treatment.

I try again. "Did you love her?"

His voice resigned, he replies, "I don't want to talk about it."

"What do you want to talk about, then?" I arch a brow.

His square jaw set as he clamps his mouth shut in a stubborn line.

Screw this. "Okay. Great chatting with you." Taking my drink with me, I slide off the high stool, being careful not to spill my wine, and begin walking back to my villa.

"I didn't love her," he declares matter-of-factly. "She didn't love me, either."

I stop and spin around at his confession.

"We weren't marrying for love. It was a business arrangement." He states their romantic status... or lack of it. When I meet his gaze, he keeps sharing, surprising me. "She didn't give us a chance or take the time to get to know me, not that it would have worked, anyway." He manages a shrug. "Don't get me wrong, I'm not upset about her not loving me, not even a little. I'm upset about the whole situation; my family expecting me to perform like a puppet on a string for them. It's ridiculous."

I don't react; I wait patiently for him to tell me more.

He blows out a long breath, eyeing me nervously. "No judgment?"

"You'll not find that here." I've made plenty of mistakes in my own life. I'm in no position to judge.

He nods decisively. "In answer to your question, am I always this confident? I used to be, but now..." His muscles tense. "... I'm not. My mother and father chose my future wife as part of a business deal. Gregor maybe told you, but our family owns one of the largest print works in Scotland, but it's a dying industry. Our marriage was designed to strengthen and expand the business between my father and hers. It was a calculated business deal. Nothing more, nothing less."

"How romantic." His sad aura is so thick you can feel it. I try humor to lift his dying spirit.

Under his watchful gaze, I reseat myself and pat the stool beside me, inviting him to join.

I slip my gold shoulder bag off and lay it down on the gray patio paving below.

Owen casually walks out from behind the semi-circle bar and pulls a seat closer to me before sitting. Pulling his phone and wallet out of the pockets of his shorts, he lays them side by side on top of the bar.

Now only a few inches apart, I swivel to face him, resting my feet on the footrest of his bar stool, my knees between his widespread legs.

I place my hand on his bare knee that's covered in soft golden hair and give it a squeeze. "Relax. You can share anything with me." I smile reassuringly. Discretion is my jam. I've become a human vault, filing away all the relationship, career, and life dramas my team members share with me, and I never disclose. *Hello, this is the Agony Aunt Sommers. How may I help you?*

He swallows hard, staring at my hand that's trying hard to soothe him. "Our marriage was doomed from the beginning. It would never have worked. Marrying her felt like a prison sentence." Deep in thought, he looks off into the distance. "I genuinely thought I could go through with it, but I couldn't. I just couldn't." He shakes his head, taking a deep breath. "I don't think I have a job or a home to go back to in Scotland anymore, either. My mother hated me already, but this time I think I've really blown it. She will never speak to me again after this." I can't imagine never speaking to Poppy as she grows up. That would break my heart.

"My mother is all about the show, all for the sake of the business. She wears a mask well to hide the fact she and my father despise each other. I've cast a shadow over the family name. They, well, *she*, will never forgive me for that." He stops, taking another deep breath, almost as if he is desperate to get out whatever he's been keeping bottled up inside. My hand stays rested on his knee, giving it another squeeze, coaxing him to get whatever is eating him up, out, loving how soft the golden hair on his skin feels.

"That business, my job, working for my father... it's all I know how to do and suddenly I don't know who I am and I have nothing to get up for in the mornings anymore."

Clenching and unclenching his hand around his wineglass, he looks pained when he says, "In the past, my friends have told me I can be selfish, and apparently, according to my ex-girlfriend, Skye, who married my best friend, Jacob, I might add." He looks at me as if waiting for my reaction at that news, only I don't give him one. I will not judge a situation I know nothing about, or base my opinion on what Gregor has told me about him, either. It's unfair of me and I want to give him a chance to explain himself.

He continues, "I wasn't a very good boyfriend either. So, in the last year, I've tried to be a better man. Paid attention to my friend's lives, been helpful, showed up for people. I've been trying to right my wrongs. I even helped build the new nursery furniture for Jacob and Skye."

My eyebrows rise in surprise. "They are expecting their first baby together." He shakes his head, and I wonder if it's because he wished he was the one starting a family with

Skye, but instantly he quashes my assumptions. "Skye and me. We were never right together. Too much off again, on again. I was never there for her when she needed me, but she was always there for me." He takes a sip of his wine, savoring the taste as he smacks his lips together. "But Jacob, he's perfect for Skye. They are sickeningly perfect together." His lips twitch at the sides, curling into a dazzling smile as if memories are flooding his brain. "He bought her a big, fuck off castle for their first home. He's a hopeless romantic and loves her better than I ever could. They are amazing together."

He then proceeds to tell me about Skye being kidnapped by a crazy stalker she met online and how he was away on business when it happened, but Jacob was around to save her.

"Jacob is an amazing man. He's my hero. And Skye's."

"Do you still love her?" I ask apprehensively.

"Skye? Hell, no," he scoffs. "As a friend, I do, though. I love them both equally. They were made for each other. I can see that now. But I am not sure I was ever in love with Skye."

I adore how mature he is about his best friend marrying his ex-girlfriend.

"Were you and Skye together long?"

"Since high school."

"Wow."

"Fourteen years. But most of the time I was a dick to her. How she put up with me, I will never know. In fact, scratch that, I do know because I've had time to think about this *a lot*. I think she felt sorry for me."

"Why?"

Humming as if in thought, he runs his tongue along his pearly white teeth. "I have Mommy and Daddy issues. Let's just say that growing up wasn't easy. I also wasn't honest with Skye from the start, although she knew my mother would never have allowed us to marry, she stayed with me, and I reckon that's why I always held back from her, never fully letting myself *be* with her. I know I didn't put in the effort in our relationship, because deep down I knew I would have to marry someone my parents chose for me. My sister is trapped with a man she doesn't love, and she is utterly miserable." He fades off. "Christ, my poor sister. She looks so unhappy." He rubs his hands down his face. "I don't want to talk about that."

Rubbing my fingertips across his knee, I nod in acknowledgment.

"You don't have to tell me anything at all. But I am guessing the Owen I am sitting across from is a new Owen, am I right?" He doesn't come across as being an inconsiderate prick. In fact, he gives off deep regret and remorse vibes. He's had a year to change his ways and I believe him when he says he has.

"I've been trying to be a better friend. I think I nailed that, but doing what was expected of me for my family..." His eyes dart around the pool. "... every word I spoke, everything I did for my mother, father, Evangeline..."

"Was that her name?" I ask softly. "Evangeline?"

"Yeah." He sighs, completely deflated, his flat eyes reflecting his feelings. "None of it was good enough for any of my family, especially Evangeline. *I* wasn't good enough for her and I'm a dumb fool for believing that I ever could be. Standing at that altar was like awaiting the death penalty, and running away, I thought, was an easy way out. But now I'm here, in Cyprus, with nothing but time on my hands to over-think, it feels like the problems I was running away from are bigger than they were before."

His mouth pulls to the side as he chews the inside of his cheek.

His words fill my heart full of sorrow, every part of me wanting to reassure him it won't always be this way. He's important, and he doesn't have to make hasty choices.

Few men would have the balls to share their innermost secrets with a stranger, but I am guessing he's at the lowest point in his life and feels like he has nothing left to hide or lose. He sounds desperate to share, as if no one has ever truly listened to him or given him the right to make his own choices.

"Did you know Evangeline beforehand?"

"I've known her and her family for years. Since we got *engaged*, I have been trying to get to know her better, make it work. For everyone's sake." His voice is low almost indifferent as he realizes it was pointless. He drags his fingers through his hair, his pale eyes crinkling around the sides as if deep in thought. "I found out today she'd been seeing someone else."

I gasp. "She was cheating on you?"

With a mixture of amusement and disappointment in his voice, he says, "I couldn't give a shit if she was, because you can't cheat on someone if you haven't slept with them, can you? Our relationship was a lie."

"You guys didn't have sex before marriage? Do people still do that? How proper and... wow... just wow..." Astounded by this revelation, I drain my glass of wine.

Did Evangeline see Owen? All of him? Really look at him? Because from where I am sitting, his powerful body looks like it is made for sex and sin and those biceps are begging to lift one helluva lucky lady into them and to be bounced up and down his—

OWEN

I squeeze my thighs together to ease the surge of excitement zapping through my core, wetting my panties.

"She barely spoke to me. I am certain she would rather boil her own head than touch me. She made it very clear that I was not her type." He interrupts my fantasy.

His smooth fingers slide over mine, where they still rest on his knee. Liking his touch, I don't pull away, letting his hypnotic strokes on the top of my hand pull me under his spell.

"What was her type?" I urge, needing to know what Evangeline thought Owen lacked.

"I don't know, but thank God it wasn't me." He shudders. "She's a cold-blooded reptile in human skin and loves her bitch of a cat more than anyone with two legs, and that cat too..." He waggles his finger in the air. "It's not an angel, no ma'am. It's the fucking devil in white fur. Her evil sidekick. It almost fucking killed me. It gave me an infection. I could have died." He points to what looks like a red scar in the shape of a bite mark on his hand.

I chuckle at his story. While I don't know Owen well, I sense a sad and tortured individual when I see one. He hides his lack of self-confidence well, deflecting it with humor.

Despite being crushed, Owen is putting on a brave face and I decide not to push him for more or he might retreat into his mental man cave. So he surprises me when he says, "She said I had an enormous nose." He draws a straight line down it and then places his hand back on top of mine.

It's not big at all. In fact, it's perfect; symmetrical and slightly lifted at the tip.

He becomes a bit more animated. "And I never said the right things. I was either too loud or too quiet. I would offend her if I didn't say she looked nice, but when I did compliment her, she would change her outfit. I tried organizing date nights, and theater tickets, but she would bring friends along, choosing to spend time with them instead of me. I even wore a baby blue and pink wedding suit for her." He throws his arms out to his sides as if to say *what was I thinking*, and I miss the warmth of his hand on mine again. I like when he holds my hand.

"Sounds lovely." I struggle to hide my laughter that's bubbling like a simmering cauldron in my chest.

"It was embroidered and looked shit." He gestures to his upper torso and down his arms. "And it had this enormous pink rose over my crotch area." He makes a bowl shape with his hand and cups his junk.

Laughter like confetti breaks free from my lips, sprinkling warmth into my heart as Owen joins in. At least he can see the funny side.

He points to himself. "Laughingstock. Although you should have seen my two best men. They wore baby pink suits and looked like a pair of giant dildos."

"I need a picture."

He ponders for a moment. "I wonder if my friends got one? I'll have to ask."

"There may not be any photographic evidence of dildo suited best men?"

"Such a pity." He shakes his head, smiling softly. "I put my suit in the trash, or I could have shown you that."

"You should have worn kilts in your family tartan," I firmly state.

"That's what I said." He throws his hands up to the constellations again. "At least someone has some common sense around here." Letting out an enormous sigh, the surrounding air feels lighter. "I felt powerless," he mumbles, rubbing his hand across his stubble.

"Time to claim back your power, Owen." He should know he's in control.

His eyes fill with warmth, his shoulders dropping and his face looking less tense. Even the deep *V* between his eyebrows seems to soften as he grants me a genuine smile.

"Thank you," he says.

"For?"

"Making me feel better than I have in days, maybe weeks, months. Who knows?"

"All part of the service," I reply with one hand on my empty wineglass and the other still on his knee. I'm glad I joined him for a drink; he obviously needed someone to talk to.

"Another?" Owen points to my glass.

I put my hand over the top. "No, thank you. Training tomorrow."

He tucks a lock of his blonde hair behind his ear. "Discipline, I like it. Did you always want to become a pilot?"

I clear my throat, happy to share. "Since I was ten. My father was in the Air Force, as was my grandfather and my great-great-grandfather, too."

Owen's serious when he asks, "Did you feel you had to follow in the family footsteps, or is it something you wanted to do?" The tip of his pointer finger brushes against the skin of my knee and a zing of electricity shoots between us, making all the little hairs on my thighs stand on end. When he inhales a deep breath, I know he feels it, too.

Usually in control, I find it hard to concentrate as he begins to draw a figure of eight with his fingertip across my skin. "It's something I have always wanted to do. I love it." My whole body lights up. I feel it every time I talk about my job, and with him touching me the way he is, my entire body feels like it's burning for more. Contently, I sigh. "When it's just you, the aircraft, how it responds to you, it's intense and nothing comes close to how exhilarating it is. When I sit inside that cockpit, everything changes. I just focus on the mission and what I need to do next. Maintain a cool head, make split decisions under pressure if I have to." My voice is dreamy. "I focus on flying and leave my personal problems on the ground." I almost whisper my last words as more of his fingers dance across my knee, moving up my thigh.

What is he doing? I can't think straight. And why am I not stopping him?

"Do you have problems, Jade?" He waits several seconds and when I don't reply, he says, "I hope you don't mind, but I asked Gregor if you were in a relationship."

My heart jumps in my chest at what that may mean. Does he like me?

I hope so.

Owen confesses quietly, "He told me you'd broken up with Poppy's father. He also said your ex is a bit of a douchebag." His face is serious, and his eyes stay glued to mine.

I feel my forehead tightening under my scowl when I think about my ex. "No judgment?" I ask the same question he asked me.

He shakes his head slowly. "None."

"Until I had Poppy, I didn't have any problems. But now, every decision I make, from childcare to my next career move, they all feel like problems. It was just me before. I had no one else to think about. But now." I can't hide my emotions, my voice thick with love. "She's all I can think about."

Unsure why I am opening up to a stranger, I babble my

innermost thoughts that have been playing havoc with me. "Lately, I can't stop thinking about the safety of my job. What happens if I make an error? What happens if the aircraft fails? Who would look after Poppy? Michael? I don't think so." I scoff, forgetting who I am speaking to for a moment.

"Michael?" Owen questions.

"That's my ex's name. Poppy's father," I whisper, ashamed I couldn't make it work between us.

He nods. "Does he not see her?" His eyes fill with sadness.

I avert my gaze across to the pool that's lit up like a blue lagoon. "Oh, he *can* see her. He just doesn't *want* to. He's not interested."

"Well, that's a damn shame, because she's super cute."

My heart flutters. "She is."

"She looks like you."

"Poor girl. She'll have to spend her life in the shade. Red hair and pale skin are not fun in the sun."

"She'll still shine the brightest. Just like you." He leans in closer, sliding his hand further up my outer thigh. My breathing stalls when he places a knuckle under my chin.

A mere millimeter away from my lips, his hot breath ghosts my skin. Every part of me wants him to kiss me. It's been so long since I've been intimate with anyone.

This is the first night I've been out since I had Poppy, and it's not exactly what I had planned, but I like how Owen makes me feel. I can't explain why I feel drawn to him like a magnet. I can't seem to pull myself away. Almost as if I've met or known him before. It's a strange sensation in my chest that I can't make sense of.

"Wanna do something reckless?" His *hot with desire* pupils dilate.

"Like what?" I ask.

The pad of his thumb dusts across my lips. His touch the spark needed to light the embers, allowing it to spread through my body like an out of control forest fire.

"This." He loops his arms firmly around my waist, throwing me into the air at speed as he stands.

Alarmed, I shriek.

"Hold on." Owen squeezes his arms around my waist tight, reassuring me that I'm safe with him.

High on his manly scent, I do as he says and lace my arms around his neck and my legs around his hips.

Without hesitation, he's running in the pool's direction, carrying me as if I'm as light as a helium balloon.

"Hold your breath," he cries.

Oh shit.

CHAPTER FIVE

Jade

"Noooo—" My voice dies in the air as we hit the *warmer than expected* water. Bubbles gargle in my ears, fizzing between the layers of our clothing on impact.

To gather my bearings, my eyes ping open and I'm welcomed by Owen's white smile, glowing in the underwater lights. He looks effortlessly gorgeous submerged in the water; his hair on end moving from side to side in the ripples of our movement, white shirt, and bronzed skin. He's a beautiful sight. One I want to photograph mentally and save to my favorites for later.

He tilts his head up, instructing me to move upward, then he lets go of me, allowing us to reach the surface of the water separately.

I gasp for breath like a dying fish, pushing my dripping wet hair off my face.

As soon as his head pops up, I flick water his way, splashing his face. "You're an idiot." I splutter, wiping my eyes.

His face falls. "So everyone keeps telling me."

Wordlessly, we move to the shallower end of the pool. "That's not what I meant, and you know it. A little warning would have been good, that's all. And I'm wearing a new dress." I push my uncooperative dress between my legs to stop it from floating to the surface.

"I'm sorry. I'll buy you a new one, and you could always take it off." His voice is playful before he lowers himself into the water slightly, his mouth disappearing as I swim over to him. Watching me, my stomach ties in knots as the heat of his gaze burns my water-cooled skin.

Reaching him, I tease, "Is this what you call reckless?"

"Nope. This is." My eyes follow him when he stands tall, smirks, and begins unbuttoning his shirt. "But a better way to describe it would be, throwing caution to the wind."

My mouth is instantly drier than the Sahara realizing that he wants us to skinny dip. "I'm not getting naked." I sound horrified. There is no way I can let someone like Owen, who is gorgeous, with perfect skin and muscles, see my stretch marks and C-section scar. No way, not in this century.

He shrugs. "Suit yourself."

I avert my gaze when he removes his shorts, then hear him chuckle when I swim away from him.

A large splash from behind me prompts me to glance back over my shoulder, but all I can see is a puddle of clothes by the poolside alongside his sopping wet, expensive-looking designer white sneakers.

I stop swimming and search the area, but he's nowhere to be seen.

Where the hell did he go?

I don't have to wait long to find out, as a hand grabs my ankle from under the water and I yelp in shock.

Fully naked, he swims past me, his white ass glowing

like a full moon against the contrast of the rest of his sun-kissed body.

A giggle bubbles in my chest at the absurdity of my situation.

I'm in a pool with a naked stranger. I'm thirty-nine and acting like a teenager.

I can't deny it's the best fun I've had in months.

I squeeze my eyes closed when he swims up beside me and resurfaces, not trusting myself not to look at his cock.

"Scared you won't be able to resist?" he laughs, obviously noticing my reaction.

"Oh, shut up," I reply, flustered, already fed-up wrestling with my dress.

Just take it off, Jade.

"I thought fast jet pilots took more risks than us average Joe's."

"Calculated risks. There's a difference, and I have self-control. Something you clearly lack." My words sounding more prim and proper than usual.

"I'm fun. Something you clearly lack." His Scottish accent is thick with humor.

My eyes still closed, I gasp dramatically. "Oh, that hurts."

"Take your clothes off, then."

"No."

"See. I'm right, you're a prude. No fun."

I let out a stupidly girly squeak and pop my eyes open when he pinches my waist, discovering that he's standing right in front of me.

This guy's got my head spinning like a Ferris wheel. "It's not that I don't want to take my clothes off." I keep my gaze high, forcing myself not to ogle his million pack abs or dip lower.

Thinking, he pulls his lips into his mouth. After what feels like forever, he then says, "So you *want* to take your clothes off?"

Goddammit, he got me.

"I can't take them off." But I want to.

He rakes his wet locks off his forehead with his fingers. "Why not?"

"Because we are in a communal pool, and it's not very professional of me if the guys come back to find their boss naked in the pool now, is it? And..." I trail off.

"And?" he mimics.

I look away, embarrassed, and mumble under my breath.

"I didn't catch that. Say it again," he pushes.

I say it again, slightly louder.

"I missed that too." He moves closer, his mouth now in line with my ear.

Through clenched teeth, I say, "My body doesn't look the same since I had Poppy."

"And?" He twists his head in my direction, our mouths aligning.

"And I have stretch marks, wibbly bits, and a C-section scar. It's not attractive. And you're like..." I motion to his body. "Carved from marble. How is that possible?" I can't resist reaching out and touching his sinewy abs, making his pecs twitch under my touch, inwardly mad at myself for not spending more hours in the gym. It's taken me eleven months to shed my pregnancy weight and I still have more to lose. I wish I knew how those social media moms, who snap back to their original size post-pregnancy, do it. *Do they survive on fresh air? Maybe.*

With a soft voice, he quashes my worries. "I couldn't care less about any of that shit but keep your clothes on if it makes you feel better." Reaching out, he runs his thumb under my eye, then the other. "Your mascara is running."

"Do I look like a panda?" I must look disheveled. Soaked, matted hair, smudged makeup, and my green lace dress stuck to my body. *Fantastic.*

"You look like a beautiful panda," he says honestly. "Tell me, Jade, when was the last time you felt carefree, did something without having to think about Poppy, and had a little fun?"

I can't think straight as he pushes my wet hair off my face with his large but tender fingertips.

What is this guy doing to me?

Trying desperately to answer the question he's just asked; it suddenly dawns on me as the memory comes into view. "I went skydiving."

"How long ago?" He tucks a lock of hair behind my ear.

"Three years," I say quietly. I can't believe it's been that long.

His eyes crinkle at the side with humor. Knowing he's made me realize it's been years since I had even the slightest bit of *fun* outside of work.

"Three years," he repeats in shock.

"I need to get out more," I confess, my voice strained. Suddenly, I forget my sadness, distracted by everything about the gorgeous man before me who is pulling me toward him. Curling his fingers around the back of my neck, causing all the tiny hairs across my body to stand on end. *How does he do that?*

"You're out now," he whispers, leaning down, millimeters from his lips brushing over mine.

"I am," I whisper back, silently wishing he would kiss me already.

"I want you to have fun, and I want to be the one you

have it with, Jade, and for some fucked up, crazy reason, I want to kiss you so damn much." He buries his fingers into my wet hair at the nape of my neck. "I feel so drawn to you. It's some sort of weird shit I can't explain."

Holy freaking hell.

"I want to kiss you, too," I confess, the strange feeling that part of me knows him already filling my chest again.

It's just sexual chemistry, Jade. Stop making it something it isn't.

I close the distance, grab his waist and pull him toward me, then press his lips to mine.

Billions of sparks burst through my body, illuminating every dark spot I didn't know existed. The sensation of his mouth slanting over mine makes me moan. He tastes like wine and cologne as our tongues collide together and for a moment, I can't ever imagine wanting to kiss anyone else ever again.

The soft blond whiskers of his beard tickle my chin, a feeling I'm not familiar with. The three men I've ever been with have been in the Air Force and were clean shaved with short back and sides haircuts. But Owen, well, he's all floppy hair and bristly scruff and I relish in his uniqueness; it's new and exciting.

Controlled, he takes his time, exploring my mouth, his kiss softer than I imagined.

My free hand moves up his arm, to his shoulder, then back down around his firm waist, pulling him closer to me.

He takes this as an invitation to do the same.

Our kiss deepening, I sigh, feeling blissed out.

No longer caring about my dress floating to the surface, our slow kiss goes on forever. It bleeds into my soul, flooding my senses, making me tremble.

His bare, hard cock presses against my stomach, and I

gasp.

He wants this.

I want this. I want *him*.

"Take my dress off," I sigh between our heated kisses.

Panting, Owen pulls back to look at me, as if he is reading my face for any trace of doubt.

I glance down into the water, frustrated that I can't see his cock because the fabric of my floating dress blocks my view.

I want to see him. All of him. "Please," I beg.

"You sure?"

My tone is soft but sure. "Now, Owen." His lips find mine once more, making me whimper when he nips the bottom one.

He touches his forehead briefly in mock salute. "Yes, ma'am."

Chuckling, I smile against his mouth.

His voice drops an octave. "I fucking love that you're the boss, and how you out rank all those men we were out with tonight. I can't wait to see you in your flight suit."

Well, that's new. Michael hated me in my flight suit. Although, I guess his jealousy of my career progression may have clouded his perspective, hating the fact I made the final cut at selection for the aerobatic squad, and he didn't.

"You'll see me in it tomorrow."

He winks so sexily that I can't wait another second for him to touch every part of me.

"Just get me out of this dress and show me what this fun is you speak of."

"So bossy." He kisses the side of my mouth, moving to the shell of my ear, before peppering kisses down my neck.

"Do it now, Owen," I groan.

"Yes, ma'am."

CHAPTER SIX

JADE

Pulling my dress up over my head, it lands with a loud *splat* as Owen throws it on to the poolside.

Not at all uncomfortable with him looking at me now, knowing he doesn't care about my post-pregnancy body, *and,* because he makes me feel safe, our wet bodies almost collide when he pulls my lips back to his. Only this time, he's not gentle or patient and I don't want him to be.

His firm hands find my ass as he lifts me, and with a timbre to his voice I've not heard from him before, he instructs me to wrap my legs around him.

I fleetingly worry that the extra baby pounds I am still carrying may make him topple over. However, as soon as I am locked around him, he pushes me through the dense blue water with ease, as if he's parting the Red Sea.

Deepening our kiss, he curls his tongue around mine, expelling a low groan and I can't help the sound that leaves my throat either as my panty-clad pussy rubs against his hard length.

"Jade," he gasps.

"Owen," I respond boldly. "I want you."

Chest to chest, he nips at my mouth, peppering small kisses across my jaw and neck as he glides through the water. "You've no idea how much I love hearing those words."

"All night I've imagined your lips on mine, your taste, your touch, all of it." I want to reassure him because I know he's felt unwanted for so long.

Arching my neck giving him permission to continue kissing my neck, the waves lap against my outer thighs, and with every step he takes toward the shallow end of the pool, I rub my center along his thick length, making me shiver with need, my desire for him wetting my already soaked panties.

"You're big." He is. Much bigger than I've experienced.

"And you are so fucking sexy, Hotshot."

Uncharacteristically, I giggle girlishly when he calls me that. "Hotshot?" I ask on a gasp when he lifts me onto the edge of the pool, tugs the cup of my green lace bra down, and sucks my pebbled nipple into his mouth.

Pulling him into my chest because I want more, my sex drive suddenly shooting into overtime as he awakens my dormant desires.

"I'm not showy," I admonish. "Hotshots are flashy and uncouth." My words are breathless. He makes it increasingly difficult to concentrate as he rolls his tongue around the outer edges of my areola.

"You are neither of those things." Licking, sucking, and gently biting my dusky pink nipple, he expertly unclasps my front fastening bra and moves to the other breast, giving it the same attention before climbing kisses up my décolletage and neck. Clinging to the back of his neck, I spread my legs wide for him, needing him to be closer, as he slides my bra straps down my arms.

"You are successful, though. You can't deny that. The only female aerobatic pilot ever to fly for the Royal Air Force," he mumbles in wonder against my skin while his lips seek out the perfect spot behind my ear, sending tingles down my back, unleashing a warmth deep in my core as my pleasure builds. I can't make sense of anything that is happening between us. He's barely touched me and I am so frigging turned on I might explode.

My heart melts when he confesses, "I feel like the luckiest man alive tonight, being here with you, and for you allowing me to see a different side of you, Jade."

He's right. I keep my circle tight in romance, friendships, and my career.

So why do I trust someone I barely know?

I hope I don't live to regret my gut feeling about him, because if Owen discloses our evening together to anyone, especially the press. *Gawd, the press.* Since I landed this role, being the only female of a high-profile team, they seem to have a thing for me, taking an interest in my romantic life. It got worse after I split up with Michael. The newspapers and gossip mags printing photos of me with celebrities I've barely met for a minute on the red carpet or at charity functions, making assumptions about who I'm dating.

Fingers crossed, I'm right to trust Owen, or I will chop off Gregor's balls and watch him eat them if his cousin turns out to be a snake.

I'm not usually so reckless, but tonight I want to let loose, plus I love sex. It's been such a long time since someone has made me come, only I don't want just anyone to do that. I want Owen.

Every cell in my body tells me I can trust him, already

caring for him and his sad heart. I want to heal it and make it whole again.

No longer caring if anyone hears me, I moan loudly when he sucks my neck.

Please don't leave a mark.

"I trust you, Owen. That's why I am here with you tonight. I haven't been with anyone since I had Poppy."

He pulls back, our eyes connecting instantly. I place my hand over his thumping heart. "I trust you."

He suddenly looks taller and wider, the strength of my words filling him with confidence.

I curl my pointer finger, beckoning him to me as I leisurely lean back on my hands, pushing my exposed chest out.

Screw it. If I am doing this tonight with him, I am doing it all. In the low lighting, he can't see all my squidgy bits and scars properly, anyway.

Can he? Nah.

When his eyes drop down my body, I pull my legs out of the water and rest my heels on the edge of the pool.

"You are beautiful. I think I'm dreaming." His desire-filled gaze is hot enough to trigger an uncontrollable blaze.

"I think you have that the wrong way round, Owen. I think I might be dreaming."

A shadow of something flits across his face. What is that, *doubt, pain, suspicion*? I don't know, but I want to find out. I don't have to wait long. After several seconds, he reveals his insecurities.

"You don't mean that, Jade. I bet you could have any man you wanted. I'm unemployed, a washed up finance director, a paper pusher at best, and you..." He shakes his head, retreating and I think he's going to jump out of the pool as he takes another step away from me. "... you dine with celebrities, meet kings and queens, travel the world, and me, well, I'm just an office worker from a minuscule seaside town on the east coast of Scotland. I'm insignificant. A nobody."

This poor man, his self-confidence has been shot to smithereens. "I don't care about celebs and the cities I visit. I don't care what you do or where you come from either. All I care about is having fun tonight, with you. Not just any man, I want *you*, Owen." I'm honest with him when I say, "I don't fool around, *ever*, and I haven't been with anyone since Michael and I split up."

His eyes blow wide with shock, then he confesses, "I haven't been with anyone for over a year. Not since Skye."

"Well, then..." Feeling a newfound sense of bravado, I drag my pointer finger down between the valley of my cleavage, over the soft swell of my stomach, and down into my soaked *from the water and how turned on I am* panties, making him gulp audibly. "You had better get over here and end this dry spell for both of us." I rub my clit in little circles, watching him watch my hand. "I'm so wet for you, Owen. Only you." I let out a long low moan, reassuring him it's only him that turns me on like this.

"Jesus, fucking, Christ." He lets out a half-grumbled groan, dragging his hands down his face as if he's torn.

I bite down on my lip and watch his reaction as I insert a finger into my wet pussy. My mouth drops open as I work it in and out a couple of times, the beginnings of an orgasm taking hold. I'm not going to last if he doesn't take over soon.

Teasing him, I ask, "Do you want to taste me?" I remove my hand from inside my panties before holding my finger out, offering myself to him.

He doesn't need to be asked twice as he lunges forward, causing the water to splash everywhere as he quickly devours my finger. Sucking, he hums as he licks every drop of my orgasm from my skin.

"Fuck me, you taste so fucking good," he pants, dipping his head to kiss the skin of my knee, moving to my inner thigh as he scatters kisses, dusting his fingertips over my goose bumped skin. "Are you cold?" He looks up at me with concerned eyes.

I shake my head. "No, every touch from you feels like molten heat. Now take off my panties because I am so hot for you, and I need to come." The need between my thighs now taking on a pulse of its own.

His mouth twitches with humor. "You're so fucking bossy."

I suppose I am.

He hooks his fingers into the sides of my soaked underwear. Helping him, I dig my heels into the ground, lift my hips off the still-warm concrete beneath me, allowing him to pull my panties slowly down my legs. He tosses them behind him into the pool.

Tipping his head to the side, he stares at my exposed pussy. "It's beautiful," he says as if talking to himself. "I like this." He tugs on the tiny triangle of light copper hair above my public bone, making me gasp. Everything he does sends sparks of pleasure deep into my core. It's as if his touch is magic. That's never happened before.

"You're soaked, Hotshot."

"Kiss me," I beg.

I'm not prepared when he misses my mouth, instead, he leans forward and kisses my clit, licking and sucking on it hard.

When his huge hand pushes my chest, silently instructing me to lie back, I do, crying out when he roughly licks my clit again.

"Softer, please." But he doesn't hear me and continues his assault on my sensitive clit.

Oh, I do not like that at all.

"Owen," I gasp, grabbing his hair to stop him. Only he takes that as my cue to go harder.

I reach down and grab his tongue, pulling it away from my pussy.

He gags and retches, but I don't let go.

Pulling his head up to look at me, he muffles jumbled words I can only imagine is him trying to ask what the hell I am doing.

His hand clasps around my wrist. Still holding on to his tongue, and with narrowed eyes, I glare at him. "You are not tunneling your way to France, nor are you sucking hard candy." I let go of my hold on him and he snaps it back into his mouth.

"Was I not good?" He looks pained, as if I just punched him in the nuts.

"You're too eager, Owen. I know it's been a while." I cup his face. "But go gentle. Tender. Slow. I don't like it hard like that." I brush my thumb down his cheek.

"Right." He swallows. "Slow, gentle." Repeating my words, his shoulders sag.

"Yeah." I nod, encouraging him with a smile.

"I'm sorry." He looks like a lost puppy with his sad eyes. "It's just, well, Skye never, you know, wanted me to do that, but maybe this is why?"

"Oh my God, please never mention exes ever again while I am naked with you." I roll my eyes jokingly. I don't care and I am the least jealous person I know. When I trust, I trust completely and do not need to be envious of any girl, especially exes I don't know. "Let me teach you." I sit up fully, tipping his head so I can capture his lips with mine.

"Like this." I kiss him, so softly it's barely a kiss, then I run the tip of my tongue across the seam of his mouth. "Take your time." I push my tongue slowly between his lips. "Then explore." He gasps when the tip of my tongue touches his and I twist them together. "Small circles," I mumble. "Up and down." I flick. "Sometimes sucking." I suck his tongue, making him growl into my mouth. "And don't forget to use your fingers." I grab his hand and suck one of his thick fingers into my mouth.

With hooded eyes, he watches as I move it back and forth.

Swirling my tongue around his strong digit, I push it out from between my lips, grab his wrist and drag his hand down my body to my clit. "Now show me."

"Who the fuck are you, Jade Sommers?" he asks, seemingly baffled by my direct ways.

I smirk. "Your new teacher. I'm going to show you how to be a phenomenal lover, Owen Brodie." I lie down, arching my body as I stretch out my back. "Now make me come like you've made no other woman before."

I smile when soft warm lips touch my clit, then with light swirls, his tongue explores my lips, my wet entrance, and back again to my clit, making me melt into the tiles. "Owen, that feels so good."

"Yeah?" His warm breath heats my already scorched skin.

"Keep doing that." I bury my fingers in his hair when his fingertips stroke my clitoris, then play with my labia. He leisurely pinches my clit, making me grab his long hair. "Oh, God, yeah. Just like that."

He licks my folds up one side and then the other before teasing my wet entrance.

"I'm so hard for you right now," he pants, plunging his

rigid tongue into my pussy, making my body curl off the uncomfortable hard ground.

Continuing to lick me, the tip of his tongue picks up a little speed as he shapes two fingers around my sensitive clit, sliding them back and forth on either side, working me into a frenzy.

"Tell me what you want, Jade?" He kisses the spot above my clit, his blond scruff brushes my overly sensitive bundle of nerves.

"I need more. I want your fingers inside me," I beg, my voice raspy and not sounding like my usual self.

Not needing to be asked twice, his entire mouth covers my pussy, his tongue awakening every nerve ending. Pleasure surges through me, hitting places I thought no longer worked, as he takes his time like I told him to. He slides one thick finger, then another deep into my *wet for him* core. My hips buck into his face, thrusting uncontrollably with the need to come.

"Deeper, Owen." I clasp his head harder. "God, that's so good." I cry out as he shifts the angle of his hand, edging against my G-spot.

A rush of slick heat coats his fingers, pouring out of me as he fucks me with his long fingers.

Rubbing slightly faster, the ache between my thighs builds. "Holy shit, I'm going to come."

"Come for me, Hotshot," he hums, then he hums more as if he's a human vibrator.

I look down at him momentarily. With his eyes closed, he's eating me out like a man who's been starved for too many years. "That's so sexy," I say out loud, not meaning to, shamelessly riding his face to chase my release.

Feeling my eyes watching him, he looks up. His eyes hooded and dark with desire and with his tongue teasing my clit, his fingers sliding in and out of me, and the humming sensation from his lips, pleasure like I have never felt before builds suddenly, startling me as my orgasm runs through every millimeter of my body. It's intense and mind-blowing and so many other words I can't think of right now as stars explode behind my eyes, and I cry out his name, the sound feeling familiar as it falls from my lips.

My thighs lock his head in a tight vise-like grip as my pussy flutters around his fingers that are still buried deep inside my body.

Heart beating out of my chest, sheer elation dances across my body as I come down from my *come to Jesus* moment and relax my thighs on either side of his head.

Startling me, making me jolt, I release a long pleasurable groan when he kisses my clit one last time. I cling onto his soft wavy locks as if they are a life buoy on a stormy sea.

He kisses the swell of my stomach just above my C-section scar. I'm grateful when he doesn't give it a second glance, showing me it really is a non-issue for him.

"Good?" He sounds unsure, looking up at me, uncertainty swirling in his eyes. My heart melts in my chest at his self-doubt. How could this shockingly handsome man, who's built like a tank, be so unsure of himself?

My pulse still racing, and heart pounding in my chest, I pull myself upright, then slide into the pool, needing to be closer to him.

He looks startled when my fingers climb his chest, and I cup my hand around the back of his neck. Pulling his lips down to meet mine, I kiss him with reverence, showing him how much I appreciated the orgasm he just gave me.

Tasting myself on him, I whisper, "That was the best orgasm I've ever had." I'm not lying. It was incredible.

"Really?" His entire face lights up like a kid that won a stuffed toy at the fair.

"You're great at that."

"I had an excellent teacher." He teasingly pinches my ass.

"You can thank her from me." I smile against his lips, going in for another kiss because I can't stop touching him. "Now, can I show you my appreciation and help you with this?" I reach down and rub his hard cock that I've been desperate to touch, making his eyes roll into the back of his head.

"I will blow in like two seconds." He sounds pained. "You are so beautiful and sexy. I won't last."

"I want to take care of you." Kissing his chest, moving up to his neck, I bite his ear lobe and gesture for him to sit on the side of the pool.

Within seconds, he's there. Thick thighs spread wide, showing off his God-like body. "You're not human," I stutter, checking out his sculpted muscles.

"I work out a lot. Too much."

I settle myself between his legs. "You are perfect," I whisper, running my hands down his abs, across his Adonis's belt, the *V* shape pointing to his perfect, *but oh*, so fucking thick and long cock. "Holy shit," I mumble as I see it up close for the first time.

"Do you want me to teach you what I like, too?" He places a knuckle under my chin to stop me from staring at his erection.

"I think I can handle this." My fingertips run up and down his thighs, causing him to shiver.

"I've never met anyone like you before, Jade. You are way out of my league." He cups my face.

"That's not true." I place a soft kiss on his wrist, directly over his hammering pulse. "I live under the same sun as you."

I try to hypnotize him with kisses up his inner thigh, asking questions to distract him from the sadness I feel radiating off him. "What would make you happy, Owen?"

In a daze, he shakes his head. "My family seems to think money makes you happy, but I know first-hand that's not true."

I plant a soft kiss on the side of his hard cock that's jutting out away from his washboard stomach, making it twitch. It's so big, I've yet to figure out how I will fit all of him in my mouth.

Hissing when I lick him from root to tip, he cups my cheek as I roll my tongue around his thick crown, lapping the precum from his weeping slit.

"You make me feel hopeful, Jade." His answer is not reassuring in the slightest. How can he say that when he's only spent a few hours in my orbit? Does that mean he's sad all the time?

"I want to make you happy again, Owen." I groan, enjoying the sweet and saltiness of his cum. "You taste incredible."

"Fuck. Me," he growls, bucking his hips, tightening his grip around my jaw as I take control of his pleasure.

My nipples tighten as I wrap my hand around his shaft, then suck him into my mouth.

I have to stand on my tiptoes to accommodate his length. Using my hand, I stroke his shaft and circle my tongue around the head of his cock before taking him in further.

When the tip of his dick touches the back of my throat, I quicken my pace, bobbing my head up and down. My hand and my mouth creating a warm, wet tunnel for him to glide in and out of.

With every stroke and lick, his cock thickens, hardening. He drops his hands from my face and lays them flat against the poolside, allowing me to control his pleasure.

Worshipping his cock, stroking and sucking much faster now, I cup his heavy balls and roll them, almost tickling them between my fingertips.

"Fucking hell, Hotshot. Look at me."

When our eyes lock, he gasps, "I'm gonna come." I think he's trying to warn me.

I let him slide out of my mouth and kiss the side of his cock. "Come down my throat, Owen." I give him permission.

He watches every move I make as I hollow my cheeks and suck him harder, and with only the sound of our combined moans and the gentle lapping of the pool water as our soundtrack, Owen only lasts another couple of deep throat strokes before his hips jerk, and he fills my mouth with his hot, salty cum.

I swallow every drop as his husky roar echoes around the space.

I can't take my eyes off him; head arched back, his mouth slack while his chest heaves in breaths, creating a feeling inside me that I've never felt before that loops around my heart, making it beat faster.

Slowly removing him from my mouth, licking, then kissing his tip, he lets out a final moan.

Eyes magnetized; we stare at each other. "You slay me, Jade." He still struggles to catch his breath. "I think you've come into my life for a reason."

His words render me speechless.

He leaps into the pool unexpectedly and pulls me hard

up against him, surrounding me in his fortress of a body, embracing me as if he never wants to let me go.

"You're beautiful inside and out." His voice is thick with emotion as he squeezes me tighter. "I don't want tonight to end."

"The guys will be home soon," I murmur against his solid chest. "We have to go inside before they catch us. I have an early start in the morning."

"Stay just a little longer."

"I can't let the guys see me. I'm naked."

"I don't care."

"I do." He crushes me even tighter in his embrace, then kisses the top of my head.

"Your nakedness is awesome," he chuckles.

My giddy heart feels like it's being transported through the wind on a giant fluffy cloud. He feels nice. Good. *Right*.

I curl into him, enjoying every minute in his broad arms that make me feel at ease and safe.

"Your wife-to-be was wrong about you."

"What do you mean?" His fingers that were caressing my back stop moving.

With my hands laid flat against his chest, I push him back so he can see how serious I am when I say, "You are more than enough, and nobody deserves to be unhappy, including you. Never let anyone tell you what to do."

He sucks his lips into his mouth as if trying to hold back what he truly wants to say.

I continue, "If you ever told me how good I looked in an outfit, I would wear it every day." His heart beats faster beneath the palms of my hands. "And if you organized theater dates, I would find ways to spend time with you, and you alone. And I would never make you wear a pink suit to get married in."

He acknowledges my words with a nod, his hands skimming slowly down my spine and back up again.

"I don't know you, but inside each of us lies something special, Owen. You've never been shown what's special about you. And you are special. If your parents can't see that, and you can't either, then with time, you will. Until then, go out there into that big, imperfect world and discover what makes you happy and no one else but you can do that." I tap his chest reassuringly before I rub my fingertips across the soft, light hair nestled there.

The warm night air makes everything seem so much more perfect with him.

As if the cicadas got the memo, they all instantly stop singing, making Owen's gulp clearly audible. He bites the side of his mouth nervously. "Thank you."

"For?"

"Accepting me for all the fuckedupness that is me, without truly knowing who I am, and agreeing to never make me wear a pink floral suit again."

Unladylike, I snort.

Owen pinches my waist. "So, tell me, if I told you my favorite outfit on you is naked, would you go about like this all day?" he teases.

"Oh, you're good." I roll my eyes as a burst of laughter and loud voices travel around the corner to us from the forecourt.

"Shit," I spit out, my voice low in panic. I duck for cover, sinking into the water up to my neck. "They can't see me." I dart my eyes around the vast space, searching, trying to locate my clothes.

Calmly, Owen moves through the water. On powerful arms, he pulls himself out of the pool onto the patio. Dashing across to the bar, his feet slap loudly as he runs until he finds what he's looking for. Hitting a switch on the wall, he plunges the pool and the outside area into darkness.

I squint, letting my eyes adjust to the blackened space, and make out a faint Owen-shaped silhouette, scooping up my clothes.

Chatter and laughter from the rest of my team move closer, making my heart rapidly bounce in my chest.

"Shit, I can't find your panties." He's doing a shitty job of keeping quiet.

"They're in the pool." I hiss, spinning around on the balls of my feet, struggling to see anything but one foot in front of me. "I can't find them."

"Leave them and get out, Jade," he whisper-shouts.

I scurry across to the side as fast as the water will allow.

Strong hands help me out and, as naked as the day I was born, I grab my sopping dress out of Owen's clutches. "Here's your bag." He hands me that, too.

"I have to go. How do I get out of here without them seeing me?" My voice now a low, desperate whisper.

"Go round that way." A shadowy hand points in the bar's direction. "Follow the path around the back of our villa. It will take you to your terrace." Owen grabs my hand, pulling me along and I have to run double time to keep up with him. "Quick," he hastens me.

He guides me around the back of the bar and onto the secret pathway, and I make a beeline to my villa.

"Wait, can I see you again?" he calls after me.

Whizzing around, I run back to him and smack a kiss on his lips. "See you tomorrow."

I can see the faint outline of his grin in the pitch black.

"For lesson two," I tease, cupping his junk.

Laying his hand over mine, he grinds himself against our hands. "See you tomorrow, Ms. Sommers."

"I prefer Hotshot." I squeeze his balls.

"Ah, ah, okay." He winces. "Hotshot."

I release my tight grip. "Good boy." And kiss him again.

"Fuck. You'll make me hard again."

"Hold that thought until tomorrow. Night Owen."

I can't see him properly, but I'm pretty certain he's wearing a goofy grin and rocking a semi.

"Night, Hotshot."

Wow, what a great night.

Lesson two?

What the hell was I saying?

Aw, hell, screw it. Let class begin.

CHAPTER SEVEN

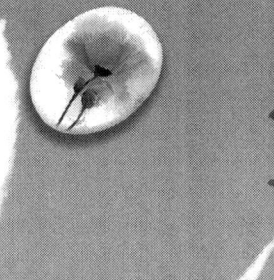

Owen

Chubby cheeks and a gummy smile look back at me as I throw Poppy into the air, making her babble nonsense words and shriek with delight as the high motion makes her stomach drop, tickling her insides.

Landing with a splash in my arms, she kicks her little legs in the water again with excitement. "One more time," I say.

Straightening my arms, I push her little body away from me. "Ready?" I throw her a giant smile, matching her giddy excitement.

We've been playing in the pool for the last hour and she's like a jumping jellybean in the water. She loves it.

Marigold, Jade's mother, sits down under the parasol on one of the white patio chairs, placing a tray on the table with two freshly squeezed glasses of lemonade on it and a bowl of food and drink for Poppy too.

"You are so good with her, Owen." She gives Poppy a finger wave.

"She's easily pleased, Marigold." I repeat the same

motion and a high-pitched squeal leaves Poppy's lungs as I throw her a little higher this time. Her smiles and laughter are contagious, causing me to laugh, too.

"Please call me Mari." She looks at me with kind eyes. "And thank you for making lunch today and for looking after Poppy for me."

"How are you feeling now?" Mari took a dizzy turn by the pool this morning, so I sent her to lie down and prepared lunch for us all while she rested.

"Better. I think it's the heat. I'm not used to it." She flicks her folder paper fan open and wafts her face with it.

I agree with her with a nod of my head. She's a lovely woman and everything I wish my mother was—kind, caring, funny, compassionate, and supportive. She's so proud of Jade, talking her up to me all day when we've been chatting. My mother would never dream of looking after her own grandchildren. Heck, she didn't even bring us up, choosing to hire a governess for such unspeakable tasks instead.

That woman has the ability to love as much as a rock does.

I look up at the bright, sun-blessed sky and pull my sunglasses resting on my crown down to protect my eyes. "I think we should get you into the shade, Poppy."

Now looking like *Casper the Friendly Ghost*, as instructed by Mari, from the waterproof sunblock I smothered her in earlier. I received a lengthy lecture from her, instructing me how to apply Poppy's sun cream, warning me about red-head's skin being more susceptible to the sun's harmful rays followed by another lecture warning me on the dangers of the pool and how to keep Poppy safe, hence the pink inflatable armbands with printed strawberries and matching swim vest she's wearing. I doubled up on the safety front. I want to prove to Jade and

Mari that they can trust me with their precious cargo. Poppy is precious. All grabby hands and bumbling chatter. With the most beautiful copper curls, smiles, and blue eyes, just like her momma.

I haven't heard her cry yet. She's such a happy child, which is just as well as Mari hasn't been well since her funny turn earlier. Her rosy glow cheeks still haven't returned.

"I'm so thankful you were here, Owen." Mari takes a long sip of her lemonade.

"Happy to help, and it's not as if I have anywhere else to be."

With Poppy in my tight grip, I climb up the steps at the end of the pool to make my way over to Jade's mom.

"You'll be fine tomorrow, I'm sure. I think you're right about the heat. Give it a few days, and we'll all be acclimatized." Grateful, the clouds move in, momentarily hiding the sun.

Mari expertly wrangles Poppy into her highchair I brought over from their villa and scatters chopped up apple, strawberry, and banana onto the feeding tray in front of her. Immediately Poppy grabs the fruit pieces, sucking them into her mouth, taking tiny bites with her only two front bottom teeth.

Mari and I situate ourselves around the table, sitting in comfortable silence.

Having never paid much attention to kids, or babies before, I watch with fascination as Poppy tries to feed herself with the grace of an elephant doing ballet, while noisily bouncing her sippy cup full of water off the tray.

Poppy holds out a piece of squished banana for me to take. "You have it," I tell her. "Poppy's, not Owen's." I point to her and she takes that as permission to smoosh it into her mouth, smashing the banana all over her lips and up her nose.

"Well, don't you look beautiful now?" I chuckle as Poppy makes *num num* noises.

"She likes you," Mari says with a smile.

I straighten out my wet shorts that are stuck to my legs. "That's because I fed her earlier, and made her tummy feel like she was on a roller coaster in the pool."

"The perfect way to a girl's heart, Owen; food and laughter." A smirk plays along her lips. "But I didn't mean Poppy. I meant Jade."

My eyebrows shoot up in surprise.

"She spoke to me this morning before she shot off at six."

I'm shocked she told her mom about us.

"She said she had a great night." Mari smiles cheekily. "She looked happy. *Glowing.* Then she told me to find the panties she misplaced in the pool last night."

Oh, my freaking God.

My face heats with embarrassment. "Adventurous," is all I say, feeling slightly uncomfortable, and not wanting to give anything away.

"She said she went for a midnight dip." She watches me squirm in my uncomfortable plastic seat. "By herself."

"Right." My throat dry, I audibly gulp and lean forward to take a mouthful of my juice.

"Did you not get a taxi home together?"

"No," I lie.

"Hmmm." She taps her chin with her pointer finger. "You know, I'm pretty certain when Gregor came to the front door this morning, he asked Jade if she got home safely." She theatrically pauses. "With you."

My lemonade goes down the wrong way, making me

cough and splutter everywhere. Poppy blows a raspberry in response as I wipe down my torso, which is now covered in sticky lemonade.

"That's what I thought," Mari mutters under her breath.

I clench my hand, coughing into it while I grab the pack of disposable wet wipes off the table to clean myself up.

"My girls are special to me, Owen." Through narrowed eyes, she stares me down.

Clearing my throat, I scrunch the now dirty wet wipes into a neat ball and place them in the middle of the table.

"My husband died last year and they are all I have." Sounding melancholy, Mari lets out a deep sigh.

Nodding in response, I understand everything she's not saying. *Don't hurt her.*

Mari leans over and casually wipes the creamy banana out of Poppy's fiery curls. "Tell me about yourself, Owen. What's going on in your world and how long do you plan on sticking around?" I understand her concern for her daughter. "I know you fled here to get away from a marriage you didn't want." She pulls a baby wipe from the packet to clean her hands.

Preparing myself, I blow out a breath and tell Mari everything I told Jade last night.

She's watching me intently as I finish, then says the most unexpected thing that blows me sideways. "You're a man of honor and integrity."

I disagree; that couldn't be further from the truth. If I were honorable, I would have married Evangeline. "That's not what my family thinks." *Or me.*

"Well, it's true. Your feelings are valid, Owen. Above all else, you honored them and stayed true to yourself. Being honorable doesn't mean pleasing your family or anyone else. It means being honest and true to yourself."

"You mean selfish," I scoff.

"No," she says firmly, swiping her hands through the air in front of her as if casting my words aside. "You believed in the truth and stood by it, knowing neither of you would be happy if you had gotten married. That rotten feeling you had in your gut as you stood at the altar is very telling; it was your inner alarm system going off, warning you of what your future held if you went through with it. And you knew it was unfair to put her, and yourself, through a loveless marriage. You did the right thing for both of you, regardless of what your family believes." She leans forward and grabs my hand, then pats it. "You have high principles, and you broke the archaic family tradition of what they distinguish as marriage. Marrying her for stature and financial stability, and vice versa, was a recipe for disaster."

"You don't know that."

"Oh yes, I do," she replies, staring me down. "My father's views on who I married weren't exactly liberal. He expected me to become a nurse and marry a doctor or a surgeon. He even signed me up for nursing college behind my back. The day I came home and told him I had signed up to join the Royal Air Force as a clerical assistant, he was horrified. And that got worse when he discovered the weeks of grueling basic training I had to go through. Crawling through muddy grounds and obstacle courses, cleaning the blocks, field exercises, camping, chemical and biological lessons, rifle work, prepping uniforms, and shining shoes." She chuckles as if remembering. "After basic training, I started on the lowest pay grade, living in single living accommodation in a room no bigger than a sardine can. Oh, no, my father was not happy at all. It wasn't very ladylike."

She nods. "His words, not mine. But it's how I met Andrew."

"Jade's father?"

She smiles fondly. "He was the most handsome man I had ever met." Her eyes go dreamy. "I remember the day I arrived at my first posting. I was like a lost sheep with no idea what the heck I was doing or if I'd made the right decision to join up. Nerves, like a washing machine in my stomach, posted hundreds of miles away from home. I was barely eighteen." Her eyes crinkle around the sides as she reminisces. "I had never been out of the little village in Kent I'd lived in all my life, and I couldn't even drive. But I knew what I wanted. Becoming a nurse and marrying a surgeon wasn't it."

"Was your father mad at you?"

Mari picks up a slice of apple that Poppy has thrown on the ground and places it on top of the pile of used wipes. "Hopping mad," she answers. "He didn't even turn up to watch my Passing Out Parade after basic training. But then, when my mother told him I was courting a fast jet pilot, well now, that got his attention." She throws me a cheeky wink. "And it wasn't really the done thing; an officer going with a non-commission service woman."

"I bet it wasn't." Amused at Mari's rebellious ways, I chuckle softly.

"And the rest is history. Andrew and I married, and he wanted to start a family straightaway, but I wanted us to enjoy each other first. Not long after we married, they deployed me for months, and I hated being apart from him." Her memories make her smile even wider. "It forced my hand, and I left the Air Force because it was becoming too difficult to match my postings with Andrew's, and when I left, I fell pregnant with Jade. From then on, we let the Air

Force dictate where we lived. We were happy and had everything we wanted in life, so our location didn't matter. We had lots of friends and each other. When Jade was only a few months old, we relocated to Lincolnshire after Andrew's squadron moved stations, and there we stayed and settled. It's where I still live."

"There's an air base near Castleview Cove at Licharty," I tell her. It's only three miles away from Castleview. As a little boy, I always loved the sound of the fast jets roaring by from the end of the pier, watching them take off and coming in to land out on the peninsula.

She chuckles fondly. "I know. It was a posting we always dreamed of. Your town and beaches are beautiful, but Andrew's squadron was stationed in Lincolnshire."

I nod in agreement. Our beaches are award-winning. It's no wonder thousands of tourists travel from miles around to visit, even if it is just for the day.

Curious, I ask, "They don't fly fast jets there anymore, do they? Why not?"

"Something about a reshuffle. They always do that, then they realized they made a mistake and had to rethink the plan." Mari reels off her intel. "There was a rumor that the base was closing down completely."

"I heard that too. I also heard it's going up for sale."

"What the hell would you do with a military base with hundreds of homes and an airfield? You'd have to be mad to buy something like that," she ponders.

I take a deep breath and ask Mari, "Do you regret any of the decisions you made?"

She replies in a heartbeat, "Not a single one. Everything I did, I did for *me* to begin with, then meeting Andrew and having him by my side throughout my career was the icing on the cupcake I wanted to share with him every day. We were very happy."

"Wow," I say, impressed at how bad ass Mari is. "You stuck to your guns."

"I did because I knew what my father wanted for me was *not* what I wanted. I went out and found my dream. Made my own memories and created a legacy that will live on for years to come."

"In Jade?" I ask if that's what she's referring to.

"Yes. She's special. Have you watched her flying? Her interviews? Being on camera? She shines." She flicks her paper fan out to cool herself down as the sun has cracked out from behind the clouds again.

"No," I answer honestly, with the sudden urge to look her up on the internet. I'll most definitely be doing that later.

"She's a star. My girl will go down in history. But had I followed my father's plans for me, there would have been no Andrew and me, and ultimately no Jade." She looks off across the pool in deep thought. "She inherited Andrew's family's talent for flying. Andrew and I, we made someone very special indeed," she whispers her last thoughts.

Yeah, they did.

"Don't play the game, Owen. Change it." Mari finally shares her last words of wisdom.

Lost in my own thoughts, I realize I am getting my fresh start. To finally do whatever the hell I want. I don't want to work in finance, because that's what my father wanted me to do at, or printing, attending boring machinery expos, balancing books or researching yet another complicated hedge fund or entering into a marriage to expand the business. Mari and Jade are both right. This is my opportunity to change course and take my shot; to break free and create my destiny.

As much as that scares me, it's what I want.

The tumbling sensation that feels much like excitement bubbling in my stomach tells me it's my time to take control of my life and to break free from my parent's clutches. Internally, I make a vow to myself to discover what makes me want to hop out of bed in the morning, find a new career path and return to Castleview Cove self-sufficient. Or maybe never return at all. Maybe a new life awaits me elsewhere.

It's *farewell* to Owen Brodie, heir to Castleview Printing Press, and *hello* to Owen Brodie; the man who sought his own destiny without knowing what that was. S*idenote: with a little help from his grandfather, who left him a few million in trust.*

I push my shoulders back, determination now running through my veins.

I can do this, and I will... whatever the hell *this* is.

Splitting the silence, Poppy bangs her sippy cup off the plastic food tray repeatedly, chanting *mom, mom, mom,* in time with her hammering. Whacking harder this time, the lid pops off with the pressure, then she pours the rest of the water over the top of her red locks, leaving it there as if she's wearing her cup as a hat.

Both Mari and I burst out laughing, then Mari says, "And of course, we wouldn't have this little one either had Andrew and I never met, would we?" Mari stands up too quickly, making her wobble on her feet and grab onto the table to steady herself.

I'm at my full height within seconds, hands on her elbows to support her. "Hey, I got you. Are you okay?" Concern drips from my lips. "We should text Jade."

"No, don't," Mari snaps, then hangs her head. "I'm sorry, Owen. I didn't mean to sound so stern." She shakes her head back and forth. "Please don't contact Jade. She's busy and I don't like her worrying about me. I think I need to lie down again." Her pleading eyes speak volumes. "I felt better after I rested earlier. That's all I need." I notice her skin is paler now as she wipes her perspiration covered brow.

I try to bury the niggle in my gut that there is a bigger underlying health issue causing Mari's lightheadedness.

Reluctantly, I agree to not call Jade. Pulling a wet and fruit salad covered Poppy out of her highchair, ordering Mari to hook her arm into mine, and carefully ushering her to their villa.

"Poppy needs her swimming diaper changed into a dry diaper, then she needs her nap." Mari sounds concerned, listing another three things she needed to do today before Jade's return.

"I can help with all of that."

Mari and I shuffle slowly to the forecourt and follow the path to the front of her villa.

Her eyebrows shoot skyward. "Have you ever changed a diaper before?"

"Never."

"I'll talk you through it."

"Good plan."

"She's wrigglier than a worm, though."

"I'll be fine. It's just a diaper."

I help manage a three hundred strong team of employees and run a production line in my father's absence. I mean, what could go wrong?

CHAPTER EIGHT

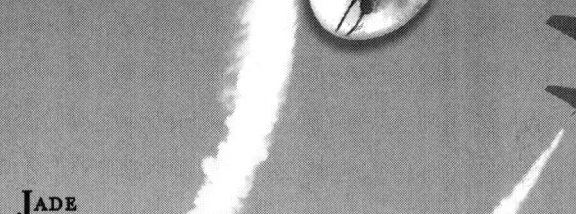

JADE

Back half an hour earlier than expected, and around the same time Poppy has her afternoon nap, I press the front door closed carefully and sneak into the quiet villa, guessing my mom is resting while Poppy does.

I love training in Cyprus; early starts mean early finishes.

Today went better than expected. I had nothing to worry about.

The guys loved my choreography. We sat around the table for hours, running through it several times, examining parts of it we want to change to minimize risk, letting everyone have their chance to express their thoughts and concerns. Level heads and professionalism shone through each of us, highlighting just how much of a tight-knit unit we are already. The loyalty and attentiveness of my team knows no limits and I am buzzing about getting to fly in formation tomorrow.

I pull my aviator sunglasses off my face, fold the legs, then push one of them into the neckline of my tee shirt.

Burning up, I unzip my flight suit, rolling the green fabric down to my waist then tie the arms of it around my hips.

"God, that feels good." I shake out the tension in my tight shoulders and waft the neckline of my crisp white shirt, causing my sunglasses to *clink* on top of the soft cotton fabric.

I swiftly toe off my issued black boots and make for the stairs, but just as the sole of my foot hits the first one, I hear a masculine voice travel across the hallway, prompting me to stop and listen.

Zeroing in on the noise, trying to figure out where the voice is coming from, I lean my body over the banister toward the living space when Poppy giggles with glee.

My lips involuntarily smile at her laughter. That giggle gets me every time.

"Oh, you like that, do you?" A Scottish accent, one I know all too well now, hits my eardrums.

What the hell is he doing here?

Louder now, he bellows in his broad Scots accented words, "It's a braw, moonlicht nicht, the nicht." And she giggles again.

Trying not to be heard, I slowly move off the step, and tip toe closer to them.

"You are so easily pleased, Poppy. Maybe I should become an actor or a singer." Out of tune, Owen sings a few lines from a song I've never heard before. "Maybe not. I'm not very good. Don't tell anyone how bad that was," he whispers. "Our little secret, right Pop-a-doodle?"

Stealthily curving my head around the corner to get a better look, I have to cover my mouth to stifle my giggle. Owen is standing with his hands on his hips, wearing a stainless-steel vegetable strainer as a hat with the handles of two wooden spoons jammed through the holes as if he's got alien antenna, and he's wearing Poppy's dress-up pink voile tutu over the top of his blue shorts and nothing else.

Even in a tutu, this man is delicious.

And hot.

Poppy is looking up at Owen from the sofa as if he's the most magical guy in existence.

Melting my heart, he keeps chatting away to Poppy, "Another secret us two need to keep." He motions to the gap between them. "Is the one where we don't tell Mommy you got poo all over Owen's tee shirt when we changed your diaper earlier. Or that it went up my fingernail, or that it took me five attempts to put your diaper on. Just like your nana told me, you are a wiggly worm, huh? Thank goodness for YouTube." He points at Poppy again. "Oh, and you can't tell your mommy that either. Don't tell her I cheated. Tell her I was amazing." He narrows his eyes and asks, "Do we have a deal, little Pop-a-doodle?"

Poppy claps her hands and blows a raspberry, sealing their agreement.

"Yes." Owen punches the air. "I knew I could count on you. Right, little one, I think it's time for your nap." His broad frame steps around the table and scoops Poppy into his arms.

Oh my God, who is this guy who calls himself selfish and believes he is unworthy of love? He's far from it and obviously has a kind heart in that chest, because he's so beautiful, caring, and sweet with my daughter.

Realizing he's coming this way, I shift back around the corner, run on my tiptoes as far as I can, not wanting to be seen, then swivel around and walk back in the same direction, shouting, "Hey, I'm home." I sound delirious, my voice too high, almost a squeak as I try to disguise my peeping Tom act.

"Yay, Mommy's home." Owen cheers and appears in the hall, greeting me with the biggest smile. My heart instantly melts with how utterly adorable they look together.

With one arm around his broad neck, Poppy is snuggled into Owen's bare chest as she pushes the thumb of her other hand into her little pouty mouth and mumbles, *Mamma,* quietly.

"Hey, baby girl."

My throat instantly tightens with a flash of what life would be like if Poppy had a proper father. One that cared for her and didn't treat her like an object he felt obliged to take every now and again. Those thoughts slice my heart wide open, my emotions bleeding out of me.

How could this gorgeous man, who has known Poppy for less than a day, be more connected to her than her own father? Tears prick behind my eyes and I can't stop them escaping as they run down my cheeks, soaking the neckline of my tee shirt.

What the hell is wrong with me?

I flick the tears away quickly as I'm pulled into the firm hold of Owen's muscular arm. He coddles me, then kisses me on top of my head, smooshing me into a solid chest. Owen holds me until my tears subside and right on cue, Poppy pulls me back to reality with a firm tug on my nose.

Catching our reflection in the mirror, the three of us huddled together like this makes us look like an instant family.

Like we belong.

Lightening the mood, Owen nods, then winks sexily. "I knew you'd look hot in your flight suit, Hotshot." His voice is soft yet deep, and I know he's trying to distract me from feeling emotional.

I nervously chuckle, stepping out of his embrace, instantly feeling stupid. Wiping my eyes with the palms of my hands, I apologize profusely, embarrassed, and unable to look at him.

"Long day?" Owen asks, his voice deep and gravelly. His face floods with concern as worry dances around the edges of his forehead, his brows hunched low.

"Yeah, something like that. I'm sorry," I apologize again, holding out my arms. "Come here, baby." Poppy willingly moves into them as she sleepily snuggles in.

I look around to avoid questions he might have about my sudden waterfall of tears. "Where's my mom?"

"Resting." He looks up toward the stairs. Thinking for a minute, he drops his voice to barely a whisper. "Don't tell her I told you." He nips at his lips worriedly. "But she's been feeling dizzy most of the day."

Blood zooms around my brain. "Why didn't you call me?" I half shout.

"Shhh." He places his forefinger over his lips. "She asked me not to," he hisses.

My voice panicked, I ask, "Is she okay now?"

"She's been sleeping most of the afternoon. I checked on her half an hour ago and took her a fresh bottle of water. I suggested she rest until you come home." He pauses. "She thinks it's the heat."

"I wish you'd called me." Although I know why he didn't. My mother can be very insistent and stubborn. I guess it takes one to know one.

"I don't have your number." He throws his hands in the air as if defeated.

"You could have called Gregor," I point out.

He rolls his eyes. "She asked me not to, plus everything is cool. Poppy and I have had an awesome day together. Haven't we Pop-a-doodle?"

Pop-a-doodle. I love his nickname for her.

Poppy smiles, between her thumb sucking, batting her long eyelashes at him.

Yup, I'm a sucker for him too, Pop-a-doodle.

"See, she already loves me. I took care of her like a pro." He stands confidently with his hands on his hips, pushing his muscular chest out, and all I want to do is reach out and run my hands down the rivets of his washboard stomach. *Holy-freaking-shit. He is mighty fine.*

Mischievously I question, "So, you managed the diaper changes with no problems?" Knowing fine well, he is shirtless for a reason.

"None whatsoever. Diaper changer of the year." He points at his chest, then examines his fingernail.

I giggle, assuming that's the one that had poop under it.

As proud as punch, he replies, "We are all fully sanitized within an inch of our lives. Like I said, no poop on any hands or clothes." He waves his hand down his body, motioning to himself. "Professional."

I look up at his homemade hat. "You look like one."

Pushing his hands out to the side, he throws me a dazzling smile. "I do, don't I? I'm the best alien ballet dancer on planet Zog."

"Really?" I tuck my lips into my mouth.

"Well, Poppy seems to think so, don't you?" He looks at Poppy for an answer, but she's already half asleep, making squelchy noises as she sucks her thumb. "She's so bloody cute." I'm not sure he means to say his next sentence out loud. "If she was mine, I wouldn't want to miss a thing." He reaches out to touch a lock of her hair. "Michael's a fool."

I clear my throat, not wanting to give the meaning of my erratic heartbeat thumping in my chest another thought. "I'm going to check on Mom." I tilt my head toward the stairs.

"Keep in touch with Gregor. Let me know how she is, yeah?" He's respectful, not asking for my cell number.

"Have Gregor give you my number." I suddenly feel nervous and forward. Giving a man my number is not something I do, but at least I have an excuse now.

Nodding cheekily, his megawatt smile lights up the already luminous sun-filled hallway.

"Will I see you later?" Hopeful eyes search mine as he removes his makeshift tin hat.

"Blake is coming over for dinner tonight."

"Blake?" He eyes me suspiciously.

"Yeah, our public relations manager." Blake and I have been firm friends since I joined the display team.

"Right." Jaw clenched, Owen nods his head slowly. "So, you're seeing Blake tonight?"

"Yeah," I confirm.

"Fine," he grits out with a fake smile, hastily removing Poppy's tutu, almost ripping it.

What did I say to make him act crazy?

"Well, have fun with *Blake*." His sarcastic tone sounds riled when he passes me the soft pink tutu, and darts past me.

Confused, I reply, "Thanks."

Circling back around in haste, Owen stares me down. "You know, if you were already seeing somebody else, you should have said." There is an underlying biting tone in his voice. "If I was simply the warmup act to prepare for Blake, then you could have at least told me the truth."

Is that what he thinks I would do to him?

Taken aback by his outburst, words of reassurance get stuck in my throat. I'm speechless.

He runs his hands through his wild hair haphazardly. "Stupidly, I thought something special happened between us, but clearly you don't like me as much as I like you." The cadence of his voice now filled with notes of impatience. "Last night, with you was, different. It was great, incredible. Kissing you felt right. It's never felt right with anyone else. With you, it was fuc—" Aware of Poppy in my arms, he seems to reconsider his choice of words, then melts my heart when he says, "Utterly perfect."

My wide eyes stare at him in alarm. *He felt it too.*

He stops himself from saying any more. "Bollocks, I've said too much. Anyway, hope your mom's feeling better soon. See you around."

Still reeling from his words, I watch Owen storm out the front door.

What the hell just happened?

CHAPTER NINE

Owen

I slam the front door so hard it makes the windows and shutters of the villa shake in their frames. A reflection of how I feel; rattled.

Heading for the kitchen, I pull open the refrigerator, take out a beer, twist the top off, and take a large gulp.

In anger, I bash it down on the worktop, making it explode like a volcano. Irritated, I curse under my breath before cleaning it up.

"Christ, who bit your ass?"

"No one." I storm past Gregor, into the living area and drop myself onto the sofa.

Speaking in an amused voice from behind me, he asks, "You're not pissed off, then?"

"No." Tilting my neck, settling the back of my head against the cushions, I eye the ceiling.

"You sure?"

Sounding firm, I reply, "Yes."

"Great, glad we cleared that up."

I twist my head to look at him. "Do you know she's spending the night with Blake?"

"Who's spending the night with Blake?" Gregor's brow lines with confusion.

"Jade."

"Jade?"

"Yes, Jade."

"They're close, so what?"

"What does he look like? Is he big? Could I take him?" I seriously do not know why I care or why I have this unfamiliar ache in my chest when I think about her with him. Or why little Poppy has already slid into my thoughts and heart.

It's not right. Nothing is right, and it's making me feel off balance.

I've known them for all of thirty hours.

So why does it feel like longer?

Gregor raises his pointer finger in the air, then he slyly smiles. "Wait, are you into Jade?"

"No." Lies, lies, all lies.

"Fucking hell, you've no chance." His words only antagonize me more. "She's really protective of Poppy, and after Michael, she doesn't trust easily."

I mutter incomprehensible words under my breath, rolling my head back to the center.

"I didn't catch that," Gregor informs me.

I run my hand down my face. "I said, something happened between us last night."

Gregor plonks himself down beside me on the sofa. "Well, shit. Cobra won't be happy about that."

"Cobra?"

"Yeah, he's our big boss; the Wing Commander. He's our supervisor and oversees our health and safety procedures and does the commentating at the displays. You'll meet him soon. I think he has feelings for Jade."

With a nickname like Cobra, sounds like he's ready to strike and sink his teeth into her.

He adds, "But he can be leery. Weird. I don't like the way he looks at Jade."

"Weird how?"

"I don't know. Creepy. Like his eyes linger on her too long. And just other things he does and the way he speaks about her. I don't know. Maybe I'm wrong."

Blake, Cobra, how many more admirers does she have?

Never one to be jealous before, I find myself wanting to lay my heart on the line for her, enter the gladiator ring, and fight any man until I'm the last one standing.

Maybe it's the lack of direction I currently have in my life that's sending me off-piste, but I can't say I've ever felt the instant spark like the one I feel with Jade.

Gregor continues, "Jade is..." He tails off.

"Special, I know, so everyone keeps saying." They don't have to tell me. I feel it. All the way down, deep in my bones.

"Wow. This is big." Gregor sounds shocked at my news. "Jade is a closed book in relationships." He pauses, his gaze thoughtful. "She's an introverted extrovert. In public, at the shows, during press conferences, meeting celebrities and the royals and such, she lights up the whole room and does more positive PR than any of us combined, but with her private life, she keeps that on lockdown. That's a treasure chest no one's getting the key to."

Except she let me unlock it last night—*not that I'm telling him that*—and I'm so fucking grateful she did, because after hearing how closely guarded she is, I feel *special*. She made me feel important. But now I know she is having dinner with Blake, she clearly doesn't feel the same spark between us.

"And she told me earlier that she doesn't like that her villa is next door to Cobra's. I am certain he has an ulterior motive," Gregor adds.

Without saying anything, I know what he means; Cobra wants to get closer to Jade.

"He allocated the biggest villa to her and then put himself right next to her in the smallest apartment, making it look like he was taking one for the team."

Cobra couldn't be more obvious if he tried.

"Is Jade interested in Cobra?" I snap, not understanding why my blood is boiling hotter than the sun, and I have an overwhelming desire to pull his fangs out with my bare hands, despite having never met the man.

"No way. Jade would never date another fellow serviceman... not after Michael. It's weird and I'm not sure what's going on, but she's mentioned how uncomfortable he makes her feel and has asked me a few times to stick around if she's working late, so she's not left alone with him. I didn't notice before she said anything, but I've caught him staring at her for more time than I'm comfortable with. He even wolf whistled at her one day when he didn't know I was there. She's not interested in him at all."

Gregor slaps my thigh. "You can't fuck this up. She's my boss, Owen, and I won't let your fuck boy ways ruin my career. She'll give me all the shitty flying stunts if you mess around with her."

I spring upward, sitting straighter than a ruler, yelling, "I am not a fuck boy."

"Yes, you are. All those times you split up with Skye, did you not hook up with girls every time?"

"Yes, but..."

"And now you've split up with Evangeline? It's only taken you a week to get your dick wet."

What the fuck? I push myself to my feet. "I didn't fucking sleep with Evangeline."

"What?" He looks shocked, his eyes wide and doubtful. "For an entire year, you kept your dick in your pants?"

"Yes." Exasperated, I fling my hands in the air. "I haven't slept with anyone since Skye and I broke up."

"No way?"

"And I never *ever* cheated on Skye." I only hooked up with the same three girls when Skye and I would break up. It was a rebound thing and something I'm not proud of.

"Well, that's a pleasant surprise." He rubs his chin. "So, you and Evangeline... never?"

I shiver at the very thought of her cold hands touching my body. "Fuck no. She was too young for me, and it was all fake and *wrong*." So fucking wrong. "We weren't even friends."

"Well, that's a damn shame. She was hot."

"And as deceiving as a starfish; pretty on the outside, but a cold, heartless bitch on the inside." I shudder again. That girl gives me the heebie-jeebies.

"Your parents seem to think she was right for you," Gregor smirks, knowing that's the furthest thing from the truth.

"That girl has the emotional capacity to love as much as a serial killer does while stalking his next victim. I'm certain they picked her out of a line of suspects at an identity parade," I say, making Gregor laugh.

Downhearted, I prepare myself to spill the next news I learned earlier. "While we are discussing Evangeline and matters back home. I got a text from Jacob earlier telling me that my dad sold my car."

Gregor's mouth drops open. "Your fucking car?"

Although it hurts, I shrug it off. "He bought it for my twenty-first birthday. He's angry at me and taking back what 'rightfully' belongs to him, I suppose. He had a removal company box up all my stuff from my house too and put into storage."

Confirming everything I already knew, I'm simply a tiny cog in my father's ever-changing machine. Insignificant to him in every way. I'm not important to him. I never was.

"He's trying to hurt you, Owen. Don't let him. It's just stuff. Stuff that is easily replaced."

I nod in agreement and plonk my ass back down on the sofa.

Knowing me well, he asks, "I can tell there's more. What else did Jacob say in that text?"

"That I have forty-eight hours to get my ass back to Castleview Cove or he's cutting me from my inheritance."

"No," he exclaims. "He can't do that."

With nothing more to lose and my loyalty to the family dissolving, I spill the tea. "I couldn't give a shit about my inheritance. I've decided I'm not going back."

"You're not?"

"I need to do something for myself, Gregor. You have this incredible career. One you wanted. I've never had to think for myself before. I need to discover what I want to do with my life, not what my father wants for me."

Hoping he understands, I glance at him and wait for his response. "Do whatever you need to in order to be happy." Pausing for a beat, he then finishes with, "Fuck them. Prove them wrong."

He then changes direction. "Do you still have your trust fund your grandfather left you?" He holds his breath.

"Yeah. Still there. I checked this afternoon."

My father's father was a stern but lovely man and when he died, he left me and my sister Camilla five million each. He was always about family and taking care of each other. He would have hated to know my mother bullied me.

He exhales loudly. "Thank God for that. That's rightfully yours. That money was left in trust for you and you alone. What about your sister? Does she still have hers? I'm assuming she does?"

Ashamed of myself for not taking more interest in my sister's life, I answer truthfully, "I have no idea."

If I reach out and check how she's doing... offer her an olive branch, it could be the beginning of making amends. We could maybe patch the little tatters that are left of our relationship back together. However, perhaps now is not the time.

Gregor runs his hand back and forth across his blonde buzz cut, determination written all over his face. "Do whatever makes you happy, Owen. That money will help to set you up for life."

"It will." Mari's words from earlier race through my mind. *Don't play the game, change it.*

From this point going forward, I am determined to make my own choices. My strength at work is finance. I'll invest it wisely.

He stares at the wall as if considering what his life would be like if he were in my position. "You did the right thing leaving, Owen. I'm proud of you, man."

Embarrassment floods my cheeks, because no one has ever been proud of me. Even my parents didn't show up on the day I graduated from university.

Plus, it's always been the other way about for us. I'm the one that's proud of Gregor and his chosen career, because he went through a tough selection process while I went to a university to do a degree my father chose for me, and although I earned my first class honors degree fair and square, I didn't have to apply for jobs. I simply showed up at the family offices the week after graduation and that was that.

Gregor cuts through our silence. "Stay here with me. Sort your head out."

"Yeah," I agree with him. I'm not being threatened or allowing my parents to bully me anymore. "Then I'll decide what my next move is." I point at the spot I'm rooted to on the sofa. "And I don't want the business anyway, so I don't care if he cuts me out of it," I confess.

My sister can have it.

And if my father can decide to cut me from his life in just a few days, then it proves to me I mean nothing to him. Neither does Camilla.

"That empire is all that matters to my father." Disheartened, I sigh. Although I know Camilla has no interest in it either.

"You mean something to me, Owen," Gregor murmurs, the emotion clear in his voice. "You always have. I know I treated you like my little brother when we were growing up; the fights about sharing my toys and moaning when you wanted to tag along with me and my friends, but that means I also love you like a brother." His Adam's apple bobs slowly in his throat. "Jacob and Lincoln do too."

I wiggle nervously in my seat. "Thanks."

Emotion building between us, it gets all too much, and he clears his throat and changes the subject. "I'm meeting some of the team for dinner later. Wanna join?"

"Nah." Not wanting to go out tonight, I say, "I'll make myself something. There's lots of food in the refrigerator."

"I like how much you've grown in the last year, Owen.

Buying your own groceries, learning to cook, firing your cleaner. Doing your own laundry. It's admirable."

"And about damn time." I sweep my chaotic chlorine-filled hair from my face.

"You've changed. I liked you before. I like you better now." His honesty throws me off kilter.

I have changed for the better, grateful to have broken free from the charmed, almost unreal life I was living before my friends woke me up from my selfish coma.

"I like me better now, too." I push aside the stuck-between-worlds feeling; still at a loss about what direction to lead myself in. "But I'll feel even better after a shower," I say, rising to my feet and moving out of the living room.

"We are flying early tomorrow," Gregor informs me, so I know he'll be gone at the crack of dawn.

"I'd love to come watch you fly."

"I'd love that too. It's been a long time since any family has watched me perform." He looks excited when he leaps to his feet and bounces on his toes. "I'll organize a pass for you to get on base and you can use my hire car."

"Can't wait. Enjoy your meal tonight." My foot hits the first step on the staircase. "I didn't sleep with Jade last night." I clear up my earlier statement, just in case he gets the wrong idea about Jade and me.

"Really?" he replies, his voice thick with sarcasm again.

"Yes. Really." I draw out my words. "We did, you know, other stuff."

He casually leans against the doorway and stares at me as if expecting me to divulge, then a big toothy grin curves his lips.

"I shouldn't have said anything. You're an asshole."

"She dumped you for Blake?" Gregor teases me from below.

"Yes. Now fuck off."

Gregor's taunting echoes in the hallway. "Now you come to mention it. She has grown closer to Blake over the last couple of months. I see that now. Blake filled a civilian post, not a military one, so that would work out perfectly for Jade if she doesn't plan on dating anyone from the military, I guess."

The asshole keeps on making jokes as a low growl bubbles in my throat. With every stomp up the last of the steps, I imagine it's Blake's face I'm pummeling the sole of my foot into, and Gregor's.

Well, isn't this year just one big fucking delight?

Showered, and now sitting on my bed, legs sprawled out in from me, ankles crossed, laptop teetering on my knees, I've trawled the internet, reading everything my eyes can soak up about Jade.

Watching interviews, scrolling pages and pages of photographs of her shaking hands with celebrities and royalty, her arms around musicians and sports personalities, she appears to have met everyone, becoming a celebrity in her own right.

On camera, she's a natural. In photographs she's scroll-stopping and captivating. Her big blue crystal eyes and firecracker colored hair make her unique in so many ways. I can't fathom why I never paid attention to Gregor's career sooner. How did I not see her before?

Because you've had your head up your egotistical ass, that's why.

OWEN

I stalked her social media platforms for way too long, scrolling, enlarging, and learning everything there is to know about her schedules, the display, how the stunts are performed, and watching press videos of her with the team.

I then watched a half-hour special with her that followed a day in the life of an aerobatic pilot on the Air Force's video channel, too, making my stomach do its own three-sixty spiral while she reached speeds of five hundred miles an hour. Soaring, looping, and flipping through the air, sometimes only feet apart from another aircraft, making me realize she's an unsuspecting daredevil in a jumpsuit; and fucking sexy as hell in it.

Hypnotized by her online presence, I scrolled back through her cleverly curated newsfeed and grids. Work focused, and asides from Poppy's birth announcement, there isn't a selfie in sight.

On closer inspection, and thinking about it, it looks as if it's managed by an external media company. Or Blake maybe. *Fucking Blake.* The guy I can't find any information about. It's killing me that she's currently next door with him, and Poppy. *Does Poppy like him more than me?*

Why does it matter? All you did was change her diaper and look after the little cutie for a couple of hours.

I smile to myself.

It was a great couple of hours, though.

However, my judgment is way off since I've fled my hometown. With no job prospects or even a roof over my head, and with my beautiful Aston Martin Vantage sold, Jade would never be interested in someone like me. After all, I have nothing to offer. *Although, I have my trust fund money.*

Maybe I should start my own business? It would certainly allow me to have control.

What the hell would I do?

Still lazing with my back against the headboard, I continue my detective work.

Having found out from Gregor that he's friends with Jade's ex on social media, I click open a new tab on my internet browser, open Gregor's page, and type *Michael* into Gregor's friend list. With only one option, I click on his name and there he is in a flight suit, all sickly sweet smiles, and oozing success.

Selecting his photos folder, there is only one of Poppy, looking only a few days old. The rest are all selfies.

"What a douche canoe," I mutter to myself.

I scroll further down and stop in my tracks as dozens of photos of Jade and Michael cuddling, laughing at parties and on holiday appear. I click and open the one that catches my eye, stealing my breath away.

A picture of Jade fills the screen. Head in hand, she's casually leaning across a dining table, wearing a plain white tee, her long copper hair spilling over her shoulders in waves; a stark contrast against the white fabric. No makeup, big pouty pink lips, and massive blue eyes stare back at me as if looking into my soul.

Her beauty knocks the air from my lungs, my mouth instantly dry, and blood rushing through my brain.

"Holy fucking shit." I palm my twitching cock over the fabric of my shorts.

Remembering how she cried my name last night as she came on my tongue, the zip of my shorts is down in a flash, my hard dick in my hand. Using the precum from my weeping slit to stroke myself, faint memories of her breathy sighs and gasps flood my brain.

I jerk myself faster, imagining her fingers in my hair,

pulling at my scalp, recalling how she responded when I did what she asked last night. *Just like that, Owen.*

She almost suffocated me, pushing her pussy, which tasted like heaven, into my face.

I stare at the stunning image on my screen and fist myself more firmly, warmth and pleasure building in my balls.

Come down my throat, Owen. I recall her demands.

About to blow, I remember what her pretty lips looked like wrapped around my cock. Like a fucking red ribbon tied around the best present. My balls draw up as a tidal wave of pleasure pulses through every cell. I shoot my release all over my hand and stomach, my cock pulsing as I expel a low groan, but not feeling sated, not even in the slightest.

I want more. So much more.

I want her.

"Fuck," I curse, emptying myself completely, coming down from my orgasmic high, and bang my head backward against the headboard behind me.

I leap from the bed to clean myself up in my adjoining bathroom.

Sauntering back into my bedroom while zipping up my shorts, my phone lights up from the nightstand. Pulling a fresh shirt out of the closet, I button it up before reaching for my phone and opening the text message from my cousin.

GREGOR:
> I arranged your visitor's pass. Blake approved a team pass for you too, which will give you access all areas. Go to Jade's and pick it up from Blake. You need that for tomorrow.

Another text drops in.

> GREGOR:
> At least you'll be able to see if you can take Blake on ;) I didn't pack my boxing gloves though, sorry.

> ME:
> Idiot.

> GREGOR:
> (Laughing emoji).

> GREGOR:
> Go now.

What's the urgency?

> ME:
> Okay.

> GREGOR:
> Don't do anything stupid.

> ME:
> I think I've done enough stupid things recently to last me a lifetime.

> GREGOR:
> True. Text me to let me know when you've been.

> ME:
> Will do.

I examine my outfit in the mirror, then pull on a pair of white sneakers internally telling myself it's not a fashion show, nor is it a competition.

Yes, it fucking is.

With one final glance in the mirror, running my hands through my hair, I tuck both sides behind my ears. I push my hands into the pockets of my shorts. Filling my cheeks with air, I blow out a huge breath.

Why the hell am I so nervous?

Because you like her dumbass, and you feel threatened by Blake.

"Ah, fuck it." Grabbing my phone off the bed, I push it into my pocket and run down the stairs.

Right, Blake, it's game on.

CHAPTER TEN

Owen

It's late now. I tap the brass Grecian Goddess door knocker lightly, twice, being careful not to wake Poppy, if she is in bed.

Shoving my hands into the pockets of my shorts, I wait, tapping my foot impatiently, desperate to see Jade again.

But she's spending the night with Blake, numb nuts. You don't stand a chance.

The door clicks twice as someone on the other side fumbles with the locks. I straighten myself to full height, preparing to greet this *Blake* guy, who Jade is having *dinner* with. If I have it my way, she'll be having dinner with me tomorrow night and not him.

As the door swings open, I'm thrown off center as a stunning brunette woman, in a navy and white spotted dress, wearing the biggest smile, welcomes me.

"Hey. You must be Owen?" She widens the wedge of the open door, beckoning for me to come in with the sway of her arm.

"Eh, yeah," I stutter, as I step inside out of the dark, and into the warm mood lighting of the hall.

"We've been expecting you." She confidently winks, shutting the door behind me before she fiddles with the shiny red belt around her waist. She's immaculate from head to toe. *Who is she?*

Just then, Jade bounces down the stairs in a deep burgundy knee length dress, making her hair look a deeper red tone. It shimmers under the low lighting, making her eyes pop.

I audibly gulp at her beauty as lust courses through my veins. *I want her.*

"Hey Owen," she says breezily, as if I didn't act like a deranged idiot earlier. She stops on the bottom stair and casually leans against the banister. "So, you met *Blake*." She emphasizes her name with wide eyes and motions with a head nod in the other woman's direction.

My head snaps in Blake's direction. "You're a woman?" My mouth clearly not getting the memo to shut the hell up.

Blake looks down at herself, squeezes her boobs, then lifts her gaze back up. "All five foot five of me." Then Jade and Blake both burst out laughing.

I narrow my eyes and stare Jade down. "But—"

She cuts in, "You thought Blake was a guy? I know." Smug with herself, she folds her arms in front of her, and pops a hip. "I figured that out after you left. Then Gregor sent me a text confirming my suspicions."

I may steal that meat cleaver I spotted earlier from Jade's cutlery drawer and chop off Gregor's balls with it when I get back to our villa.

With a pleased and confident curve to her lips, she says, "You're blushing."

"No, I'm not." She's right, my cheeks are burning.

"That's cute." Her grin broadens even more.

Blake walks behind me. "I'll leave you two alone," she says amusedly. "Your pass to get on to base for the next four weeks is sitting on the console table, Owen." She pats my back twice. "Have Jade give you my number and text me when you arrive on base and I will meet you at the guard room and show you where to park near the airfield."

Feeling like an idiot, my awkward gaze follows her, watching as she disappears into the kitchen. Then I slide my eyes back to Jade.

She beckons me to her with her forefinger.

Pulse racing, I walk across the hall to the bottom of the stairs where she still stands. Up one step higher than me, and now the same height, she drapes her arms over my shoulders.

"Hi," she breathes.

I relax when she presses herself against me. "You could have told me." I'm filled with humiliation at my knee-jerk reaction earlier.

Blake's a woman, phew.

"You didn't exactly give me a chance to explain. You went off on a tangent at a hundred miles an hour." She moves her lips closer to mine. "Your jealously makes me like you all the more." She grants me a lazy smile, making my heart do some sort of weird tumbling thing in my chest.

She likes me.

"I'm sorry about earlier." Our foreheads rest against each other.

"I'm not. Now kiss me like you did last night, Owen Brodie, because kissing you feels amazing. Utterly perfect." She sighs, happiness shining in her eyes as she repeats the words I confessed to her this afternoon.

I wrap my arms around her waist and kiss her like I've

never kissed anyone before, because, before her, no one has ever come close to how I feel when my lips touch hers.

Not anymore.

Because this woman who is currently kissing me, digging her fingers into my hair, and moaning into my mouth, is the only woman to render me speechless and make me lose all sense of reality.

This past year has been so fucking hard, but this woman... the one that didn't run a million miles away from me when I freaked out earlier, make spiteful jests about my behavior, or look at me as if I meant nothing... is making all my emotional wounds disappear. She's wrapping me up in a cocoon of euphoria; she's fucking addictive and healing me in ways I don't yet understand.

Deepening our kiss, twirling her tongue around mine, I never want her to stop.

Threading my hands into her fiery red locks, tightening my grip, I tug her head back, allowing me access to the delicious curve of her neck.

"Owen," she moans, my cock now rock solid for this woman.

Moving my lips across her jaw, I trail a path of languid kisses down her slender throat and back up again, toward the sweet spot I discovered she likes behind her ear.

Nuzzling into my neck, she kisses away all my insecurities and doubts from earlier, the heat between us becoming unbearable.

"We have to stop." My lips move against her soft skin, inwardly annoyed because it's not what I want.

"I don't want to," she gasps, as if reading my thoughts as I nip at her neck, rubbing her pelvis against my aching cock. "I want you." Her brazen words holding nothing back.

I swallow her erotic mewls with a kiss, our bodies coming alive together as she sets my heart on fire.

"I think you're magic," I mumble between breaths. "A kiss shouldn't feel this good." *Should it?*

"Kissing you feels like witchcraft," she whispers. Her petal soft lips twitch against my mouth, then blossom into a full smile at the same time as mine.

Forehead to forehead, my chest heaving in excitement, we stare giddily into each other's eyes.

"Can you forgive me for my outburst this afternoon? You drive me fucking crazy." I try to justify my jealous behavior. I don't know what the hell is wrong with me.

Well, that's a bald-faced lie, I do. It's her.

She's special.

"I like you crazy." She bites at her bottom lip.

I rock my head slowly left and right, as if in disbelief. *She likes me crazy.*

She follows up with, "Would you like to do something with me tonight?"

Still holding on to her, I lean out of our embrace slightly. "What about Poppy? And your mom? Gosh, how is your mom? Is she okay?" I'm still not fully convinced it's the heat that's making her dizzy.

She tucks a lock of my hair behind my ear, which I find oddly settling. I may decide to keep my hair longer if she touches me like that again. "My mom was fine at dinner after resting this afternoon, and she's had no more weird dizzy spells. She said she felt better, too, but went to bed half an hour ago because she wanted to get an early night. I reckon she needs a good sleep. It's been a busy time for us coordinating our move here."

"That's reassuring news but tell her I am here tomorrow if she needs me to help with Poppy."

"I'll let her know," she says, then reminds me of her earlier question. "So, tonight?"

"What about it?" A boost of energy, enough to start a car, brews in my belly.

"Wanna get out of here?"

"Poppy?"

"I asked Blake if she could babysit for a couple of hours. I'll have you home by midnight."

Calm settles in my bones, knowing she made plans to enable her to see me tonight.

"What happens at midnight?"

"I turn into an ogre."

I shake my head at her stupidity.

"Where are we going?"

"You'll see." Then she kisses me again.

CHAPTER ELEVEN

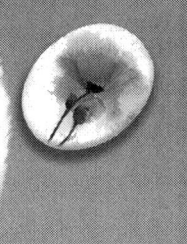

Owen

"Where the hell are we?" I look out of the car windscreen, into the dark as Jade parks her hired Jeep Wrangler.

"Welcome to Aphrodite's Rock." She unbuckles her seatbelt, jumps out of the car, and motions for me to get out too before I've even blinked.

Fuck me, this woman moves fast.

Fast jets and fast driving. I held on for dear life as she tore along the cliff-topped roads on the way here.

I mean, I enjoy driving fast and we have incredible countryside roads in Castleview Cove to do exactly that. But at night, in the dark on a road you don't know, Jade just gave a whole new meaning to living life in the fast lane.

She scares the shit out of me in so many ways. Which freaks me out, but I'm also here for it too.

"What are you waiting for?" Her voice muffled as she shouts from outside of the car, as I still haven't moved. Then she turns on her heels and starts running away.

"Shit," I hiss, unclipping my seat belt, and leap out of the jeep as her silhouette disappears into the darkness.

Pulling my phone out of my shorts pocket, I tap the flashlight on and call out her name as I slam the car door closed. The warm salty air hits my nostrils, the faint sound of breaking waves radiating in the distance.

"I'm over here." Her phone light flickers in the black of night as she swings it through the air.

Jogging toward her, the ground changes as I hit pebbles, kicking them up around my legs and into my sneakers.

"You're so slow," she teases.

"I didn't realize it was a competition." Slightly out of breath, I grab her waist, pulling her into my arms to tickle her sides.

"I'm not ticklish." She doesn't react to my wiggling fingers.

"What? How is that even possible? That's surely not a thing?"

"It is and I'm not." She elevates herself to her tiptoes and smacks a kiss to my lips. "Clothes off. We're going for a swim." She moves back, quickly places her phone on the pebbled beach, then removes her dress, followed by her gold sandals.

"No way. There could be sharks." My voice goes a little squeaky. I love surfing and swimming, and as a hardened Scot, I'm thick-skinned and can tolerate the bracing temperature of the North Sea in the winter surf, but sharks, nope, not doing that, never.

"There won't be any sharks." She pulls a white stone out of her bra before whipping it off. Standing there in only her lace panties, my brain disconnects from my spinal cord momentarily.

Realizing she pulled something out of her bra, my

curiosity pulls me back to reality. "What's that?" I point at the white stone.

Holding it up between her fingers, she shows me a shiny white pebble, barely an inch in size. In the dark, I can just make out a tiny pillar box red poppy on the front of it. "My lucky charm. I wear it in my bra, next to my heart most days, and always when I fly." She looks melancholy. "My dad gave it to me." Her eyes drop to the shiny stone as she rubs the pad of her thumb over it. "He said it would bring me good luck." When she looks up, her mouth is tilted up to the side. "It has."

I gulp so loud I'm surprised she doesn't hear it over the waves crashing and lapping against the rocks that line the edge of the beach as it suddenly dawns on me that I want to keep her close to *my* heart. Forever. Because she feels like my very own good luck charm.

Standing almost completely naked on the beach, she meticulously places her stone on top of her clothes. My head in a spin, I use my torch to look around the beach, to check no one else is around.

"It's just us," Jade reassures me excitedly. "Nobody comes down here at this time of the night."

I shine my torch in her face. "Is this what we do now? We skinny dip by moonlight together?" Although I quite like the thought of that.

"Yes. Strip," she says authoritatively, stalking toward me, her full breasts bouncing as she moves. "Or I will undress you myself." Her brows raise as if she's challenging me.

Having only known each other for a few days, it strikes me how comfortable we are with each other already. Jade seems to have shed any initial body insecurities she may have had as she swings her flared hips my way.

Enjoying every delicious curve of her body, I continue to watch her as I push my arms out to the sides. "Have at me then," I counter as I shuck my sneakers off my feet.

My shirt is gone in a flash. Next, she crouches, unzips my shorts, then pulls them and my boxers off, throwing them over her shoulder. When I'm naked, she pushes herself up on her tiptoes, placing another chaste kiss on my lips.

Kissing seems to be another thing we both like doing.

I look down at myself, growing hard, my cock excited to be near her nakedness. "Why the hell am I completely naked and you're not?"

"Have at me." Smirking, she pulls the elasticized hair band off her wrist and ties her hair up into a messy bun. Like a magnet, my eyes automatically follow the silhouette of her hourglass curves as she offers herself to me.

Sliding her panties down her hips and legs, I then drop to my knees onto the shingle beach, too lost in her and our *what comes next* moment to care about the sharp stones against my skin. My lips seek her pussy and her whimpers get lost in the warm wind as I use the tip of my tongue to flick her clit.

"Owen." She moans, thrusting her hips, wanting more. I grin against her skin, then inhale her sweet scent of tangerines and deep amber. "You smell fucking amazing." I softly bite her now swollen clit.

She grabs my face, guiding me to stand, then hungrily kisses me. "I might drive you crazy, Owen, but you make me feel like a wild woman," she mumbles before she bites my bottom lip. Without warning, she grabs my hand, pulling me past the pebbled part of the beach and down into the sand along the edge of the shore. Then she leads me into the blackened sea as we wade deeper.

She squeals as she hits the *colder than expected* water, and I roar when the Mediterranean Sea hits my skin. "Fuck me sideways," I hiss. "I think I lost my testicles."

Jade bursts into a fit of giggles, and I reach for her, threading my arms around her waist.

Her hand disappears below the water, making me flinch when she cups my junk and says, "I think you're right." She squeezes my now shriveled cock, her teeth chattering together.

"You'll have to warm him up to make him come out again, Hotshot." I wink, my eyes now adjusted to the darkness.

With a loud laugh, she wraps her arms around my neck, jumps up, then threads her legs around my waist, hooking her ankles behind my back, before kissing me for what feels like forever. Her kiss hits hard, pulling me into her orbit, making me feel as if I'm weightless.

Between kisses, she says, "Do you know why you're here?"

"Nope." I kiss the side of her mouth.

She points to the enormous rock to our right that's standing like a soldier guarding us.

I pull her closer when she starts speaking. "Legend has it that this..." We both look at Aphrodite's Rock, "Is the birthplace of the Goddess of Love, Aphrodite. She was created from the foam of the sea. Cronus caused the foam by castrating his father Uranus and throwing his genitals into the water."

I shake with a combination of laughter and feeling colder since we aren't moving. "Great, we might find a pair of testicles in here after all." I wrap myself around her tighter to keep us warm.

"We might." She fights hard to hide her smile as she

continues, obviously desperate to tell me the story. "Local folklore says that anyone who swims around the rock will be blessed with great and eternal beauty. But Greek mythology says that if you swim around the rock three times, you will find true love."

Her last words stop my heart for a millisecond.

Eyes locked, I can't tear my gaze away from her angelic face that I dreamed about last night.

"Is that what you want, Jade, to find true love?"

She whispers, "I did for a very long time. Then I gave up." My heart plummets from my chest into my stomach. "That was until yesterday."

Giving me hope and being coy, I ask, "What happened yesterday?"

"I met a guy." Her voice is playful but with a hint of uncertainty.

"Is he nice?"

She bobs her head twice, slowly. "He's wonderful, but no one, not even himself, has ever allowed him to shine."

Her words trigger my vulnerabilities. "You don't know him well enough to say that."

"I do. I'm a great judge of character and I feel like I already know him, because he shared part of himself with me last night, something he rarely does, if ever." She plays with the wavy hair at the base of my neck, curling it around her fingers, hypnotizing me with her touch. "He told me since the day he was born he was expected to be, act and do everything a certain way. Never allowed to make his own decisions or carve his own path. So he gave up trying; with his girlfriend. His friends. Family. Work."

As if someone turned down the noise levels, the crashing waves around us seem to stop, reflecting how she makes me feel; calm and steady.

She's got me all figured out.

What a woman.

Enchanted by the way she's looking at me with her big blue eyes, brick by broken brick, she dismantles the wall I've built up around my heart. "He may have been selfish in the past, but he's trying to change. He thinks he's being selfish by running away, except for the last year he tried to do what he thought best to bolster the family business and maintain its legacy. All while he was dying inside." She rests her hand over my heart. "He knew deep down in here." She taps the center of my chest. "That love and people can't be bought, but he was doing what was expected of him, even at the cost of his own happiness. His cousin told me everything today, including that his mom and dad married as part of a business deal. His sister did too and his mother did nothing to protect her children from their inevitable fate." She shakes her head in disapproval. "Loving your children unconditionally, protecting them—" She stalls, as if emotion is building in her chest. "Love should be freely given, not bought or exchanged. She should never have put you in that position." Her eyes turn watery. "Love and marriage are sacred. They mean something. They allow you to form a bond that no one else understands. It's limitless and transcends beyond intimacy. It's about being partners spiritually, emotionally, and physically. Marriage is not a tool to be used to bargain with, and the guy I'm talking about knew that, too. So, he broke the cycle."

So many emotions I've been holding on to expel through my next breath, suddenly making the tight muscles of my chest loosen and relax. "He did," I exclaim. I fucking did. I broke the chain.

Jade lays her forehead against mine. "Love is about feeling that connection... that feeling that you can't ignore."

My voice cracks, "Fate." I know what she's getting at.

"Kismet—" She smiles confidently. "Us meeting. We were predetermined. I know it because I feel it, Owen. Destiny, on the other hand, is what *we* choose to do from this moment moving forward."

Always one to be cautious with my heart and feelings, I decide to be honest. "I don't know what happens next. I have nothing to offer you."

"One day at a time, Owen."

"I have to start again."

"Press the reset button and start here." She looks over her left shoulder, up at the towering rock. "Tonight, under the moonlight, you'll start your own legendary story. Swim around the rock and make it mean something specific to you. Not legend or folktale, not myth. Give your swim meaning."

"To find my purpose."

She twists to face me again. "Set an intention and let it go. Hand it over to the deities and demigods. You're in the perfect place to ask the Greek gods for help, guidance, support. Anything your soul desires, Owen. Just ask," she whispers, quietly adding, "Swim once. Let inspiration come and ideas percolate. Swim twice, then, and only then ask for what you want. And don't be specific, go general. Ask for happiness, feeling good, comfort, the perfect job, a bed to sleep in, a home, but no detail. Let the gods and goddesses do the work for you tonight. The last swim, release and unattach yourself from the outcome."

She renders me speechless. I'm at a loss why she thinks I am worthy of her time, or why she brought me here to do this.

"It's time. Your time." She says.

I gasp when she unwraps herself from around me, fully

exposing me to the freezing temperature of the water, making me shiver.

Looking out across the now calmer water, right on cue, the clouds clear, exposing the full moon, its light dappling and twinkling across the surface of the waves.

"Full moon forgiveness." Jade pushes herself through the dark water that looks like liquid ink.

My body brewing with emotion and excitement at taking the first step along a new pathway, even if Jade's mumbo jumbo doesn't work, I join her, slicing through the sea, as if carving my highway.

"What does full moon forgiveness mean?" I ask, choosing to swim breaststroke so I can keep my head above the water and navigate in the dark.

Jade is clearly spiritual and as the only woman to make the cut on a highly male dominated team, I am guessing she uses positive mindset rituals, like this one she is having me do, to push herself, to make every day matter, and grow.

Breathlessly, as we get close to the rock, she tries to keep her voice level as she continues to swim. "Forgive yourself for your past, forgive others to help you move forward, let go of any grudges, shed the hurt you feel or have placed on others. Fully forgive to let the good in. The full moon is all about completion. Let the cleansing energy of the moon water bathe you."

"You're so weird," I say, laughing nervously. I want to believe her, but at the same time, I can't help pooh-poohing her hocus-pocus.

Coming to an abrupt halt, unable to touch the bottom of the ocean, she treads water to circle around, spraying water in my direction. "Do you trust me?" She looks fierce, the fire in her tangible.

"I barely know you." If I'm being honest with myself, I

feel like my heart knows her, and she's what's been missing from my life.

"Oh, you know me, Owen, you know you do." Her eyes roll as she calls me out. "Ask, believe, release. Trust the process. Go."

I won't ever grow tired of her telling me what to do.

As she leads from the front, I watch her move through the water as we bask in the moonlight together.

In silence, I do everything she asks, because no one has ever taken the time or had the energy to put up with my entitled ass and spoiled smart mouth.

What do I have to lose? My life is currently in pieces, and if this is the first step to help pick up the parts and glue them back together into a completely different shape, then I'm all for it.

I want change, and I want my life to have meaning. It's all been pointless and lacking substance so far. As long as I am safe, warm, and happy well, that's all that matters.

As we reach the finish line of the last lap around the rock, I feel relaxed, as if the swimming immersed me into a kind of meditation.

Lost in our bubble of calm, we swim away from the rock, toward the smaller ones scattered along the shoreline.

As we reach the shallower water, Jade flips onto her back, trying to catch her breath, her chest heaving from the exertion of our swim.

Floating on the water, she looks every inch a Pre-Raphaelite goddess as her pale skin creates a glowing silhouette around her.

I swear to all the Greek gods as I stop breathing when the swell of her breasts and small belly pop out above the surface, making them look like tiny white sandy islands.

"You've no idea how beautiful you are, Hotshot."

Tipping her head further back to wet her hair before she tilts her hips and lowers her legs into the water. I anchor my feet, steadying myself into the sand below as she swims into my arms, "And you are very handsome." Chest to chest, she laces her legs around my back again.

I like how easily she accepts my compliments; her confidence gives me confidence.

"Thank you." I hug her tightly.

"How do you feel?" She lays her head on my shoulder, her breathing returning to its normal pace, reminding me what great shape she has to be in to do her job.

"Better." I feel great, energized, ready to take on the world.

"What did you ask for? In fact—" She lifts her head suddenly, then places her pointer finger over my lips. "Don't tell me. That's your secret."

"Okay," I answer against her finger, my intrigue getting the better of me. "Did you ask for anything?"

"I did." Her voice is full of excitement. "I asked for—"

Not wanting her to share her innermost desires with me either, I swallow her words, kissing her lips which taste of salt and possibility.

"Thank you for bringing me here." Grateful she knows what I need even when I don't, our kiss deepens, turning erotic. I can't hold off any longer. "I want you."

"Then take me." She anchors her hands against my chest as I capture her lips with mine. Against her mouth, I say, "Not here. I want to spread you out and take hours enjoying your delectable body."

"Hours?" Her little moans are deep and needy when I lay a path of soft kisses down the curve of her neck.

"Yes, hours, although I may not last five minutes inside of you. You're so sexy and my cock really fucking likes you."

I slide my now hardened length between her pussy lips. Being this close to her makes my heart thump against my rib cage.

She gasps, lacing her fingers into my hair at the base of my neck. "God, Owen, I want you inside of me. Now," she demands.

"I don't have a condom," I can barely get my words out as the thick tip of my cock teases her clit.

"I had a contraceptive shot before I arrived here, and I had a medical a month ago. I'm clean."

"Me too."

"You had a contraceptive shot?" Her chest full of laughter shakes, pressing against mine.

"Smart ass." My hands cup her ass and I give one of her cheeks a pinch.

"Ouch," she squeals, her hips bucking in reply, aligning the head of my cock perfectly with her entrance.

Inhaling deeply, letting my nerves almost get the better of me, she slants her mouth over mine, our noses squashed against each other's faces. Consumed by her, she settles my nerves as I'm surrounded by everything Jade; her scent, her touch, her sounds. *Her.*

Opening my eyes, I find her staring at me. The moon highlights her beautiful face that I never want to stop looking at.

Tightening her thigh grip around my middle, feeling desperate, I close what little space there is between us, pushing one arm under her ass and my other around her waist. "Tell me again how much you want me."

"I want you, only you."

My mouth lifts at the side with satisfaction, knowing she wants *me*. "Is this what you asked for when you swam around the rock?" I slip my cock inside of her, almost stumbling at the enormity of what we are about to do, because this isn't just anyone. This is her; my fresh start. We're about to change everything and I know without a shadow of a doubt this is where I'm supposed to be. Until my last dying breath; with her.

"Yes. I want you. Please, Owen." Her needy pleas turn into a long groan as I enter her fully. Her wet, tight pussy pulls me into her body. Fighting the urge to come, I can't control the deep groan that leaves the back of my throat.

I squeeze my eyes shut. "Jesus. Fucking. Christ, Jade," I grit out between my clenched teeth, steadying myself momentarily, resting my lips against hers. "You feel so fucking good." My chest fills with emotion as this incredible woman trusts me with her pleasure.

She moans as I thrust my hips into her as best as I can while standing, legs braced in the ever-sinking sand. "You're so big." Her walls tighten around my cock.

"I need to fuck you right, Hotshot." Walking through the dense water, I carefully sit her down on one of the large smooth stones at the edge of the beach that has been carved by the sea.

Still buried deep inside her, I feel like a god myself as she looks up at me with her ecstasy-filled eyes. I brace one hand against the rock and the other under her ass.

"Owen, I need you to move."

Groaning when she tilts her hips, I bury my face into her neck, breathing her in. A desperate need overwhelms me and I can't hold back anymore. I begin to fuck her, my body lighting up when she digs her feet into my ass, urging me to move faster, her arousal coating my cock with her excitement.

She arches her back off the rock, scraping her nails across my shoulders, instructing me to fuck her faster, making the salty water splash all around us. I reach up to pinch her nipple, hard, her legs spreading wider for me as I roll my hips, welcoming the feeling of her tight walls sucking me in.

The sounds of waves, our combined moans and breathless cries, and our wet bodies slamming together create our own symphony as we chase our release in the dark night, and I commit it all to memory because I never want to forget this moment.

Wanting to savor every minute, I slow my pace and rest my body over hers. Cupping her face, I kiss her breathless as I lazily slide back and forth, teasing her G-spot, but not enough to make her shatter.

Rocking together, I whisper in her ear, "You feel like heaven. Say my name."

Without missing a beat, she calls my name. "Owen."

"My name on your lips as I fill you with my cock is the hottest thing I've ever heard." I kiss the shell of her ear.

Leaning back to gaze into her lust-filled eyes, we stare at each other as if neither of us can believe we are doing this. An involuntary smile breaks free from my lips.

"Your body feels incredible against mine. And you are so fucking tight." The spiraling feeling in my chest I've had for days is no longer an issue, as it's replaced with a deep desire to be consumed by this amazing woman below me.

Exploring each other with desperate hands, we can't stop touching as we move together in perfect harmony. We are perfectly matched.

Giving her what she needs as she digs her fingernail into the skin of my ass. "Owen." She calls out my name when I kiss her soft skin and run my hands up the slight curve of her waist.

OWEN

"Fuck, Hotshot," I curse. "Your pussy was made for my cock."

"I want you to go faster, Owen. Please," she begs.

Impatiently, she grabs my hand and places it between us. Moving my thumb to her clit, I rub it softly at first. Her cries echo around the bowl of the cove. Showing me what she likes, her fingers press on top of mine as our hips move together in a perfect rhythm.

The sensitive tip of my cock rubs her inner walls, teasing her sweet spot that's making a whole new sound leave her lungs.

Her eyes never leave me when she cries out, "Oh my God, I'm gonna come." She curves her other hand around the back of my neck.

"Come for me, Hotshot."

"Whatever you do, don't stop." Pulling me down to her, our lips crash together.

Our tongues curl around each other as I piston my hips, desperate to make her feel good, as our souls join in a life-changing moment.

"You are fucking soaking, Hotshot."

She gasps. "You make me so wet." Her lips leaving mine, she buries her face in my neck.

Excitement and pleasure race through my body and as if she's hit by a spark of lightning, she comes. Arching her neck back, our eyes lock and her blue gems slay me as if she's looking deep into my soul, awakening parts of me I never knew existed.

Her fluttering walls set off my own orgasm, and we both cry out together. I pour my release inside of her, as her pussy continues to clench around my cock, milking me of every drop as I struggle to catch a breath, sliding back and forth more slowly, not wanting to stop.

Head back and eyes closed, her chest heaves, as her grip on my hand loosens.

"You look beautiful." I take in her relaxed body that's draped across the bleached sandstone. The shorter strands of her now drying hair whirl about in the wind like wild flames resembling the fire coursing through my veins as we connect in a way I haven't felt with any woman, or correction, in a way I've never allowed myself to feel because I knew that eventually my parents would choose my wife for me, anyway.

Not anymore. I choose Jade for myself and they don't get a say in my life anymore.

As I stare down at her, I'm filled with a possessive need to protect her and then it hits me like an arrow to the heart; I want to take care of her and Poppy. I want her to be mine in every way.

Suddenly nausea rolls in my stomach, feeling like my heart is already breaking in my chest at the thought of what follows next, because we are only here for four weeks and I'm clueless about what that is.

I lean down, reaching for her, to pull her soft lips to mine. Longing to touch her, to know that what we just did was as monumental to her as it was to me. "You are perfect, Hotshot." I nibble her bottom lip.

With her eyes still closed, blissed out, she sighs in a dazed-like state and kisses me back.

Sliding my cock out of her, pulling her sleepy body off the stone and into the water with me, I carry her onto the beach, then carefully lower her to the ground. "We need a hot shower," she giggles. Fucking giggles and it's a sound I love so much already.

"We do." I tuck the wet hair on both sides of her face behind her ears. "Let's go home."

"I don't want to." She presses her body up against mine and nuzzles into my neck. "It's been a long day, but I want to spend the night with you," she mumbles.

"Did you ask the gods for that, too?" I brazenly ask.

She snuggles into me deeper. "I asked to find true love with someone who loves Poppy as much as I do."

My heart squeezes at the word *someone* because I want that someone to be me. "He'd be one hell of a lucky guy."

"You would." She yawns, unaware she said *you*.

Her words filling me with confidence, I push my shoulders back as if I'm a showy peacock. "C'mon, Hotshot. Let's get you home."

She moans as if annoyed, her teeth chattering slightly as the cold finally hits her. "I don't want to drive. You tired me out." The energetic woman who bounced into the water and swam faster than me around the rock is now gone.

"I'll drive." We dress quickly, eager to find warmth back in the jeep.

Not wanting to end our evening together, I drive slowly back to the villa. The entire time, Jade holds my hand on top of her thigh.

"We should move to Cyprus. It's so pretty," she mumbles, almost dozing off.

Taking my eyes off the road for a moment, I glance her way. "You and Poppy?" I ask, amused at her sudden lack of stamina; her head rested against the window.

She doesn't answer as she finally succumbs to sleep and I go back to focusing on the cliffside roads I'm not familiar with.

Almost back at the villa, Jade makes me jump when she mumbles in her sleep. "I'd move here with you, Owen." Before I can get too excited, she follows it with, "No, we don't need a parachute. Just the pancakes," and I laugh out loud.

My brain snaps when I realize I would move to be anywhere with her. It won't matter as long as I'm with her.

My first request to the gods; find a house to call home.

CHAPTER TWELVE

Jade

Waking up inside a muscular arm is not how I planned to start my day, but all the same, I welcome it; drinking in Owen's scent, enjoying his warmth.

Draping my leg over his thigh, calm washes over me as I listen to the strong beat of his heart. Hypnotized by it, I almost fall back to sleep again, only the strong pull to check the time makes my eyes flutter open.

Trying my best not to wake him, peeling his arm from around me, I turn around carefully. The first thing to catch my attention is the pile of my clothes on the marble floor, all neatly folded in a pile with my lucky poppy stone sitting proudly on top of them. Owen must have done that because I certainly didn't.

I have a hazy memory of Owen driving us home. Then I remember greeting Blake and thanking her for staying with Poppy and my mom as I waved her off. She had whispered something about Owen clearly having a magic dick because he'd stupefied me with it.

She's not wrong.

The last I recall was checking on Poppy before heading to my bedroom where Owen undressed me, put a clean tee shirt over my head, and then tucked me into bed with a goofy smile, feeling more contented than I had done for months. Clearly the buildup of pressure, doubt and stress from training the team, an exhilarating night swim and then Owen pulling a powerful orgasm from my body exhausted me, sending me into a deep slumber.

I scratch my thick salt-filled beach hair, chuckling at the memory. *Yuck, my hair feels nasty.*

Pulling my watch off the nightstand, I check the time and sigh with relief seeing that I still have another hour before I need to get up for work and before Poppy wakes up.

Poppy.

I leap out of bed and look down at what I'm wearing, laughing as no man I've ever dated has dressed me before.

I tiptoe down the marble hallway to Poppy's room, with a heart so happy it feels like it's skipping, and discover her lying on her back lost in her own dreams, sucking her thumb, her red curls wild. Satisfied she's slept through the night and happy that she seems to have already settled in her new crib and surroundings after just a few days, any of the doubts I had about moving her here with Mom vanish.

Also, knowing she was fine while I was out reassures me, knowing I can leave her in the safe hands of people I trust. Something I haven't been good at doing in the past.

But for the last two nights, I've been letting go of the apron strings, allowing myself to enjoy my time here and have some well-needed fun.

My mouth lifts mischievously to the side as I recall the fun I had with Owen last night.

Moving quietly out of Poppy's room and back to the safety of my bedroom, I sneak back into my bed. I lay back on the mattress before feeling restless and side eye Owen. Turning to get a better look at him, I smile from ear to ear, suddenly realizing it's been a very long time since I had a man in my bed. I'm glad that I held out and waited... that I waited for someone like Owen. He was incredible with Poppy yesterday, taking care of her in ways her father never could. He's so gorgeous, with a beautiful soul he can't see for himself.

And I'm feeling a little smug with myself that I made him buy into my woo-woo moon ritual. I wanted to make him feel better and help him uncover his version of happy. He deserves nothing less.

I sigh happily, as I think I might have found mine. Last night was so romantic. Having wild sex under the moon and stars, on the island of love, surrounded by myth and the magic of the goddess, Aphrodite. *Wow, what a perfect night.*

I can't take my eyes off him. Following the bleached by the sun, wavy neck length hair, it frames his face perfectly, making him look like a movie star. I struggle to comprehend how this handsome hunk of a man *likes* me. Or so he said yesterday.

I hope he's telling the truth because he's the first man I could see myself falling in love with.

While Michael and I had a good relationship, that's all it was; good. Not great, just good... okay.

Having never wanted to settle for mediocre, I knew something was missing. Me making the cut for the aerobatic team finally made him snap, resenting my success. That's what ultimately broke us up. His jealousy got the better of him. Then there is Owen, who thinks what I do for a career is awesome, nicknaming me Hotshot, which I like.

In fact, I love it.

And I like him all the more for putting me to bed and not bolting off in the middle of the night, having just had his wicked way with me; he stayed.

With one arm raised above his head, making all the sinewy muscles of his chest move as he breathes deeply in and out, I long to touch him again.

Considering if I should, I nibble on my fingernail, then push my pointer finger under the edge of the white bedsheet. Lifting it up, I take a long look at his cock, confirming it's the biggest I've ever seen, and he knew exactly what to do with it. He didn't need lesson two like we joked about the other night. With me, he's not selfish, and with me, he seems honest. I trust him. *I think.*

My fingers dance along the fringes of the thin sheet, itching to touch his skin, my mouth watering at the thought of taking him in my mouth again.

I mean, everyone else is fast asleep. No one will hear us, will they? *Nah.*

With the finesse of a prowling lioness on the hunt, I move to kneel between his spread legs, pulling the cover back up over us both.

On a mission, I flick his thick crown with the tip of my tongue, and he groans groggily, his cock twitching.

I start slow, licking his already semi hard shaft. Never having been one to want to give head before, every part of me wants to satisfy him and make him feel good, bringing all of his fantasies to life. Well, I sure hope this is one of his.

When a long intense moan rumbles deep in his chest, his cock thickens to its full length, telling me he's enjoying it. Twisting the tip of my tongue around his rim, I run my tongue down and back up along his thick vein, then push him into my mouth.

A waft of cool air bursts across my face as he lifts the sheets. "Fucking hell, Hotshot." I grin around him as he looks down at me, still half asleep. "Am I dreaming?"

I hum and then suck him hard. His hands cup my face as he pulls his knees up, digging his heels into the mattress.

Letting him fall from my mouth, I mumble, "Be quiet." Then, desperate to see him come undone, I suck him deep into my mouth, almost gagging as he hits the back of my throat.

"Aw fuck," he hisses as quietly as he can, jerking his hips into my mouth at the same time.

I stroke him up and down, creating a wet channel with my mouth and hand for him to fuck. Moving my other hand to his balls, I cup them lightly, then give them a squeeze, my tongue lightly licking them on every downward stroke.

Owen lets go of my face, pushing the palms of his hands into his eye sockets. "I'm gonna come."

He grabs a pillow and throws it across his face, trying not to make any noise as his body locks and his cock swells before he shoots ropes of thick cum into my mouth, grunting as his orgasm hits. "Jesus *fucking* Christ." His cursing is muffled behind the thick pillow.

I swallow every drop, as he slowly rocks back and forth in my mouth, not wanting it to end, his cock twitching out the end of his release.

He lifts the pillow off his face, flinging it to the side, chest heaving as he looks down at me. His eyes darken as he grabs my hand and pulls me up onto his chest, kissing me like he would burn down the world for me. It's possessive and not in the slightest bit tender, but it's everything I want him to give me, and more.

"You're a dirty girl, Hotshot." He pushes his tongue between my lips. "You taste of me."

"Delicious."

Everything about him is amazing, almost dizzying.

And he feels right; staggeringly so.

I have no inhibitions wanting to give myself to him.

How can this be possible?

Is this what love at first sight feels like? Pure, intense, no doubts, just sheer joy and overwhelming pleasure, experiencing everything together.

He pulls my tee shirt up and over my head, cupping my breast in his firm hand, then gently rolls my nipple between his fingers.

Smashing his mouth over mine, he swallows my shocked cry of pleasure as he pushes himself inside me.

"How can you be hard again?" I lift myself off his upper torso, giving me the leverage I need to slide up and down his hard again cock.

"You've been dating older men for years. I'm only thirty-one and horny as fuck around you."

"I have a boy toy." I cover my mouth to stifle my giggle.

"And I have a cougar." He grabs my hips.

I gasp in horror and stop fucking him. "I am only thirty-nine."

"Almost forty." He winks, winding me up. "Cougars are forty-plus. You're almost there."

Mouth gaping open, I can't believe I'm almost a cougar. "Oh, my God. I'm so old," I say in shock.

Owen takes my momentary brain snap as an opportunity to grab my waist and flip us over so my back is now to the mattress. He moves fast, pinning my hands above my head and spreading his legs wide so he can fuck me hard. "You have the pussy of a twenty-year-old. It feels like heaven. Tastes like it too." He engulfs me with his muscular body, and I submit to him, spreading my legs wider, allowing him to fuck me deep, exactly the way I like it, punching the air out of my lungs.

"And you have the stamina and crazy short recharge time of a twenty-year-old," I whisper pant as he hits my G-spot perfectly and I know I'm about to come as the sensations of my orgasm burns deep in my core and I have to bite my lip to stop me making any noise.

"Yes. I. Fucking. Do." He punctuates every word with a punishing hip thrust, hitting my cervix with his long dick. "Now come all over my cock, Hotshot." He pins my wrists to the bed with one hand, and with the other he covers my mouth, gagging me. "Quietly. Do you think you can do that?" he challenges me.

I nod as best as I can.

"Can you come on demand?"

I try shrugging, lifting my shoulders to my ears, although the dominant heat in his eyes is so hot I might come right now, anyway.

"Tilt your hips," he commands as he takes control.

Following his instructions, I push my heels into the bed and tilt my hips at the same time he thrusts into me, his hand muffling my cry.

"Good fucking girl. Again. Hold your hips there."

My eyes widen as I struggle to breathe, and he continues to fuck me. He moves his hand away from my nose, then devilishly smiles. "Now—" His voice takes on a low, delicious tone that makes my pussy clench, as his mouth finds my ear. "When I get to one, you come. Yeah?"

I nod my head again, excitement surging through my veins.

"Good girl."

The sensation of my orgasm already on the cusp, he counts, "Ten." In a rougher than normal Scottish accent, "Nine." He rails me into the bed. "Eight." He moves faster as he keeps on counting down, and I'm trying so hard to hold off that I don't hear the next few numbers and then suddenly he counts, "Three." I fight hard to hold back my orgasm, thrashing my head from side to side as tears run down my temples. "Two." He fucks at an unrelenting rhythmical pace as he counts, making me grateful for the solid wooden bed not squeaking. "One," he rasps in my ear, biting my earlobe and I go off like a rocket, my body locks, fingers and toes curling into the bed as I squirm beneath him, my pussy clenching around his thick cock.

I swear I black out for a second as golden stars explode behind my eyes.

I can barely breathe as he muffles my moans with his hand and whispers words I can't make out against the shell of my ear as pleasure continues to pulse through my body.

"You take instruction well, Hotshot. That was fucking hot." His cock pulsing inside me with need, his body covered in a thin coat of perspiration, he kisses my temple, removing his hand from my mouth. He kisses my cheek, the side of my mouth, then my lips softly, the scruff of his beard tickling my upper lip. "You're so fucking beautiful. You are *not* old. You're young and sexy and vibrant, and everything I could only ever dream about." He begins moving again, his hips rocking with the perfect amount of pressure, my oversensitive body already reacting to his touch. "Your success doesn't scare me. It makes me want you all the more and I will show you every day if I have to, exactly how much you turn me on." He groans between his firm words. "Because you have the sweetest pussy I have ever tasted. I'm fucking addicted." His hips pick up the pace again, and I feel the telltale signs of another orgasm building between my thighs. "I've never felt this way before and I never want it to end, Hotshot. So, you will take my cock like the good girl you are. Never doubt yourself, and if I ever hear you describe yourself as old again, I will spank you."

"I might like that," I whisper as butterflies dance in my stomach.

"I bet you fucking would." He chuckles, then tries to stifle his groan. "Aw fuck, I'm gonna come, Hotshot." I'm guessing he likes the idea of him spanking me as much as I do.

My heart jackhammers in my chest as I watch him come undone and I follow him over the edge as another orgasm rips through my body.

"You're mine," he pants, as his cock jerks inside of me, filling me with his hot seed, while my release coats his length.

Moaning as he comes down from his climax, he kisses me with such tenderness my heart might explode with emotion.

Still inside of me, he leans up on his forearms, brushing the pad of his thumb across my temple, and I find it oddly spellbinding. "What time do you need to be at work?"

"Briefing is at half six, sharp." Owen is only the second person to make me not want to go to work. The first being Poppy.

"You better get in the shower then, you dirty cougar."

Unladylike, I snort. "Are you teasing me, boy toy?"

"Boy toy." He shakes his head, repeating the words under his breath. "I'll be your boy toy any day of the week."

"And night?" I ask, my voice laced with hope.

"Day, night. Summer, spring, winter, fall."

"For years to come."

We stare at each other, both realizing the enormity and weight of what we are saying; we want every day with one another. My brain tries to figure out where the hell this guy came from. Whoever he is, I fucking love him. Sorry, I mean, I *like* him. I'm not in love with him, because that's such a stupid thing for me to say after a handful of days. What I mean is that I am enjoying it... I mean, him. Oh Jesus Christ, I'm having a meltdown.

Owen snaps us out of my stupor. "For this morning, though, I need to figure out a way to sneak out of here before your mom and Poppy wake up and before Gregor realizes I'm gone."

"I'm not bothered about them finding out," I tell him honestly.

"You're not?"

"No. And I will tell my team when I'm ready. But our family should know first."

"Is this us then? Not just a *thing* while you're training *thing*." His brows hunker down as if worrying about how we make this work.

"I want to see where this goes, Owen. I'm here in Cyprus for four weeks. You don't have any plans to return to Scotland before then, but you will have to return eventually, won't you?"

"I'm not fussed about living in Scotland anymore, and if it means being able to see you every day, I'll move anywhere."

I question myself; am I acting more like an eighteen-year-old than a thirty-nine-year-old? Do I have a crush on the popular guy dreaming about him sweeping me off my feet and living happily ever after? Because part of me thought that's what would happen with Michael, and he proved himself to be a douche canoe that I'd like to push down the river without a paddle.

"You have a lot to figure out, Owen."

I don't want to pressure him into anything, and he has to work out what he wants first before I figure in his plans. I don't think dating a single mom and becoming an instant step-father were in his new life plans.

"I do, and it starts today." He winks cheekily.

"Oh yeah, what's your plan?"

"I will tell you once it's done."

I raise my eyebrows in surprise. "Did last night at Aphrodite's Rock help you?"

"It made me see everything clearer than I have in years. Maybe forever."

"I just want you to find happiness, Owen." I push a curl of dirty blond hair off his forehead.

"Me, too. I feel happy today."

I smile, knowing how lost he's felt. "Long may it last."

His face turns serious when he says, "I asked for the universe to make me a better lover. For you."

I hate he thinks he wasn't good enough for me to begin with. All he needed was to take his time and to learn what I like. Although he's doing bloody great already.

"Sex with you is amazing, Owen." I freaking loved the countdown he just did, silently praying he'll do that again. It was incredible.

Looking pleased with himself, a megawatt grin appears across his lips. Then he gives me a chaste kiss. "So, tell me, when do we tell our families about us?"

I open my mouth, but the words die on my tongue.

"Owen didn't come home last night. I'm worried about him, Mari." Gregor's panicked voice booms into my bedroom.

Both our heads snap in the direction of the chaos, and I squeal, trying to hide any parts of my nakedness as a member of my team stands in the doorway looking frantic and about to lose the plot alongside my mother, *and* with my daughter in her arms. Poppy gives me a sleepy smile.

"Oh, shoot," my mom exclaims, covering Poppy's eyes comically. She clenches her teeth together, cringing at her error at bringing Gregor to my bedroom, then mouths 'sorry'.

World give way and swallow me whole.

And why the hell did Mom let Gregor into my bedroom?

"Well, that solves that problem, then. The family knows," Owen drawls. Embarrassment burns through my entire body, knowing Owen is still inside of me and neither of us can move without being obvious.

Undaunted, Mom calmly says, "Well, now we've found your cousin, Gregor would you like some breakfast?" She turns around with a smirk pulling at her lips, ushering a shocked Gregor out the door before she clicks it closed. "Breakfast will be ready in ten minutes, you two." Her voice is slightly muffled as she shouts back through the door.

Both Owen and I burst into fits of laughter.

"My mother has never caught me having sex before."

"Me either. Or my cousin."

"Or my daughter."

Still on top of me, Owen drops his head to my shoulder and grumbles.

He stays there for a second before lifting his head, his eyes locking with mine. "First time for everything."

"Yeah," I whisper.

Why does it feel like he's referring to us and not our family that burst into my room?

First time falling head over heels.

First time knowing this feels right.

First time feeling like you met the person who you can imagine spending your life with.

Is that what he meant?

Nah, of course he didn't.

Did he?

CHAPTER THIRTEEN

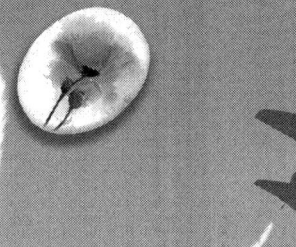

OWEN

Following a slightly awkward breakfast at Jade's, as Gregor's eyes bore through me like a heated fire poker from across the circular dining table, Mari, Poppy, and I then waved Jade and Gregor off as they jumped into their hired bus to take them onto base for the rest of the day.

Gregor dropped me a text as soon as he was seated, with a very stern threat of *don't fuck this up*, then glared at me through the window as they drove off.

I have no intention of fucking anything up with her, but I love how protective he is of his boss and little Poppy. Or maybe he's just thinking of himself and his job. Either way, it's sweet of him, and I'll have to rib him later and let him know how *cute* he is being, trying to protect Jade's heart.

As the bus disappeared out of sight, Mari suggested she come with me so that she could watch Jade and Gregor in action, too.

Buzzing with excitement, we were ready within an hour.

Offering to drive, Mari and I made the half-hour trip to

camp, with Poppy chattering away, buckled into her car seat in the back of Gregor's worn out jeep, that feels like it's going to tip over around every corner. He has really shitty taste in cars, or a shitty budget to rent one. Either way, the jeep is far from ideal or safe to drive a baby around in, and I might just mention that to him when he returns from work later.

Texting Blake before we left the villa, we met at the gates, then followed her up the two-mile corridor of road, from the guard room up over the hill, where a vast airfield and full working air base came into view.

My mouth dropped open at the enormous space I did not know existed until a week ago. Hundreds of military family homes, a petrol station, supermarket, bars, restaurants, swimming pools, even beaches and its very own airport; it's like a village within a village.

Given full access to the briefing before the aerobatic team flew, I couldn't take my eyes off Jade. Fascinated by her assertiveness, and the way she commanded a room full of strong-headed and very talented men, I listened intently, hanging on to every word she said.

She was captivating.

Ever the professional, in the zone and not distracted by my presence or her mom and daughter, she ran through their choreography with precision, making my heart swell with pride, making me want to yell from the top of my lungs *she's mine.*

She's breathtakingly fierce and fearless; a goddamn goddess.

Obviously sensing how I felt, Mari gave my hand a little squeeze, letting me know she felt the same amount of pride as I did.

When the briefing was over, and the team dispersed,

then and only then did she come over to kiss Poppy on the cheek and say *hello* informing us she could only spare a few minutes as she had her flight suit to put on.

The moment she gave me a farewell kiss, the infamous Cobra appeared in the doorway asking what she would like for lunch, displeasure written all over his face.

Now I know how he got his nickname. I swear he was imagining sinking his prominent fang-like canines into my jugular vein as his nose flared and jaw twitched. The snake tattoo on his forearm tensed as he clenched his fist by his side.

Oblivious to his obvious dislike of me, or maybe she was aware and choosing to ignore it, Jade introduced me as Gregor's cousin, blushing, as if desperate to give a label to what we are and inform him we're a thing, whatever that *thing* might be.

He shook my hand, almost breaking it as he squeezed it tightly, but I didn't flinch, showing him I was unaffected by his strength.

Fuckwit.

Side eyeing me with disdain, Cobra instructed Jade that she was to stay back after flying today as he had important matters to discuss and that he would personally drop her off at the villa afterward.

Slimy fucker.

She replied, telling him that Blake would also join them, as she had a couple of media ideas she wanted to discuss too.

It made the hairs on the back of my neck stand on end as I thought about her being vulnerable or scared around him, and what I would do to protect her from him.

Thirty minutes later, I'm standing with an entourage of press and spectators, on the furthest point of the base, way up high on the cliffs of the peninsula, watching in awe as Jade, and the team, in tight formation, roll, corkscrew, and zoom through the air in a series of moves and steep turns over the Mediterranean Sea.

In the past, I've watched Gregor, but to be honest, I was too distracted by other event activities and I never really paid attention before. But now I can't look away.

Mari taps me on the forearm. "Could you hold Poppy for me? She's getting very heavy?"

"Of course." I lift Poppy into my arms and point at the red planes as they fly toward us, preparing themselves for another synchronized maneuver.

Knowing she can't hear me from under the noise protectors that are keeping her tiny ears safe from the noise, I still say, "Here they come, Popsicle, are you ready?"

At supersonic speed, the nimble jets fly straight for us, then snap out of formation to create something that looks like a firework of planes in the sky as they change course, flying from horizontal to vertical in the blink of an eye. The screeching noise they create shakes the cliffs underfoot, rattling every bone in our bodies.

Poppy gleefully claps her hands, completely mesmerized by it all. Clearly having been exposed to this lifestyle since the day she was born, she is not one bit fazed by the speed of the jets or the overwhelming sound. She might very well be a little daredevil herself.

Blake walks toward us across the rubble-topped cliffs. "That was the final maneuver. You ready to go?" She smiles, pushing her sunglasses on top of her head. "They did great today." She nods in Mari's direction.

"Her display was perfect." Mari makes an okay sign with her hand using her thumb and forefinger.

"She had nothing to worry about." Blake pushes her arm

out as if she's a teapot to escort Mari over the uneven ground.

Mari accepts, pushing her arm through the hole she made, then she chuckles. "Except she did anyway. She always does with her routines and her team," she says, now walking toward Blake's sturdy four-wheel-drive jeep she brought us up the steep cliffs in.

I listen in, fascinated by Jade's apparent under-confidence in her ability, and clearly only sharing that with loved ones. She should never doubt herself and I make a mental note to tell her that later because she was awesome, both in commanding her team and in the sky. I look up into the expanse of bright blue sky, Poppy's electric copper hair catching my attention.

"Shall we take these off?" I pull off her ear protectors.

"Momma?" she asks.

"Flying. Up there in the sky." I point above.

Poppy's gummy smile lights up her whole face. Then she babbles away, as if chatting to me about the weather. She's so freaking cute in her blue gingham dress with gold pineapples embroidered on it.

I answer her constant chatter, pretending to have a conversation about the display and how hot it is today, then ask her if she wants to go for a swim when we go back to the villa, and I take the way she grabs on to the back of my hair and pulls it as a firm yes.

As we reach Blake's car, both she and Mari are staring at me like I've grown two heads.

"Everything okay?" I ask, worried I've done something wrong.

"Yeah, great." Shaking her head, almost as if in disbelief, Mari's eyes shift between me and Poppy.

"Everything's perfect." Blake sighs blissfully. "Just—"

"Perfection." Mari finishes her sentence.

Not understanding what they mean, I ignore their weird behavior, strap Poppy into her car seat and then jump in the back with her as Mari and Blake buckle themselves into their seats up front.

"Right, little Pop-a-doodle," I say, sounding like we have an important mission. "We have swimsuits to locate, sun cream to apply, just like your nana taught me, and then we are going to do some huge zoomies in the air, just like Mommy's plane. Yeah? Maybe we should stop and get that giant inflatable duck with the cool sunglasses we saw at the shop on the way here. What do you think?" Poppy grabs my hand when I hold it up. I was expecting her to high five me, but, instead, she holds on to my thumb and doesn't let go.

"I'll take that as a yes then, Popsicle." I chuckle, turning to face the front, curious why we are the last car to leave the cliffs, only to find Blake and Mari's heads twisted around between the space of passenger and driver's seats watching me.

"Do I have something on my face?" I pull my hand to my cheek, dusting whatever it is away.

"No. Not at all." Mari's smile broadens. "You're just really great with her. It's lovely to watch."

"You're very cute with her," Blake says, making me scrunch my nose up.

"Cute? I'm not cute." I make light of her comment, flippantly scoffing.

Asshole? Yes. Cute, most definitely not.

"You are with her." Mari nods in Poppy's direction.

I slowly turn to look at Poppy and she's looking back at me with adoration written all over her face, as if I stole the moon out of the sky for her and my heart swells in a way I'm not familiar with.

What the hell is that feeling?

I reach for my chest with my free hand, laying it over my tee shirt as my heart pounds against my ribcage.

"She likes you, Owen, and you are a natural with her." With love-filled eyes, Mari stares at her granddaughter. "Much better than her own father," she mutters under her breath.

In a heartbeat, Poppy's face changes, turning bright red.

"What's wrong?" I panic; she looks like she's choking.

"Oh, she's doing a poo." Mari's amusement is clear in her tone as she turns to face the windscreen.

Giving her privacy, I look away too, a laugh bubbling in my chest. "Well, that's not very ladylike, is it?" I stare out of the car window, inwardly replaying Mari's words.

Trying not to overthink what this all means, I brush them off and say, "I'm gonna call you Poopy instead of Poppy from now on," making Mari and Blake chuckle.

All the way back down to Gregor's car, enjoying her little chubby hand wrapped around mine, I imagine what I would be like as a father.

Having never had the best example, I'm not exactly a good candidate for the job. I couldn't even change a diaper yesterday.

I twist my neck to look at Poppy and my heart does that crazy fluttery thing it's been doing for the past few days again.

Me, a stepdad?
I've never considered it before.
Until now.

CHAPTER FOURTEEN

Owen

I'm lying by the pool, enjoying the mid-afternoon sun, mindlessly watching the rays make the water twinkle and I exhale a contented sigh, finally feeling like myself again.

All around the surrounding trees, Cyprus Warbler birds sing away to themselves, enjoying the afternoon heat.

An entire week has passed since I watched Jade fly for the first time with her team, meaning the deadline to return to Castleview Cove my father set me has long passed.

I ignored it, refusing to bend or stretch to his demands. The night I swam around Aphrodite's Rock, I made a commitment to myself to not look back, vowing to only move forward. Returning would be like admitting to him he was right all along when that is not the case; forcing his only son into a loveless marriage was wrong, so wrong.

I am here now, standing on my own two feet, and I took the first step this week toward securing financial stability for my future. I made a call to a realtor friend of mine, Jude, back in Castleview Cove, to help me find a house. Part of the plan was to find some property to invest in, not to live in as such. Wanting to be near Jade and Poppy, because that's where my head and heart want to be, I'm pretty certain I won't be moving back to Scotland. However, when I return to Castleview Cove, with my father taking it upon himself to rid me of the place I call my home, I thought it would be a good idea to secure a holiday home near the beach. It will be handy when I visit friends.

Promising to pay Jude a higher commission if he keeps quiet about my whereabouts, within three hours he'd found me a stunning home with four bedrooms and a large family kitchen, with a garden scattered with old trees to make homemade swings in and space to build a Wendy house, as well as a sea view.

Having spent a lot of time around Poppy, perhaps it was a subconscious decision I made as I reeled off my new home requirements, almost imagining the three of us living there together.

Mindlessly, I watch two dragonflies flirt with one another, hovering, twirling, they then zoom off, skimming the pool, lost in their own game of kiss chase.

I shake my head to rouse myself from my daydreaming as my text message alert dings loudly from the table next to me.

Aware that both Poppy and Mari are having an afternoon nap on the outside double daybed, I curse under my breath, praying my deafening notification sound doesn't wake them up.

Cuddled together beneath the cream canopy that's protecting them from the blistering sun, I give them a quick glance, relieved to find them still sleeping soundly.

Worrying my bottom lip, I scowl, not happy that Mari has been feeling unwell again. Her prolonged bouts of dizziness make me feel anxious, so I called Jade earlier at work to ask if we could get her seen by a military doctor on camp tomorrow, and she has an appointment booked for early in the morning.

And so today we stayed by the pool, in the safety of the villa, not making it to the beach like we'd originally planned. But that's okay, as Mari, Poppy, and I have another three weeks to explore the island together while everyone is at work. Although, I'm not sure if Mari will be able to if her lightheadedness continues.

While Jade's been at work, I've been helping Mari out with Poppy as it's all been a bit too much for her. Even laundry has been a stretch. Although she reassures me she's more than capable and doesn't need me, she has, in fact, needed me. Following a week's worth of training, I'm now an expert at diaper changing, applying sun cream, prepping Poppy's food, and baby bag for excursions, and even changing a wiggly Poppy into her romper suits she wears at bedtime.

I should have an accreditation in popper fastening. I'm a quick learner and the key is to be fast, faster than her mommy flies.

While Mari, Poppy, and I have spent the last week together, Jade and the team's schedule is slammed. Flying and training aside, it has kept them busy doing press conferences, online interviews for magazines and newspapers, and meeting with different news teams from all over the world. In addition, the press is fascinated by the only female on the team returning to work, a working mom no less, featuring her in parenting and women-specific magazines.

She juggles so many things at once, I can't keep up with her.

Today, I listened to the team being interviewed on the

local radio station on base, too; they sure don't get much downtime during the day.

Listening intently to my cousin across the airwaves, he was articulate and professional, and I find him and his elite team fascinating and inspiring, almost jealous that at thirty-one I am still finding my place in the world when they are so confident and solid in theirs.

However, I no longer feel the weight of the world on my shoulders, and I can't deny how much I have enjoyed my evenings with Jade and Poppy just relaxing, with Mari sometimes joining us for meals out and walks along the beach, although she likes to disappear to give us space and *alone time* together.

No matter what we do, Jade and I have laughed until our bellies ache. We have fun and I can't imagine my life without her in it. I want to be with her everywhere.

Although sometimes I have to share Jade with her team, especially when the guys all join us around the communal pool. They appear to love Jade and respectfully treat both Poppy and Mari like their own, too.

Except for Cobra. Who I've yet to figure out because although Gregor suspects he has a *thing* for Jade, he sure as hell doesn't act like it, nor does he make her job any easier or treat her well; keeping her back later than anyone else, scheduling in nights to accompany him at the Officer's Mess, to which she's turned him down twice, preferring to stay in with us.

And he wasn't exactly polite when Mari stumbled yesterday between the cars at the front of the compound either, laughing when she skinned her knees, joking inappropriately about how she must be inebriated when he could clearly see how concerned Jade was for her.

When one of the other team members called him out, he half-heartedly apologized and headed back to his villa.

What kind of person does that?

He's a thoughtless asshole.

Getting nothing but bad vibes from him, I don't like his sleazy nature and snide remarks, which he makes a lot of, and appears to get away with it, too, because of his rank and status.

If he's trying to win Jade over, he's doing a shitty job of it, and to be honest, he's already lost her because, in every way, she's mine now.

And how do I know this? Well, because we talk. We talk about everything together. I laid my heart on the line and told her what I want; I want a chance with her to give this a shot.

She confessed that she wants the same things, making my heart beat in a way I've never felt before. Because she wants me as much as I want her and she wants to see what our future together can bring.

I want to take care of them both; although I'm not sure how to do that when I don't have a roof over my head to even protect myself.

Ding, ding, ding. Another three text messages sound loudly from my phone.

Annoyed, turning it over in my hand, I squint to find Jude's name displayed across the screen alongside shouty capital letter messages.

JUDE:

> WHERE ARE YOU?

JUDE:

> I'VE TRIED CALLING YOU SEVERAL TIMES.

> **JUDE:**
> YOUR PAYMENT DIDN'T GO THROUGH FOR THE HOUSE.

My mouth drops open.
How is that possible?

> **JUDE:**
> CALL ME ASAP.

I can almost hear the neurons in my brain misfiring, as I try to work out why they would decline my transaction. I gave them the correct details; I know I did because Gregor double checked the account number with me, twice. Plus, I'm a numbers guy. I check, check, and check again. As boring as it is, it's in my DNA to be analytical and methodical. There surely must be a clerical error at their end.

Moving inside the house for privacy, I unlock my phone and hit call on Jude's name. Sure enough, he picks up on the first ring. "Thank Christ, I've been trying to get hold of you all day."

"My phone hasn't rung once, I promise." I'm not lying, the connection has been dropping out all day.

"Can you call your bank? Because of data protection, they won't tell me anything. You know what they're like." Sounding stressed, he knows he'll hit the big time off the commission from my sale.

"Yeah, sure." I nervously run my fingers through my hair. "Has this kind of thing happened before?" I ask, out of curiosity.

"Only once when we did another cash sale. We didn't know it at the time, but the guy was under investigation for laundering money and his bank stopped the transaction."

"They've got the wrong guy if they think that's what I'm doing." My finances are as clean as a whistle.

I need to figure out what the issue is.

Responsible for the accounts at Castleview Printing Press, I know all the tax avoidance schemes out there, however, within work and personally, I stick to the rules, knowing one wrong move can cost businesses thousands. Or even worse, force them into liquidation. And that's why I always try to keep my father on the straight and narrow and question him on everything. However, he's not as particular as I am, and that used to cause arguments between us all the time.

"I'll call you back as soon as I know." I check the time. Being two hours ahead of the UK, I ask, "What time do you finish?"

"I'm never off the clock, Owen."

"Great. Give me half an hour."

"Speak soon. Hope they sort it for you quickly."

Ending the call, I open my banking app to locate the online help desk number. As my account details load onto the screen, I lose my breath, unable to comprehend what my eyes are reading. It's as if someone hit me with a bullet through my chest as I stare down at the zero balance glaring back at me.

My heart pounds in my chest and my ears fill with a whooshing sound as every muscle in my body tenses up as I gasp in horror.

Frozen to the spot, it prepares to fight the unknown threat I'm facing or run the other way and take flight.

I blink once, then twice, then rub my eyes.

It's surely an error.

I close the app, reopen it and log back in using my security pin number.

Yet again, I'm greeted with a bank balance of zero.

"What the fuck?" I exclaim, confused by what I am seeing or not seeing.

"What's wrong?"

Wrapped in my bubble of disbelief, I didn't hear Gregor and Jade entering the hallway.

I look up to find them both staring at me when Jade says again, "What's wrong, Owen? You're freaking me out. You look like someone drained all the blood out of you."

I go to answer, but my voice box has stopped working.

"What's happened?" Gregor's voice agitated as he storms in my direction and pulls the phone out of my hand, his eyes immediately seeing what I do. "He didn't?" he asks rhetorically, clearly livid.

"He did," I reply, my voice barely a whisper.

CHAPTER FIFTEEN

Owen

"What did who do? Who's *he*?" a befuddled Jade shrills.

Struggling for air, I clutch my chest, gulping, trying to catch my breath.

"I think he's having a panic attack." Gregor motions for me to sit down on the staircase while Jade runs to me, crouching down between my legs. Her features turn foggy as my vision blurs.

Cradling my face in her hands, she coaches me back from the brink of passing out, my breathing eventually returning to normal, her beautiful face coming back into sight. I nod my head, letting her know I'm fine again.

She looks up at Gregor. "Tell me what has happened. Right now," she demands, with an edge to her tone.

Gregor turns the phone so she can see for herself. "His father wiped him out. He took every penny of the trust fund his grandfather left him."

Jade gasps. "He surely can't do that." Snapping her attention back to me, she soothes my anxiety with her touch.

"He did," I say flatly. "He took everything." Including any choices I thought I had left. With no money, I can't follow my heart and jumpstart my plans.

Jade shakes her head fast. "No, no, no, that's not fair, Owen." Her eyes turn glassy and fat tears run down her cheeks.

I pull a fake smile and brush my thumb against the skin of her cheek. "Don't cry for me. I'm not worth your tears."

"You are worth every one of my tears. You mean everything to me, and I never want to see you hurting, Owen."

"You're wrong about me. I have no home, no money, no family, except Gregor here." I side eye him as he lays his hand on my shoulder. "I was trying to buy a holiday home for us in Castleview Cove because I wanted somewhere we could go together to spend time with the handful of friends I have left, because I want to move to England to be with you, Jade. I had already picked out a place to rent nearby your base. I wanted it to be a surprise." I catch my breath. "Now, I can't even do that."

I don't have the money for the up-front three-month deposit anymore.

Nothing seems to be going my way and I can't seem to catch a break.

"It doesn't matter, Owen." More of her tears appear at my grand gesture.

It mattered to me.

"We'll figure it out." Gregor gives my shoulder a squeeze. "What I want to know is how your dad found your bank login details?"

I lay my hand out flat for him to pass my phone back.

Within a few taps around my banking app, I find what I'm after. "He accessed it legitimately." I look at the five million plus change he siphoned from my account into one in his own name with a note on the transaction, *'come home, and you'll get it back.'*

Motherfucker.

Turning the phone around, I let Jade and Gregor read the transaction note on the screen.

When will he take the hint? I'm not going back.

Staring at the phone, it suddenly dawns on me how he gained access. "He used my laptop at work. I've accessed my account from it before." Angrily I shout, "Fuck." Slapping my forehead with the palm of my hand, making it echo louder than I expected it to. "I have a flash drive I store my personal passwords on, in the locked drawer of my desk. But I'm the only one with the key."

"Apparently not." Gregor mutters.

Defeated, I close the app as I won't be needing that anymore and shut down my phone.

The sheer dread and embarrassment of having to tell Jude makes me feel like a failure.

I'll tackle that phone call tomorrow.

"What's done is done. It's out of my control. My father has my money, and that's that. End of story." I want to draw a line under today and move on.

But I will not allow my father to control me; expecting me to run to him like one of his obedient hounds. I'm holding on to the little control I *do* have left. He can't physically make me return home because he doesn't know my whereabouts to make me; not yet.

That money was mine, left for me by my grandfather. Being close to him throughout my childhood, I think I know why he left me that money in trust; to break free. Hence why he left it for my sister Camilla, too.

Could he see how miserable my parents were?

Perhaps he did, and he wanted me to break the mold.

Long gone now, I can't ask him if that's why he left both of us such an enormous inheritance, although I wish I could.

When I was around sixteen, I remember finding him sitting at the desk in his home office. Lost in thought, staring off into space, swirling his whiskey around the bottom of a crystal glass. I vividly remember him turning to me, his powerful voice almost a warning, *"Don't make the same mistakes others make, boy."* I did not know what he meant back then, but through the gift of time and having now lost it all, I know what he means; don't repeat the cycle.

Inhaling deeply, using all my willpower, I force a smile. "We need to wake Poppy up or she'll never sleep tonight, and what are we doing for dinner?"

Gregor and Jade both look at me in shock as I flippantly move on with the rest of the day. The truth is, I'm fucking dying inside, but what do they expect me to do?

As angry as I am about the money, I can't do anything to change it. I'm powerless and my father knows it.

"Is that it? That's all you're going to say?" Gregor asks, puzzled by my U-turn.

"What do you expect me to say, Gregor? I have nothing left. Should I just give up and go home?"

Jade gasps, her touch soothing me as she glides her fingertips over the skin of my thighs. "Please don't do that," she begs, sounding desperate. "Please stay, say you'll stay. We've only just met Owen. You can't leave me, and Poppy adores you."

I have no intention of going back, but she doesn't know what she's saying. There's probably someone much better out there for her. And me? I'm just a boy-toy like she said.

The indignity of having everything to losing it all

weighs heavily on my chest. "I have two hundred euros in my wallet. That's all the money I have." A wave of nausea rolls over my stomach. "I'm at rock bottom. Homeless and penniless." I push my hands out to the sides. "I have a suitcase of clothes and not much else, Jade."

She lays her hand over my chest. "Don't say that. You have a heart made of gold, Owen. That's all that matters to me. And you have me, and Gregor, and my mom, who seems to think the sun shines out of your ass." She tries making a joke, only it doesn't land. My sense of humor dead, not wanting to be revived.

"I'm going to make myself scarce." Gregor moves to leave. Before he goes, he says, "I will give you money to tide you over, Owen. I would never see you stuck. And you're moving in with me when we go back to England. I don't live in the Officer's Mess like some of the single guys do. I rent off camp." Because he has a girlfriend and he's yet to tell me what her name is. *Sneaky fucker.* "Like it or not, that's what is happening." He walks away from the bottom of the stairs, his phone in his hand, bank app open ready to transfer me money, on a mission to help me.

I'm grateful that Gregor is on my side.

"Please promise me you won't go back," Jade pleads again. "Please stay. For me." She gives my knee a squeeze.

What the fuck she sees in me, I'll never know. I bob my head, remembering why I left. I don't want to be controlled. I'm not planning to go back. "I'll stay." *Because I can see my whole life in front of me. With her.* "I promise I'll stay." *I want to stay with her forever, because I'm falling head over heels for her and I can't stop myself falling. I don't want to.*

She drops her head to a bow, exhaling an enormous sigh of relief. "Thank you." She lifts her head back up. "I feel happy when you're around. You can't leave me when we've only just begun."

I'm not giving up. It wouldn't surprise me if she gives up on *me*, though.

I feel like all the fight has been knocked out of me. Not a single inch of me wants to fight my father. I simply want him to leave me be so I can get on with my future.

With no money to fall back on, it looks like I'll have to start again and do everything the hard way, which I don't mind. If I have Jade by my side, then I'm a winner either way.

Good things rarely come easy, and I'm willing to prove to my mother that I am not the piece of worthless shit she thinks I am.

"I need to get a job," I state. That was always going to be the case. It's just happening sooner than I expected.

"You'll find one, no problem at all. You have great qualifications with heaps of experience in business and finance. Someone will snap you up."

I don't tell her I have no plans to return to work in that industry. Having completed a couple of online questionnaires aimed at helping people who want to switch professions, I'm yet to uncover my big *why*. However, what I know is that I don't want to go back to working in a stuffy office every day, feeling uninspired by meaningless paperwork.

I want to do something that has a lasting impact on people, and finance is not it.

Jade smiles, beaming at me as she stands, inviting me to do the same, "We're agreed then, you can use the next few weeks while here in Cyprus to find a job around the area we are based in England, and you can move in with Gregor. Maybe."

What does she mean, *maybe*?

She sighs blissfully as I push my arms above my head, stretching out the tension.

"It's all figureoutable, Owen."

"You made that word up." I give a brief laugh, feeling better with her around me. She calms me in ways I didn't think were possible.

"I did not." She puts her hands on her hips over her green flight suit. "If it's in the urban dictionary, it's a word."

I catch her staring at my abs. "Maybe I should become a model?" I flex my muscles and try to look serious.

"This body is just for me." Jade pokes me in the ribs, making me laugh, because unlike her, I am super ticklish. "I don't enjoy seeing you upset." She says on a sigh as I pull her into my arms, surrounding me with her fragrance that I'm addicted to.

"I'm not now that you're here." The whole world could disintegrate as we hold each other at the bottom of the stairs, getting lost in each other's embrace. "And I'm not going anywhere. Wherever you are, I'll follow."

She sounds satisfied that I agreed to stay, because I want to. *God*, do I want to be with her, but the pull to claim back what is rightfully mine is strong, willing me to hop on a plane to confront my father. Not because I wanted my old life back, but because I wanted that house, for her, and to rent a place to be near her and Poppy. Now I'm back to relying on my cousin to bail me out of the godforsaken hole my father pushed me into.

"You're braver than you give yourself credit for. There are millions of unsettled people in the world unhappy with their lives, yet they do nothing to change it." Our bodies are sealed together so tight, there is barely room for a strand of hair between us. "Most of them are too scared to chase their dreams, learn a new language, or open the shop they've been dreaming about owning. But you—" She leans back to let me look at her. "You, Owen Brodie, already started making big changes before you even arrived here in Cyprus. Changing your life wasn't about your job, a house, cars, or the money you had in the bank. It started in here." She taps my temple. "And in here." She points to my chest. "You knew *you* had to change yourself before you could truly change your life."

Emotion builds in my chest, as she uses her positive energy to make my damaged heart beat stronger.

"Learning to cook, managing your household, being there for your friends, agreeing to marry Evangeline and attempting to get to know her, fleeing when your soul felt like it wasn't where it should be. You still did it. And sometimes, like now, the repercussions of your actions are turning up to bite you on the ass, but you've been given the gift of possibility and opportunity. To think big and be limitless. You said you've hit rock bottom." She shakes her head. "I don't agree. This is your time to build solid foundations. To step outside your comfort zone and embrace what's about to unfold."

I grin, astonished by her gems of wisdom. "Are you sure you aren't an eighty-year-old wise woman trapped inside a thirty-nine-year-old's body? You're something else, Hotshot."

"It's part of my job to leverage my mindset. It's what sets me apart from others and makes me an effective leader. I didn't get to where I am by chance, Owen. I worked for it, and I still work on myself every single day. You should read motivational books to help you."

She's right. "Recommend me some." I want to be like her when I grow up.

"I have them all downloaded on my Kindle. I'll let you borrow it."

Bowing my head, my lips meet hers. My plan to kiss her gently, to show her how grateful I am to have met her, is instantly shredded as our kiss turns passionate. "I'm falling for you." My unscripted words of affection accidentally slip from my mouth.

"My heart is falling faster than a sonic boom." She's almost purring as she speaks before she twirls her tongue around mine.

I grin wider when she uses the speed of sound flying terms to tell me she's falling for me, too. She has no idea how sexy her nerdiness is. Or how hard she makes my cock. The flight suit she's wearing is so sexy, making it difficult to control myself.

Desperately wanting to be inside of her, my cock thickens in my swim shorts, our kiss deepening by the second. Our breathing heavy, she murmurs, "Tonight." Referring to the fact we will fuck like wildcats later. That's if we can, because nine times out of ten, I have to gag her to stifle her loud, pleasurable moans and go easy on her so not everyone in the surrounding villas can hear us.

"We need our own place." My throbbing cock agrees with me.

"We'll be back in England before you know it. We'll have space then." She threads her hands into my hair as we continue to kiss unabashedly in the hallway, not caring if anyone catches us. "I have a super tight schedule this year, though."

"I'll travel to wherever you are."

With her lips on mine, it's as if she sucks all the emotional pain I've been feeling away. With every kiss, she heals me, breathing fresh oxygen into my body, regenerating my heart.

Slowing our kiss, our lips finally part. She looks possessed with beatitude, a mix of blissfulness and arousal.

Her lips swollen, she whispers, "I need to check on Poppy."

"She's been on great form. She caught a Chitchat Gecko." I shake my head.

"How the hell did she do that?" Jade gasps, knowing how fast they move.

"She's faster than a cheetah sometimes. She presented it to me like it was a gift at the lunch table."

Jade covers her mouth with her hand. "Was it okay?"

"It was fine, but Poppy got more of a shock when your mom screamed and made her jump. She burst out crying when she dropped it, then cried even more when it scurried off into the bushes."

"She never cries."

"It was a very upsetting day. She made a friend and lost him just as quick."

"She needs to socialize with other kids." Jade looks concerned.

"I can take her to the indoor jungle gym on camp." I saw a big sign for it when I drove past the station facilities the other day.

"You would do that?" she asks gently.

"I would do anything for you two. I've learned so much about myself, from her and you. You've shown me what it means to be a real, loving, and connected family in a short space of time. I'm willing to do whatever it takes to make both of you happy."

"Michael has *never* taken Poppy to an indoor playground." She sounds almost disbelieving.

Michael's missing out on so much. Poppy is a dazzling little chatterbox who radiates zany happiness everywhere she goes.

"I'll take her tomorrow." I'm adamant she'll have the best day out and meet some other kids.

"You really are quite something, Owen." She holds her hand out for me to take, and when I do, her touch settles me in that perfect way that only she seems to be able to do. "I will repay you later. But first, you need a shower."

She guides me up the stairs and into the bathroom. "Let those bad vibes wash away down the drain."

Consumed with gratefulness at having this awesome woman in my life, I pull her into my arms and hold her for longer than I mean to.

"Thank you." I kiss the top of her head. "You don't know me well, and yet you're so accepting of me, my crazy parents, and all my flaws."

"You're not flawed, Owen. You're going through a shitty spell in your life. Your past doesn't define you. Let your future shape you into something new and incredible. And I know you." Leaning out of our hug, she continues, "My heart knows yours."

Her heart knows mine.

"Plus." She breaks her sincere moment. "I've worked with Gregor for a while. I know he's a great guy. You're just like him. Only stellar. Just don't tell him I said that." She bites her bottom lip cheekily.

"You are out of your goddamn mind, woman." She's crazy. Gregor is a better man than me by a mile. He has everything, a car, home, a thrilling career.

Although I do have a big dick. It's the only thing I can offer her in my current situation.

I can't believe I *have* and *am* a situation.

"Plus, you're taking my Poppy to a jungle gym tomorrow. You get extra brownie points for that."

My Poppy. I would love for my Poppy to be *our* Poppy. *Fuck, since when did I want kids?*

The truth is, I can now imagine myself having lots of little red-haired cherubs to chase after.

I want that with Jade.

"I see something in you, Owen. Trust me, you'll find it too." She kisses me on the lips, pushing my chest, forcing me into the bathroom. She tells me to hurry and get my ass over to her villa in time for supper because tonight we're having a Greek meze and I'm helping to prepare the sixteen dishes of food. I hope she realizes I've only been cooking for a year and couldn't even boil an egg before then.

However, I love it when she bosses me about, so I do everything she asks of me, excited to spend the night with my favorite girls.

What I wasn't prepared for, but welcomed, was what followed.

Because when life gives you lemons? Well, sometimes you just gotta reach for the salt and tequila, throw it back and say *fuck it, let's do this shit.*

CHAPTER SIXTEEN

OWEN

Screaming and shouting, coming from what sounds like Jade, instantly sends my mind spiraling and I sprint out of my room at the same time as I haphazardly fumble, doing up the zipper on my shorts.

My world falls away as I find Jade standing at the bottom of the stairs of my villa, covered in blood, frantically bouncing a crying Poppy in her arms.

Oh no.

Flying down the stairs, my head in a spin, I can't get to them fast enough. "What's happened? Are you hurt? Is Poppy bleeding?"

Panting, tears running down her face, she wails, "It's Mom. She needs a paramedic. Now." She stares at me, looking terrified. "She's fallen down the stairs." She turns on the balls of her bare soles and flies out the door. "Come." Her feet slap loudly against the hot concrete as she runs back to her villa.

Hearing all the commotion, Gregor jumps down the

stairs at lightning speed too, his phone already in his hand. "I'm calling an ambulance now."

He runs behind me as I follow Jade.

"What the fuck is the number?" Gregor sounds distressed.

"Google it. Now," I demand, gritting my teeth.

"It's one, nine, nine in Cyprus." Cobra appears as if by magic. "I heard the commotion." He justifies why he is here, when in fact it's all hands-on deck as far as I'm concerned.

Sprinting, I run ahead to get to Mari.

I'm not prepared to find her lying in a puddle of blood as it oozes out of what looks like a deep gash on her forehead and onto the stark white marble floor, making it look like something out of a crime scene.

Mari moans when I crouch down and call her name.

"She tumbled all the way down the stairs." Jade is seemingly unaware of how frantically she is bouncing Poppy, making me worry.

As Gregor races through the door, I instruct him to take Poppy away from the scene she shouldn't see. The last thing I want is my little Pop-a-doodle traumatized at such a young age as her grandmother bleeds out onto the floor.

Gregor scoops Poppy out of Jade's arms and passes his phone to Cobra to take over and speak to emergency personnel on the other end.

"C'mon, beautiful. Let's go find some toys for you to play with." Gregor disappears into the makeshift playroom Jade and Mari set up for Poppy. "There, there, you're okay, Poppy," he coos calmly, closing the door behind him, her sobbing dying down.

Jade falls to her knees by her mother's side, worry deeply etched into her forehead.

"My leg." In a daze, Mari groans, reaching down lazily, then moves her hand to her head.

I grab it before she makes contact with her deep cut, which desperately needs stitches, and wrap her hand in mine reassuringly.

I look at Jade. "Hotshot, look at me."

Her eyes bounce between her mom and me, then to her mom again.

With my free hand, I cup her face to get her attention. "Jade, listen to me."

Her already pale face grows paler. "She's hurting," she whispers.

"I know. But listen to me. I need you to go into the kitchen and grab me lots of towels. Do you think you can do that?"

Jade nods her head a tiny amount, her face wet with tears.

"Great." I move my eyes in the direction of the kitchen. "Go, Hotshot."

In a flash, Jade is on her feet and scurrying about in the kitchen, scooping the supplies into her arms.

While my attention is fixed on Mari, in the background, Cobra's deep voice is giving our address details over the phone.

Using soothing words to reassure Mari, I rub my thumb over the back of her hand, coaxing her to stay awake and asking her questions about the day and date.

Taking her time, she answers me, correctly every time, which I take as a good sign.

Cobra finally says the words we've been waiting for. "The paramedics are on their way."

Jade returns with the towels, and I gently cover Mari's

split head with one, applying a little pressure to suppress the bleeding which is still pouring from the wound.

When I ask Mari where the pain in her leg is coming from, she motions to her hip area.

Shit.

"I shouldn't have brought her here. This is all my fault," Jade cries again.

Before I get the chance to reassure her, Cobra has pulled her off the floor, wrapping his arms around her.

"Well, you wanted to bring her. And this is where we're at," he says matter-of-factly.

What the fuck?

"Jade," I say sternly, concerned about Mari, but wanting to reassure her. And punch Cobra in the nuts.

She breaks free from his tight hold, pushing herself out of his arms.

"None of this is your fault," I tell her as she sits back down on the floor next to her mom, holding her other hand. "It was an accident, Jade. She could have fallen anywhere."

She wipes her nose with the back of her hand. "But she's been dizzy and I should have made sure she went to the doctors sooner."

"And now we'll find out why she's been having those spells. She's going to be just fine."

"She is?" She sniffles.

"She is, Jade. I promise." I feign positivity, trusting Mari has a slight fracture and needs some stitches and nothing more.

Within ten minutes, the paramedics arrive and they confirm Mari needs to be taken to hospital immediately to have an x-ray and stitches in her head.

Jade climbs into the ambulance to accompany Mari and as soon as they leave, I jump into Jade's Jeep to follow them.

OWEN

It pisses me off when Cobra hops into the passenger seat, but I bite my tongue. After all, it is Jade's boss and having spent a week with them, I know all too well about their pecking order and how it works; respect for authority maintains discipline.

No one answers back to Cobra. He's a first-class bully who rules with an iron fist. He didn't get to his position of power being nice.

In his spare time, he most likely sacrifices young calves, then eats their hearts for breakfast. He's an evil motherfucker and seems to get off on causing the guys humiliation.

Did I mention I don't like him?

We followed the ambulance into the main city of Limassol, in silence, to the private hospital with its own urgent care department, not intimidated by Cobra one bit, knowing my girl needed me to be there for her at the other end.

Parking up and dashing inside the hospital, I grabbed Jade's hand as she watched her lovely mom being wheeled off for an x-ray.

My backside numb, I wiggle in my seat as we've been sitting in the waiting room for hours. I rest my hand on Jade's thigh and give it a reassuring squeeze.

"How long do you think they'll be now?" Jade asks hopefully as she ends her call with Gregor and Blake, who have been taking care of Poppy tonight. Unsettled by earlier events, they've only just got her to sleep. What I wouldn't give right now just to cuddle that little pudding in for the night. I slept like a log yesterday on the sofa when she napped on my chest, and we had a little snuggle together.

"Shouldn't be much longer." I sigh heavily, eager to find out how Mari is doing. I've grown incredibly fond of Jade's mom. She's a gentle woman, with a caring heart, who is always concerned with my well-being, and I adore how tactile she is toward me; always touching me on my arm or hand when she talks to me. Something I'm not used to with my mother. My mother would never dream of touching me for fear of catching the plague; she's archaic with a fixed mindset in so many ways.

So, yeah, I hope Mari's okay, because I care more for Jade's mother than I do my own.

We've been waiting for over three hours as it's been a busy evening at the hospital, causing us to have to wait longer to get the results of Mari's x-rays.

The doctors checked Mari over on arrival where they confirmed she needed sutures to close the deep wound on her forehead, reassuring us they would carry out further tests to understand her dizzy spells, too.

Jade yawns, tipping her head to the side to rest it on my shoulder, and I thread my fingers into hers, because I always want to be touching her, or holding her, or kissing her, or fucking her, or all four simultaneously.

"I'm thirsty." She squeezes my hand.

I kiss the top of her head. "There's a coffee making station down the corridor. Let me get you something." I stand to my full height and stretch out my stiff legs to get the circulation flowing again.

"Would you like anything, Cobra?" I inwardly scoff at his stupid fucking name. I wish I knew his real one.

"A coffee. Black. No sugar." He's firm with his order.

"Please?" I say as if he were a child. His manners are appalling.

He glares at me. Jade reaches up and gives my hand another squeeze, shaking her head subtly, as if to say, *not now*. So, I let it slide. For her.

Before I fetch our drinks, I lean down and kiss Jade on the lips, and just as I thought, Cobra watches our whole interaction, his dark stormy eyes wild enough to sink a ship.

She's mine, asshole.

Hands off.

Taking longer than expected because the filtered coffee machine had to be refilled. Holding three polystyrene cups teetering on top of the other, being careful not to burn my hands, I navigate myself through the winding hospital corridors back to our seats.

I round the last corner, only to find Cobra cupping Jade's face in his hands as she tries to pull away.

My world turns on its axis, my brain trying to figure out why the hell he is touching her and why the fuck he isn't listening to her when she's telling him to stop.

Sounding desperate, I hear her adamantly say, "I've told you before, Cobra. I don't see us like that. You're my boss." Sounding distressed, she desperately tries to pull the palms of his firmly gripped hands from her face. "Get your hands off of me." She grabs his wrists, stepping back.

"Jade, don't be like that. You know we'd be great together." He bows his head as if going in for a kiss, the snake tattoo on his forearm appearing to move across his skin as he wrestles with her.

I see red.

Running along the corridor, not giving a shit if the boiling liquid spills out of the plastic lids and burns me, I bellow, "Get your fucking hands off her. Now."

CHAPTER SEVENTEEN

Owen

Stepping back instantly, Cobra's hands drop from Jade's face, and I watch him unclench and clench his fists by his side while Jade rubs her jaw.

"Are you okay?" I ask Jade, my blood fizzing through my veins at the speed of a hurricane. Placing the coffee cups haphazardly down on the waiting room table, I look around the busy room that's now empty.

He saw a fucking opening to strike, and he took it.

The prick.

"I'm fine," she whispers, almost inaudibly.

I storm past her, not caring about his position or what rank he holds, because out here on civilian street, it counts for nothing.

He holds his hands up in surrender. "I'm sorry. I misread Jade's advances."

Jade gasps from behind me as the easy lie falls out of his slimy mouth.

"You are a lying piece of shit." I grab his throat and shove him against the wall to hold him there.

Cobra struggles for breath as I squeeze harder, restraining him.

"If I ever see you touching my girl ever again, I will fucking end you." Baring my teeth, I spit my hate filled words in his face. "I feel sorry for you, having to use your rank to sexually harass women and then lie about it." My spittle leaves droplets on his face.

I'm raging hotter than a volcano, something feral inside of me roaring to unleash itself.

"Now, I'm not sure if you know this, but my uncle is *very* close friends with Air Chief Marshal Patterson." Cobra's eyes pop out of his head at the mention of the second highest ranking officer in the entire Royal Air Force. His face turns red as I continue to cut off his oxygen. "I never want to hear about anything like this ever again, or Air Chief Marshal Patterson will be receiving a call. Understood?"

It helps to have a high-profile family sometimes, and my family knows everyone.

"Let him go, Owen, please," Jade pleads from the side of me, her hand resting on my arm.

I snarl at him before releasing him.

Wheezing, he reaches for his throat, coughing and sputtering.

"Now, fuck off back to the compound, and don't ever go near, look, or touch her again. Only ever talk to Squadron Leader Sommers if it's work related, otherwise, you don't talk to her. Do you hear me?"

He holds his hands up in surrender again.

Ah, you're not so tough now though, are you, dick?

I turn to Jade and cup her face. "Has he ever done anything like before?" Her eyes slide to Cobra, then back to me as he tries to compose himself.

Is she scared of him?

"No," she says, not sounding certain.

"You sure?" I narrow my eyes.

With her face in the palm of my hands, she jerks a nod and I know she's lying. I will make it my mission to sort this out. Knowing Gregor, his suspicions were right, and I think he's been making advances toward her for a while.

I swivel on the balls of my feet and pull Jade in behind me.

"What are you still doing here? I asked you to leave."

And with that he disappears, almost running down the corridor, and I lose the opportunity to ask her what has been going on when the doctor appears, informing us that Mari's test results are back.

Listening intently to the Greek doctor who speaks fluent English, she relays what she knows and we both hold our breath as she delivers the news.

"Your mother has labyrinthitis which is what is causing the dizzy spells. I believe she had the flu before you traveled to Cyprus, and this might have been the trigger. It's very common and would explain her vertigo and struggle to remain upright." I squeeze Jade's hand, letting out a relieved breath because I genuinely thought there was something seriously wrong.

"We've started her on antibiotics to fight the underlying inner ear infection." The doctor points to her ear. "And she'll need complete bedrest, which won't be difficult as, unfortunately, during the fall, she fractured her hip, which requires surgery."

Jade releases my hand, then covers her face. "My poor mom."

"Don't worry, we have given her pain medication, and

she is feeling much more comfortable now. We scheduled her in for emergency surgery tomorrow."

"Oh, my God." Jade runs her hands through her red hair, and I can help but think how tired she looks right now, the shock of tonight having finally caught up with her.

"When will she get home?" I ask curiously. Hip surgery sounds like a big deal.

"Following surgery, she'll be released within three to ten days. Within a day, we will have her up and about and moving her hip." The doctor answers, holding her clipboard to her chest.

Jade stays silent. I can almost hear her brain ticking away. I know exactly what she's thinking; how will she do her job and who will look after Poppy?

"She'll be stiff, so your mom will need someone to look after her as well as physiotherapy to help her move about again. She won't be able to drive for a few weeks either—"

"Can we fly her back to England privately tomorrow instead?" Jade interrupts. "So she can be in her own surroundings and with her sister-in-law? I am working here every day for the next three weeks, and I can't take any time off. Plus, she will need around the clock care when she leaves the hospital. My Aunt Babs can take care of her at her house. It would make more sense for her to have surgery in the UK." Her voice is higher, and she sounds panicked.

The doctor pulls her shoulders up to her ears. "I don't see why not. As long as she is stable and if that's what you want, then yes, I would work with you to make sure she has a smooth transfer to the airport."

"I will pay for it all." Jade sounds frantic.

The doctor gives a quick nod in acknowledgement. "Then let's sort that then."

Jade swivels in her seat to face me, and a tumble of

words all come out of her mouth at once. "I will call in a favor from work. They will help me. We need to pack her stuff. Make sure she's stable. Get her from here on to base in the morning and I will make sure they look after her and have transport organized for her at the other end to take her directly to the hospital. Mom has a private health care plan. I need to call my Aunt Babs." She pulls the phone out of the pocket of her shorts as she shakes her head viciously. "I should never have asked her to come with me. It was selfish of me. My father would never forgive me for this." She can't hold it in anymore, tears falling freely, running down her face. "Just because I'm the only woman on the team shouldn't mean I get extra privileges. It was silly of me to ask in the first place, and now karma has firmly bitten me on the ass. This is all my fault. Who the hell do I think I am demanding to bring my mother and daughter with me? And who will look after Poppy? I need to hire an au pair. How the hell will I do that? I can't have any more days off work. We are in the middle of training and have a full display schedule for the next year. Michael is no use. He won't help me with her." Her frantic rambles take on a higher octave as tears continue to stream down her face, desperation written all over her face. "I can't have it all. I can't have a career in the Air Force and be a mom. It's just not going to work."

Who the fuck told her that? Those words don't sound like something she would say.

Then I realize; fucking Cobra. He's gotten into her head.

I try bringing her back from the brink of a mini meltdown. I slip off the seat, crouch down, and position myself between her legs. I let her calm down a little before I speak. "Jade, I will look after Poppy."

She gasps. "I can't ask you to do that." Her bottom lip trembles.

"You're not asking me. I'm offering." I kiss her bunched up fingers that are gripping onto her phone. "I want to."

She nibbles on her bottom lip as she considers my offer.

"It's not up for discussion. I am here. She likes me, I love her, and I have this diaper changing malarkey down to a fine art." I don't tell her I almost vomited the other day when Poppy had the squirts and she decided to undo the Velcro fasteners herself. Literally; holy shit. I go on, "Plus, I have already scheduled in our jungle gym dates. I made our first booking for tomorrow morning."

She snorts, creating a snot bubble. "Oh my God, that is so unattractive."

From behind, the doctor passes her a tissue. "Thank you." Jade blows her nose. "You've officially seen me at my worst." She scrunches the tissue tightly in her hand.

"And I've seen you at your best." I reel off a list. "I've watched you fly, lead a team of powerful men. You have them eating out of the palm of your hand and following your instructions. It's such a turn on. I've watched you juggle your job alongside being an incredible mother. You command a room when you're at a press conference, you coach those boys like nobody else could. Christ, you've selflessly coached my sorry ass for the past week, picking me up when I'm down. You've conducted dozens of interviews, and not once have I heard you complain. And whatever that was with Cobra, which you *will* tell me about later, you put up with that when you shouldn't have to. So, yes, Hotshot, I am looking after Poppy, and I will look after you too. I can cook, clean, do your laundry, whatever you need from me, I will do."

"Like a nanny?"

"No, I'll be the manny." I smirk.

"The manny," she repeats under her breath, as if liking the sound. "You would do that for me?"

"I would do anything for you, Jade Sommers." Confidence blooming in my chest. "And your little pooping machine."

She giggles.

With the idea firmly planted in her head, it germinates and then fully grows when she finally agrees to let me help. "Okay." A rush of pink flushes her cheeks, which I know happens when she's happy.

"Okay. Let's do this." As I go to stand, I smack a kiss to her lips and plonk myself back down on the seat beside her to find the doctor staring at us. Her eyes glazed.

"The love between you two is exquisite," she comments.

Like summer lightning, her words jolt my heart.

Jade and I turn to look at each other. Our eyes say everything our mouths don't because we know she's right; what we have is beautiful.

She's the one.

But wait, hold that thought. What's that sound?

Thunk.

Yup. I knew it. That was the sound of my heart; I've most definitely fallen in love with her.

CHAPTER EIGHTEEN

JADE

It's been over two weeks since I called in a favor with one of the squadrons on base and waved my lovely mom off on a plane from the airfield on base.

Luckily for me, I know most of the flying squadrons and many service personnel, and we were fortunate that there was a nursing officer returning to the UK at the same time.

Flight Lieutenant Winters, or Becky as she insisted my mom call her, accompanied her, ensuring she had a smooth journey home, taking care of her pain relief and comfort throughout the five-hour plane ride.

Mom told me over the phone how well Becky looked after her. Chortling, as she retold how Becky bossed everyone around when they transferred her off the flight and into the ambulance to take her to the private hospital we booked her into; calling my mom her precious cargo, and if they didn't move her with cotton gloves, she would find their children, feed them lots of sweets, and teach them to swear like a pirate.

Grateful for Becky's help and humor, I put in a call to

her Squadron Leader, who I've known for many years, and recommended her for a Station Commander's Commendation.

The night before Mom flew home, I pulled an all-nighter, calling, emailing, and filling out copious amounts of paperwork to get her back safely. And with little to no sleep, I'm surprised I managed training the next day. Luckily for me, it was a ground training day, where we amended some of our maneuvers and discussed our flying and media schedules for the upcoming weeks ahead, as well as any functions we have been invited to attend; which is lots apparently.

Following my mom's surgery, which I worried about the entire time she was in theater, I've spent at least an hour on video call with her and my Aunt Babs every day since. She bounced back quickly and was up walking within a day.

Home after surgery within three days, Aunt Babs assures me she is continuing to do well in her physiotherapy sessions and getting around just fine. Her movements are improving daily, and she is no longer in any discomfort. I'm relieved she healed well and made an incredible recovery because she hates nothing more than people fussing over her and loves her independence. Although Aunt Babs insisted Mom stayed with her for at least another few weeks before moving home, which settles my nerves knowing they are together and should anything happen to Mom, Aunt Babs is there.

My Aunt Babs is an angel. We wouldn't cope without her, and I'm so incredibly blessed to have both her and my mom living close to the aerobatic team's airbase in England. It's just as well really, because on my return I won't have time to look after Mom, as we gear up and start display season. Often doing two shows and a fly past a day, it's both exhausting and exhilarating and I couldn't love it more.

After mom's fall, it made me realize she's not immortal nor is she getting any younger, and I want her to go on day trips and vacations with Aunt Babs. Since my dad died and then we lost my Uncle Harry, Aunt Bab's husband, they only have each other and they are more like sisters than sisters-in-law. It just makes sense to set her free and let her live a retired life without having the daily commitment to look after Poppy.

It makes perfect sense. Mom was Plan B, now it's back to my original Plan A; hire a nanny.

"You're doing that tongue sticking out of your mouth thing when you concentrate." Gregor knocks his shoulder into mine as I stare at my phone and he sits down beside me.

Knowing he's right, I pull my tongue back into my mouth as the rest of the team joins us in the break room. It's getting increasingly hot as we approach summer in Cyprus, and following our morning flying, we're back to have a break, rehydrate and eat before our midday slot. I don't know about everyone else, but flying makes me hungry.

"I've not found a nanny yet," I say half-heartedly, scanning my eyes over yet another resume the agency sent me to look at. None of them have been right for the position. It's a huge ask to assume someone would be one hundred percent flexible; work nights, travel with me, travel without me, and meet me in different countries.

The panic of still not having arranged any nanny interviews for next week when I'm back in the UK is turning into fear, overshadowed by enormous amounts of anxiety; who will look after Poppy?

Every part of me wants to ask Owen to do the role full-time. He's incredible with her and I love watching them together. I can't remember what life was like before him. He's organized and ensures Poppy has an activity booked every day. He takes her to the park, loves going to the soft play center with her and he's the best manny any girl could wish for. He never complains when she grumbles in the night either, getting up to see to her, telling me to go back to sleep as I have work the next morning.

The man has stolen my heart. And Poppy's.

He's amazing. Period. And I have seriously fallen in love with him.

But can I ask him to put his plans on hold for us?

Would he do that?

I am way too nervous to ask him. I don't want him to think that I am taking advantage of his jobless and homeless situation, because that's not why I would ask him.

I trust him with her.

I never want him to think that's the only reason I want him around.

But he has his own life to live and his own dreams to chase. I can't let my career take over his. But if I don't find a nanny, I'm going to have to ask Aunt Babs for the interim, and that does not sit well with me at all. I feel like I'm taking advantage.

Of everyone.

I'm definitely getting pushed off the team if I don't find a solution soon.

I pop the last of my halloumi and bacon roll into my mouth, and moan as the salty flavor bursts against my tongue. There's no denying it. Halloumi tastes better in Cyprus than it does anywhere else in the world.

Sliding my phone onto the table, I put my head in my hands and rest my elbows against the table. I lick my lips to dust the crumbs of my sandwich off them and blow out a shaky breath as I stare at the resume on my screen. If this one. I glance at her name, Iris. If Iris can't do every third weekend of the month, then she's not suitable. "I need a nanny, stat."

One by one, the guys join us around the table.

"Why?" asks Spike.

I roll my eyes as if it's not obvious why I need one. "Because I have a baby, Spike."

"Duh," someone says, making everyone laugh.

"But you have a nanny." Spike's brows wrinkle.

Expelling a sigh. "For the time we are here, Spike." *What then?*

Sometimes these guys exasperate me. It's all good and well for them. They have their wives back home, seeing to childcare and managing their households, but I don't have a partner to help me.

Although Owen did say he would follow me wherever I go.

Not used to having a partner travel with me or give up everything to be with me, I can't help but hold on to that thought to bolster my hope for our future together and I can't believe someone would do that for me. Especially after Michael ran at the first opportunity he could, making me lose all faith in finding someone perfect and who would understand my demanding role.

And while my team are amazing, I carry more responsibilities than most of them on my shoulder, because they're also unaware of Cobra's advances toward me. They couldn't know because I've told no one.

Since the incident at the hospital, two weeks ago, he's been a little better, keeping his distance and not making excuses to be alone with me, but I've caught him watching me and he's always helicoptering around me when he doesn't have a reason.

It's enough to have me on edge, knowing he could make a move at any time. My mind reminds me of the time, not long after I split up with Michael, when he cornered me in the break room and made it clear that he was into me. I remember it like it was yesterday...

Cobra leans his hip against the counter in the small kitchen. "Michael was no good for you, Jade. You need someone who is your equal."

I flick the kettle on. "Like you?" I joke.

"We could be so good together, Jade."

My laughter dies in my throat.

He's so close, he's making me feel uncomfortable. I take a step back, but he closes the space between us and grabs my face roughly. "I'm being serious. I want you, Jade."

My mouth dry, too shocked to say anything, my heart seizes in my chest as I try to figure out what is happening.

"I can't stand another day watching you prance about this hangar in that sexy little flight suit."

"I... I..." My usual sharp brain and smart mouth struggle to form words.

My blood pounds in my skull as he lowers his mouth to mine, and I whimper when I think he's going to kiss me.

"Wouldn't you like to find out how wet I could make you? Because you make so hard." He rubs his less than impressive length against my stomach, making me wince.

Breathing rapidly, stress hormones flood my body, and my heart rate inclines, as my body goes into shock, making it impossible to move, and a whole new level of panic descends upon me.

In all my time in the Air Force, no one has ever spoken to me in this way before, and certainly wouldn't expect it from a high-ranking officer.

My vision goes blurry when I hold my breath for too long and then I hear a muffled voice from behind. "Hey, is everything okay?"

Keeping his voice low, Cobra leans closer to my ear. "Do not utter a word. It would be easy for me to end your career." *Dropping his hands off my cheeks, he whips away from me.* "Yes, Jade had something in her eye," *he lies with ease.*

My lungs fill with air, and I dip my head to cover my face, pulling my hand to my heaving chest as I try to catch my breath.

"Are you alright, Jade?" *The concerned voice I know to be Gregor's asks me from over my shoulder.*

"Yeah, I'm fine." *I turn to face him, my eyes glazed.*

"You don't look fine." *Brows dipped, he scowls.*

I nod my head a few times. "I'm fine." *And swipe my fingertips under my eyes.* "It was something sharp. A little painful." *I move toward Gregor, who is standing in the doorway.* "Now you're here. I wanted to show you something." *I move quickly, urging him to follow me.*

Not long after the incident, I found out I was pregnant, and they moved me to an administrative role. And while I remained within the squadron, I was far enough away to avoid Cobra at all costs.

Since my return, on more than several occasions, he's tried to get me alone.

To protect myself, I always ask someone to accompany me in meetings so it's not just him and me, making excuses that since I had Poppy, I have a terrible memory or that we need someone else to advise or take notes.

It's not been easy to navigate, and I don't want to rock the boat, but I do it to protect myself.

I love this job and want to fulfill my full term on the display team.

It's worrying to think Cobra has so much power, especially when he made it clear he did me a *favor*, persuading the drafting clerk who allocates postings, to hold my position open for an extra two flying seasons to accommodate my time away on desk duties and off during maternity leave.

He likes to remind me that at the snap of his fingers, he could take my dream job away from me and have me return to my fast jet squadron. Although he hasn't mentioned this since the hospital and I am praying this is a good sign.

However, if I don't find a nanny soon, I'm guessing he will make good on his promise to cut me from the team.

How did I ever think returning to a flight squad traveling every week was ever going to work as a single mom?

As the most sought-after flying role in the Air Force, it's all I ever wanted to do and few people ever make the team throughout their career and for me, this is everything. I'll retire a lucky woman knowing I reached the peak of my career, doing a role made only for the elite.

But Cobra isn't making it easy, nor is finding childcare that suits my stupidly busy career calendar. *Where is Mary Poppins when you need her?*

Cobra is often angry with me, throwing his power around when I ignore his unwelcome advances. He talks to me in a condescending tone, and makes lewd remarks with a sexual overtone, informing me I could *return the favor* he wangled for me with the drafting clerk, by going out for dinner with him or throwing me another one of his creepy winks, suggesting something more.

What the *more* is, I never want to find out.

I've been trying to ignore his advances, but he's only been getting worse.

The incident at the hospital was just the tip of the iceberg.

He makes my blood turn to ice, sending shivers down my spine, hence why I keep every conversation with him work related. He's easily distracted, always desperate to steer the conversation in a direction about him and me, but I avoid that at all costs.

However, he saw an opportunity at the hospital when I was vulnerable and took it as an opening to get to me.

Cobra clearly didn't expect Owen's protective reaction. Not caring about Cobra's rank or the position he holds, he swept in to protect me, saving my ass and sanity.

What would have happened if he wasn't around?

And what will happen if I am ever put in that position again?

Owen brought it up the day after Mom left the island, but I brushed him off, telling him it was nothing. I am not sure he believed me, but I changed the subject immediately and have avoided talking about it ever since.

Anyway, I have a gigantic problem to solve first; like finding a flexible au pair.

I inhale a deep breath while sending a quick email to the agency asking if they have any other options. Close my phone and push it further away from me. I've looked at around twenty applicants so far.

Why is it so difficult to find someone? Oh, I know why,

because this job takes over my life, that's why. It doesn't make allowances for babies or single moms.

Regardless, I'm in this position now, and I desperately need to sort my shit out before I crash and burn, and if not, I'm going to have to ask for time off, and *that* is most likely not an option.

It's times like this I wish I had a bigger family. With only me, Aunt Babs and my mom left, I don't have any other alternative than to hire help.

Ultimately, while I love my job, I don't want to be away from Poppy either. The pain I feel when I think about leaving her with a stranger seizes my chest and I can't think straight.

I would feel better if I knew Owen was looking after her and that's the only thing that would help settle me.

I stretch out my neck left and right as Arlo joins us. "I heard you talking about your childcare problems. Why not keep your new nanny? He's hot." Arlo then takes a large swig of his water.

"I'll let Oliver know you said that... you know, your boyfriend." I hitch a brow.

"Oh, he knows already. I sent him a photo I took of Owen at the pool. Yeah, Gregor's cousin is hot." He swoons, eyes twinkling as if picturing him fresh in his mind.

Yup, he makes me feel like that too.

"I'm being overlooked. I'm not exactly an ugly bastard." Gregor scans his eyes around the table, making everyone laugh.

He's not ugly, not even in the slightest. Gregor is super handsome. Good-looking genes run in their family. However, I've never seen Gregor in that way.

But Owen? Well, Owen makes my insides go all gooey and my legs feel like Jell-O when I'm around him.

And then there's that thing he does with his tongue behind my ear, as he counts down and begs me to come on command, which is hotter than a volcanic eruption. Not to mention, no man has ever had the ability to turn my usual sharp brain cells into sponge when he's eating me out like I'm the best meal he's ever tasted. What that man can do with his tongue is as surprising as it is pleasurable.

How I'm still able to walk after having him fuck me on every surface and piece of furniture in the villa, I will never know.

Having not had mom around for two weeks, once Poppy goes to bed, it's as if a new level of Owen has been unlocked, filling me with his cock every hour of every night. I'm not complaining. Having someone who desires you and looks at you the way he does me, as if I stole the stars out of the sky for him, is oddly addictive and the way he kisses me breathless makes me crave him all the more.

Floating off somewhere on a flying carpet through rainbow-colored clouds thinking about Owen, a hand waves in front of my face, bringing me back to reality.

"I think we lost her." The team chuckles. "She's loved up."

While the guys openly talk about their relationships, I like to keep my personal life exactly that, personal, so I never share, but maybe I should.

"I really like him," I whisper, not sure if I am doing the right thing. Embarrassment coloring my cheeks.

Arlo leans across the table and lays his hand over mine. "We know."

My eyes meet at least a dozen pairs. "Do you like him?" Knowing how much we all mean to each other and how tight we are, approval from them is everything.

"We love him, ma'am." Arlo pats my hand. "He's incredible with Poppy."

They all know how Michael created a whole new brand of selfish, not wanting to be part of Poppy's life.

My cheeks grow hot and I just know they fill with color again, exposing the way I feel about him. "He is, isn't he?" I pull my shoulders up to my ears and discreetly rest my hand over my flight suit where my lucky charm is nestled, safely tucked into my bra. It brought me more than luck, it brought me a six foot two, chiseled to perfection, Scotsman, with the body of an athlete and the brains of a statistical whizz. It blows my mind how quickly he can do mental math.

Each guy around the table adds their own thoughts.

"He's funny."

"Smart."

"Respectful."

"Kind."

"Despite what he's been through lately, he's still smiling. He's not broken."

"He has great abs." I knew Arlo would mention those, making me giggle.

"And he has a gigantic cock," I add. "And you should see what he can do with it." *Kidding*, I don't say that, but I chuckle, imagining what they would all say and do if I did.

I'm a lady after all, prim and proper, cooking and cleaning for my imaginary husband, shouting *tally ho,* waving goodbye to him as he goes out to make some hard-earned pennies for his family... yeah, right. Long gone are those days.

Thank goodness.

Bring on the New World where we have women fighting on the front line, running the country, and flying fast jets while we birth more strong women, then get back to business. I am honored to be one of them.

Women empowering women, I'm all for it. Bring it the hell on.

Well, bring it on, but for the love of God, find me someone wonderful to look after Poppy first.

Only being one of the handful of female pilots in the Air Force, recruiting more women to enroll is something I spoke to Cobra about when I first joined the team.

How I would love to give motivational speeches to the high schools, encouraging boys and girls to join the Armed Forces and consider going through our flying school. To travel the world, see and do things no one else ever has. It's the best job in the world and I'll tell anyone who will listen.

However, Cobra has pooh-poohed me, every time I have suggested it.

I shiver as I remember the way he touched me at the hospital and push the thoughts about him aside, deciding to stand up to Cobra the same way Owen did.

I make a snap decision.

It's time to take a stand.

I earned my place here. My skill and talent secured my place on the aerobatic team and I won't let anyone take that away from me.

I must put a stop to his harassment. As soon as I return to the UK, I will make an appointment with our Group Captain because he outranks Cobra by a mile, certain he'll be appalled to learn everything I've been taking notes of while under Cobra's command.

Owen worked him out from the start. I didn't, but he's shown his true colors and he seems incapable of being a good, kind, or compassionate leader; proving to me that his ethics are muddier than a swamp.

Bide your time, Jade. Be patient. You'll get your meeting with the Group Captain as soon as you're back in the UK.

I tune back into the conversation the guys are having. "You should move him into your quarters and make him your full-time childminder," Gregor says, referring to Owen. "It would give him something to do until he sorts his life out."

What then? Will he leave to pursue a new career like I've told him to, leaving me and Poppy to piece our hearts back together?

Saddened by that thought, my heart crumples like a piece of paper destined for the trash can.

"He would need full security clearance and I recommend you have a DBS check done." Cobra's steely voice breaks through our lighthearted banter.

I hate that man. He's the only bad thing about my job. He hasn't even taken it upon himself to apologize for his dreadful behavior at the hospital, and it's been two weeks. And that creepy snake tattoo he has branded into the skin of his forearm gives me the heebie-jeebies.

"A DBS check?" Arlo questions him. "What the hell would he need to have a Disclosure and Barring Service check for? That's ridiculous." Arlo shakes his head. "Sorry, sir, but I disagree."

"What's a DBS check?" Looking at Arlo, Gregor hooks one elbow over the back of his chair.

Cobra narrows his eyes, pissed off that Gregor didn't ask him, but he answers anyway. "To check whether he is safe to work with children."

"What the hell?" Gregor runs his tongue along the front of his top teeth. "Seriously, Cobra? Do you even know my family at all?"

"Easy, Flight Lieutenant Brodie," Cobra's voice stabs

like needles. "May I remind you who you are talking to? And you can never be too safe these days. There are all sorts of weirdos out there."

Yeah, you being one of them.

The atmosphere instantly changes, turning to ice even as the warm air continues to billow into the room through the mosquito-netted windows.

"Forgive me, sir." Gregor reluctantly apologizes, remembering our ranks, then angrily pushes his chair back. Standing with such force that the chair drops with a loud clatter against the floor.

One of the other men picks it up and before Gregor storms out of the room, he turns to me, and with fire in his eyes so fierce it burns, he says, "She's safe with him, ma'am."

I give him a curt nod.

I know she is, Gregor, because I feel it through every inch of my body and way down deep into my soul.

But him, looking back at Cobra, I wouldn't trust him to look after a goldfish.

CHAPTER NINETEEN

OWEN

Looking down the lens of the camera on my phone, I'm bursting with giddiness when I say, "I've met someone." I rest my chin on top of my clenched fist that's resting on the table.

An involuntary smile shapes my lips. I can't help it. I'm so fucking happy because Jade is the only good thing in my life right now. And Poppy. She's the little firecracker that has my heart in a spin.

I hear running footsteps behind Lincoln and right on cue, Violet appears. "You met someone?" she gasps, nudging Lincoln's side to take a seat next to him. She's a sucker for gossip.

Lincoln's statement grin sparkles back at me, his olive skin making his teeth look even whiter. Got to hand it to him, he works those Greek genes of his; he knows he's a handsome fucker. "It's only taken you a few weeks to meet someone?"

"Not just anyone, Linc. She's *the* one." I sigh, blissfully.

"What's she like?" Violet's dark eyes light up.

Christ, Violet, why don't you grab some popcorn while you're here?

I chuckle at her enthusiasm before I say, "She's." I stop, unable to find the right word. "Sensational." Intense peace settles in my chest.

Violet repeats my words. "She's sensational," she gasps. "And what is the name of this *sensational* woman?"

"Jade." I sigh, feeling like the boy next door who scored a date with the head cheerleader.

"Is she vacationing in Cyprus?" Lincoln presses me. He and Violet will want to know everything, and I have been bursting to tell someone, anyone, about Jade.

"She's a member of the Royal Air Force. She works with Gregor." I'm being vague before I tell them exactly what she does for a living. Because it fucking knocks my socks off and I'm hoping it will knock theirs off too.

"What does she do?" Violet leans forward.

"She's a pilot," I say proudly.

"A pilot?" Lincoln's mouth drops open in shock.

"She's a world record holder. The first and only woman to have ever flown with the aerobatic team. She's a fucking knockout and amazing at what she does." My chest bursts with pride.

Lincoln shakes his head in disbelief. "Only you could fall in a dumpster and come out smelling like a perfumery."

I watch Violet grab her phone, no doubt to scour the internet and find a picture of Jade.

"She has a daughter called Poppy. She's amazing too." Everything about them both brings me joy. That joy growing every time I'm around them.

I couldn't comprehend it at first, however, it's clear to me now that the three of us were meant to be. We belong together.

"You bagged a woman *and* a child. You're an instant family." Lincoln fights hard to keep the surprise out of his voice. "You've changed, man."

"I have," I agree.

Violet flips her phone around to show me something on her screen. "She's their team leader?" Violet sounds stunned. "Is this her?"

I look at the image on the screen and nod. "Yeah."

"Holy fucking shit, she is stunning." Lincoln grabs the phone from Violet. "How the fuck did your ugly ass get her?"

"Fuck if I know." My smile is goofy.

"Hey, I am right here." Violet jabs Lincoln in the ribs with her elbow, causing him to let out an *oft* noise.

"I only have eyes for you, Petal. You know that." He throws his arm around her shoulder and hugs her in tight to his side. "Plus, you give the best blo—"

Violet slaps her hand over his mouth to shut him up, his eye flaring in response, dancing with humor.

I'm so fond of these two and their capers. I miss them.

The baby monitor makes a few shuffling noises before Poppy chatters away, indicating nap time is over. She never cries when she wakes up, instead, she sings sweet little tunes. Although I think it's the feeling of her tongue against her gums she likes when she sings, *leedle, leedle* repeatedly.

"Give me a second. I'll be right back." I run up the stairs to fetch Poppy to be greeted by her holding on to the side of her crib, jumping up and down excitedly, wearing a big smile.

Sleepy eyes and wild bedhead hair, she's so adorable I could eat her.

"Hey, Popcorn." I push my hands under her armpits, lift her out of the bed, and smack a kiss on her cheek. "Did the sandman send you lovely dreams, huh?" I bounce back down the stairs, grab her sippy cup from the refrigerator that I filled up earlier with water, and give it to her.

Poppy grabs the cup by the handles and then snuggles into me. It's the best feeling.

"Come and meet my friends," I say to her. "They're gonna love you."

Sitting back down in front of the phone, Violet gasps. "Hey, beautiful." Then finger waves at her.

Poppy sleepily smiles, with the spout of her sippy cup still in her mouth, showing off her two bottom teeth.

I situate Poppy on my lap so we're both facing the front, wrapping my hands around her chubby thighs to keep her safe. Her vibrant hair looks luminous against the contrast of my white tee shirt.

"She's adorable, Owen," Violet coos.

"She is." I lower my chin to sit on top of Poppy's head and enjoy her fresh baby smell. That smell is addictive, and I wish I could bottle it so I could wear it every day.

With hearts in her eyes, Violet swoons, her gaze firmly focused on Poppy. "I think I'm ovulating, Lincoln. Can we have one?"

"Let's do the marriage thing first, yeah?" He looks petrified and I inwardly chuckle, knowing that having a little one around can be heaps of fun. Although I haven't been around for the teething, the midnight feeds, and any of the other stuff I spend my nights reading about on those parenting blogs.

"So, are you babysitting today?" Lincoln asks.

"Yes, and no." I explain what happened to Mari, combined with Jade's training schedule, and how I offered to take care of Poppy temporarily for Jade. Although, on reflection, I don't want this to be a temporary thing. I want

OWEN

to look after Poppy permanently. I don't want Jade to find a nanny, as I wouldn't trust anyone with her except me.

It's not something we have talked about. I am pretty certain it's what she wants too, but I wonder if she thinks that if she asks me, it would be putting my life plans on hold. However, right now, I don't have any apart from being with her. Me becoming the full-time nanny would be the perfect solution.

I just have to work out a way to broach the subject with her.

Both Lincoln and Violet stare at me in surprise, then Lincoln chuckles. "You're a manny."

"That I am." I'm not ashamed. It's an epic job and super rewarding. I've even taught Poppy how to say bye-bye this week. It's a crude attempt and sounds more like *ba-ba* but she's almost there. I'm going to teach her how to say my name next, that's our top priority for this week. Well, that, jungle gym, musical tots, and there's swimming lessons for infants on base, which I thought we could sign up for.

"What the fu—" Lincoln pauses, amending his cursing in front of Poppy. "I mean, what the heck happened since we spoke to you three weeks ago?" Lincoln sounds astonished.

"I had a meeting with the Greek gods and I met a goddess." I'm abstract with my reply.

Right on cue, Poppy says, "Mamma."

"Spot on, Popple." I give her little leg a squeeze.

"Aphrodite?" Lincoln knows his ancestral gods. His Greek grandmother drummed it into him. "My yaya would have a field day with this. She always said she was the most powerful of all the deities."

Poppy places her sippy cup haphazardly onto the table, then claps her hands as if she agrees with Lincoln's yaya.

"I could eat her." Violet turns to Lincoln and says excitedly, "Let's have an army of them."

Lincoln drags his hands down his dark beard. "No way. We'll leave that to Skye and Jacob, my dad and Eva, and her sisters. That lot can make up for us." Lincoln looks pale at the thought of having an army of kids running around.

Never finding pregnancy or babies appealing previously, I time travel into the future, an image of Jade pregnant, her swollen tummy full with my baby, coming into view. My desire to make that happen makes me feel like a fucking caveman.

Over the next twenty minutes, Violet and Lincoln share their news about the hotel they run alongside Lincoln's father, Knox, updating me on the plans to build an over the cliff restaurant. It sounds like hell but also exciting. I know how much they love running the hotel together; they're an incredible team.

I shared my empty bank account update with my two friends. Filling them in on my having seven-figures lifestyle to losing it all situation.

Instantly jumping in, Lincoln offered to help me out, pulling his phone out to transfer me some money, which I graciously turned down, informing him that Gregor has loaned me some from his savings and I am now living on a tight budget until I find myself a job. I've worked out I have eight weeks to find one.

"We're looking for a new finance director." Violet looks excited at the prospect of me joining the team.

"I'm not coming back to Castleview Cove." I grab Poppy's soft sensory book full of bright images off the table and hand it to her to play with. She grabs it, clenching her fists to make it crinkle. It's her favorite book. "Thank you, though," I add with a nod of appreciation.

"The offer won't expire, Owen. Peter isn't due to retire for another six months, so it's yours if you want it." Lincoln adds.

I nod in response, grateful for his offer.

In every way, I can count on Jacob and Lincoln. Even if they didn't have a role for me in their businesses, they would make one. This I know for sure.

Then I ask, "I need to speak to Jacob about something. Could you get him to call me?"

"Can I not help?" Lincoln questions.

"Maybe." I retrieve Poppy's soft book off the floor she threw away. She grabs it and sticks it in her mouth as soon as I hand it back to her. "Remember that private investigator Jacob hired to find Skye?"

"Yeah. His name was Walter Forrester."

"He helped Jacob get results fast and pushed paperwork through, didn't he?"

"Yeah," he answers again.

"Do you reckon he could rush through a DBS form for me?"

Lincoln blinks in confusion. "What the hell is that for?"

"It's a check to ensure I am suitable to work with children. Jade and I." I stall. "Well, she doesn't know me very well."

"Carnally though, right?" Lincoln winks cheekily.

I shake my head with a smile. Lincoln is the definition of cheekiness. "Never change," I order.

"Never," he smirks.

I continue, "So this DBS form thing, it's a way to check if you have a criminal record and whether you are suitable to work around children, too. I want to run the check and get the certificate to show Jade that she can trust me with Poppy and that I'm a good guy with no convictions." I've been reading up about it, but it can sometimes take up to ten days. However, Walter is well connected, and I think he can help me get it quicker.

Violet eyes me curiously. "You really like her."

"I think I'm in love," I say without hesitation.

Although I haven't told her how I feel.

Both Lincoln and Violet sit silently as if they can't quite comprehend my confession or believe that I'm telling the truth.

"This is big," Violet whispers. "For you, this is *huge*, Owen." She pushes her hands out to the sides as if she's holding the biggest fish as the catch of the day.

"This is real," I firmly state, brimming with confidence, but also nerves. *Can you fall in love this quickly?*

Lincoln pipes up. "This is crazy." He makes me chuckle, then he adds, "Leave the DBS form with me. I'll sort it all and I want to pay for your certificate. However much it costs, I'll cover it. I'm sure he'll email you with instructions, just do whatever he asks, and fingers crossed, you'll get it done pretty quickly."

I manage a nod, my chest full of gratefulness. "Thank you," I breathe. I've not always been the best or most supportive friend in the past. However, knowing both Lincoln and Jacob would do anything for me, regardless of my circumstances and have forgiven me for being a shitty friend, is causing me to fight to swallow down the emotion brewing within me.

"And what then? What's the plan, Owen?" Lincoln asks, part concerned, part curious.

"I'm going to move in with Gregor back in Lincolnshire in England. He's offered me a room as he's renting off camp, and then..." I shrug. "I'll get a job, I suppose." That's as far as I've gotten with my life plan. Voice unsteady, I say, "If only I could work out my big why, then I wouldn't still feel that niggle of discomfort."

"Do whatever makes you happy," Violet's cheerful American accent sings merrily.

Then Lincoln says, "When Dad made me leave Scotland to travel to America and *'find myself'*." He holds his fingers up, wrapping air quotes around his words. "I was already certain I still wanted to work at the hotel. I never wavered. Meeting Violet, though, she's the reason I went to California. Not to find myself like my dad thought I would, or soul search, or anything like that. It confirmed to me how I already felt, but my reason for being there was to find Violet. To find my soul mate."

And find lost family members. I don't mention that. It's an open wound that I don't want to rub salt into.

Violet hums with delight. "You're too cute for your own good sometimes, Linc." Then she kisses him on the cheek.

"I know, I'm adorable." He rolls his eyes, wearing a cheeky grin, and I smile at how perfect those two are for each other. Lincoln's right. I think meeting Jade is why I am here, too.

Finishing what he was saying, Lincoln continues. "Take the pressure off. Don't go on a treasure hunt. Just let whatever is meant for you come your way."

"Like kismet?" I ask, using Jade's words the night we swam around Aphrodite's Rock.

"Exactly like that." He nods. "If you push too hard, you'll end up back here. See what happens and let nature do its thing."

"Okay." I raise my chin, feeling more confident and not worried that I'm still piss-farting around. Although... I look down at the adorable girl who's covered her cloth book in slavers and is dribbling all over her hands... I love taking care of Poppy. I've been enjoying every minute of every day with her. The last few weeks haven't felt wasted in the slightest. It's felt meaningful, and I seem to be a natural at this nannying malarkey. Although I have had to speak to Mari twice over video call to check if I have Poppy in the right outfit and make sure if she likes certain foods. Cheese and ham are her favorites; she's a girl after my own heart.

Another call comes through on my phone and I eye it suspiciously as I lean forward to check the displayed number I don't recognize.

"I think that's my bank calling. Can I call you later?" I ask Violet and Lincoln as I reach for the phone to answer the incoming call.

"Of course, go and I'll sort out the DBS form," Lincoln reassures me.

"Thanks." I wave them off and hang up, then hit accept on the other call and place it against my ear cautiously to greet the unknown caller, "Hello?"

"Well, it's good to know you're still alive, son?" My father's callous voice sends chills down my spine, and I freeze, not knowing what to do. Do I hang up, stay on the line, speak?

I'm at a loss.

I squeeze my phone between my shoulder and ear and lift Poppy off my lap.

"Still can't find the balls to speak to me?" His tone has its own brand of liquid sarcasm making my heart thump in my chest.

I carefully sit Poppy down on her circular play mat covered in a zany robot print, then run my hands through my hair, standing to my full height, as I figure out what to say.

I'm not prepared, nor do I have a clue how to reply. I hit the speaker phone icon on my screen and stare at it.

"I thought you'd be home by now, Owen, begging me for your money to be returned. You've surprised me and I can't deny I'm almost proud of you." *Almost.* It's the only time he's ever been proud of me, and even then, it's almost.

I listen to him while watching Poppy stack her fabric cubes, one on top of the other.

And then he says, "You've broken your mother's heart."

"She doesn't have one." I snap back faster than a lizard catching flies.

"Oh, so he speaks."

"I'm not coming home."

"Interesting." I picture him lounging on his black leather desk chair while rolling his cigar between his fingers. He confirms my suspicions when I hear the *sizzle* as he pulls a drag from it; he's exactly where I thought he would be, at work, at his desk. He spends more time there than at home.

Although why would you want to go home to the woman who gives a whole new meaning to arctic?

"You know you can't stay wherever you are forever." He drawls as if bored with our conversation.

"Of course I can. I'll start over. I'm smart, not that you would know, since you've never taken the time to get to know me. I'm also incredibly resilient." If anything, my mother's love, or lack of it, made me grow a skin so thick it's almost impenetrable.

Until Jade broke through it.

"That's not true, son. I know more about you than you think. I know that last year you were just a couple of nights away from pickling your liver to death at that dive bar in town."

He's right, I was, but it's not a dive bar. The Vault is an upmarket nightclub run by respectable members of the town. My father is a presumptuous cunt.

And it was because of him I was there. As soon as I discovered I was to marry someone, my parents chose for me it was all downhill from that moment. Drinking away my problems wasn't the answer, although neither was running away, it seems.

"I know you spent a hideous amount of money on expenses when you were out wining and dining to secure the many contracts we tendered for."

On his instruction and it's what won us those contracts. I search my memory, trying to recall if he's won any in the last year, and come up short. *Why hasn't he been tendering for more work?*

He keeps listing shit I don't agree with. "You didn't even give Evangeline a shot; your heart wasn't in it from the start."

"That's a lie." I shake my head, my pulse quickening at his dishonesty. "And you know that, Dad. I stopped drinking. I did everything you asked of me. I tried, my God, did I try with her, but nothing I did would have ever been good enough, and let's not forget that she was far too young for me. Your ideas about love are archaic and, frankly, disgusting."

He chuckles, fucking chuckles, at my outburst. "You didn't moan about it when you asked to borrow my yacht to woo her, or when you used my credit card to entertain her for an evening at the opera."

"See, I tried, and you handed me the card," I admonish. He's got a knack for twisting the truth.

Exhaling a breath, he says, "Yeah, I suppose I did. Oh well, never mind. So, when will you be over this little tantrum of yours and come back? Can you give me a date?" He flippantly moves on as if everything is kosher between us.

"Are you for real? I am *not* coming back."

Ignoring me, he railroads me with more words. "So, you fancied a little vacation? Great, get that out of your system, and then set a date to come home."

Frustrated by his tone, my heart thuds against my ribcage, my pulse quickening at sonic speed, thumping so hard I can hear it in my ears.

"I'm not having this conversation with you. I can't keep going over the same things. I'm done, I'm out." Even though he can't see me, I slice through the air with my flat hand. If I could divorce my parents, I would. They should make that a thing.

He growls, making my speaker rattle in the phone casing. "Now you listen here, son, and listen good." He starts slow and steady. "You will come home. It's not a fucking option. You were born into a family where loyalty and honor count for more than love." Then he roars down the phone so loud I have to remove it from my ear. "So, get your head out of your ass, and fucking grow a pair. You *will* come back and save this business right now or I will…"

Save the business? What does he mean?

"Or you'll what?" I ask petulantly. "And what do you mean, save the business? Our business is rock solid." I go through those accounts with a fine-tooth comb, scrutinizing our finance reports. I know every overhead, day-to-day cost, ways to make us more efficient, ensure we get the right funding for our machinery, and meet every tax deadline, so what the hell happened in three weeks?

Or what am I missing?

"Located him." I hear an unfamiliar voice down the other end of the phone.

"Who the fuck is that?" I snap, panicking now.

"We'll see you soon, Owen." Out of breath at his outburst, he pants, then laughs loudly.

I cut the call and throw the phone onto the sofa as if it burned the skin off the palm of my hand.

He traced the call.

"Fuck," I yell louder than expected, making it reverberate through the stark marble villa.

Hands on my waist, I look up at the ceiling and expel a long-weighted breath before roaring into the space again as anguish and hate for my father heightens my anger.

I drop my head and look around to find Poppy's bottom lip quivering.

Oh my God, I spooked her, and she looks petrified.

Feeling terrible I run to her, crouching down, to reassure her that everything is okay, but it's too late, her petted bottom lip trembles, tears gloss her eyes and as if it was a delayed reaction, she cries as if I blew out the candles on her own birthday cake.

Lifting her into my arms, I cradle her tight, rubbing her little back to comfort her, but my rocking her back-and-forth skills have no impact as her little chest moves in and out while her sobs continue.

And as if I'm covered in a blanket of calm, a warm set of arms joins us from behind, wrapping themselves around my waist.

Jade.

She moves around to the front to face me, then embraces us both. I pull her under my other arm and press her head into my shoulder, while Poppy rests on the other.

We have a three-way hug; Poppy settles almost instantly, her little sobs dying down.

"I upset her." I feel terrible. "I'm so sorry, Jade, I didn't mean to. I would never—"

"It's okay," Jade consoles me. "I know you wouldn't. Hey, baby." Jade swipes the tears off Poppy's reddened cheeks as she sucks in two quick breaths. "You're okay, aren't you? It was just a minor blip. No harm done." Jade's voice settles Poppy in an instant.

I read up about that too. Moms are like natural calmers for babies, something to do with connection and close proximity. Whatever it is, it's like watching real witchcraft. However, Poppy wouldn't have been crying in the first place had it not been for me. "I'm angry with myself. I can't believe I made her cry." I hate myself.

"Stop stressing. You had a good reason to be upset. I heard everything," Jade confesses against my pec.

"Everything? With my dad?" My mouth twitches. I didn't want her to hear that conversation.

"And with your friends," she confirms.

How long was she listening for? "Oh, yeah?" A hint of wonder in my voice, "What did you hear?"

"That you're a stellar guy, like I've always believed, because you want to have a DBS check done, even though it's unnecessary." She nuzzles into my chest, giving my waist a squeeze. "We trust him eh, Pops?" I look down. Jade's eyes are sparkling as she nods her head, smiling at Poppy.

"When did you get home?"

"From when you sat down in front of the camera with your friends. I was here when Poppy woke up." I stop the gentle rocking motion I've been doing. "I couldn't resist listening in."

Sneaky eavesdropper.

I try to recall our conversation, and then the penny drops.

Oh my G—

"So, you love me?" She looks up at me with those big beautiful blue eyes.

CHAPTER TWENTY

OWEN

"Eh, forget I said that," I stutter.

I've never told anyone I love them before.

I know Jade and I have spoken about falling for one another and catching feelings, but what if she isn't quite where I am yet? What if she doesn't love me? Not fully... not yet?

I don't think I could face the humiliation of telling someone I love them for them to not say it back.

Although it feels like she does.

We connect in a way I have never experienced with any other human being, and being with her feels different.

We feel right.

Perfect together.

We laugh, bicker playfully, and have moments where we never have to speak, but know we don't need to because we are content together. Everything about us feels aligned.

"Why should I forget what you said?" Her eyes widen in amusement.

"Because it sounds stupid now that I've said it." Plus,

having not told anyone I love them before, I was expecting it to be in a far more romantic setting than overhearing a conversation with my friends. Maybe a five-piece string quartet playing something super meaningful in the background while fireworks explode overhead, surrounded by dozens of roses. Isn't that what they do in the movies?

Only I could fuck up a beautiful moment. Again.

"Your heart is beating faster." She drums the fingers of her rested hand on my chest.

"It's not."

"It is, and it's not a stupid thing to have said."

"Yes, it is." I slip Poppy into Jade's arms and move away as sweat breaks out across my forehead. "It's been three weeks. It's ridiculous of me to think that I am. Isn't it?" It's a rhetorical question. "You can't fall in love in three weeks, can you?" I look at Jade and she's staring at me as if I'm amusing her. I start to pace when she doesn't reply. She's got me all in a fluster. "I mean, I dated Skye for fourteen years, and I'm not sure I was ever *in love* with her. It was a high school relationship that went on way too long. We were more like friends by the end, which was all my fault. I never let her in. I didn't tell her things that were going on at home." My rambles take on a new up-tempo pace as I wave my arms around in the air like a wacky promotional inflatable tub guy. "I don't think I've ever been in love. Christ, I didn't even take the time to buy Skye gifts when we were dating. I let Jacob do that. I'm not romantic. Even the boat ride and theater tickets I organized for Evangeline weren't romantic. I was never exposed to what love really looks like, except from my friends and their families; they are all crazy about each other. My family is a mess, and I know it's a shitty, heartless thing for me to say, but I hate my parents. Their relationship is forced, orchestrated. As a kid, they—"

Jade cuts off my racing words. "You're freaking out."

"I'm not freaking out." *Why the fuck do I feel lightheaded?*

"Yes, you are. Stop moving." She's firm with her instruction, so I do as she asks.

Hand on my hips, almost out of breath, I can barely look at her. *What is wrong with me?*

"Answer me this," Jade says calmly. "Do you think about me most of the time?"

"Yes." Constantly.

"Do you want to spend every waking hour with me?"

More if I could. "Yes."

"Do we laugh at the same things, love the same television programs, you can't stop smiling and feel you're a better person having met me?" Poppy plays with the collar of Jade's flight suit.

"I can't disagree with any of that." The intensity of feelings I have for Jade is borderline obsessive.

"Is having sex with me the best sex you've ever had?" She gives me a knowing smile.

"Shhh, not in front of the baby." I place my pointer finger over my lips. "But yes," I whisper, then take a slow step toward her, feeling more like me again.

She continues, "So tell me the dark cloud that was hanging over you. Has it flown away?"

"Yeah." I nod my head. *Yeah, because of you.* Although I push my father's threat of turning up away, because he can make that black cloud reappear.

"And when we talk, text, kiss, touch, does it feel like we twisted that megawatt lightbulb on causing sparks to shine brighter than any filament?"

"It's like an explosion in my chest." I'm only two steps away from her now.

She looks up at me. "And does it feel like someone pressed the accelerator and everything is going so fast, and like we've been together forever?"

"How the hell do you know how I'm feeling?"

"Because I feel the same way, Owen."

"You do?" Confidence blooms in my chest. I push my shoulders back and tilt my head to the side, then close the space between us. Only inches apart, it's still too far away. *She feels the same.* My heart does that weird flipping thing again that it only does around her.

Reaching up, I cup her face with the palm of my hand, and she nods her head. "I do, Owen. I've fallen for you. This is all so—"

"Incredible." I can't stop the Cheshire cat grin forming across my lips. For the first time, in well, ever, I feel a deep contentment, giving meaning to all the parts of my life that make little sense before now. I move in closer to her lips. "You make me feel more daring." She makes me want to free-jump off a cliff while holding an enormous flag, telling everyone I'm in love with her. Because I am. Or maybe she could teach me how to fly that awesome jet of hers and I could write it across the sky in giant letters.

She whispers, "If I make you feel like a daredevil, I should take you out flying before we leave the island, if that's the case." She can't hide her grin, either.

"I would love that."

"You would vomit."

"I'd be fine." I lie, knowing she's right. I'll probably hurl my guts up. "I like roller coasters." I do, but doing several loops in the air at over five hundred miles an hour, nah, no thanks.

"It's not the same." She chuckles, her lips brushing mine.

"But *we* feel the same." I press a kiss against her soft lips. "I love you, Hotshot."

"I love you, too, Owen." She stares at me for a moment and I can see the emotion dancing in her eyes, then she kisses me with the gentleness of a fluttering set of dragonfly wings.

I wrap my arms around her and little Poppy, who is still in Jade's arms, and squeeze them, then kiss the tip of Jade's nose, then her cheek.

"I love both of you," I whisper against the shell of Jade's ear.

"Which makes me love you even more. The way you are with her melts my heart," Jade admits. "You're so caring and patient with her. You're everything I've ever wanted."

And they are everything I didn't know was meant for me.

"Dada?" Poppy's little voice chirps.

I lean out of our hug and kiss Poppy on the cheek. "Not yet. Patience, Poppadom. We've only just told each other we love one another." Then I wink at Jade, and she smiles happily.

"How many nicknames do you have for her?"

I pull Poppy out of Jade's arms and thread my fingers into Jades. "I have at least another dozen." I walk us to the bottom of the stairs. "Now Mommy, you go take a shower and put on something pretty." I lean down and whisper in Jade's ear. "Minus the panties." She shivers when my lips brush over that happy spot behind her ear and she lets out a little moan. "Easy." I use that commanding tone she loves so much and squeeze her hand. "I will make us a lovely dinner this evening, then we are going to watch *Glow Babies*." I focus my attention back on Poppy. "Because it was just getting to the good bit where Sunlight was going to rescue Flash from the grumpy Cloud King."

Poppy claps excitedly in response.

"You're so odd." Jade shakes her head.

"And clever. *Glow Babies* makes her sleepy." I'm certain the animators on that show are on drugs, it's fucking mesmerizing. "And I have plans for us tonight." I drop my voice and I swear Jade glows, making her hair look like firelight.

"Yeah?" Her eyes flash with a carnal, ravenous look.

"Yeah. It's Mommy and Da—" I correct myself. "I mean, Mommy and Owen time."

She licks her lips. "I'll call you Daddy later."

Her words make me groan, my cock twitching against the fabric of my shorts. "Not appropriate while I am holding the Poopinator."

She mouths a *'sorry'*. "I'll go jump in the shower." She skips up the stairs giddily.

And my heart skips on its own accord, too.

She loves me.

CHAPTER TWENTY-ONE

JADE

"O... O... O..." I'm on the verge of a mind-blowing orgasm when Owen stops flicking my clit. It's the fourth time he's edged me like this, leaving me breathless and panting with need.

"It's Owen, Hotshot. My name is O-wen. Say my name."

"Owen," I groan loudly, twisting the bedding into my fists in frustration. "Please let me come," I plead.

"No," he almost snarls, making my pussy clench. I love how he takes control in the bedroom. He's now a stark contrast to the first time we had fun by the pool. I'm convinced his request to the gods to make him a better lover for me was granted.

Although I swear all he needed was to find me to make him *want* to unleash the beast within him in the bedroom.

Grabbing my hips, he flips us both over. His back now on the mattress, my legs straddled on either side of him. Having spent weeks in the sunshine, he's so bronzed now, making his corded muscles more pronounced.

"Now sit on my face," he demands.

I blink. I've never done that before. "What?"

"I want you to bring that pretty pussy up here." He points to his face. "And I want you to fuck my face until you're screaming my name, Hotshot."

"I might smother you."

"I'm hoping you fucking do. Smother me in your taste and smell." He guides me up his body, over his chest, to his mouth. With my inner thighs surrounding both sides of his face, his hot breath brushes my clit as I'm fully exposed to him.

"Now, Hotshot. I want you to hold on to that headboard." He inserts a finger into my soaked center. My hips buck, chasing my overwhelming need to come. "Not yet." He smacks my bare ass with his free hand, making a loud cracking noise across the room, then grips my hip to stop me moving. "When you fuck my face, I want you to sit, not squat." He removes his finger and I moan at its loss.

Grabbing onto my ass with both hands, he pulls my hips down to his mouth and I watch as he grins wickedly, then closes his eyes and lunges forward, sucking my clit in to his mouth.

He had nothing to worry about as I fully sit on his face, my body desperate for his touch. I roll my hips in response to his fingers that are digging into them, and grind against his open mouth as he covers my pussy with it.

Lavishing my clit with his tongue, he sucks it into his mouth, toying with it, then flicking it. And I swear to Christ himself when he nibbles on it and thrusts a thick finger inside of me.

Throwing my head back, I ride his face, relaxing now as he laps at my clit and inserts another finger, stretching me in the best way.

Letting go of the headboard, I grab onto his hair to fuck his face harder as the burning need in my body becomes almost too much, and a few seconds later I come.

Hard.

I cry out his name as blinding stars appear behind my eyes, soaking his chin with my orgasm.

My thighs tremble as he removes his fingers slowly from my wet center, then replaces them with his rigid tongue, lapping up every drop.

He lifts his hand in the air, holding out his fingers. "Taste," he mumbles against my pussy as he taps my lips, instructing me to open.

Every first with him is always erotic and hot and so fucking dirty. I love it.

I love him.

I paint my lips with his two fingers that have just been inside of me before I pull them into my mouth and twirl my tongue around them, sucking them deep, cleaning off my release.

He grabs my thighs, lifting me off his shoulders and down his body with ease. Face to face, I drop my mouth over his, and kiss him as if it's the end of the world and we'll never have another moment together. His rough scruff, still wet, smells like sex, and sin.

He threads his hands into the back of my hair, kissing me so hard, it feels like he's bruising my mouth, his whiskers giving me chin rash.

He doesn't give me any warning, pushing his thick cock into me, feeling the burn from the way his thick length opens me up. I push myself down, letting out a long, soft moan as he fills me completely. Not giving me a second to breathe, Owen pistons his hips, thrusting into me with a punishing force that I meet with the same desperate need.

There's nothing soft or tender about this moment. It's carnal and intense as we connect on a new level. As if the words we've spoken today have unlocked something inside us both. And it's delicious.

Delicious and rough, intense and intoxicating, and I want more.

"You're fucking soaked, Hotshot," he growls.

My body begs for more as it chases another release. I move my hips faster up and down his hard cock in a desperate attempt to give my body, and his, what they seek.

I bite his bottom lip, sucking it into my mouth, and he groans, digging his heels into the bed to jackhammer into me like a crazed animal.

"Fuck. Your pussy feels so good," he cries out, his fingers digging so deep into my hips, branding me with fingerprint bruises. "Come for me again, Jade," he commands through gritted teeth. "Show me how much your pussy loves my cock." His eyes roll into the back of his head.

"You make me so wet, Owen."

He curls his neck up off the mattress and sucks my sensitive nipple in to his mouth, then bites it, making it pucker, shooting sparks of pleasure into my pussy. My impending orgasm builds; the sensations spreading through every cell of my body.

The physical chemistry between us is so hot we could start a forest fire. I'm burning up.

He sucks, then flicks my nipple with his tongue, and, as another orgasm rolls through me, his hits, simultaneously. My inner walls clench around his thickening cock as he explodes, shooting his release, the aftershocks causing his cock to jerk as he pumps every drop inside of me.

Kissing me lazily, he slows his hip movements as he slowly caresses the curves of my waist and hips, brushing his fingertips up and down my body, as if committing every touch to memory.

Covered in a sheen of perspiration, panting and satiated, our bodies press against each other. Every cell of my being sings with happiness.

I hum out a contented sigh.

"I love you, Jade," he whispers, trailing loving kisses down the skin of my neck and shoulder, then back again. "I love you so much." He reaffirms the sentiment.

I can't help but smile, blown away by how in tune we are, jumping from wild and fast to soft and gentle in a heartbeat.

The bond I feel between us is so strong already, it shakes me to my core.

With neither of us wanting to face our problems, we lose ourselves in one another.

And tomorrow we'll tackle my lack of a full-time nanny issue, and we'll face whatever is coming with his father, but until then, it's just us.

At least until the sun rises.

"I love you too, Owen."

CHAPTER TWENTY-TWO

Owen

Wrapped in a thin white sheet, Jade and I are lying face to face in bed as the sun welcomes the new day.

"What happens if your dad shows up here?" Nervously, she nibbles on her bottom lip.

"What can he do? Blindfold me, tie me up, and fling me into the back of a plane to fly me home?" Not likely. And we no longer have the private family jet. Out of the blue, he sold that last year.

"I don't know what he is capable of." She looks at me with those big, innocent doe eyes.

She's right, she doesn't know him, but I do, and although he's an ass, I don't believe he has it in him to be so bold. He's comfortable in his own surroundings in Scotland and barely leaves the country. He's far from the man about town he thinks he is.

"Positive. He may have tracked me, but we leave here in five days, and I have no intention of returning to Scotland." He can't make me.

"We have so much to pack before then." Jade groans at the enormity of it all.

I moved in with her and Poppy the day after Mari's accident, and we've grown into this villa; accumulating things as if we were already a little family.

Jade's job is her priority and I want to do everything to make her life easier. "You focus on refining your choreography. Is today the last run-through?"

She's glowing with happiness when she nods. "Yes, and Families Day is on Friday to say thank you to the base for hosting and show them the entire display from start to finish." She pulls the covers up to her mouth with excitement.

"Then home on Saturday," I confirm our plans.

Then back to the cold weather of England. I shiver at the thought.

With only one suitcase and a passport to my name, I never in a million years thought I would move to England.

Although—I stare at Jade—I've got her and my lovely little Pop-a-doodle and they are more than enough to stoke the fire in my belly to find a job and make some money so I can look after them. I'll do whatever it takes to make this work. I'll even take a job in finance if I have to. I've already been looking and there are plenty of options. I'll not struggle to get work.

"My choreography worked out perfectly." She sighs.

"Your display is jaw-dropping." And stomach dropping. I couldn't do the job she does.

Poppy and I have made our way up the cliffs several times to watch them practicing and every time I spot something different, and now they've added in flying with colored smoke, it gives the stunts that extra *wow* factor. I especially love the giant love heart two of the jets perform.

OWEN

The precision and shape of two planes drawing a heart shape in the sky with red smoke while only feet away from each other blows my tiny brain. I do not know how they do it. The risky maneuver is performed perfectly every time.

I bop the end of her nose. "So, you concentrate on being awesome, and I will pack all the suitcases today. It won't take long." I've already packed most of Poppy's toys ready for the plane.

While Jade is flying her jet back to England, Poppy and I are returning on a flight from Larnaca airport to Manchester, where we'll be greeted by a driver to take us on to camp to meet Jade. Without check-ins and transfers, she'll be back before us but not soon enough to meet us at the airport.

Having never flown with a baby before, I'm unsure of what I am doing, so I am winging it. Although I looked up a few blogs on how to keep babies entertained and happy. We booked flights for around Poppy's nap time, hoping she might sleep. I've kept out her favorite cloth book and her Hungry Caterpillar interactive toy she loves shaking about and spends hours playing with, and I've downloaded a few episodes of *Glow Babies* on my phone too.

I'm a little worried, but I'm sure we'll be fine.

Jade nibbles on her thumbnail. "Can I ask you something?" Her voice sounds a pitch higher than normal.

"It's at least ten inches, Hotshot," I answer cheekily, making her chest shake with laughter. I pull her thumb out of her mouth. "Ask away. What do you want to know, Jade?"

"If... what... I can't ask you. Forget it." She rolls onto her back and stares at the ceiling.

I roll on top of her, pressing our bodies together, and lean my forearms on either side of her head.

"Talk to me."

Her eyes bounce back and forth between mine. "Have you started looking for a job?"

"I have."

"In finance?"

"Yeah."

"Is that what you want to do?"

"No."

I wanted you to ask me to look after Poppy full-time, but I know you're looking for a nanny.

I continue, "But I need to pay my own way and eat. And if I am moving in with Gregor, then I will need money to contribute toward the household bills."

"Okay. But would you be open to offers?"

I widen my eyes in anticipation. "Spill."

"I can't find a nanny," she blurts.

I open then close my mouth, then eye her suspiciously, pulling my brows together. "Wait, I thought you'd had over twenty resumes from the agency and you were interviewing the shortlist when we got back?" Which I was disappointed about.

She groans. "None of them are suitable. Some can't stay over. Some need every weekend off; others need every Thursday off. What the hell happens on a Thursday?" Sounding stressed, her voice goes all squeaky. "One of them wants more than fifty days' holiday a year because she likes to travel for a month every year. I don't even get fifty holidays a year."

"Right." I draw out my word, hoping she'll get to the point soon. I'm pretty sure I've figured out what she wants from me, though, and I am so fucking excited I can't contain my smile. "So, why haven't you told me this sooner? We go home in five days." I taunt her, hoping she'll ask me *the* question.

Ask me to take care of Poppy. Go on, Hotshot.

She scowls hard, her brow becoming lined with annoyance. "Because for the first time in my life, I feel out of control. My job requires me to be organized, focused, responsible at all times. I've flown thousands of hours at Mach speed. I'm a leader, a great one. I'm motivated and I motivate others. I've completed front line tours, lived in tents under the blazing heat of the desert, completed assault courses, then walked for ten kilometers, then completed another assault course right after which made me vomit my lungs up. I even survived on only a couple of hours' sleep a night for the first weeks of officer training. I've done all of that, and yet, finding someone I trust who can look after the most precious thing in my life seems an impossible task." She pauses. "I can't do it. And—" She looks angry at herself for admitting how she's feeling. "I'm scared to leave her with anyone I don't know, and even more petrified that if I don't find someone, I will probably get kicked off the team. Although maybe that would be easier, I wouldn't have a crazy schedule, except then I will have to return to my fast jet squadron, and I know I will have to go on deployment for six months somewhere which leaves me in the same position I'm in now." Her eyes dart from mine to the ceiling and I watch as her panicked mind takes hold. "Oh my God, I need help, and fast."

And a paper bag to blow into.

Her heart is beating like a set of bongo drums.

"Hey, hey. Just breathe, Hotshot," I say, using a soothing voice to calm her. "They can't and won't do that. There are strict employment laws." She's overthinking it, but we need to solve the nanny, or lack of, situation.

Her voice sounds hopeless as she tells me everything she should have told me days ago. "I've barely been back at work two months and I'm already failing at this mom and work thing. I have hundreds of displays to perform from the beginning of June through to the end of September. And we still have more shows to be confirmed overseas and in the UK. I haven't found anyone who can even nearly accommodate my ridiculous schedule." A tear runs down her temple and I brush it away, my heart spiking with pain for her. "I thought I had this all figured out, but I don't. I didn't account for Mom having an accident. And I now know why the other female pilots with children don't apply for aerobatic selection because I failed the team as soon as I got pregnant and now that I can't find a nanny, I'm going to fail them all over again. And I am failing Poppy too. I can't do this."

She squeezes her eyes shut. "I'm a failure." She covers her face with her hands, then muffles into them. "I'm too ashamed to look at you."

"Jade," I coax. "You are not a failure, far from it. But you keep mentioning losing your job. Legally, that can't happen, unless there is something you're not telling me. What is really going on, Hotshot?" I can feel there is more to this than she's letting on.

Eventually, she whispers into her cupped hands on her face so quietly I don't catch her words.

She's scared or hiding something, *or both*.

"Jade, baby. Look at me."

Holding her hands in place, she doesn't move.

"Please." She's worrying me now. "I can't help you if you don't tell me what's wrong."

At a snail's pace, she spreads her fingers to peek through. "It's Cobra." Her voice is small.

My body goes rigid, the timbre in my voice dropping. "What about Cobra?"

She moves her hands away from her face and then worries her bottom lip. "If I don't find a nanny, Cobra will kick me off the team. He's been threatening to do so since I returned from maternity leave. He—he—he, makes me feel uncomfortable." She sucks in a breath as if gearing up to make a confession, then she does. "I haven't told anyone, and I lied to you when you asked if he'd ever made other advances toward me, but he has, and I couldn't say anything because he said he would shorten my time with the display team and send me back to my squadron. This is an opportunity of a lifetime and my dream job. I don't want to have my term with the display team shortened."

That motherfucker. I knew it. My blood takes on its own heat as my body temperature rises.

"I want to know everything. No stone left unturned Jade; I want complete honesty from you."

And then she lets it all out. She tells me about an incident in the break room, him whistling at her, comments about returning favors. She lists a series of offensive comments, asking her about her sex life, offensive gestures, unwanted touching, using his rank to not only sexually harass her but emotionally and physically harass her as well.

"This stops right now." I kiss her on the lips, roll off her, and pull her up out of bed. "Jump in the shower. I am calling Gregor."

"No, don't," she exclaims as she tries to grab the phone that I now have in my hand.

"Do you want my help?" She wouldn't have told me if she didn't, and I think secretly she knew I wouldn't keep this from Gregor. It's too big not to act on.

"Yes, but—"

"But nothing, Jade. How do you know he isn't doing this to other women? And what about before you? Where was he based before this posting? We have to stop him. Now. He knows what he's been doing. He's been misusing his power to harass you and not just once or twice, it's dozens of times, before and after having Poppy. You said you kept a diary of events, yes?"

When she nods, standing in front of me naked, my heart aches in my chest at how my usually confident girl looks completely lost and vulnerable.

"Up there." I point to the sky. "You are the one in control. You are the brave leader that turns me on so fucking bad. I want to jump in your plane and write across the sky how badass I think you are. But sometimes, Hotshot, like now, you need to let go of the control and let others lead. Let Gregor help you, because this has to stop. For you, for others he may have done it to previously, and for anyone else that comes after you." I close the distance between us and kiss the shell of her ear. "You didn't ask for this. You don't deserve it, and I will not let this go on for another minute."

Surrounding her with my body, I wrap her up in a warm embrace. "We'll fight this together, Jade. I can be your witness. I saw everything at the hospital. They *will* believe you."

"They will." It's not a question. She sounds more confident now.

"And Gregor saw the break room incident, plus he saw and heard him wolf whistling at you," I confirm more of her evidence against Cobra.

"He did."

"Then you have enough evidence for a team to investigate. And when they find what they are looking for, because they will." I squeeze her tight. "Then and only then will they take administrative action. But we need to follow your chain of command or whatever procedure the Air Force follows. They'll have a strict zero tolerance policy. It may be a drawn out and lengthy procedure, but I'll stand by you every step of the way. We all will."

"Thank you." Her tone is laced with heavy worry. "I don't want to be a burden or be the woman who won the world's first aerobatic pilot title to have it overshadowed with a sexual harassment accusation. I don't feel in control of this."

"It's not an accusation, Jade. These are facts and they will uncover the truth with a thorough investigation."

"What if I lose my job?" she questions, sounding pained.

"By law, they can't do that. Cobra, though, will most likely be dismissed." I lean out of our embrace and, with a firm voice, say, "You're the victim, Jade. He's the perpetrator. He made some terrible decisions and now he has to face the consequences."

"Okay," she whispers, finally agreeing that we are doing the right thing.

Keen to call Gregor, because I want to strike before Cobra gets the chance to, I move out of our embrace. "First things first. Shower." I point at the bedroom door. "Second thing, I am calling Gregor while you're in there. I'll tell him everything and thirdly—" I kiss her on the lips. "Yes, I'll be your nanny."

Looking both astonished and confused, her eyes widen.

"That's what you were going to ask me, right?"

"Yeah, sort of. You know what? Forget I mentioned it, it's fine." She wafts her hand through the air as if she's swatting flies off her face as she tries to renege on the offer she never made me in the first place.

I smile, enjoying how uneasy she is when she needs to ask for help. I listen to her listing shitty excuses as to why it would never work, and when she's almost out of breath, I speak, "It's a great idea. I can keep Poppy at Gregor's when you're overnighting. I can look after her during the day at your house."

"Unless you move in with me?" she blurts out, then covers her mouth with her hand.

My brows dip in confusion. "I didn't think partners were permitted to live in quarters unless you were married?"

Her hand drops from her mouth. "You're not, but if I employ you as the nanny, you can live in with me. I would fill out the correct paperwork to make that happen and get you a pass to get on and off camp. You'd have to have a security check." The solution to all our problems falls into place; she needs a nanny and I need a job. It's a win-win situation.

I let out a half chuckle, half exhale, letting the plan simmer. "I'm gonna be the nanny with benefits."

She scrunches up her face, making all her freckles join together. "That sounds terrible."

"It sounds amazing."

Then she makes me an offer. "I will pay you."

"So, I'm the gigolo, now?" I joke.

She drops her chin to her chest. "Oh, my God. That's not what I meant."

Too far away from me, and because I always want to be touching her, I sweep her into my arms and crash land us on top of the bed, making her squeal. Her warm laughter is muffled against my skin.

My large hand takes her face as I plant a kiss on her lips. "Let's not talk about any of the detail. Just do what you need to do to get me on to camp and if I have to stay with Gregor in the interim, that's fine, too. Just know this, I will take care of Poppy. Whatever you need me to do, for however many days and nights, to give Poppy consistency, the care she needs, and to make your life and job seamless, I'm the man for the job."

Relaxing in my arms, contented, she sighs. "I have a nanny."

"I'm going to be the best goddamn nanny there ever was."

Kissing me deeply, she hums, "You already are."

Then it's all systems go, and while Jade gets ready for work, I call Gregor and fill him in about Cobra. He's not surprised when I confirm his suspicions. He then tells me exactly what Jade needs to do to file a complaint, reassuring me that he, along with the entire team, will support her.

But it sounds like there is a long list of protocol to follow first.

Let's hope that Jade's lucky stone she wears in her bra brings us lots of luck because, from the looks of it, we're going to need it.

Fuck, could anything else happen to me this year?

Apparently, it could.

CHAPTER TWENTY-THREE

Owen

It's the day before Families Day. After an intensive assessment by an Air Vice Marshall, the team gained their public display authority, allowing them to fly for the season. It's a huge weight off Jade's shoulders and she stood everyone down for the rest of the afternoon. To celebrate, I drove her and Poppy into Limassol in Jade's hired Jeep, and we are currently having lunch at one of the little tavernas around the ruins of what used to be the town's castle.

The heat has clicked up a few more notches on the temperature gauge as summer officially makes its appearance, and part of me is looking forward to going back to the cooler air of England, although it won't be as cool as Scotland. In Scotland, it will feel like wintertime, not spring as it should.

We are all set to leave the day after the social event tomorrow, where over a thousand families will show up to watch the first aerobatic display of the year, and Jade and the team are buzzing to show it off.

With our suitcases all packed, we are ready to leave the

island, and it was easier than I thought in the end. Although between Poppy and Jade, they have six suitcases, and me, I have one. How many toys did Poppy need, and how many military uniforms does one person require? Lots, apparently.

Following Jade's submission of her formal grievance complaint against Cobra, just as I thought, an administrative team was flown out immediately to Cyprus, as there was enough evidence to investigate.

Gregor's father, my Uncle David, also pulled some strings. His close friendship with Air Chief Marshal Patterson came in very handy, and I'm certain the dedicated team who spent yesterday afternoon meticulously questioning the team were hand-selected by the man himself.

It turns out that Cobra, who I have since learned has a more vibrant nickname than his birth name, Brian Smith, has been investigated before on two separate occasions but the victims changed their minds and dropped the charges against him.

We suspect the devious bastard used his wicked forms of manipulation to make that happen, although we have no way of knowing for sure.

Following the interview, Cobra was suspended from the team until further notice and was sent back to England until the investigation is finalized.

Jade was exhausted and quiet after her long day of interviewing yesterday. I can't imagine how emotionally taxing it all must have been for her.

When she returned to the villa I had a cool bath waiting for her, a hearty meal was on the table, and the house was bathed in candle light and calming music before we went to bed early, where we stayed wrapped in each other's arms all night as the moonlight shone through the slated shutters.

It was yet another evening where we stayed up far too late, discovering our love of different foods, kissing, sharing our favorite movies, more kissing, uncovering our shared love of obstacle courses through mud, to physically push ourselves, promising to sign up for a challenge as a team when we return to England.

When we exchanged stories from our childhoods, Jade became emotional when she spoke about her father, and how supportive he was of her career.

All it did was make the lack of support in my life from my own parents even more glaringly obvious, knowing they never took the time to speak to my friends or take any interest in my extracurricular activities.

When I was a teenager, I was a natural at sports. I could have gone professional in football, rugby, or even BMXing. My physical education teacher saw the potential in me and wanted to help get set up with the right people to train. I had a pipe dream of going pro, but like everything I wanted to do or was good at, my mom shot my dreams down in flames, reminding me I was only ever birthed for a purpose; to carry on my father's empire. So, I stopped sharing my aspirations to become a sportsman, burying them deep so they could never be dug up again, and simply went with the flow to appease my parents, hoping I would win the approval.

It wouldn't have mattered what I did. My best was never good enough.

And having been away from them for over a month, I feel relief that they are no longer controlling my life and career and it's given me space to think about what *I* really want for my future. I realize that I would love to set up an activity center for kids to help them discover their mental and physical strengths with climbing walls, assault courses, BMX tracks, archery, canoeing, maybe even a youth club or wellness center. It's what I would have loved as a young lad myself.

I sit up tall in the chair that's nestled under the canopy of a tree, perking up at the idea of working at an adventure center, or maybe eventually open one of my own.

Christ, it's a big dream, but maybe something I could retrain to do during the evenings and transition into once Poppy goes to school full-time.

You're getting ahead of yourself. Slow down.

However, it's the first idea that has excited me, so maybe I need to think about it some more.

My focus right now; look after Poppy and Jade, and I couldn't be happier about it, so I'm doing that and letting fate decide what happens next.

Daydreaming and wrapped in my bubble of jumbled thoughts while Jade visits the restrooms inside the taverna, I glance down at Poppy, who is sound asleep in her stroller. Her mouth open, with her thumb hanging out of it.

I place her soft gray rabbit plush toy that she loves on her chest, and she instantly wraps her little arm around it, snuggling in as she goes back to sucking her thumb rapidly.

It's the cutest sight that has my heart expanding in my chest at the love I feel for this little cherub who isn't mine by blood but feels like it.

I make a vow to myself to always be there for her, to protect her from whatever life throws her way, but always having her back no matter what life choices she makes.

Jade was right the night we swam around Aphrodite's Rock. Love is unconditional, this is why I freely give my love to them both, because I know they feel the same about me, regardless of what I have to offer them.

Resting back in my chair, Jade appears in the doorway and quickly scuttles across to her seat. "We have to go." Eyes wide in shock, she sounds panicked.

"What? Why? Is everything okay?" On red alert, I sit up straighter in my seat.

"No. Get up, let's go." Looking back over her shoulder, she lifts her purse off the table.

"What is—" I don't have time to finish my question because it's then I see my mother and father standing in the taverna's doorway.

Shoving my seat back calmly, I rise to my full height. "What did they say?" I sound calmer than I feel when I push my sunglasses on top of my head, but I'll be damned if I let them see that their presence has rattled me.

"Oh, you know, they just offered me more money than I would know what to do with if I disappear out of your life." Her eyes dart from me to Poppy to the pathetic excuse of procreators who call themselves my mother and father, standing there poker-faced. "They know everything about me," she whispers, sounding scared, and darts her eyes around the outdoor space.

Fuck them. They don't get to do that to her.

"Take Poppy," I tell her, never taking my eyes off the doorway. I dig the keys to the jeep out of the pocket of my shorts and hand them to her. "I will meet you at the car."

"Owen." Her voice pleading.

Cupping her face in my hands, I kiss her soft mouth. "I love you and I am not giving in to them. I just need a few minutes to tell them to go to hell and then I will meet you at the car, okay?"

"Promise?"

I draw a cross over my heart. "On Poppy's life."

She nods, satisfied with my answer, agreeing to do as I ask.

"How much did they offer you?" The bottled-up nerves in my stomach swirl about like a tornado, but I smile easily as I try to distract Jade from worrying about me.

"Five hundred thousand."

I roll my eyes and kiss her again. "Assholes, I'm worth at least two million."

She snorts and snuggles into my shoulder. "Your heart is priceless to me, Owen. I wouldn't accept anything but your heart."

"You have it, Hotshot," I whisper in her ear and side eye my mom and dad, who are watching every move we make.

Yup, get an eyeful, you heartless fuckers, because this is what love looks like.

"And you have mine."

Jade pushes up onto her tiptoes and closes the small gap of our height difference and kisses my lips. "Don't be long." She narrows her eyes as she shifts her disapproving gaze over at our two voyeurs.

The car keys jingle in Jade's hand as she loops the strap of her cross-body bag over her head, then grabs the handles of Poppy's stroller. My eyes stay fixed on two of the most incredible people in my life, as I watch Jade stride confidently down the cobbled alleyway and round the corner of the castle with an oblivious Poppy.

Pushing down my anger, I stride toward the two people I would be happy never seeing again.

"Did you think she'd take the money?" I stare them both down. "Whatever you found out about her, you clearly didn't dig deep enough to find out what type of person Jade is. In case you're interested, she's loyal, faithful, and a woman of honor. Some people you can't buy off." My voice firm and strong.

My father pushes his hands into his black dress trousers. Closing the space between us, he meets me half-way with his glacial blank stare fixed on his face and sighs. "Everyone has a price."

I laugh at his audacity. "You don't know her like I do."

My mother appears next to him. "We know she's a single mom who could easily fund her daughter's education and set them both up for life with that money."

"I'm surprised you're here. Did you have to ask permission to come?" I pop a brow. "Did you two talk to each other on the way here? Or did you travel separately? When exactly was the last time you spent any time together? Have you ever been on holiday with one another before? Or is this a first?" It feels liberating to finally speak my mind because I don't care how they will react anymore.

"Son, may I remind you who you are talking to? That's your mother and you will treat her with respect."

I flinch, snapping my head back. "Son?" I *tsk* then shake it in disapproval. "Don't call me son. Not once have you ever treated me like anything more than a disposable item that you can manipulate for your own gain. And I know exactly who I am talking to." My nostrils flare in disgust. "I'm talking to the woman who has name-called and gaslit me since the day I was born. According to her, I am a worthless, ugly, good for nothing."

I wait to see her reaction, but her face doesn't move, probably because of the amount of Botox and filler her skin is stuffed with. "Isn't that what you said?" Her jaw tightens as she pretends to push an invisible blonde hair off her forehead. "Just like I thought," I state the obvious. "When Father is around, you barely say two words. Although, you always had plenty to say when he wasn't, telling me at five years old that I was unlovable. It's one of the highest forms of child abuse, you know? Although you would know all about that, *Dad*." I look back at him. "You are the master in the art of manipulation in order to get what you want."

Stepping back, a cynical laugh leaves my throat. "You two deserve one another. You turned a blind eye." I point at my father. "To her daily name calling and hurtful belittling." My angry eyes burn into his. "And you have done everything to control my education, my life, and my career. I had no one to turn to or ask for help when I was growing up. Not once did you ever tell me you loved me or ask how I was. Do you remember when I caught chicken pox? You refused to come near me for weeks, just in case you contracted shingles." My rage flies out of my mouth. "And that sorry excuse for a mother blamed me and Camilla for you not loving her. And on the odd occasions you did ever speak to us, she would get jealous, claiming that we were plotting against her or some stupid shit. We were children." My voice rises into a yell, bouncing off the yellow sandstone walls of the ruined castle and I spot a few onlookers recording our encounter on their phones.

My parents will hate that we've drawn a crowd.

I wipe my brow that's now covered in perspiration. "You should be ashamed of yourselves because you are fucking terrible parents."

"Stop," my father bellows, his face reddening against his white shirt.

I push my hands through my hair, annoyed at myself for letting them see how angry I am. I've said what needed to be said a long time ago. I'm done. "I won't come back and I never want to see you again. Either of you."

I finish. "You two are miserable and proof that money

can't buy you happiness because it comes from here." I point at my heart. "And I feel sorry for you that you will never get to experience the love and joy I have felt since meeting Jade. She's not a possession to be bought." I snort at my father's lame attempt to buy her out of my life. "She's a powerful, talented, driven woman who loves me even though I have no home, money or car to offer her." My arms open wide into the air. "She likes me just as I am." It fucking wrecks me inside to think these two people whose blood I share liked nothing about me, or that I was only ever an item in their lives waiting to be pawned.

I push my shoulders back; my body becoming taut with confidence as I turn to walk away. I only get five steps away when I hear, "We're broke, Owen." Stopping me in my tracks, my father's voice calls after me.

"For fuck's sake," I curse under my breath and swivel around on the balls of my sneakers. "Explain."

Like a reflection, I look just like my father. However, I'm grateful I didn't inherit his inability to wake up and finally see the world from a new perspective. I almost feel sorry for him. He's stuck in a life I'm not sure he wanted either.

He looks livid when he replies, "I made some poor investments," he whispers, turning his back from the crowd.

"How?"

"Gideon and Richard, they..." He stops himself. "Over a year ago, they advised me to invest in a hedge fund and it went wrong. They invested too." Clenching his jaw together as if mad at himself, he keeps his voice low.

That would explain the money transferred into the business from Sanderson Shipping that my father told me to ignore.

Around twelve months ago, a massive amount of money

appeared in the business account from Sanderson Shipping, Richard's company, and I'm not just talking hundreds or even thousands. I'm talking millions.

Suspicious, when I questioned my father about it, he told me Richard was lending him the money for a new business venture. Even when I told him we needed a specific explanation for tax purposes, he never explained its *exact* purpose and told me to put it down as an investment. He also didn't explain why he withdrew my access to the business savings account after that.

My father assured me it was all kosher, but a niggle in my gut told me otherwise and he shut me down every time I mentioned it.

However, it's no longer my concern.

"Gideon? And Richard?" My sister's husband and her father-in-law are Lucifer in the flesh. "How could you have trusted them?" I don't understand. "I told you how risky hedge funds were. I told you not to invest." I add, "Our printing business was fluid. My numbers were perfect. Our tax returns, everything, it was all legit and above board. And my books are never a penny out." I always triple-check the ledgers. "Is that why you withdrew my access to the business savings? To hide all of this from me?" There was millions in there.

What the hell has he gotten himself into?

I don't think my father knew what type of family Sanderson Shipping was when my father married my sister off faster than a whippet out the gate to their son. He was rubbing his hands when she had to marry that rich prick, Gideon Sanderson. I'm certain falling pregnant wasn't exactly what she had planned or having to become a part of the corrupt world of the Sanderson's wasn't either. But she's stuck with them now. And my father seemed to be making the most of it. Gideon's father, Richard, was never out of his office.

However, it sounds like Richard finally showed his true colors and pulled my father into his corrupt world.

My father stays quiet and refuses to answer me, but I keep shooting questions at him. "And what about your other investments?"

My father looks uneasy when he grabs the back of his neck, cringing. "I traded billions on the crypto exchange and the stock market, trying to save us. I sort of got carried away."

I gulp. "Did you lose it all?" Asking, but not really wanting to hear his reply.

His silence speaks louder than his admission would.

"Oh, my fucking God. You stupid, stupid man," I spit, outraged at his insanity.

"Richard told me the hedge funding was a sure thing and that I would triple my investment. The crypto thing was unfortunate timing. The collapse of Bankham Main triggered a crash in the market. I wasn't the only one to lose out," he protests, looking sheepish. "I also made some stupid decisions betting on stocks."

Some? They were all stupid, in my opinion.

"You tried to manipulate the market. What did you think would happen? It's fraud. Did you not consider investing in real estate or even buying a sports team, instead of something as unpredictable as hedge funds and crypto?" Enraged with him, I can't help the name calling. "You're a fool." He has everything, a castle, a successful business. What else did he need? Then it dawns on me. "Greed," I growl out between my teeth. "None of it was enough for you. What did you think you would achieve?" I'm so relieved I got out when I did.

"I had to borrow money from Gideon and Richard last week to pay the staff wages, to keep the business afloat and pay off some of the other debts that have accumulated." He carries on as if I hadn't spoken. "But I took a punt and invested it to see if I could double or triple it."

A hiss escaped my lips. "You have got to be kidding me."

He has a gambling addiction. It's so obvious to me now and he needs help. Stat.

"And I lost it all." He drops another bombshell of information.

Pacing up and down now with my hands in my hair, I breathe in and out while I decide how to respond. "So, as well as losing all of your money and Richard's, *and* not being able to pay the staff from the printing press, I'm guessing the merger with Evangeline's father's business didn't go through either?"

"That's a business deal I no longer care about."

"Why not?"

"It doesn't matter now." His eyes bounce around the walled enclosure of restaurants, my mother standing closer to him than I've seen her before.

"What do you mean? It doesn't matter now?"

"What Evangeline's father is due to me is nothing compared to the amount of trouble we are in."

"We? There is no fucking *we*. And what is he due you?" Evangeline was clearly part of the payment.

"It's not important."

Fuck him, I'm probably best not knowing anyway, and I'm relieved the deal didn't go through before the wedding. As much as I hate what our fathers were making us do, I would never wish for another business to fold because of my father's stupid decisions.

"Your money problems have nothing to do with me. I

kept our books cleaner than a freshly laundered bed sheet. I hope everyone knows that. You blew it." I point at him. "Not me." I stop pacing and look at him. Really look at him as sweat patches bleed like ink on blotting paper into his shirt.

Oh, my fucking God, Daddy dearest blamed me. "You used me as the scapegoat, didn't you?"

Looking away, I scoff.

"I have no way of paying Richard and Gideon back." He nervously looks at my mother and says under his breath, "If they find out we have no money left, he will take the only thing we have; the printing house, and illegally trade fuck knows what from there with his shipping company. They don't trade in coffee and cars, Owen."

I've read many an article in the newspapers about the lawsuits against Sanderson Shipping. There are so many rumors about their dodgy dealings, that I believe them to be true.

I tilt my head to the side. "You're just like them. Greedy, manipulative, and corrupt."

Exasperated, he lifts his hands into the air, gesturing to what looks like an explosion. "I can't let him get his hands on our business, Owen," he grits out through his teeth. "It's the only thing we have left, but it's not enough to pay him back. I need you to come back and help me figure out how the hell I liquidate the business without losing our house and figure out how I can pay them off."

"Oh hell, no. I'm not doing that. This is your mess," I exclaim. Immediately after the words leave my mouth, an odd calm settles over me. I'm relieved I'm not a part of this anymore, and then I realize. "You don't care about me at all, do you? You're only here to ask for my help so I can save your sorry ass and keep her in designer handbags." I point at my stiff as a board mother who hasn't let one flicker of emotion show on her face throughout this whole conversation. "And she's only here with you because she's desperate."

I mean, what will her elitist friends say about her if she doesn't have the latest purse in every color?

Jagged creases line the skin around my father's eyes. He looks tired, but he's hiding behind a wall of bravado. I should know, it's what I was doing myself before I fled that sorry excuse of a wedding and this family.

His voice is low and steady as he makes his demand. "You will get on the plane with us tonight and come home, Owen."

Unable to hold it in, a burst of laughter leaves my throat. "You are so out of touch with reality, it's actually funny." I hold my stomach for good measure. "Get yourself out of the mess you got yourself into. I will not be your scapegoat or your savior." The one good thing in all of this is that my father signed off all the end-of-year accounts I filed. Choosing to take a bigger salary and no dividends, I was a director in name only and not a shareholder. Thank fuck for that, or he would have happily dragged my name through the mud with him, possibly ending up in prison, just as he might.

I take one last look at my mother. Her blue eyes are laced with a mixture of fierce pain and defiance. "I would say it's been nice knowing you, but it's not. Good luck with everything, and you can use the money you stole from me to pay off some of your debt that you are due Richard," I add as a final dig before I turn away.

"It's not enough to pay him off." My father's loud voice roars closer to me as I make to leave, but he storms after me.

Not enough? He needs over five million? How much is he owe him?

And yet he was offering Jade half a million of money he didn't have.

What a liar.

"You will save this business." My father's voice sounds desperate as he tries to demand I help.

"I will not." I keep walking away from him, but he catches up with me and grabs the top of my arm with a punishing grip.

Uncurling his hand from around my biceps, I blow out through my teeth. "Get your fucking hands off me." My words raw and angry, I square up to him, meeting him fierce eye to fierce eye and broad chest to broad chest as I find the strength. "Let the business go. It's a toxic, deadly poison. It has destroyed our bloodline and ruined not only your life but hers, too." I jut my head in my mother's direction. "Do you remember who you were before her? Or did you have the same shitty upbringing I did? Huh? Was it her that turned you into a heartless, spineless cunt, or were you already one?"

Something I can't quite put my finger on flashes behind his eyes. "You get used to it after a while," he replies, his tone changing as if he's completely deflated.

Maybe he was capable of love once, but somehow he lost himself along the way. Then I remember the words Jade's loving mother, Mari, spoke to me. *Don't play the game, change it.* "I'm not playing your games anymore. This is my life now and I don't want you or *her* in it. Fuck the business and fuck you." I shove his chest, pushing him away from me.

I glance at my mother for a second to discover her usual stone face is wiping tears off her cheeks.

Shit, things must be bad.

"You won't get a second chance with me, son," he snarls.

"I don't care."

Crazily furious for allowing them to ruin my beautiful afternoon with my girls, I walk away as his spiteful voice follows me until it's just noise in the distance.

And before I know what's happening, my feet are running.

Away from my past and into my future.

To Jade.

To Poppy.

To the only people that make sense.

CHAPTER TWENTY-FOUR

JADE

We leave tomorrow morning.

It's been an eventful month.

And an even more eventful week.

It's not been a terrible week, however, it hasn't been a pleasant week either.

Everything between Owen and I is good, no, great, although between his parents showing up, the Cobra debacle, and the pressure to perform the premier of our display earlier today, I'm exhausted and feel like I could sleep for a month.

The team smashed it today, and I smiled so wide I thought I might split my face with glee when we landed and kissed my lucky poppy stone so hard. It can only mean one thing; the rest of the year is going to be a success.

Contentment rests easily in my bones, and I let out a blissful sigh.

With a white towel wrapped around his waist, Owen ambles through into the bedroom, and I watch as he rubs his longer sun-bleached hair with a towel to dry it.

"You'll damage your hair drying it like that and make it frizzy."

He smiles leisurely. "Oh yeah, how should I dry it?"

"Blot and squeeze it, don't rub it, or you'll get split ends." I love his long hair.

"I was thinking of going short again." He runs his fingers through his damp shoulder length locks. "I only grew it because of, you know, *she who shall not be named.*" His goose bumped flesh makes him shiver, and he pulls a grimacing face, making me laugh.

He really doesn't like that girl, Evangeline. And she was a girl, not a woman. She was far too young to get married at twenty-one.

I rub the back of my head against the pillow, shaking it in disapproval. "Keep it. I like it long."

"What else do you like?" He throws the small towel into the laundry basket then whips off the one from around his waist, holds it out to the side, and drops it on the floor theatrically. My eyes automatically move to his thick, heavy length hanging between his legs. *Wow, I am one lucky girl.*

Words get stuck in the back of my throat.

He winks cheekily. "Noted, you like that too." He crawls up the bed, prowling toward me like an agile cougar, all the while smirking menacingly at me.

"I like that very much." I suck on my bottom lip and cradle his scruff covered face with my hands. "I could look at you for a lifetime." Marriage is something I drew a line through after I had Poppy, but since Owen entered my life like his very own unique version of Prince Charming, I could see myself spending the rest of my life with him.

Becoming serious, his eyes gleaming and full of love, he says, "I've loved no one the way I love you, Jade." He leans forward and kisses my forehead then plants more down the length of my nose, his lips finally landing on mine. "I have nothing to offer you. Yet. But I will. I will do everything in my power to provide for you and Poppy."

"You don't have to do that," I say between kisses as he drags the thin bed sheet down between us.

The simmering heat between us burns red hot.

He nips at my lips. "I want to, and I decided I don't want to work in finance again. I want to retrain to become an outdoor activity instructor."

Even though I don't want to, I pull back from our kiss. "You do?" I wrap my legs around his waist and hook my ankles together behind him.

He bobs his head. "Yeah. I've been looking into it for the past few days. I love fitness and doing those muddy obstacle courses you love, too. I'm sporty and healthy and love rock climbing, surfing, canoeing, skiing, all of it. I've always been naturally good at sports. I'm a good leader, patient, resilient, and I reckon I'd like to do a coaching qualification too. Hit it from both sides; mentally and physically. I could even be a youth leader." He astonishes me. "I'm far from an Olympian, but I am great at BMXing, mountainbiking and skateboarding, and would love to run stunt classes for kids, oh, and paddleboarding, maybe surfing, too." His chatter is full of life and excitement.

"You've really thought about this," I state, grinning at him proudly for seriously considering his future.

"I would be the world's best outdoor activities trainer."

"The next Bear Grylls."

"I'd need to invent a wicked nickname like that." He chuckles.

"No stage names necessary. I like you just the way you are."

Frown lines deepen his brow as his hand cups my jaw.

"You are one in a million, Hotshot. Thank you for accepting me for all that I am, even though I am not the man I used to be. I could have given you the world."

If his father hadn't lost it all or stolen it from him.

His money and status mean nothing to me though. I meant it when I told him I only want his heart.

Tilting my head upward, I reach his mouth to kiss him again, but pause with my lips dusting his. "I like this man in front of me now. I don't want the old you. I want this version. I love him."

"Owen, two point zero." His smile almost splits his face.

"Then we could make thousands of robots just like you. Every woman on planet Earth needs an Owen Brodie." I tighten my legs around him.

"They won't function properly without a Jade Sommers. Every one of them needs the love of a brilliant woman."

Making me giggle, I wiggle beneath him, pushing my hips into his.

"You make me want to be a better man." He groans when I rub my pussy lips against his cock.

"You already are." I gasp as the head of his cock brushes my clit.

"I wasn't before."

"It's all in the past, Owen. Time to move forward." Pressing my lips against his, I feel his cock grow hard against my center. I'm desperate for him to make love to me.

"But first I want to be there for you. Until Poppy starts school, I will be the best lover, partner, chef, cleaner, caregiver, and nanny." He pushes his tongue into my mouth.

Naked flesh pressing against naked flesh; this is how we should always be.

"Not the nanny, her stepdad." Overwhelmed by his commitment to me, I've said what I've been thinking about but didn't mean to say. Letting my secrets spill out between searing kisses. I panic for a second, but I needn't have worried because the next words out of his mouth settle me.

"If that's a proposal, I will fucking marry you, Jade Sommers."

I smile against his lips. "You will?"

"Never been so sure of anything in my life. Just give me a chance to get my life in order, and then I am making you my wife."

My doubts begin to creep in almost instantly. "Once my time is up with the display team, you'll have to move with me to my permanent station, and sometimes they can move me at a moment's notice. My life is in their hands. They call the shots." It's yet another reason I have been reconsidering the time I have left in the Air Force. Just as Owen is doing with his life, I want to make my own decisions.

Owen rubs himself against me, distracting me from my concerns. "I don't care." He buries his face into my neck, kissing then biting my ear lobe.

My neck arches into his touch.

"I will go wherever you are," he whispers against the shell of my ear as he pushes his cock into my wet heat, causing me to cry out in pleasure. "And whenever you go away on deployment, I will be at home waiting for you. I'll always be waiting."

He slides his cock back and forth, fucking me lazily, the palm of his giant hand skimming my hot skin, moving down my outer thigh to my calf, where he wraps his fingers around it and then coaxes me to bend my knee, pushing my thigh against my body and my shin into his shoulder, allowing him to go deeper.

We rock together, slowly, dreamily, as we make love.

His steel-colored eyes bore a hole in my soul. "Nothing will ever change how I feel about you, Jade." His admission causes a rush of wetness in my core, coating his cock in my excitement. "You're always so fucking wet for me, Hotshot."

He drives into me, every muscle of his body glistening. He's like a work of art, carved from the finest of iridescent opal; rock solid, alive with color, and too beautiful for words.

His hips pick up the pace, thrusting into me as the cool air from the ceiling fan pebbles my *hotter than the sand of the Sahara* skin, hardening my nipples against his chest.

"Come for me, Jade." The thick head of his cock teases my sweet spot, his balls slapping off my ass when his thrusts become faster.

I'm not prepared when he sucks his finger into his mouth to wet it, tells me to hold my knee back in place, and then moves his hand between our bodies. His fingertip finds my asshole, where he rubs it in gentle circles, round and round, giving me a pleasure I've never felt before.

Igniting the fuse, he pushes his finger in slightly. I'm surprised by how much I enjoy the pressure and how it adds to the sensation of his thick cock inside me.

He pummels into me, making me gasp when he tells me, "Touch yourself."

Moving my hand between our bodies, my fingertips find my clit, and we light the blue touch paper as his hard body meets my soft one.

He moves back onto his haunches, widening his knees on the mattress. Shaking his head from side to side, his hair falls in waves around his face as his hooded eyes take in the show. He gently pushes his finger further into my back entrance, working it in and out until I'm desperate with need.

"Come, come with me," he bellows.

And I come for him.

Hard.

Skyrocketing into the unknown.

It strikes me like a bolt of lightning, intense heat tearing through me, spreading from my inner walls through my pussy and down into my spine, thighs, and back entrance. With no control over my body, my eyes roll into the back of my head as I call out his name.

Clenching around him, milking him as he comes inside of me, he jerks and I twitch, our bodies so perfectly in sync with one another, going limp with exhaustion and pleasure.

My heart is buzzing like a happy bee in my chest.

This is us.

He's mine.

He didn't cave under his father's demands.

He chose me.

And Poppy.

Us.

What will be the consequences of his choices?

I'll guess we'll just have to wait and see. Regardless, I'm here for him, just as he is for me.

CHAPTER TWENTY-FIVE

OWEN – SIX WEEKS LATER

On reflection, telling my father where to shove it was a good decision.

I stood my ground.

I did the right thing.

I know I did.

Two weeks ago, Jacob called me in the dead of night to inform me that the printing plant was on fire. The entire business literally went up in flames.

Spreading over five hectares, it was the biggest fire Castleview Cove had ever seen.

I sat up all night, watching every news bulletin, reading every article, and each one of them mentioned my father's struggling publishing business.

A few days later, a journalist who dug deeper uncovered the billions my father lost. It was all there in black and white. Which means both Gideon and Richard know, too.

The only thing I haven't been able to ascertain is how the fire was started. However, knowing how hot some of the machines we used for printing get, I can only assume it was a paper fire.

I've brushed off the thought that's crossed my mind several times; would my father really commit arson to help with his problems?

Was he really *that* desperate?

Two weeks have passed and I'm still mad at my ego-driven father for losing the family business that his father and my great grandfather fought to build from the ground up. The family's reputation was everything, but from over four hundred miles away, all I could do was stand by, watching and reading about how the Brodie heritage burned to the ground.

A huge part of me is relieved. The other part? Feels sad my father had the opportunity to make something of a business with enormous success and an incredible legacy and then lost it all.

Loathed, because we haven't spoken in months, I refuse to pick up the phone and speak to my sister. I guess there is also part of me that is sad because we aren't close. If we were, I would know what the financial status of the family is as well as their mental state too, but I'm completely in the dark.

Either way, it must be testing my mother and father to their limits, and knowing my mother, she'll either be having a mental breakdown about her world blowing up, or wearing her impenetrable iron mask, pretending everything is fine.

I push the thoughts of my family out of my mind and go back to preparing dinner.

Between Jade's busy display schedule, Poppy's weekly routine, me keeping house, and my new volunteering position at the youth club on camp, which my *safe to work with children security* check came in handy for, I haven't had a day off since the wheels of the plane hit the runway the day we returned from Cyprus, and it's been the quickest six weeks of my life.

So much has happened. I settled into Jade's military family home with ease, and it's so Jade. Elegant with colorfully painted shabby chic furniture, where no two pieces are the same. Each room has a theme with loads of soft, quirky Scandinavian-style fabrics, and cushions, dozens of fucking cushions, with tassels. What is it about women and scatter cushions? It's just a cushion after all, but I am not allowed to use them. Jade has informed me they are for *decoration only* and that pillows are to women what power tools are to men. I can't argue with that. Since our return, I've had to borrow a few tools from the neighbors to fix the extremely squeaky bed she had.

She informed me the squeak was never an issue before my arrival. However, the number of times we have had sex in it, it sounded like it was going to break. My solution: I'll fix it so, bring on the power tools, because my body craves her in a way that I can't explain and that bed is important to us. It's where we share midnight secrets, where she has the ability to shine light into the darkest of my memories, and where she tells me she loves me.

It's our sanctuary.

Living with each other permanently came naturally. Mirror images of one another, we are both organized and immaculate and I am guessing her tidiness comes from being in the military, where discipline and cleanliness are paramount. For me, it was because of my mother's insistence; we were never allowed to play with toys outside of our rooms, and it wasn't as a safety precaution in case one of the staff tripped over them. Oh no, it was a means to control us, to stifle any fun, and confine us to our rooms. It was also a way to criticize us if we didn't tidy up after playtime. God forbid there was even so much as a toy soldier lying on the floor. That triggered a barrage of insults from *did you do this to upset me? Are you just stupid?* Or the one she loved to use the most, *you've caused me nothing but heartache since the day you were born.*

Seeing Jade with Poppy is like a breath of fresh air and the opposite of my stonehearted mother. Jade is full of fun, encourages messy playtimes, isn't afraid to be silly or play dress up, and as soon as she returns from an overnight display, she has Poppy in her arms in a heartbeat telling her how much she missed and loves her.

It's heartwarming and life affirming. It's how I wished my childhood was.

My mother may have fucked me up for a while, but I refuse to let her ways become the norm. Because it's not.

It's a bonus having Gregor living a mile away from camp. Visiting him, chatting most days, we are closer than ever.

I have my little family now and I couldn't be happier.

Taking care of Poppy seems to come naturally to me. Going for a run every day round the perimeter of camp as she chatters away to me in her stroller. Taking her with me to the gym while she naps, and she loves nothing better than holding the grocery list when we visit the store.

We celebrated Poppy's first birthday without Michael, because apparently, he *couldn't make it*. Since our return, he has made every unbelievable excuse in the book not to visit. I mean, who uses the excuse that your mother's budgie has died and that she is inconsolable to the point you can't leave her? Although, knowing my mother, she would cry more over the death of her precious corgi, Felix, than me.

And I see the hurt in Jade's eyes as the excuse texts arrive on her phone.

She was right about him; he doesn't deserve Poppy.

I keep reminding her that it's his loss. He's missing out on all the good stuff. From the new words she's trying to say to exploring new foods. She's even started walking. Crawling was too limiting for her and just like her mother, she hits every milestone like a champion.

Jade signed Poppy up for nursery for a few hours a week to get her used to *mixing with other children,* but I worry about her during her three-hour morning session in the same way I worry about Jade and her dangerous job.

It terrifies me to think about what could happen to her should a stunt go wrong.

It happens. Gregor informed me it *has* happened. Twice. One being fatal.

And while I love my daredevil vixen, she equally fucking terrifies me.

My world would implode if anything were to happen to her. In a short space of time, she's set up camp in my heart and I never want her to vacate it.

The thought of losing my mirror soul, my twin flame. I couldn't go on without her.

I love her more than life itself; waiting at the door for her to come home if she's been away overnight. When she comes home from work, I get giddy and happiness bubbles low in my stomach at the sight of her.

This is all new to me, and I'm basking in every moment I can.

The way I feel about Jade has nothing to do with her providing security and a roof over my head because I would happily sleep in a tent if I had to in order to be with her. It's the joy, hope, and excitement she brings to my once soulless existence.

She's introduced me to a world I knew nothing about. Being within the confines of a military base is like living in a village where everyone pitches in and looks after one another.

It's life changing and fucking mind-blowing how these talented people and their families pull together to become a complete unit.

I can't deny how much I miss Castleview Cove, which I never expected. I miss the beaches, surfing, running along the cliffs, the golf courses, and most of all, I miss my friends. Those boys and that town will always be a part of my life that I will treasure forever. Part of me wishes we were closer and another part of me wishes Jade's flying schedule wasn't so jammed packed because I reckon we would have already visited my hometown.

Although they assure me they have all been busy, too, which is why they haven't squeezed a visit down to us either. Vacation season is the busiest at the hotel for Lincoln and Violet.

However, next week we are driving the five-hour journey up to Scotland where I'm excited to finally introduce Jade and Poppy, in person, to my friends.

It should be a blast, as we have a busy weekend planned. We are staying with Lincoln and Violet in their house situated within the grounds of Lincoln's family estate.

It made sense. With some of Lincoln's step siblings being over twenty years his junior, he's used to having little kids around. Poppy will have a ball with Lincoln's stepbrothers and sisters and the menagerie of animals they have. At least they will keep Poppy entertained for the weekend and not short of a friend, animals to chase after, or a babysitter or two. I know Violet is desperate to give Poppy a squeeze.

And it will be good to see Knox and his wife, Eva. After all, I spent hours at Lincoln's family home growing up because I always had these 'I would rather be here than at home' feelings. Such a kind and generous man. Knox was more of a father to me than my own, and he knew about my mother's critical and toxic tongue. Plus, the negativity of that stuffy old castle my parents choose to call *home* had bad juju. It oozes out of moisture trapped between the cracks of the stone-cold walls.

There is also another exciting reason to visit. Skye and Jacob welcomed their daughter, Aurora, into the world four weeks ago, and it kills me that I still haven't been to see them all. Had I still lived in Castleview Cove, I would have been the first one on their doorstep. Jacob is obsessed with his little princess and is already desperate for another. I hope Skye is prepared for a huge family; I know it's what she always wanted, and I couldn't be happier for my two best friends as they start their family and get their happy ever after together. It's what they both deserve.

Knowing how important my friends are to me, Jade is equally nervous and excited to meet them. When we confirmed our visit, I almost rolled my eyes at her for foolishly saying, *"what if they don't like me?"*

Anyone who meets Jade loves her. You can't not. She outshines even the brightest of stars and when she walks into a room, you take notice. She's demure, captivating, focused, and so fucking smart. I find her analytical mind such a turn on. She has nothing to worry about. They will all adore her. I know it.

I've yet to meet anyone who says a bad word about her.

Although Cobra may not have the same opinion about her anymore.

Following the review of Cobra's behavior by the Air Force's Special Investigations Team, he was dismissed and a variety of training has now been implemented to improve the values throughout the Air Force. Jade helped to make these changes possible, and I'm so proud of her for speaking out.

Since then, it's been smooth sailing for Jade. She's brighter and doesn't feel like her position on the team is at risk anymore, although she has made reference a couple of times that she's considering leaving the Air Force once her time with the aerobatic team is over. She's keen to bow out of active service, to become either a flying instructor or retrain to become a commercial pilot.

I don't care what she does, she could learn to play the flute with her nose for all I care; all that matters is that she is happy and that we can be together.

Talking of happiness and future career plans, I have started an online qualification in Youth Mentoring in the Community. I am loving it so far and learning a lot. It's a radical change to the mathematical profession my father enrolled me in. It's refreshing and I know for sure now that it's what I want to do.

The youth leader on camp helped point me toward the courses I will need to complete to become an outdoor activities instructor for kids, advising me to gain a certificate in mentoring young people first. So that's what I am doing. Well, I started after Gregor loaned me the money to do it, making a promise to him to pay back. As soon as I am financially back on my feet, I will pay back every penny.

Jade has been extremely supportive of my new career plans, offering to pay for my courses and retraining, but I want to do this my way. The last thing I want anyone to think is that I am after her just for her money. Jade isn't rich, but her salary isn't too shabby either. They call her salary *danger money* for a reason, with more emphasis on the danger part. I am all too aware of how risky her job is.

She reassures me she is safe, and that she didn't spend years undergoing grueling training to become a fast jet pilot without knowing that she has a higher probability of having an accident than she would if she had a desk job. Several times I've seen something flash behind her eyes that I've not put my finger on yet, but I think it's the unknown of who will look after Poppy should anything happen to her.

It can't be Michael.

I don't have a legal leg to stand on where he is concerned. After all, he is her father, so I hope that we *never* have to venture down that alley. *Ever*.

Daydreaming, staring out of the kitchen window, a sudden cold chill sweeps through my body at the thought of Jade having a crash.

If the Universe is listening, which I hope it is, *look after her for me.*

Please.

"You look deep in thought." Jade's voice trickles into my consciousness.

Laying the kitchen knife down, I turn from chopping the vegetables to welcome the enigmatic woman who arrived in my life like a full on fucking hurricane, knocking me sideways.

"Hey, Hotshot." Wrapping my arms around her, I squeeze her tightly, splaying my hand to the back of her head to keep her close. "I missed you today."

"You saw me at lunchtime." She chuckles, squeezing me

back. She missed me, too. I know she did. The days she's here for lunch, like today, are my favorite days.

The advantage of living in an Officer's Quarter just a half mile away from the airfield is that she can come home for lunch when she's not away.

"Four hours of not seeing you is too long." My mouth finds hers as we kiss each other hello.

Smiling against my mouth causing me to kiss her teeth, she giggles. "What's made you miss me?"

"Everything. I missed this sexy little flight suit you have on." I squeeze her ass. "And this prissy little hair bun that makes you look all prim and proper, although I know you're really a freak between the sheets." Pulling out the bobby pins from her hair, I release her silky locks, letting them fall loose over her shoulders like a waterfall of fire.

I stand back and take her in while her big blue eyes blink back at me. "You look beautiful." She has the ability to steal the breath from my lungs.

Knowing how my praise affects her, heat blotches her cheeks, making them flush with color.

"I think you're beautiful," she whispers in response, making me clench a little, not quite believing it. Having been told since I was a child that I was a worthless piece of shit, getting used to Jade's praise is something I am still working on.

"We've been over this before, Hotshot. You are the one raising the bar of this relationship. I'm just the nanny," I tease, knowing how much she hates me saying this.

She prods my side playfully and I flinch at how much it tickles. "I have told you, Mr. Brodie, that you are more than the nanny."

"I know." I make a list with my fingers. "I'm the cook,

housekeeper, personal shopper, diaper changer, oh, and live-in lover." The last one is our secret.

According to the official paperwork and my station pass, I'm the live in nanny and not Jade's boyfriend. Living together outside marriage within a military family quarter is against the rules, which I find archaic and unrealistic, given most couples live together before walking down the aisle these days.

I also suspect my fake single status is the reason why I get side-eyed, smiled at, and hit on too when I'm out and about. It's as if the moms are all in heat.

Jade tells me that it's most likely because their husbands are away on deployment and I'm the most *handsome guy on camp*. I know what lonely feels like. It's not nice. Everyone needs someone. My someone just happens to be a redheaded spitfire and I can't bear the thought of her being assigned elsewhere for six months without me. It sounds torturous.

"You are the best live-in lover to have walked the streets of this camp." She tries to tickle me again, but I grab her wrists and hold them against her sides. "But shhh, don't tell anyone." She sounds flustered. "You are so strong."

I keep her arms pinned to her sides. "And fast," I state.

"Not as fast as me in my jet." She wriggles about, trying to free herself.

"Wrong." I bend at the knees, catching her unawares, and throw her over my shoulder. "I'm faster."

She squeals, slapping my ass as I bounce up the stairs. "What are you doing?"

"Punishing you for trying to tickle me."

"Where's Poppy?" She squeals again when I slap her backside.

"Your mom came over this afternoon with Aunt Babs

and asked if she could babysit for us tonight." Mari has been keen to have Poppy stay over for the night. Desperate to get back to her *normal* life. "Aunt Babs is having a sleepover, too. Just in case your mom finds anything too difficult or has to get up in the night," I reassure Jade.

She sounds out of breath as we reach the top of the stairs and I stride across the landing to our bedroom. *Our bedroom.* What a fucking rush.

"So we have the house to ourselves tonight?" Her tone bounces with excitement.

I gently lay her down on the bed and stay standing at the foot of it. "I'm going to fuck you, then feed you." I pull my tee shirt up over my head and throw it aside. "And then fuck you some more. How does that sound?" Eye fucking my abs, she bites her bottom lip, squirming as I crawl up her body.

"Or we could go to the gym," she suggests, knowing that will never happen when we have the entire night alone together.

Grabbing her hips, I push hers into mine and rub my now hard cock against her. "I have a better workout planned for you."

Her girlish laughter turns into a gasp when her eyes catch sight of my glinting metal. "What is this?"

I look down at the gold dog tags dangling from the chain around my neck.

"My new necklace."

Squinting to read the small print, her eyes turn glassy. "You got dog tags with my name on them?"

"And mine. One of each."

Examining them closer, she asks, "What does the date represent?"

"It's the day we met," I answer.

I watch her rubbing her thumb over the cheap gold identity tags. It's all I could afford from one of those online jewelry stores. When I have the funds, I will replace them with real gold, but for now, gold-plated will have to do.

"Is that co-ordinates?" she questions.

"It is."

"For?"

"Cyprus. Where we met. Check out the other sides."

She flips the two gold tags over, then shakes her head, almost disbelieving. "You had a poppy stamped on the backs of them."

"You both mean the world to me, and now I have you both close to my heart. Even when you're not physically here. You are here." I grab the swinging tags, pulling them up on my naked chest to position them where they will rest when I stand up.

Silence stretches between us as her gaze bounces between the tags and me.

Shit, did I fuck up? Too much?

"Owen, these are beautiful. These are so special." Her eyes fill with tears. "Since the day we met, you've had my heart and head in a spin. It's all happened so fast, but I love every minute of every single day with you. I don't know what I would do without you. My heart is yours. I love you so much, Owen. More than you can ever imagine." Pink creeps into her cheeks. "I hate being away from you when I go away. I've not wanted to go to work before." She pauses. "Until you. You've changed my life."

"Have I ever told you that you are the best thing to happen to me?" I rub the pad of my thumb across her temple, wiping the salted tears from her skin.

"You are the best thing to ever happen to me." She repeats the words she's said multiple times before. With every day that passes, I fall harder for her, and I know I'm going to marry this woman. She's got me, mind, body, soul, and she owns my fucking heart.

It's all hers.

She wraps her legs around my hips, pulling me down between her thighs. "Make love to me." Her lips find mine and when she slides her tongue between the seam of my mouth, I know there is nowhere I would rather be.

With her, it's heaven.

Whereas before I was in hell.

And I never want to go back there.

However, when the devil calls.

You have to pick up.

And that was something I wasn't prepared for.

CHAPTER TWENTY-SIX

JADE

Watching Owen sleep is one of my favorite things to do. He looks so peaceful, the usual crease between his brows smoothed out as if he hasn't a worry in the world.

I know that's not true. His past still causes him concern. Although he hasn't told me, I know it haunts him.

For weeks now, I have watched him scrolling social media as he checks the news for updates on his father's business affairs. His scowls grew deeper than the Grand Canyon when the police released new information in their investigation. I know he disapproves of the way his father handled his finances. But sometimes I do wonder if he misses home.

If he does, I hope he'd have the decency to tell me.

Even though Owen wears his heart on his sleeve and tells me everything, and I truly believe him when he says he loves me and loves his new life with us, I still have a fear that part of him misses the friends he classes as family.

The familiar.

Traveling around for most of my career, home is where

the Air Force send me. For Owen, though, he's only ever lived in Castleview Cove. It's part of who he was, and I'm sure that part of him misses it.

He assures me he is content here, happy with our daily routine and my schedule. I have never felt so supported or grateful to have found this special man who swept me off my feet and loves me and my daughter unconditionally.

Always here for me when I get home from work, here for Poppy, here to provide the best orgasms that feel like they are tearing me apart from the inside out.

He's a beautiful man, with a beautiful heart, giving and kind. Although he still doesn't believe it when I tell him. The damage his mother has done to him is profound, even if he won't admit it.

I want him to believe me. I want him to see what I see. What his friends see.

His mother is wrong.

He's not a worthless piece of shit and when I saw his mother all those weeks ago in that taverna in Cyprus, I knew it was her before she said a word to me.

It wasn't her Scottish accent that gave it away. Oh no, it was her poker face and stick-up-her-ass look as if she'd been sucking stinging nettles through a straw that did.

But they don't know Owen the way I do.

He's kind, patient, gentle, and cares for me in a way I've only ever read about on relationship blogs. The type of blogs I used to read when I was dating Michael scouring the internet for advice on unsupportive partners, because I knew our relationship was flawed from the very beginning, even if I didn't want to admit it.

He hated my success and never once congratulated me when I made the aerobatic team, and he didn't. Loving the media attention to begin with, he then realized they weren't as interested in him as they were in me, blaming me for stealing all the limelight and making him look like an idiot, informing me I only made selection as they were ticking boxes to hit their diversity targets.

What a liar.

And an absolute twat.

The reason he never made selection was because he was too concerned with the title and status of becoming an aerobatic pilot for the most elite display team in the world, rather than focusing on the actual job itself. He let his ego get in the way.

And the reason I got in? Because I aced every single test.

The anger and resentment I feel toward him has simmered since finding happiness with Owen. I'm disappointed in him for not fulfilling his visitation agreement we made with our lawyers, and for making pathetic excuses, although a part of me doesn't care at all anymore, because Poppy isn't missing out, not even in the slightest.

Poppy has the best grandma, best great aunt, mom and of course, the best manny-come-stepfather a girl could ask for.

Lying on my side, I smile, running my fingers through his soft hair that sparkles in the slither of morning sun that spills through the gap in the drapes.

I let out a sigh, still worried that maybe Owen wants to be part of the world he used to be a part of.

He shared with me the famous champagne parties his mother threw to keep up with the *Muircrofts*, Evangeline's parents.

I'm so grateful I don't swim in those circles. They all sound like sharks.

While I'm at the top of the food chain in my career, it's a complete contrast to Owen's previous life.

My job may look glamorous, receiving invites to celebrity parties and award ceremonies, but I am selective with my acceptance RSVPs. I would rather stay at home with Poppy and Owen, sitting on the couch watching *Glow Babies* with a cup of tea.

But now I can't stop wondering if this life is enough for Owen or whether he feels like he is missing out on the lavish lifestyle he's used to.

Regardless of what I do for a living, when it boils down to it, I am, after all, a single, working mom with a toddler, living in a home that I rent from the military. Yes, I have savings. Yes, I will have a great pension, but what else do I have to offer him?

Owen thinks I have my life figured out, but the reality is, I don't, and I am still deciding what I want to do with my career when my time is up with the aerobatic team. A six-month deployment away from Poppy and Owen scares me more and more. Being away from Poppy has always seemed impossible. The thought of being away from my Owen becomes more unbearable each day.

My Owen.

I love him and don't want to leave him behind, and while I enjoy the displays, I hate being away from my family; they are my people.

Trailing my fingertip down the length of Owen's nose, then over the wide cupid's bow of his lips, his mouth twitches as my soft touch tickles his skin.

I'm in awe that this gorgeous man chose me, the unknown, over the familiar life he had in Castleview Cove.

But then there is that question that has been rolling about in my head like a bag of marbles. Does *Owen want to return?* He assures me he is happy; however, a huge chunk of his life was that town.

Only time will tell, I guess.

I close my eyes and snuggle into his broad chest as he drapes his arm around my waist, pulling me in closer to him as my head tucks under his chin.

Heaven.

Not meaning to, because it's nearly time for me to get up, I must doze off for a few minutes, still exhausted from last night's bedroom antics. When Owen's loud phone splits the silence, we both jolt awake from the uninvited noise.

Groaning, he turns over onto his back, reaching for his phone that's noisily ringing away on top of the nightstand.

Grabbing it, then lifting it above his head to see who is calling, he rubs his eyes and mumbles his sister's name, "Camilla?"

I check the time on my phone. It's almost seven in the morning. What is she phoning at this time for?

No good ever comes from an early morning call.

"You should answer it," I whisper as he continues to stare at the lit-up screen and worries his bottom lip.

Hitting the accept button, he then taps the speaker icon to let me hear.

"Camilla?" he questions, sounding worried.

"Owen, come home." His sister's Scottish voice, faint, but confident, comes through the speaker.

He groans. "I'm not doing this now." Digging his fingertips into his sleep-filled eyes, he yawns loudly. "I knew you would be on their side."

"You don't understand, Owen. That's not why I am calling." She goes quiet before she says, "Mom and Dad were in an accident last night."

Instantly awake, he's pulling the bedcovers back,

swinging his legs around, slipping out of the bed, and standing to his full height. "What's happened?" he asks, his fingers running through his hair mindlessly.

I sit bolt upright, my heart now thumping against my ribs.

"They were in a car crash, Owen," she answers.

"But they are never together." Becoming irate and confused, Owen pulls at the end of his hair.

"I know. But they were." She states the facts, sounding as if she can't believe it either.

Owen gives her the space she needs before she continues. "A drunk driver hit them at midnight. Their car spun off the road and down the cliffside."

I gasp, cupping my hand around my mouth as sour bile curdles in my gut at the brutality of a crash like that.

"Gideon said they were out with his father for dinner last night. It's such a dangerous road, there are no lights up there." Her voice is low as she gives him more details.

"Shit," he hisses under his breath.

"They're dead, Owen." Camilla confirms my worst fear. "They didn't make it."

As stiff as a board, he drops his backside onto the edge of the mattress.

I fling the comforter back and crawl across to him. From behind, I loop my arms around Owen's waist and rest my head between his shoulder blades. "I'm here for you," I whisper, hoping he hears me as I try to squeeze my love and comfort into him.

"Come home." Camilla pauses momentarily. "Please."

I peer up over his shoulder.

At a loss for words, Owen stays silent as he continues to stare at his phone.

OWEN

Camilla's voice cuts through the silence and Owen's thoughts. "I need your help to organize the funeral." Her voice is matter of fact, showing no real emotion. Owen appears to be the only one in the family who was born with a heart.

"I'll come with you," I say with authority, urging him to respond.

Owen agrees with a nod. "I'll be there this afternoon," he stutters.

"We'll drive," I assure him.

"I... I'm in England, Camilla. I will come but it will take us a few hours to get there."

A soft sigh of relief sounds down the phone. "Thank you, Owen. I'll meet you at the house."

Owen tenses.

A knowing Camilla tries to justify the reason for meeting there, "Dad didn't sell your car or pack up your stuff. It was all lies he fed to Lincoln and Jacob to try to persuade you to come home." She lets out a weighted sigh. "You can stay in your own house with Jade and Poppy." Adding, "I hate our family home as much as you do, too, and I would never make you stay in it again."

How does she know about us?

"Thanks." Owen lets out a huge, audible breath.

"I bumped into Lincoln. He told me you found your happiness," she answers the unasked question. "You did the right thing, Owen. Marrying Evangeline would never have worked. Gideon and I—" A beat passes. "I should never have married him. For reasons I don't understand, Mom was cruel, Owen, but Father was dead inside. I'm proud of you for sticking up for yourself."

Owen's hand finds mine, the one that's resting over his heart, and he gives it a squeeze.

"I know this may mean nothing, but I'm happy for you." Camilla sounds genuine.

Although she can't see him, Owen nods, his shoulders sagging as if relieved. "I appreciate that."

"I'll see you in a few hours." She suddenly sounds formal again. "Bye, Owen. Please drive safe," she finishes.

The line goes dead and Owen sighs again, one that comes out in a rush.

"I'm here for you." I move around to his front and straddle him, lacing my arms around his neck.

He cuddles me back, holding me as if I am his life buoy. "I have to go home."

"I'm coming with you." Leaning back, I hold his face to make him look at me. "I won't let you do this alone." And I won't let him withdraw from me. "We do this together."

"Poppy?"

"Mom will come. Aunt Babs, too, they can look after her."

"What about work?" His selflessness knows no bounds.

"We don't have a display for two weeks; I will submit vacation days and get the time off." I'm the boss and this is an emergency. He needs me.

"Thank you." He kisses my neck and nuzzles into it. "I have to call Lincoln and Jacob." His lips brush my skin. "And Gregor. I have to call him first, and my Aunt Flora. Shit, I forgot to ask Camilla if Uncle David and Aunt Flora know yet." He goes into action mode.

"While you jump in the shower, I will pack and make a few calls, okay? Then you can call them." He needs a clear mind to break the news. A shower always helps to make me feel better, so I sent up a silent prayer that it helps him, too. "Gregor will most likely want to come for the funeral. He can follow us in his car."

He nods, his chest filled with sadness. I can feel it.

"Are you okay?" Of course he isn't, but it's the only thing I can ask given the circumstances. I remember how heartbroken I was when my dad died. It tore me to shreds. Confused, everything felt impossible.

"I feel—"

"Numb," I finish for him.

"Like my entire world just turned upside down."

"I know how that feels. Hour by hour and day by day, it will slowly sink in," I say. *Then the pain will hit him like a ten-ton truck.*

"I feel nothing for *them* at all," he confesses. "Is that wrong?" His question barely a whisper. "They never cared about me," he states, then adds, "I don't understand why they would be out that late at night."

I run my fingers through the hair on the back of his head. "Maybe your dad was trying to work out with Richard how he was going to pay him back."

"Possibly."

"We may never know why," I tell him honestly. I pull out of our embrace and gaze into his saddened eyes. "Perhaps what you said to him in Cyprus made an impression." I wait a moment. "I'm sorry for your loss." Those words don't feel enough.

"They're gone." His tone is almost disbelieving.

"You are not alone. You have me, Poppy, my mom, your friends, Gregor, and Camilla sounds okay."

He shakes his head. "We've never been close, and that's the first time I have spoken to her in months. Lincoln and Jacob used to call her a princess when she was younger." He snorts softly at the memory. "She was always so defensive around them." He moves his hand up and pinches the bridge of his nose. "But sometimes, when I was just a kid, and I'd had a bad dream, she would let me sleep in her bed."

I give him a gentle smile. "People change and you have the rest of your life to make amends with her. All is not lost."

"She's a good person. I know she is, and she's as heavily embroiled in a marriage she didn't want as I would have been. Maybe I should have stopped it, but I was just a kid."

"What could you have done?"

He scowls. "Helped her runaway, spoken to my grandfather or my Aunt Flora. Maybe. I don't know." Worriedly, he shakes his head on a stuttered breath.

I smile. "Owen Brodie, the solution finder." I praise his analytical brain; he's forever trying to problem solve. From changing my utilities to cheaper ones to organizing the car's servicing plan and food menus, he loves making lists and synchronizing our calendars.

"You need to focus on one thing at a time. Just one. That's all. And speak to Camilla when the time is right. First, though, we have to go to your sister, Owen. She will be waiting for you to arrive. And Aunt Flora. Your mother was her sister, after all."

A faint smile twitches around the edges of his mouth. "What would I do without you?"

"You'd be living with Gregor, having to listen to him and his latest hook up moaning through the bedroom walls." My efforts to bring light into his darkest moment works when he snorts a laugh. Although I think Gregor's latest fling may be a public relations manager that goes by the name of Blake. I'm yet to have confirmation, but the way they've been flirting lately and their absence from our team dinners when we are away has been noted. By everyone. Not once, or twice, but several times.

"I saved you from those."

"Thank you." He kisses my bare shoulder and looks up at me through a fan of blond lashes.

"I'll be there for you." I reinforce my support. "I will stand by your side and help you through this. We will do this together. As a united duo."

"A trio," he says confidently, adding Poppy into the mix.

I repeat, "A trio."

We stay here holding on to one another for a while before he says.

"My family."

That's exactly what we are, and I won't let anyone break us.

Ever.

CHAPTER TWENTY-SEVEN

Owen

I don't know what is wrong with me, but I feel nothing... no grief or sadness.

This morning is just another day in my life.

Maybe the reality will hit me when I get to Castleview Cove, maybe not. We'll see.

"I think that's everything." I look down at the suitcases sitting in the hall. One each for me, Jade, and Poppy.

"I'll be five minutes," Jade shouts from the bedroom above as she scrambles about getting ready to leave.

Picking up a case, I groan and yell back, "Christ, you're only going for ten days. How many clothes have you packed?"

"I like a lot of options." Exasperated, I hear her talking to herself as she runs through a checklist of things she needs to remember.

If she was being honest with me, it's because she is nervous about meeting my friends for the first time and making a good impression.

Struggling with the heavy case, I pull open the front door and flinch when I find a guy mid-knock, standing on the doorstep. "Christ, you scared me." I throw my hand to my chest.

Frowning, he looks me over, and I recognize him immediately.

"Michael, right?" I hold out my hand to greet him while wondering what the hell he is doing here.

Taken aback, he replies, "Yeah. Do I know you?" He takes my hand to shake it, eyeing me curiously.

"No, but I know you." I push my shoulders back, shake his hand firmly, and stand tall as his hand finally slips out of mine.

"Ah, has Jade shown you photos of me or does she talk about me?" Gaining confidence, his smile grows.

"Not exactly," I mutter dryly.

"Right." Tilting his head to the side, he asks, "Sorry, I didn't catch your name."

Jade appears from behind me to answer. "This is Owen. What are doing here?" She sounds out of breath from us running about this morning.

"Our squadron is visiting the base today."

Sounding unamused, Jade scoffs, "And you didn't think to call ahead and tell me you were stopping by?"

I jump in. "And Poppy isn't here."

His forehead puckers in thought. "Sorry, who are you exactly?"

"I'm the nanny." A smile tugs at my lips.

He protests, horrified, "The nanny?"

Jade sighs and I push past him. "Excuse me, I need to load the car. We are driving to Scotland today."

Michael follows me, watching me intently as I unlock the car and pull open the trunk.

When he turns back to face Jade, seemingly startled, he asks, "You have a man for a nanny?"

"Yes, Michael. Welcome to the modern world."

I almost burst out laughing at how narrow minded he is. *Fucking bird brain.*

Aghast, his voice higher now. "What about your mom? I thought she was looking after her?"

"*Her* has a name, and it's Poppy." Jade folds her arms in front of her and leans against the doorjamb. I take that as an opportunity to move back through the gap to pick up the other two suitcases still sitting in the hallway. "My mom had an accident, so I hired a nanny. She's much better now in case you were interested."

He's not.

Grinning, I maneuver past them with the luggage. "I'm the manny," I say cheerfully, pissing him off even more.

"What the hell, Jade? You could have asked me to source a suitable candidate to take care of her."

Her laughter is loud as she belittles his response. She's right, he sounds ridiculous. "You have never been interested in Poppy or how I care for her. You have never asked if you can help with childcare or paid a penny of child maintenance since the day she was born. You've been waiting for me to fail. Hoping I would. Well, look at me now." She opens her arms wide. "I'm doing it all and Poppy and I, we're thriving, because of that man right there." I look over my shoulder and throw her a wink when she points at me. "He's the best man for the job and he takes care of us. Unlike you, he stepped up."

"Is he security checked and certified to work with children?"

On an eye roll. I chuckle when she says, "No, I invited a stranger into my home. He has to jump the security fencing every night to get in, and no one knows he's here. For God's sake, Michael, get a clue. Of course he is."

The trunk now loaded, I don't shut it for fear of making my non-busy status known.

I want to see exactly how this pans out.

Jade's an endless surprise as she confidently continues. "Now, what do you want? Because if you came to see Poppy, she's at my mom's. She had a sleepover there last night."

"I actually hoped I would catch you at work today." He's sheepish with his reply.

"So you had no intentions of seeing Poppy?"

His silence gives her the answer.

Asshole and deadbeat dad.

"What did you need to see me about, then?" Her eyes are hard and dark as she glares at him.

Nervously, he pulls on the back of his neck. "I've been assigned to a US squadron in Nevada, near Las Vegas. For three years."

Her brows hit her hairline. "And, this affects us how?"

"Well, it was just to let you know I won't be around."

I could laugh at his audacity. Slamming the trunk shut to make myself known, I walk past him, brushing his shoulder with force on my way back into the house. I stand behind Jade, waiting to see her reaction.

I can feel the heat bouncing off her. She's mad.

Fuming.

I don't blame her.

Her voice steady as she responds to his news. "You haven't been here since the day she was born. Your whereabouts doesn't make any difference in our lives."

I move closer, her back now to my chest. I slide my hand down her waist and rest it on her hip.

His eyes squinting, Michael doesn't miss the movement, tracking my hand as I hook my thumb into a belt loop of her black fitted jeans.

"Oh, I'm also the boyfriend," I confirm. "And I'm certified all right. Certified boy toy."

Jade snorts.

I finally get to say what I've been thinking. "For months, I have watched your absence grow wider by the day. Moving to Las Vegas won't affect Poppy's life. Being in it, though, might. You see, kids need consistency, and I know that's something you can't give her. But I can." Michael shifts on his feet nervously.

I pull Jade closer to me, and she hums when I drop my lips to her neck and press a soft kiss over her beating pulse. Looking up, I make sure Michael knows exactly who she belongs to.

Me.

He watches every moment, gulping, when I kiss her neck again and she closes her eyes, almost purring when I lick, then bite her delicate skin.

Over her shoulder. I throw him a wink and a devilish grin.

She's fucking beautiful, isn't she? Look what you lost.

"Now if you'll excuse me." I stand tall, staying behind Jade to conceal my aching, hard cock. "We have *our* beautiful little girl to pick up because we are off to Scotland." I leave out the part that my parents have died, and that's why we are returning, 'cause that just makes me sound pathetic. "We have lots to do. But thanks for stopping by. Have fun in Las Vegas." I hope he gambles his life away and falls down a rabbit hole in Sin City.

Before he leaves, I go in for the kill. "Tell me though. The budgie excuse? That was a lie, right?"

His face turns redder than a strawberry.

I nod in acknowledgment. "For a smart man, you really are a fucktard. Maybe that's why you didn't make the aerobatic team. Oh, and one last question." I don't give him chance to respond. "I'm guessing as you want nothing to do with Poppy, you won't mind giving up your parental rights when we get married?"

Jade gasps, tensing. Although I have never mentioned it to her before, I know it's what I want.

Michael doesn't answer and I can't figure out if it's from shock or the fact I am giving him an easy way out.

Asshole.

"I think that answers that question, too." I pull Jade closer, showing him how tight we are as a couple, as she melts like liquid gold from my touch. "Now, shove off, Michael." I spin Jade around, our bodies collide, and I slam my lips over hers to kiss her passionately. Before closing the door, I open my eyes to find him staring at us.

His pulse pounding in his neck. I grab her ass and squeeze it.

"I need you," Jade gasps, pulling at the belt of my jeans.

I shoot him a wicked grin and bang the door closed in his face.

"That was so hot." She pulls my zipper down, freeing my cock from my boxers. "The way you declared your love for us. You want to marry me and adopt her?"

Desperately tearing at each other's clothes, we're all fast moving hands and clashing teeth.

"Yes." I can barely get the smallest of words out as she wraps her soft hand around my throbbing cock.

With my jeans bunched around my ankles, I lift her onto the console table in the hall and pull her panties to the side.

"You will always be mine." I moan, lining my weeping, thick length at her soaked entrance, her jeans dangling from one foot.

"Always," she cries as I slam myself inside of her.

CHAPTER TWENTY-EIGHT

Owen

I've shaken at least one hundred sets of hands.

Hugged people I've never met before.

All with a somber look on my face.

The one you're expected to have; drawn face, down-turned mouth. Sad.

The mournful, grief-stricken expression you only ever see at funerals.

That's how I look as I gaze around at the people, chatting as they stand huddled together in the vast front room of the Brodie mansion.

My grief, you ask?

It's painted on.

Because I'm numb.

I thought I might feel something when I saw the family home or my sister. A trigger. But there is nothing.

I'm stuck between denial, anger, and regret.

Guilt.

My guilt is so big it's tangible, and it's growing by the day.

It's like a huge black cloud hanging over me, threatening to turn into a rapid cyclone at any given moment. A storm is coming. I can feel it.

Since my return to Castleview Cove, I have focused on planning what I can only describe as a Brodie funeral; one fit for a king and his queen.

Henry and Elizabeth Brodie.

Never to be forgotten. Their death will be talked about for years to come, as will their funeral.

I suggested a small private service, but that was not what happened here today. Camilla informed me that her father-in-law was funding the funeral, and he was demanding we give them a proper send off. Although, it meant we could avoid any talk about finances, the demise of Castleview Printing Press, or my parent's estate, as money was no object for their funeral.

Conducted in the biggest church in town, with a convoy of black cars, and enough flowers to start our own florist, laid upon the finest of solid oak and gold caskets, Camilla and I pushed our feelings aside and saw that our parents had the sendoff people expected, given their status with the people around here.

Every minute has felt like a lie.

Yesterday, I stood outside the ashes of what once was Scotland's finest and largest printing press. Relief washed over me, knowing the burden of the business was never going to fall to me. No staff to be responsible for, no paper pushing business deals to close, no bank balances or tax returns to submit. It was a boring business to be involved in, and it never appealed to me.

It's in that moment everything fell into place. Someone switched the lightbulb on in my head. Memories of every encounter between my father, Gideon, and Richard, *his tycoon father*, flooded my brain. Snippets of conversations replaying vividly in my mind.

I was only young when Gideon and Camilla married, but I remember the meetings and the phone calls I used to eavesdrop on. I remember listening to my father explaining to my mother how he helped Richard fund the purchase of new land to build a multi-billion-pound luxury housing development on. I remember the raging argument they had that tore through the house when interest rates rose an unprecedented amount, triggering the housing market to crash, and my father lost all of his money. My mother never forgave him for those losses.

Back then, a few billion here and there would have been just a drop in the ocean for him. I can only assume he must have started taking more and more risks to recover his loses, which ultimately led to his demise. I am more than certain that Richard was whispering in his ear about dodgy deals and financing opportunities, even back then.

Why he trusted Gideon and his father, I will never know. Richard isn't a property guru; he works in export and import and it wasn't long after I started working for the business that my father began asking me to research hedge funds. Then it was stocks and shares, then bitcoin, and finally crypto. And every time I would advise him to steer clear and invest in something less risky instead of putting his money in things like crypto, where the outcome was more like chancing it all on black in a game of roulette.

My feelings for my parents aside, I did the right thing by my family today. Stood shoulder to shoulder with my sister and her dreadful husband.

I've been keeping my beady eye on him since my return, but he gives nothing away and has had nothing but good things to say about my parents. Which I find confusing, especially since my father said he was due him and his father a considerable amount of money. None of it adds up.

Walter Forrester, the private investigator I hired to speed up my DBS check, is a man of many talents, and I am praying for a miracle because I have promised to pay Walter a handsome price to help me locate my trust fund my father stole from me to pay for his services.

If not, I'm royally fucked and will have to ask Lincoln or Jacob for the money.

I haven't asked anyone for money before now, but I am not ashamed to ask for help when I need it. And I will pay back every penny I am due to everyone, even if I have to work twenty jobs. I won't shy away from my responsibilities.

Grateful to have been kept busy since my return, I have been juggling my time organizing the funeral with Camilla, making sure Jade's mom and aunt are looked after and, of course, I can't live without my daily dose of Jade and Poppy. My girls.

These four women have kept me sane for the past twelve days. However, I am all too aware that Jade will have to leave in a day to return to work.

Walter assured me he'd have any information about the whereabouts of my trust fund within a few days, but he needed more time. I was hoping Jade would be here for whatever unfolded, and to help me pack up my house, but that's not looking likely now. When she's with me, I feel like I can take on the world. When she leaves, however, I'm not sure what I will do without her for support.

Exactly as I predicted, my friends fell in love with Jade and Poppy. Jade slotted right into our friendship circle as if she had always been part of it.

The plan is to pack my stuff up as soon as possible and

store anything big in the outbuilding at Skye and Jacob's castle that they assure me is watertight.

Why the hell anyone would want to buy a castle is beyond me.

I'm certain Gideon and his father already have their eyes on the one I am currently standing in. The one my parents called a home that looks more like a fortress.

Regardless of how I feel about Camilla, she deserves better. It hasn't gone unnoticed how thin, almost frail, and gray-faced Camilla now is, making her look older than her thirty-seven years. Worry lines run deep around her eyes screaming sadness, and her shiny blond locks yellowing, laying limp around her shoulders. It's not how I remember her, and I don't fucking like it. I don't like it at all.

She is rotting under Gideon's watch while he thrives. She looks miserable.

As does her son, my nephew, Sean, who I barely know. He's never left her side, and I think he uses his mother as a wall of defense from his father and grandfather.

I've seen the way Gideon disrespectfully looks at other women. And while Skye called me out on this when I was with her, other than flirting, I had no intentions with any of them and I know now even that was disrespectful.

But as I watch Gideon slipping yet another member of the catering staff's phone number into his jacket pocket, he has every intention of making those calls.

It hasn't gone unnoticed by Camilla either. I've been watching her reaction as he hits on one woman after another at his in-law's funeral, his eyes following anything in a skirt.

His designer suit may be tailored to perfection, but perfect he is not.

He's a dirty scoundrel, just like his father. They should pay for dragging my father into their world.

The noise of fine bone China meeting fine bone China sounds to the right of me breaking me from my anger-fueled thoughts, as Jade settles her teacup down on its saucer that's rested on the table.

With only a couple dozen people left at the wake, I feel myself slowly relaxing. My suit no longer feels like it is strangling me, as it did when I first put it on this morning.

"How are you holding up?" Jade slips her hand into mine.

I look down at her and give her an easy smile. "Walk with me." I squeeze her hand.

Nodding as I pass by friends and associates, I lead Jade out through the cavernous kitchen of my childhood home and out into the gardens.

"This house goes on forever," she gasps in awe, stepping out of the arched stone and wooden doorway and onto the lawn.

Looking back up at the giant castle behind us, we both take in the enormity of the building.

I always thought the twelve-bedroom, sixteenth century monstrosity was completely unnecessary for a family of four people. It's not as if my father had a choice, though. Along with being heir to the business, he also fell heir to the Brodie Mansion; a fucking castle.

After all, what is a king without one?

"Do you like it?" I squint, casting my eyes over the monster I have hated my entire life.

"It's... different."

"It's fucking hideous." I make her laugh at my unexpected outburst.

"You don't like it?"

"I hate this house. It was a prison, and those walls contain the ridicules and echoes of my mother's voice."

"Not a fan then?" she questions, knowing I would rather stick needles in my eyes than spend a night in this time vault.

I shake my head as Jade tucks a lock of my hair behind my ear. I should have had it cut for the funeral, but fuck it, this is me.

"I loved the beach house you picked out for us." We sat outside admiring the beautiful house that I dreamed of buying as a holiday home for us. That's the way it will stay; a dream.

"It was perfect." I test the waters with her. "Would you ever consider moving here?"

"I've fallen in love with Castleview Cove. The people, the beaches, the fresh air, it's beautiful. It's picture-perfect dreamy. The schools are good, the houses are stunning. There is an airport an hour away. I could maybe train to become a commercial pilot and get a job there."

She's done her research, which seems like a positive sign. "Do you think you would miss the tricks and the speed if you became a commercial pilot?"

"No, actually. Yeah, it's fun, but I would be happy being a commercial pilot or if I could wave a magic wand, I would set up a flying school to give more people the opportunity to learn how to fly. Can you imagine flying over the panoramic views of Castleview Cove every day? It would be amazing." Her excitement makes me wish I could make that dream come true for her.

"So moving to Castleview Cove in the future might be an option?"

"It's most definitely an option."

"But we wouldn't be moving into something like this house." I jerk my head in the house's direction.

"I like traditional houses, but this is too old. Maybe something less—" She side eyes my family home. "Stone, and iron and tapestry."

"Less everything. It's too much." The one I wanted for us on the beachfront was perfect for us. I drove past it again by myself and wished everything was different. White picket fence and shutters, wild multicolored flowers, and forest green front door.

I stare at the building by my side and frown. "Do you think my great, great, great grandfather had a small dick, and that's why he bought this place?"

Jade bursts out laughing. "I'm glad you didn't inherit that."

I wrap my arms around her and we stand chest to chest, listening to the tweeting of the birds and the buzzing of the summer bees.

One thing my mother did get right was the garden. She would spend hours here, creating sanctuaries for ladybirds and hedgehogs, leaving treats out for the squirrels and foxes who ventured into the garden late into the night. She loved animals more than her children, it would seem.

This was the only place I ever heard her sing or smile. I cast my eyes around the color-filled gardens and a thought drops into my mind. With hundreds of roses lining the many hidden paths, maybe they were her favorite flower and what I should have asked to be put on her coffin and not the lilies I picked. That would figure; beautiful to look at but armed with sharp-toothed thorns. Sounds about right.

I air my thoughts. "It's such a strange thing to have lived with someone for years and not known anything about them."

"Are you talking about your mom or your dad?"

"Both, I guess."

"Maybe they kept you at arm's length for a reason."

Or maybe they were brought up that way, so they never knew any different. Either way, I buried two strangers today.

Strangers that might possibly have spent their last night together trying to figure out a way to pay off their debt. Out for dinner with the devil himself, apparently.

My curiosity has been slowly creeping in all around me, like poison ivy, it's crawling through my veins so fast it's threatening to encase me in a tomb of its toxicity. What was agreed around that dining table that evening between my parents and Richard Sanderson?

Because both Richard and Gideon have been *too nice* and it's making me feel uneasy.

"Your heart is beating so fast." Jade looks up at me. "Are you okay?"

She's asked me at least a dozen times a day how I am and every time I answer with the same reply. "I'm fine, Jade." When in fact I'm not quite sure how I feel.

Maybe I need distance to get a better perspective on things. Just be with my girls until the dust settles and then see how I feel.

Once I have sorted my house, then I can go back to the new life I was creating and happy with. Because while I love Castleview Cove, Jade isn't here, and wherever she is, I am.

Jade makes me smile when she says, "Your friends have been wonderful today. I love them all."

"And they love you." I kiss her on the end of her nose. "Told you they would."

In a rare girly moment, she scrunches her nose up, making her look cute.

"I love you in this sexy little dress." I give her ass a good squeeze.

She steps back, looking upset with me, crossing her arms around herself. "We are at a funeral, Owen Brodie. Do not be so disrespectful," she scolds, sounding like a teacher. She looks around. "What if someone saw you feeling me up at your parent's funeral?" She waggles her finger at me, making me laugh.

I hold my hands up, surrendering to her observation, "Okay, okay, I get it. Be respectful." I roll my eyes. "So, we can't fool around over there in the bushes then?"

Letting out a loud gasp, she turns to look at the bush I'm pointing to. "Please don't tell me you have done that."

I draw a cross over my heart. "Never."

"You're lying."

I'm not, but I laugh at how upset she is thinking that I have, then throw her a wink.

"You are such a tease." She throws her arms around my neck, realizing that I am telling the truth.

"And this is why you love me."

"I do." She kisses me with her soft lips.

I wish this moment would last forever, surrounded by Jade in my bubble of kisses and happiness.

Bliss.

Someone clearing their throat alerts us to their presence.

When I look toward the interruption, my happy bubble pops in an instant.

This is the moment I've been dreading and trying to avoid.

Stanley.

OWEN

Evangeline's father.

"Owen." He tips his head in acknowledgment. "Can we talk?"

Uncertainty washes over me, and I turn my attention back to Jade.

"Go," she says, never taking her eyes off Stanley. "Clear the air." She moves out of my arms. "I'll be here." Her hand slips out of mine. "I will always be here for you."

CHAPTER TWENTY-NINE

Jade

With all the mourners gone, leaving only Evangeline and her mother, who are still waiting for Owen and Stanley to reappear from the office down the hall, I have listened to Camilla make mindless chit-chat about garden parties, charity work, and all the grand balls they've been invited to this year.

I wish Owen would come back.

What the hell are him and Stanley talking about?

While Evangeline's mother, Joyce, has sat talking to Camilla politely, Evangeline on the other has been staring at me from across the room, shooting poison-infused daggers my way for the last twenty minutes.

I realize that simply breathing the same air has made her despise me. After all, I am the woman whose arms Owen ran *into* while running *away from* her unwelcome ones.

It's clear what Owen meant about Evangeline being a child. She's too young to get married. From her looks to her need to be the center of attention, her threatening glare right now only highlights her immaturity levels.

I throw her a gigantic smile while peeling the uncomfortable black patent heels off my feet.

Easy little girl, don't play with the big girls.

"Excuse me." I give a gentle nod in their direction, cutting through Camilla and Joyce's conversation. "I'll go check on the men and see what the holdup is." I hope I don't bump into Gideon or his father, who slipped away only a minute ago. Those two are slimy as hell and give a whole new meaning to the word creepy.

Evangeline continues to examine me, dropping her disapproving glare down and then up my body as I rise. Holding my head high, I make my way out of the room.

"Thanks, Jade." Camilla gives me a curt nod.

Walking out of the drawing room faster than intended, I travel down the narrow stone hall in my black stocking-covered feet, taking in the vast tapestries and oil paintings lining the walls.

My gaze lingers for a second too long on the stuffed wall-mounted wild stag's head and a cold shiver runs down my spine, making me run for a couple of steps in the hope of getting to Owen quicker.

I shake my shoulders and fidget with my hands. Not easily spooked, this place gives me the jitters.

In contrast to this dark gothic castle, Owen did a really good job of playing down how beautiful and welcoming his hometown of Castleview Cove is. Scattered with history, coffee shops, and beaches, it's a place I could see myself retiring. My mom said the same thing, too. Since we've been here, she's spent hours with Poppy and Aunt Babs on the beaches, exploring the cobbled streets of the town and ancient ruins. All the while, I've been helping Owen to organize the funeral alongside Camilla.

We've also had dinner at both Lincoln and Violet's, and Jacob and Skye's. I thought it would be awkward with Skye being Owen's ex; his high school sweetheart, but it wasn't. Not even a smidge.

I have bonded with those girls and their *smitten with them* men, quicker than I thought possible, and can see why Owen loves his friends, and they love him back just as hard.

They made fun of him, joking with him when he held Jacob and Skye's daughter, pulling his leg about what color our baby's hair would be if we started a family. Mixing his blonde with my red, the decision was unanimous: strawberry blond.

Career focused, I'd never considered having one baby, let alone two. But when he looked into my eyes as my new friends joked around us, I could tell what he was thinking; let's have one.

My ovaries exploded in that moment, and I would have agreed to do anything with my giant brute of a man, all muscles, tan and long hair, looking delicious while holding that tiny little bundle of joy in his arms. We've never discussed it, but I realize it's what I want and I can tell he wants it too.

I want it all with him.

Traveling down the narrow corridor that goes on forever, I could never imagine myself living in this place. It feels damp and depressing.

I can see why Owen spent hours away from home and more time with his friends when he was growing up.

Between moving about with Mom and Dad to a few different military camps when I was growing up, and then joining the Air Force, I don't have roots as such or many friends from my childhood who I keep in touch with. Not like Owen has.

My squadron are my friends, my forces family, and I know they would do absolutely anything to help me. They proved that with Cobra and every time they trust me to lead them when we fly.

Almost at the office at the end of the corridor, I tip toe further along and the faint voices of both Owen and Stanley drift my way.

Moving closer, I am just about to push the door open when Stanley's next words stop me in my tracks. "They are dangerous men. You need to be very careful. Your father was a fool to get himself involved with Sanderson Shipping. They are not good people, Owen."

"I know Gideon and Richard are not to be messed with, Stanley. I've read the stories about them over the years and warned my father time and time again. Since my return, they haven't mentioned anything to me about any debt or discussed money. Nor has Camilla." Owen sounds astonished. "How do you know my father was still due them money? And how much was it, do you know?"

"I heard a rumor it was tens of millions," Stanley replies.

I cover my mouth with my hand to stifle my gasp.

He lowers his voice. "He made promises he couldn't keep."

"My father lost billions. Owing them millions is insignificant by comparison," Owen remarks dryly as I spy on them through the gap in the door.

Sitting at the desk, in the seat across from Owen, Stanley then goes on to say what I feared. "But how will you pay off that debt and with what?"

"It's not my debt. Surely the insurance payout from the fire will cover it?" Owen looks exasperated as he unbuttons his shirt and loosens his black tie.

"Are you sure about that?"

Owen sounds frantic when he says, "Does the debt not die with them?"

Stanley scoffs. "These are not normal people you are dealing with here. This is the Sandersons." He pauses. "And what the Sandersons want, they get. They may not be mafia, but they are the closest thing to it."

Owen scratches his beard, appearing agitated, as Stanley adds, "You know your father's finances better than anyone. Surely you knew what he was up to."

Owen's frown deepens. "I had no idea about any of my father's investments, his bank balance, or what he did. Although I worked for the business, he never shared his personal investments with me and I was given a finance director title in name only to head the finance department and only for the printing side of the business. I had no clue about anything else he got up to. My job title made him look like he was doing the right thing by his son. It was all for show. I may have worked for the family business, but I was no more than a glorified bookkeeper who sometimes won a contract for him here and there. I am not like my father. I am not a liar or a gambler."

"But you are a coward," Stanley fires angrily. "You left my daughter at the altar."

Shaking his head, Owen disagrees. "I never wanted that marriage, neither did she, and you and I both know it. Let her marry Adam Blumenthal, who she was screwing behind my back when we were *supposed* to be engaged."

Stanley winces at that news. "And who were you fucking about with?"

"I was faithful to her."

"Why do I find that hard to believe?" Stanley scoffs.

"Believe what you want."

"Do you really expect me to believe that you weren't already fucking that woman you brought with you today? It's a little convenient, don't you think?"

Red rag to a bull, Owen's nostrils flare. "Unlike your spoiled little princess, that woman is worth one hundred of her and I met her *after* I left your daughter. I won't say this again, so listen carefully. I was faithful to Evangeline, and I tried my best to please her, but ice queens don't appear to have hearts."

Stanley holds his hands up as Owen defends himself. "Okay, okay. I believe you."

I hold my breath, watching my powerful looking man, and wait for his next words.

Thinking, he sits forward.

With elbows on the desk, he threads his fingers together and looks up to the left, as if deep in thought. "We can't keep revisiting the past. What's done is done between our families. But humor me because I'm curious. In return for some contact names to help us break the American publishing market, the fancy marketing plan you pulled together to win my father over, and of course, how can we forget the lovely Evangeline that was thrown into the deal, what else did he offer you in return exactly? Because the way I see it, and before all of this shit with my father began, we didn't need the money. But you and your business did. You were or still *are* a much smaller business than ours." Owen eyes him suspiciously. "You must have thought all your Christmases came at once when our print business burned to the ground? Did you get much business from that tragedy?"

I almost punch the air at Owen's confidence as he asks all the questions he's been mulling over with me since the fire.

"Your father needed a wife for his son." Stanley justifies, looking nervous as he plays with the tail of his black tie.

"My father lives in the shadow of his ancestors. But if you do the same, you always get the same, and he *thought* he needed a wife for his son. He didn't. You're lying, Stanley."

When Stanley doesn't reply, he pushes him. "So what was it?" Owen clears his throat. "The cultures of the business weren't aligned. The printing market for newspapers and magazines is in decline and job losses were inevitable when we merged. So, what exactly did he offer you to make you want to merge your company with his and sell your daughter off like some cheap ass auctioneer? I have to hand it to you. You did have great ideas about moving into the indie author world to open up new opportunities, but you could have done that all by yourself. So what was the offer, Stanley?"

Owen never takes his eyes off him as he leans back in his father's black leather chair and drums his fingertips against the arm of it. I hold my breath as the silence stretches between them like an elastic band.

"I was the one who showed your father how to bet against the stock market."

"Jesus Christ. You do know when the stock market rises, it has the opposite effect, and you lose everything? You don't turn a profit doing that."

"I knew the risks, but your father didn't listen. He behaved like an addict, desperate for his next big stakes win. But when he did make a profit, he got greedy and reinvested it. The more he lost, the more he bet, desperate to win back his money."

"When did this all start?"

"Over a year ago."

"And?"

"He lost it all."

"How much?"

"I honestly don't know." Through gritted teeth, Stanley admits, "But he blamed me for his bad decisions. He turned up at my house with Gideon and Richard. They threatened my family. They said they had ways of making people disappear. My wife, daughter, my son, my mother, my own flesh and blood, Owen. I was forced to make a deal."

Holy shit. The blood pounds loudly in my ears. *This is crazy.*

During one of our late-night chats, Owen told me that Camilla's husband was an importer and exporter of goods. He also implied it was not fashion and fruit. I didn't ask, but I can only assume it's as dodgy as hell and they are not people you want to do business with.

As well as making bad investments, it sounds like Owen's father surrounded himself with bad businesspeople, too; he was a bad judge on all accounts.

Owen stares him down. "So, you offered him your business and your daughter to pay off *his* debt?"

"I didn't offer them to him. He took what he wanted."

"What else?"

"My yacht."

Owen raises one eyebrow. "Ah, I did wonder why you sold it to him."

"I didn't. He took it."

"Right." Owen's eyes narrow. "You can have the fucking

thing back; I don't want it." I'm beaming with pride at Owen's detective work. His suspicions were right all along. There was way more to him having to marry Evangeline.

"Look, I'll be honest. I needed to speak to you for a reason. I need reassurance from you that my family is safe. The business deal didn't go through. You didn't marry Evangeline. Other than the yacht, I haven't paid back the debt he burdened me with." Stanley's voice cracks with what sounds like fear.

Owen's beautiful face turns dark and serious. "As far as I am concerned, your debt is cleared."

"Thank you." Stanley's shoulders slump.

Because there was no debt. Henry Brodie blew up is own world and lost his billions all by himself.

I smile to myself, my body pulsing with great pride at how great a man Owen is and I wonder if he realizes how different he is to the man that raised him.

His eyes softening, Owen adds, "You are wrong about me, Stanley. I am not a coward, nor am I a liar. My parents withstood each other at best." Owen stands to his full height and buttons his dress jacket slowly. "I couldn't live a lie like they did. They were trapped in a loveless marriage where the only thing holding them together was greed, money, and power. So, call me a coward if you must, but I know I was brave to run, to pull the plug on their control over me." Owen moves out from behind the desk. "You should be thanking me, really. I saved us all. You got to keep your business. I get to marry that phenomenal woman who stood by my side today, because I choose to do that, and your daughter gets her happy ever after with someone else who doesn't make her miserable like I would have." He pushes his hands into his pockets. "And as a bonus, you get your yacht back. I will find the paperwork and write a letter reinstating your ownership and have it sent to you." His tone turns sardonic. "Now, without sounding like a heartless bastard, please never speak to me again and get the fuck out of this house."

Stanley pulls himself out of his chair. "Thank you." Stanley's face is softer now, looking relieved. "Please be careful, Owen. Gideon and his father they are—"

"Don't worry about me. I'll be fine." He tilts his chin up in defiance.

With an understanding nod, Stanley turns to leave.

I dart away from the door and carefully slide behind a large medieval knight statue made of solid steel. Looking up at it from behind, I wince. It's hideous and garish. Compared to Owen's quaint gate house home, this one is antiquated and suits his mother and father's medieval ways.

Holding my breath as Stanley passes, I give him time to disappear.

It's then I hear a loud. "Motherfucker." Owen's voice bellows out from the office, and I wait a few minutes longer before I slide out from behind my hiding spot and go to him.

Standing looking out the leaded windows, like one of the statues in the castle, I feel his steely presence, his protective armor in place, shielding him from any further hurt.

My strong man has had to deal with so much, not just in the last two weeks, or months, but for years.

My mission in life is to protect him. I don't ever want him to feel the pain I know he's feeling right now.

"Hi," I murmur.

With his hands tucked into the pockets of his dress pants, I push my fingers between the gaps, lace my arms around his waist and let the mood settle between us.

Having never seen Owen in anything other than casual clothes, he looks exceptionally handsome today in his designer suit that probably cost more than my combined closet of clothing.

Not knowing anything about his previous life, I've been exposed to another world these past twelve days. One where how much money you have in the bank, the car you drive, the type of shoes you wear, and the portfolio of homes you have define who you are. I witnessed that again at the funeral today.

When I looked around the room at the powerful men and women in attendance at the funeral today, I realized that none of them could live my life.

It takes a certain type of person to live in a tent with hundreds of other personnel on a military cot bed, in the middle of a desert, knowing you won't see your family for months at a time, or to rent a house where the retro fitted heating pipes are so old they run down the outside walls and it takes fourteen days for someone to be sent to fix them.

But this life Owen was a part of, I'm not sure I would fit into it; where men are cruel, and the woman are even crueler... to each other.

I can see why he left.

But after Stanley's words of warning, I'm scared for him, because what else will he uncover while he's here?

"Everything okay?" I rest my cheek against the fabric of his dress jacket.

"Yeah," he lies, sighing heavily. I can feel him withdrawing from me, and for a second I panic that if I can't pull him back, I could be the one to have my heart ripped to shreds.

"With every ounce of my body, I love you, Owen." I

want him to trust me and to tell me everything that was discussed a mere minute ago, but it needs to come from him. I don't want to push him.

He turns to face me, his face softer and with warm eyes, he cups my face with his huge, gentle hands. His usual blue gems that glisten with light are now full of sadness. "I want to go home. We have one last night together." His words feel like a thousand barbs piercing my heart.

"In Castleview," I counter. "We have forever." We made promises to one another.

He nods slowly, seeming distracted, then bows to kiss my lips. When our mouths meet, like the faint flutter of butterfly wings, it's the gentlest of kisses he's ever given me, and that settles my nerves to a degree.

Breaking away, he's solemn when he says, "Let's go home. Poppy has been with your mom and Aunt Babs all day."

I wish I could delve into his head and unpick his thoughts, and I am desperate to call him out for not telling me what he discussed with Stanley. Instead, I reply, "It's been a long day."

"And if it's possible, I hate this fucking house even more." Looking around his father's office, his eyes settle on the painting of his father above the fireplace. "I fucking hate him." His expression grows hard and stern, which is most unlike his never ending cheery self I have come to know and love, and expect of him.

"Let's go," I suggest. The sooner we are out of here, the better. This house makes me fidgety. It doesn't feel like a home, it feels like a prison.

As we walk out of the office, Owen turns to steal one final glance at the painting of his father.

Stoney eyes, stern scowl, emotionless.
The infamous Henry Brodie.
Yeah, I hate him too.

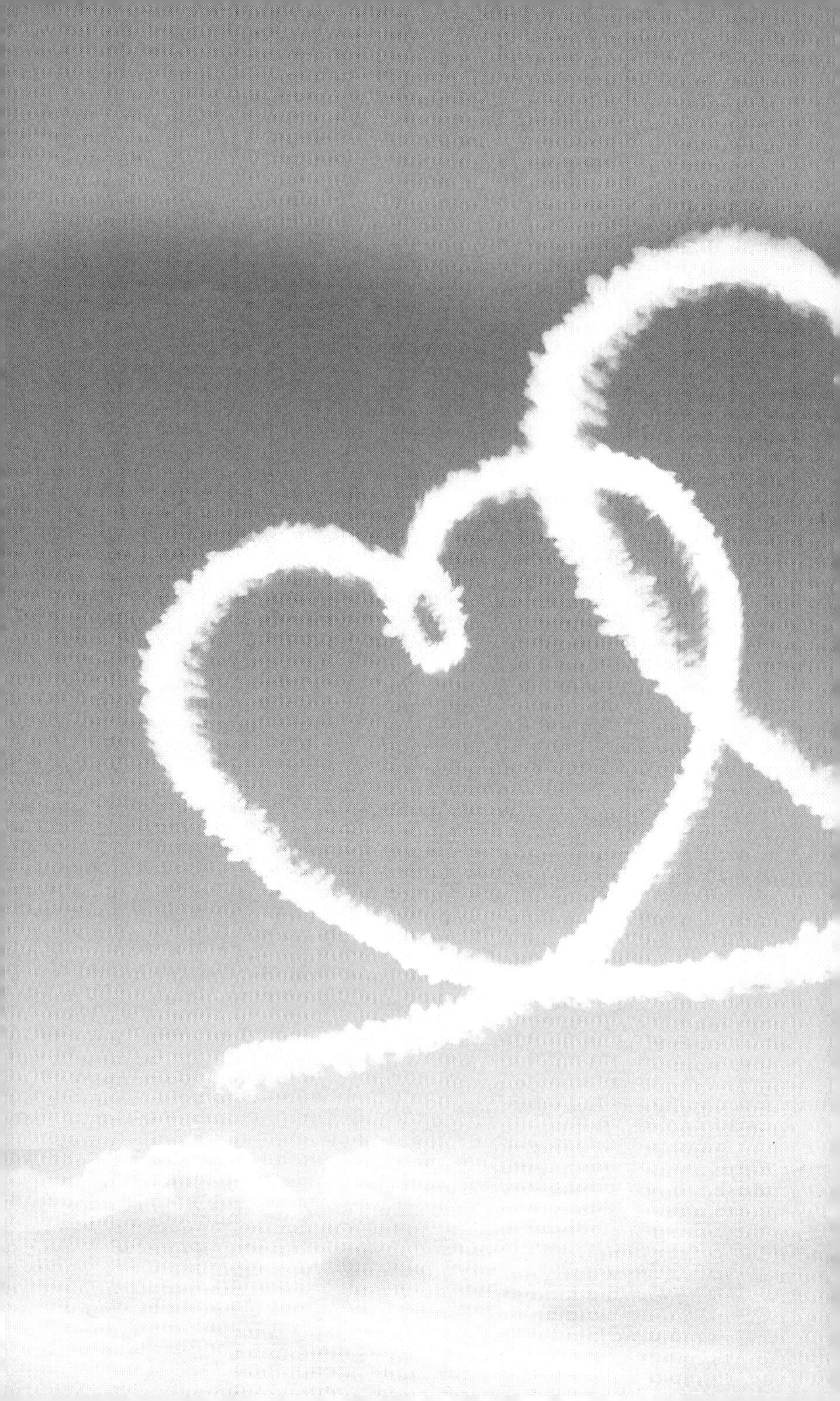

CHAPTER THIRTY

Owen

I never want to stop.

Not with her.

My Jade.

As day breaks, I pull her hips closer to mine as I drive myself into her wet pussy. The need to lose myself in her never withers. I want to spend every waking moment buried inside her, surrounded by her sweet fragrance, listening to her telling me she loves me like she is now.

She gasps against the shell of my ear. "I love you."

Unable to hold back any longer, I cup her ass and move faster, our bodies slapping together as her fingers curl into the back of my hair.

She taught me how to love and be loved.

It's not about buildings, possessions, and using people as bargaining tools, it's about fetching a cup of coffee when you need one, being there at the end of the day for a hug when you've had a hard day, preparing dinner together, laughing and most of all, it's about being happy.

When I'm with her, I am happy, and everything just feels right.

Perfect.

Her soft hands trace the skin of my back, her fingernails digging into my shoulders as she urges me to go faster. Goose bumps prickle my skin. Her touch, I feel, everywhere, way down deep in my soul. It turns my heart into a thumping mess, making me feel like I'm going to pass out.

Jade's gasps grow louder when I kiss the sweet spot behind her ear and douse her sweat-covered skin with my hot breath, making her shiver. It's a good thing the other bedrooms are downstairs on the other side of the house or Mari and Aunt Babs would no doubt be able to hear us.

Moving slowly in and out of her body, I lift her hips to tilt them, and thrust into her deeper, my cock sliding over her G-spot, giving her what she needs, giving her what I know makes her fall apart.

Looking into her eyes, I move faster, as our breathing becomes heavy with desire. Not a sliver of space between us, our hot skin, covered in a thin sheen of perspiration, glides together in perfect harmony.

No words needed, we come together.

Her nails dig deeper into my skin, enough to leave marks, as our bodies come apart around one another.

She's shaking as I spill myself inside of her.

"Jade," I mumble against her shoulder.

Relaxing in my arms, her body goes limp as we descend from our intense release.

"You're my everything." She truly is.

The reality is that she leaves today without me, while I pack up the entirety of my home. And I need to find the paperwork for that fucking yacht, then speak to Camilla about what will happen to the rest of the estate.

I don't want it. Any of it.

What I do want is this woman, the one below me that's kissing the skin of my shoulder. The woman who I think about twenty-four seven. I love the smell of her hair, the sound of her voice, every freckle, and the way they all join together when the sun touches her skin. The way she bosses me about. Even her dangerous job turns me on. She's given me a purpose, a meaning to my once meaningless life. She gave me something to work toward, to fight for, and to get up for every day. She brought joy into my life in the form of a little girl named Poppy, who touched my soul from the minute she was in my arms.

I love them both so much. There is no going back for me now, or ever.

They stole my heart, and I don't want it back; I want them to keep it forever.

I have to remind myself that it's just a few days and I will be back home with them.

The enormity of the day ahead sours my gut, bile rising in the back of my throat at the thought of having to speak to my sister, I am only meeting to say a final farewell and to inform her she can do whatever she wants with the estate. I thought I owed her a face to face goodbye.

But the worst fucking part of my whole day is Jade and Poppy leaving.

I can't fucking handle the thought of her going. It cripples me, knowing she won't be in my arms last thing at night and when I wake in the morning.

The muscles in my body tense, causing my calf muscle to spasm and I groan as it seizes painfully. I clumsily and reluctantly slide myself out of Jade and roll out of the bed to stretch it out and give it a rub. Fuck, that's sore.

Watch your back. Replaying Stanley's words from yesterday, I barely slept a wink last night and my body and mind are tired, leaving me feeling empty.

Cock bobbing, I hop up and down. "I have cramp," I say between clenched teeth, making Jade laugh.

"It's all the salt you lost from the tears you shed yesterday." Jade's words hit me hard.

"Is it weird that I didn't cry?" My cramp now easing, I jump back into bed with her and pull her close.

Laying her hand over my chest, she considers her answer. "I think we all deal with grief in different ways. Some people cry, some people get angry, and some people move on faster than others. There are no rules."

She slides her long leg over my hips and moves on top of me to straddle her legs on either side of my body. "Fancy a shower together before everyone wakes up?"

"Abso-fucking-lutely. I can feel my cum sliding out of you." I slip my hand between her legs and push it back inside of her with my fingers. Closing her eyes, she rolls her hips, and lets out a gasp, riding my hand. I could watch her all day. She's mesmerizing.

She grumbles when I remove my fingers from her wet pussy, then tell her to open her mouth. Needing no further instruction, she twists her tongue round them, licking our combined arousal from them.

I sit up and place my hands on either side of her waist.

"Let's have a baby."

She stops rubbing herself against my semi-hard cock instantly, her eyes widening. "What?"

"Let's do it. Marry me, Jade?"

Frozen for a heartbeat, her face unreadable, she

suddenly bursts into a giant smile. "Can we get married at Aphrodite's Rock in Cyprus?"

"I'm assuming that's a yes," I question as I pinch her waist, unable to hide the wide smile that spreads across my face, mirroring hers.

Excitedly she nods, "It's a big fat hell, yes."

"Like *My Big Fat Greek Wedding*?"

"Only smaller."

We throw our arms around one another and hold on tight. "I can't wait to make you my wife." I nuzzle into her neck, enjoying the tightness of our embrace, our hearts beating as one against each other. "I like the sound of a small wedding." I agree with her and kiss the pounding pulse in her neck. "I want to pay for it, though. I am going to do some financial consultancy work. It's flexible hours that I can do from home, at night, or when Poppy is at nursery, and while you are away. You may have to wait a little longer, because I have to pay Gregor and Lincoln back first, but it pays well, really well, and I get to help people make decisions about their budgeting, retirement plans, and savings."

"Sounds boring." She looks concerned. "And that's not what you want to do anymore."

"What I want is to marry you. I will, and I will be paying for it all." I pull her close, so her forehead touches mine. "You are what I want, Jade."

"And you are all I have ever wanted." She's deadly serious, and I can hear her internal cogs ticking over as she considers my proposal to pay for it all, then surprises me when she squeals. "We are getting married!"

Her lips cover mine in a wet, sloppy kiss that isn't one bit romantic but shows me how excited she is.

We are all teeth and lips and giddiness when I say, "I

have something for you. Don't move." I grab onto her hip firmly with one hand, then stretch over to the nightstand and pull open the top drawer to locate what I'm after.

I sit back up when I find it and unwrap my fingers from around the dark green velvet box, unveiling it in the palm of my hand, making her gasp.

She stares at it. "You planned this?"

"I did. Well, I had a whole big thing worked out in my head about taking you down to the beach this morning before you left. Romantic walk along the sand."

"I like this better. This is perfect. This is *us*." Smiling, she looks from me to the box and back at me again.

Like a kid with a Christmas present, I know she wants to see what's inside.

Holding her breath, I peel back the lid of the box, as if revealing a pearl snuggled deep within an oyster shell. But what sits inside is something so much better and even more precious.

Excitement swirls between us, hope dancing deep within our bones, and love in our hearts. She lets out a deep exhale and smiles with delight as I show her the hidden gem. "It's so beautiful."

"This was my Great, Great, Great Aunt Helena's ring. Her and my Uncle Thomas were very much in love." My Aunt Flora informed me of that fact when I told her I planned to marry Jade but had no ring. I didn't even know I had a Great, Great, Great Aunt Helena, but now I do. I knew my mother, *God rest her soul*, was the only heartless cow on her side of the family. Whatever happened to her to make her so cold, I will never know, but when Aunt Flora scampered off to the safe in her home and came back with this ring along with excitable chatter and romantic tales, I knew it was perfect for Jade.

"It's green," she says, stating the obvious.

"It's an emerald cut, emerald solitaire." And the biggest fucking thing I've ever seen. There is not a hope in hell I would have been able to have afforded the three-carat Columbian gem.

"It's a family heirloom?" she says, her voice quiet, almost disbelieving.

"Yeah, from the good side of the family." I want Gregor and my aunt and uncle at our wedding. With my mother not around to dictate, I know they will be.

"Do you like it?" I ask.

"It's huge." She can't stop staring at it.

"Thanks." I look down at my cock and back up at her.

She chuckles, swiping my shoulder playfully with the back of her hand.

"Do you want to try it on for size? We may need to have it adjusted."

She tucks her lips into her mouth and nods.

Carefully pulling the ring out from the place it's been hibernating in for decades, Jade holds out her hand and I slide it onto her ring finger.

"It fits perfectly." She holds it up, tilting her hand back and forth to watch the shiny gold band and green gem catch the light. "It's beautiful."

"We need to get it insured."

She pulls her newly engaged hand to her chest. "Is it worth a lot?" she asks, her eyes full of concern.

"A little." I don't let on that it's worth more than her new Audi Q8.

Batting her eyelashes at me, she holds her hand against her naked chest and wiggles her fingers. "How does it look?"

"Fucking beautiful." But I'm not looking at the ring, I'm looking at her.

"We're getting married." She sighs blissfully.

"That we are, Hotshot."

Grabbing the sides of my face, she kisses me deeply, then mumbles against my lips. "You're going to be the best stepdad any little girl could ever want."

"I think I aced it already. I think I'd like another girl."

She chuckles. "You did. And oh my God, we've only just gotten engaged. No talk of babies."

Not yet, but I sure as hell want to start trying as soon as I get myself back on my feet.

Pulling back, in a flash, sadness lines her forehead and edges her now watery eyes. "I don't want to go today."

"I'll be back home with you and our little pooping machine in less than a week."

"Promise?"

"I promise." An ache in my chest gives a nervous jolt. I don't want her to go either.

She smacks a quick kiss against my lips, before she's off my lap and leaping out of the bed, and hopping about the bedroom, pulling on her oversized sleep shirt that she never wears because she prefers sleeping naked. "What are you doing?" I ask.

"I'm off to tell mom and Aunt Babs."

I check the clock. "It's six o'clock in the morning."

She pulls open the door. "I don't care, I'm getting married." Leaving laughter behind her, I watch her skip along the hall and run down the stairs with excitement.

A cocktail of joy and sadness mix together.

She said yes. But she leaves today.

I pull the bedsheet up to my chin and take a deep inhale.

The only thing that's keeping me going is knowing that

when I slip between the sheets of my bed tonight, it will still smell like her.

Poppy's seatbelt gives a familiar *click* sound, telling me it's locked safely, but I give it a quick tug to check anyway.

Tickling Poppy, then telling her I love her, I give her another kiss on her cheek, making her face scrunch up, and she giggles again as my stubble tickles her baby soft skin. It's about the hundredth kiss I have given her in the last hour.

Loading the last of their luggage into the truck, I give Mari and my newly adopted Aunt Babs a wave goodbye, as they reassure me they will look after my girls in my absence.

Lincoln and Jacob have offered to help me, and with more sets of hands, I'm hoping we box up my stuff quicker so I can get back to my girls sooner.

With one final glance around the car, I slam the trunk of Jade's dark green metallic Audi Q8 shut.

Jade checks her watch again. She's been nervously doing that all morning as we've reluctantly organized her departure. "If we don't leave now, we'll hit the evening rush hour traffic." She fiddles with the vehicle key in her hand.

I wish you could stay.

Worry lines her brow, a deep *V* forming between her eyes. "Just a few days?"

I pull her into my arms and give her the biggest reassuring cuddle. "Then I'll be back to annoy you."

"I love you." She kisses my neck. Her voice so small it gets lost on the Scottish wind.

"I love you near, far, and always." Wherever she is in the world, I always feel her. She's like real magic.

Her grip iron clad, she balls the fabric of my polo shirt into her tight fist at the base of my neck. "Be careful around Gideon and his father, Owen," she whispers. "I don't trust them."

"I know. Me either."

"I heard what Stanley told you last night," she confesses.

"How?" I lean back slightly from our embrace.

"I came to find you and ended up listening outside the office." She worries her bottom lip.

"You should work in military espionage, not be a jet pilot." My voice is a mix of concern and humor. "But please don't worry about me."

Her small chuckle makes her chest vibrate against mine and brings a little light relief to the tension that's built between us; neither of us wants to go our separate ways today.

"I don't plan on seeing them." They are the type of men who enter a room, and you exhale when they leave. "I'm going to ask Camilla to come to the house." I look up through the thick blanket of trees to the sandstone fortress. "I need to speak to her about the will and estate." *She may have an update on the fire investigation report, too, that the insurance company instructed to be carried out*, I think to myself.

Jade informed me earlier that she had transferred money into my account, the one she pays my *wages* into, to pay for petrol and food and anything else I needed. On her insistence she transfers money into my account each week to cover anything I need for Poppy if we're out and about.

She also said she was happy to pay for the designer fragrance I wear every day because she loves it so much.

My money situation is about to change. While it's been kind of Jade to make sure I am looked after, paying me to look after Poppy feels wrong. When I offered to do it for free, Jade and I compromised. She agreed to transfer me a small amount every week to cover any emergencies or groceries. But I don't like being a kept man, hence the reason I signed up to start consulting as a financial advisor. Lincoln and Jacob both thought it was slightly ironic given my father's demise, and we all laughed about it, but this is something I want to do for me... for us... for our family.

Jade inhales deeply, her breath stuttering. "I don't want to go."

Her mom and Babs were beaming with happiness for Jade and me earlier when she woke them up to share the news.

I still can't believe she agreed to be my wife.

Holy shit, I have a fiancée.

When we did a group call earlier with my friends, they clapped, whistled, and screamed down the phone at our news, vowing to join us when we do eventually get married in Cyprus.

"You can carry me everywhere with you now." I hold up her hand and kiss her engagement ring.

"How can I forget? It's huge." She laughs.

"So, you keep telling me."

She rolls her eyes at me. "You are so predictable."

I give her one last kiss and spank her ass for good measure. "C'mon, you need to go. You're meeting Gregor in five minutes." They are driving down convoy style, and that settles any concerns I have about being apart from them, knowing he's watching out for her. Having him here has been a huge support. I know that man has my back and will look after my girls in my absence.

She slips something smooth into the palm of my hand before her hand drops out of mine.

"Jade?" I don't look at whatever it is as we stand staring at each other, but I feel the weight of it in my hand.

"Now you have a little part of me with you too." Unclenching my fingers, I stare.

It's her lucky poppy stone.

She must think I need it more than her.

"But you need this for flying." I attempt to give her it back, panicking, as I know how much she relies on it as part of her flying ritual.

"I'll get it when you come home." She winks, then grabs my hand to drag me to the side of the car.

Home.

Jumping into the driver's seat, she lowers the window and pokes her head back out of the open space to kiss me *again*.

We never want to be apart.

"Love you, Owen."

"Drive safe."

"Always."

"And fly safe."

"Always," she repeats.

And then she's off, with the other three wonderful women I have in my life, and all I can do is watch as she drives out of the black wrought iron gates, onto the road and around the corner out of sight, wishing that I was returning with them today.

"See you soon," I whisper, clutching her lucky charm firmly in my fist.

My phone vibrates in my pocket, bringing me out of my

daze, and when I pull it out to see who is calling I smile and hit accept.

"I miss you already." On speaker phone, Jade shouts down the phone, making me laugh.

"You too."

"Love you," she shouts again and then Mari and Babs join in, "We love you too."

And we all burst out laughing.

God, how I love those women.

My earpiece alerts me to another incoming call.

I pull it away from my ear to see who it is.

Camilla.

Yet another family problem to solve, no doubt.

If I can survive an hour with Camilla, I can do anything.

And before I know it, I'll be back with my girls.

CHAPTER THIRTY-ONE

OWEN

Back behind the wheel of my silver Aston Martin Vantage, I take it for a spin along the cliffs of Castleview Cove to blow away the cobwebs as it had been sitting, unused, for too many weeks.

I didn't believe Camilla at first when she said my father didn't sell it, but when I arrived at my house, it was parked outside waiting for me. I assumed he kept it in storage inside the disused stables at the back of the estate, but I never asked Camilla because making small talk isn't our *thing*.

There is no conflict or animosity between us as such, we simply dropped out of touch with one another when she married Gideon.

As I drove further up the steep cliffside curves, my mind wandered to thoughts of how we navigate our sibling relationship going forward; it's anyone's guess at this point.

I pulled over at one of the small viewing points along the perimeter, and as I stood there looking down, my stomach flipped at the enormity of the height. An image of the sheer horror my mother and father must have endured as their car crashed down the jagged rock face came into mind.

The reality of their death suddenly hit me so hard, I felt like it slapped me in my face, as guilt ferociously engulfed me like a noose around a neck. My breath caught in my lungs and I felt like my chest was going to burst because regardless of their cruel parenting, nobody deserved to die the way they did.

They were human, after all. Flesh and blood.

My parents.

Now gone.

Up high on those cliffs, I jumped back in my car, determined not to dwell on the past.

I can't change what has happened.

And even if I did come back when they asked me to, even a miracle couldn't have saved the business or them going under.

Driving back down to the estate, along the winding roads on the outskirts of town, I realize I don't enjoy driving my sports car as much as I used to.

There are no raspberries being blown or inarticulate words drifting over my shoulder from the backseat from a tiny red-headed twelve-month-old, because there is no backseat.

The sooner I box up my house and leave my old life behind, the better.

Bone deep sadness settles in my body as I pull up outside my oversized and quite frankly vulgar dragon-sculptured childhood castle home.

It's monstrous.

Camilla said she has some details about the business and estate to discuss. I'm of the opinion there is nothing to talk about because, quite frankly, she can have the whole

OWEN

lot. But I agreed to meet her here as I didn't want to meet her anywhere near a Sanderson.

This is more of a peacekeeping exercise for me more than anything else.

Inside the house now, I move out of the foyer and amble down the hall toward dad's office, where Camilla said to meet her. Humming away to myself, I'm almost pleased that this may be the last time I step foot in this godforsaken place ever again.

My humming stops dead in the air as I enter the room to find Richard, sitting behind my father's desk, with his Satan son, Gideon standing by his side, like daddy's good little soldier.

I tentatively step over the threshold and into the dragon's den.

"Owen." Richard gives me a curt nod as I walk further into the room. It's only then I notice Camilla sitting as straight as a poker on the brown leather Chesterfield sofa on the far side of the fireplace.

Fatigue that's settled in pockets under her eyes didn't go unnoticed by my friends and even Jade mentioned how fragile she looked. Her demise scares me, but not enough for me to bolt away from these two evil men behind the desk, because right now, I'm confused as to why they are here.

Then the penny drops; she's helping them. I was a fool to think her intentions were anything but good.

"Richard. Gideon." I greet them, then nod briefly in Camilla's direction.

Unlike those friendly and cheerful, always capering women I waved farewell to this morning, these people are more like strangers than family.

"Sit, please." Gideon points to the chair across from the desk.

"I think you'll find this is my fucking house and I don't need either of you telling me where to sit." I stare Richard down, ignoring Gideon. "And you're sitting in my rightful place. It should be *me* telling *you* where to sit, not the other way about." My body trembling, I push my shoulders back, hoping my confident words sound braver than I feel. "I'll stand."

Gideon rubs his forefinger across his bottom lip. "You've got bigger balls than you father ever did."

"I'm nothing like him," I sneer.

"Which is a damn shame really, as we could have been a powerhouse together, all four of us." He sounds confident as if that would actually be a given when I know differently. I would never join forces with them.

"I'm not a thief, nor am I cruel or corrupt. I don't gamble, so please don't mark me with the same branding iron as him." My eyes stay fixed on Richard.

Richard's devious laugh sounds demonic when he says, "Not a fan of daddy dearest then, no?"

"Fuck you, Richard. What do you all want?"

Gideon steps forward, then pushes a pile of paperwork across the desk. "Read." His one-word answer has my back up and I have visions of me punching him in the face over and over until he's bleeding out. I fucking hate this guy. I've seen what he's done to my sister's confidence. She's a nervous wreck.

I let out a deep breath as if to indicate my boredom, when in fact, I'm pissing my pants.

Picking up the papers, I skim read them impatiently. The words become a blur as I reach the final page. "Denied?"

"What you'll see there, Owen, is a classic case of insurance fraud. Your father deliberately had the printing works set fire to with the intention of claiming on his insurance. His claim was denied."

In disbelief that my father would stoop so low, unable to stand, I drop into the seat behind me and stare at the report. "He was desperate," I mumble to myself. And a man on a ledge, he turned to criminal activities to pay back the money he was due Richard.

When I look up, Richard looks disinterested. "Hundreds of people from the surrounding areas lost their jobs because of him. I called a meeting with the staff and asked Camilla to take the lead and inform those poor souls that the business has gone into liquidation," he says casually.

I'm guessing the entire town will now know my father committed arson and fraud.

It's the one thing I am grateful for; I wasn't at that meeting to see the looks of disappointment on the people's faces I had worked closely with for years.

Richard continues. "When that report came back, your father knew he couldn't rebuild, pay off his debts or undo what he did, Owen." He pauses before he drops the grenade. "So, he killed himself."

Gideon jumps in and pulls the pin. "Along with your mother." He examines his fingernails as if his words and their lives mean nothing.

"What?" I shout louder than I mean to and look to Camilla, whose eyes have turned glassy. "No way," I exclaim. "Camilla, tell me this isn't true?"

She shakes her head and tears free fall, sliding down her cheeks.

It's true.

I dart my gaze back to the two ogres behind the desk. Dark hair, dark eyes, dark suits, dark souls, dark everything.

"The death investigations authority said it was an accident," I counter.

"You have me to thank for that," Richard winks. "Their death certificates said accidental death. The evidence proved otherwise."

"Sorry, why would you have it changed?" I scowl, lost and unable to understand what the fuck is happening. Doing people favors is not something Richard does. There has to be a reason for covering up their cause of death.

"You wouldn't have received life insurance for them if it was deemed suicide." Richard leans across the desk.

And there is the reason.

I'm confused. "But *I* didn't submit paperwork to claim their life insurance." Then the penny drops. I exhale, realizing that it's already been submitted.

"As the oldest heir and beneficiary, Camilla did." Gideon's devious smile is beginning to annoy me.

No, she didn't. They did, and I bet it was worth millions, and Camilla obviously got the lot.

Greed clearly doesn't run in my veins like it does in hers.

She's just like them.

Gideon adds, "It's all approved and on its way to her as we speak."

I throw the insurance report onto the desk. "Is that it? That's what all the dramatics are for? To tell me there was no payout from the business, but you got their life insurance. Great. I'm really happy for you all. Book a holiday. In hell for all I care because, just in case you didn't get the memo, I'm not interested in the money." Angrily I stand and make to leave.

Richard's voice stops me in my tracks. "He owed me more than the life insurance is paying out."

I spin quickly back around. "Not my problem."

"That's where you are wrong, son. With no business insurance to cover it, and as a director of that company, the responsibility falls to you."

"I was a director in name only." I snarl, my skin hotter than the depths of hell.

"Ah, even just in name, you are still the only other remaining director of that business and you were the finance director, too. Well, isn't that convenient?" He's so casual and cool with his delivery of his non-question, it irks me. "That debt now falls to you."

"You cannot be serious?"

"Deadly." He smooths his hand down his tie to straighten it and sits back. "So, here's what's going to happen. While Camilla here fell heir to their life insurance, this fucking hideous house has been left in your name." He twirls his finger in the air.

"You can have it. I'll sign it over." I don't want it. It was worth eight million at its last assessment and I'll gladly give it all away to get them out of my life.

"Good boy." He winks.

"Is that it?" I ask hopefully.

When he tilts his head to the side, a simple but menacing crack to his neck tells me it's not. "You are ten million short."

"Me?" I point at my chest. "*I'm* ten million short?"

He snaps his fingers over and over. "You're a smart man. Keep up, Owen. Your father's debt went unpaid, this house and the life insurance cover some of it, but like I said, you are ten million short."

"But I have no money," I stutter. Other than the money that's accumulated in the bank from Jade, I have nine hundred pounds to my name. "You can have my car." That's all I have left, but I was planning on selling it to pay back Gregor and Lincoln, and save the rest toward our wedding. I'm determined to give Jade the wedding in Cyprus she excitedly spoke about this morning.

Sounding bored, Richard sighs. "Your car is too old, and only worth a fraction of what your father paid for it ten years ago. I'm not interested."

My mouth falls open in shock. Is he for real?

It's worth forty grand, but to him it won't even make a small dent in the ten million he's demanding from me.

He drums his fingers against the wooden desk. "What about your trust fund your grandfather left you?"

"Father cleaned out my account. I don't know what he did with it, but I don't have it anymore."

"Well, you had better get your thinking cap on then, eh? What other accounts did he have?"

"I don't know," I bellow, my voice bouncing off the stone-cold walls.

He eyes me suspiciously. "As the finance director, you must have shown him all the tax loopholes and dodges?"

"You are not listening to me. I was a director in name only. I was only ever given access to two accounts. One for the business savings, which he withdrew my access from, and one for the everyday in and out transactions. Both of which, I am guessing are frozen by the liquidation of the business." My voice takes on a new pitch of its own.

"We only know about the everyday in and out one. The bank hasn't been able to source the savings."

"Because there won't be any," I yell at him again "He told me in Cyprus—"

Gideon interrupts, "He visited you in Cyprus?"

"Yes."

Richard lifts one eyebrow. "Interesting."

"There is nothing fucking *interesting* about it." My blood threads through my veins like hot barbs. "He begged me to come back to help him work out how to liquidate the business without losing everything. He admitted that he messed up. He told me that he had lost billions, gambling stocks and shares, and hedge funds. You name it, he did it. But it's all gone. All of it. You've come to the wrong place if you are looking for the money he is due you because I have none. I have the clothes I am standing in, a car that, like you said, is worth nothing to you, a few books, a surfboard, a bike, and that's it." I'm so out of breath, but I keep going with all that I know. "He withdrew my admin access to the business savings account and moved it elsewhere months ago. I don't know where it was moved to, but I can assure you, there will be fuck all left. He blew it all on Crypto. He lost every penny. Including yours. He gambled the money he borrowed from you to cover the staff wages on even more stocks and shares and fuck knows what else. It's all gone."

Feeling like I've run a marathon, my chest heaves.

They both stare blankly at me as Camilla continues to sob.

I can't believe this is happening.

"Ten million. You have ten days." Richard pushes up from the desk and lifts himself out of the chair.

I laugh at his demand. "You'll have to make that ten years or decades, not days, because I have no way of getting that money. Good luck though."

"Thought you might say that," he mutters blandly, laying his hand out flat.

Gideon places a brown envelope into the palm of Richard's hand and presents it to me like he's a waiter serving canapés at a dinner party.

Dread encases me as I stomp forward and snatch it, tearing it open and pulling out whatever is concealed inside.

From the other side of the room, Camilla's sobs become louder, as if she knows what comes next.

It takes a few minutes for my brain to comprehend what the photos in my hand are of and what he's implying. It's only then that a single word tears from my throat. "No." I shake my head rapidly as a lump the size of a cannonball forms in my windpipe.

"Please don't do this to my family, Richard," Camilla cries, covering her heart with her chest.

Speechless, I look from Camilla to Richard, then Gideon, and back down at the photos.

"Ten million, Owen. Ten days. You wouldn't want anything to happen to those two beautiful redheads now, would you?" I riffle through the photos of Jade and Poppy. Some with me. Playing in the garden at her house. Photos of us kissing in the kitchen. Us doing the grocery shopping together. Poppy at nursery. One of Jade sitting in the cockpit of her jet getting ready for take-off on the airfield on base and there is even one of her taken in what looks like a restaurant overseas with her team.

"How?" I ask in horror, unable to comprehend how he penetrated a high security military compound.

"I'm a man of many talents, Owen. I have eyes and ears everywhere," Richard says firmly. Coming out from behind the desk, he saunters over to me. "Find my money. You have ten days or *poof*." He splays his fingers out in the air. "Gone." Eyes widening as if he's the fucking Joker himself, he smiles maliciously. "It would be such a travesty should anything happen to your *Hotshot* girlfriend."

How the hell does he know my pet name for her?

He taps the side of his nose. "I saw and heard it all at

the funeral. And like I said, I have eyes and ears everywhere." He does the button up on his black suit jacket. "As the world's first woman aerobatic pilot in the Air Force, it would be such a talent to go to waste." He dabs the corners of his eyes theatrically. "It would be a pity if she were to have an accident in that pretty little red plane she flies."

"I fucking hate you," I snarl, spittle spraying everywhere.

"Join a queue. You know what needs to be done." He looks around, dusts his tie, and nods in Gideon's direction. "Time to go."

Then he leaves alongside Gideon and my sister, who, as sad as she is, willingly gets up and walks to the door with them.

"I'm your brother, Camilla. Why would you let them do this to me?" She stops walking but doesn't look back and stays silent.

"I will never forgive you," I hiss.

Her voice is so small now, she's no longer the fierce girl I remember growing up with. "I will never forgive myself," she whispers, shaking her head, still crying, before she leaves.

Then it's just me.

Standing in a castle that's no longer mine. Not that I wanted it, but at the very least I could have sold it to replace the trust money father took from me.

It's official. I have nothing. Again.

My pulse beats so hard I can hear it thumping in my ears.

The man I hate with every bone in my body is dead, and yet he's still screwing me over.

And in this moment, I have never felt so alone.

If I can't raise or find that money, what will Richard do to them? I will die inside if anything happens to them.

I can't let that happen. I just can't.

And if I can't find the money, it will kill me but I will stay away from Jade and Poppy to keep them safe.

It would mean never seeing my girls again. I will kill me, but I will do it. For them.

Richard threatened the lives of the people I love the most. The only two people who love me unconditionally. And I have to do everything in my power to protect them, but right now I am powerless as well as penniless.

The knot of anxiety in my gut tightens, making me feel sick.

My stomach churns around like a washing machine on its highest spin.

Running over to the wastebasket I lunge forward, heaving, vomiting up this morning's breakfast.

Hunched over, my hands on my thighs, I suck in a deep breath as I stand tall, wiping my sweat covered hands over the pockets over the fabric of my trousers. When I feel the small lump, I push my hand into it and I pull out Jade's lucky poppy stone.

Unclenching my fingers, I stare.

Jade was right. I needed luck.

Ten million pounds of it.

CHAPTER THIRTY-TWO

OWEN – FIVE DAYS LATER

"What the hell are you doing?" Jacob gasps as he steps inside my father's home office.

"Searching." Sitting cross-legged on the floor, I reply, not lifting my head as I scan yet another piece of paper looking for any clues as to the whereabouts of my trust fund or money my father may have had stashed somewhere.

"It must be important, whatever it is you are searching for," Jacob says. "This place is a mess."

I tilt my chin up and scan the room. Paperwork is scattered across every surface. Over the last five days, I have ripped the house apart, including the filing cabinet I found in a secret space behind the knight statue in the hall. I hauled it into the office, then took a crowbar to rip the drawers open.

"I couldn't find a key for that." I point at the tall empty cabinet that's now completely unusable.

"So, you wrenched it open?" Lincoln says sarcastically. "And I'm guessing you couldn't find a key for that either." He points at the wooden desk that no longer has a top.

"I took a chainsaw to it," I answer honestly. "The crowbar didn't work."

Speechless, Jacob and Lincoln stand in astonishment, taking in the carnage of empty takeout cartons and pizza boxes mixed with archive storage boxes and folders.

"Is this where you have been for the last five days?" Lincoln looks at me like I've become a crazy person. He's not wrong, no sleep for days and living off coffee. I feel manic.

"Yeah." I push my fingertips into my eyes. "I need more caffeine."

"You need sleep. You look terrible." Jacob casts his gaze around the room again. "And it smells like ass in here."

"That would be me. I haven't showered in days. I've been here since Jade left." My eyes sting with tiredness, but I won't rest until I find what I need.

I have to raise that money to save them from him.

Lincoln's voice rises in surprise. "Is it something important you are looking for?"

I nod, my head throbbing in response at the slight movement.

"We thought you just didn't need help boxing everything up, but when we didn't hear from you again this morning to arrange for your stuff to go into storage at Jacob's, and your phone went straight to voicemail, we started to get worried," Lincoln explains.

I scramble about the floor, searching for my phone. "Shit, I didn't call Jade last night." I urgently need to charge it and call her. I'm annoyed at myself for forgetting to call her like I promised. I missed wishing Poppy a good night, too.

"I've been a little distracted." My shoulders sag with

worry as I locate my phone. Pointing to the plug, I pass my phone to Jacob, silently asking him to charge it for me.

I never forget about Jade. That's not who I am with her.

This money hunt is driving me insane to the point I've forgotten about my girls, and I've got nothing to show for the lost hours of my life I've spent on this searching mission.

Mission fucking impossible.

Walter, the private investigator I hired, came up short. He had no information on the whereabouts of my trust fund, and therefore refused to charge me his fee as he didn't deliver on his promise. It's lost in the abyss, along with my father's billions.

The stark reality is, there is nothing to find. Like a puff of smoke in the wind, every penny my father had has disappeared.

"We took a drive up here and saw your car out front. You hate this house." I read between the lines of Jacob's words. He wants to know what I am doing in the building I spent most of my childhood trying to avoid.

"I need to keep looking." I drop my head and go back to scanning the files.

"Can we help to find this important *thing* you're looking for?" Lincoln asks curiously.

"Yeah. See those?" I point at the two stacked high columns of files on the floor. I haven't been through them yet. "Take a pile each."

They both look at me in confusion. "What specifically do we need to find?"

"Money," I say before I resume my search.

Deadly silence seeps from across the room and I can feel my two friends staring at me. I don't look up as I explain. "My father owed Richard and Gideon Sanderson a lot of money. He turned up five days ago and told me his debt now falls on my head."

"What the fuck?" Lincoln gasps.

Head bowed, I keep talking. "He took this place and their life insurance. But it wasn't enough to clear the debt. He wants another ten million. He's given me ten days to find it." My clenched jaw becomes tighter as the enormity of the situation hits me yet again. "I have five days left."

"He can't do that." Jacob jumps in immediately.

"He has," I reply, my anger so strong it burns like the fires of hell. I'm so mad, I feel like I could transform into the Hulk. "If I don't have that money, then..." I trail off, unable to tell them the reality of my situation.

Jacob pushes me to keep going. "Then?"

I lift my head and stare at them, the knot in my stomach tightening. "He made a threat to both Jade and Poppy's lives. Specifically, Jade."

Too startled to comment on my confession, they immediately take a pile each and join me on the floor. "Tell us everything while we search," Lincoln insists.

When I'm finished, they are both speechless. After a long pause, Jacob finally says, "I wish I could help you, but I invested everything into the castle, and the renovations are already three times over our budget." Unlike the castle we are sitting in, Jacob and Skye's is bright, airy, and full of love.

I tap an appreciative small punch on his shoulder. "Thanks, man, but it's not your problem."

I wouldn't expect anyone to pay off my debt. It's not hundreds or even thousands we are talking about here either, it's *millions*. I will never forgive my father for this, and I still cannot process Gideon's words. *He killed himself, and your mother.*

I don't believe it.

"I have nothing either," Lincoln adds. "With the restaurant extension underway, as directors, we all agreed to forego any withdrawals or share payouts. It's already over budget too. The cost of the foundations alone makes me want to vomit."

My mood lifts, suddenly buoyant. The gratitude I feel for having these two incredible and honorable men in my life fills me with hope. There is humanity, after all. "Thank you." Emotion thick in my throat, it cracks when I say, "I will find a way." Although any hope I have is wavering knowing that, as each hour has passed, I am fighting a losing battle.

"I can't let anything happen to Jade," I whisper. "She's the best thing to have ever happened to me." I swallow hard and bite back the tears that are threatening to slip down my cheeks.

Understanding my desperation, Jacob takes charge. "First, you need to go in the shower. You smell like a swamp. Lincoln will tidy up and order food for later, and I'll keep searching while you have a few hours sleep. Having no sleep for days is not healthy, and you need to keep razor sharp."

"I'm not sleeping," I admonish.

"Yes, you are. I will set an alarm," he counters. "You look fucking dreadful."

I catch a glimpse of myself in the ornate floor mirror. Bloodshot eyes, deep shadows under them, dry skin, greasy hair. I really look haggard.

Reluctantly, I agree to run down to my house to freshen up and come back to call Jade once my phone is charged and to sleep on the office couch.

But that doesn't happen.

As soon as I've showered, I lay back on my bed to rest my achy body for a moment. Closing my heavy eyelids that feel like they are being punctured by stinging needles, I'm engulfed in a tsunami of weariness. One where darkness envelopes me and pulls me under, and that's the last thing I remember as I give in to a deep, hollow, lifeless sleep surrounded by Jade's sweet fragrance and the memories of us under these sheets.

Owen – 2 Days Later

Frantically running into my father's office, I discover Lincoln passed out on the sofa and Jacob sound asleep on the floor surrounded by folders, files, paperclips, pages of reports, birth certificates, deeds for the castle, you name it, it's here. All that's missing is what I really need.

Money.

That or a solid piece of paper telling me exactly where my trust fund is, or the location of a miracle bank account somewhere overseas with my name on it.

That's all I need. Just one piece of information to unlock the key to a ten-million-pound problem.

My hope dwindling, I've never felt so helpless.

Crazily, I grab my phone off the coffee table to call Jade and catch a glimpse at the date.

I've lost two days.

I've been asleep for two days, only up once to use the bathroom and grab a glass of water, I didn't realize I had slept for as long as I did. I push my hands through my hair.

"Fuck," I shout, not meaning to waken Jacob and

Lincoln up. Like two slumbering grizzly bears, they stretch and come to life and look about the place in a daze, as if not remembering where they are.

I give them a curt *good morning* and hold the phone to my ear as I call Jade.

"Why didn't you come get me?" I hiss at them angrily. They know I need to find that money. I have to admit, they were right. I needed the sleep and feel slightly clearer headed today, but I've lost two days. Fear swirls in my gut as I realize the enormity of my mammoth sleep. And why the fuck is Jade not answering?

"You were dead to the world. You needed to rest. And we kept looking. We had your back." Lincoln yawns and grabs his junk. "I need a piss." He clumsily gets to his feet and leaves the office.

I hang up the unanswered call and check our family calendar. Within a few taps, know her whereabouts. I check the time on the brass clock on top of the larger-than-life stone fireplace.

Lunchtime. Which means she'll be prepping her jet along with her engineer for displaying at the airshow in Wales tomorrow. She never takes calls when she is prepping to take off or on the day of a show, insisting she needs to focus and time to *get into the zone*.

Jacob stands up and gives his back a crack, stretching out his body from sleeping on the uncomfortable hard floor. "We spoke to Jade yesterday and the day before," he says calmly while yawning.

"Is she okay?" I panic. "I hope you didn't tell her anything about this." I rush my words as I point around at the chaos that still covers the floor of the office. I don't want her to know what's going on.

Jacob leans left and right, making his back crack again.

"Of course, we didn't. She's fine, as is Poppy. I did text Gregor, asking him to keep an eye on her for you too, and just said that we were looking out for her for you. She is apparently flying solo to Wales today, ahead of the team. She said she was going a day earlier than planned to scope the place out and then she was having dinner with the Station Commander and his wife before tomorrow's display."

Fully committed to her job, that makes sense. It's something she often does.

"When you spoke to her, what did you tell her?"

"We said you'd been so busy with the funeral and then there was a complication with the will and the estate. That you were sorting that out with Camilla when you got a stomach bug and had been bedridden for the last couple of days?"

"Did she buy your lie?" I ask Jacob, my doubtful voice a semi-tone higher.

"I guess she did. She didn't question us if that's what you mean. She just asked you to call her as soon as you were feeling better."

Not having spoken to her these last few days, the urge to jump in my car and drive to her is strong. With the force of a magnet, I feel my body pulling to her. I need to see her smile, hear her laughter. I miss her. And Poppy.

Like the air I breathe, I need them.

I'm not convinced Jade would have believed Jacob's lie, because she's a deception detective. She can read people so fast it scares me. I'll never be able to throw her a surprise birthday party knowing that she can detect a change in someone's pitch of voice or the use of repeated words or sentences when people are lying. She's a master at reading body language too, and she knows when I'm having a mini-internal melt down, like when I was at war with myself about the decision I made not returning to Castleview Cove when my father asked me to. When she asks me if I am fine, she knows in an instant if I am lying and makes me talk through my feelings.

She's like therapy and always makes me feel better.

I can't let anything happen to her.

Jacob clears his throat as Lincoln returns. "You received a text from Richard with a tick tock message yesterday." He stalls for a beat, his face turning somber. "Alongside a photo of Jade and Poppy. It was time and location stamped." He clears his throat. "Yesterday morning, inside the camp wire."

"Motherfucker," I hiss, instantly checking his threatening message.

Right enough, there it is. Bile sours my gut as tap open the photo of her, blazing a knockout smile, hair blowing in the wind with Poppy in her arms outside her house on base.

I lay my hand over my tee shirt where, underneath, lay my dog tags with their names on.

My girls.

I will not let anything happen to them. I look around the room to see where to start today's search.

"Richard's a bastard for doing this to you. But we might have found something." Looking confident, Lincoln grins wide.

A flicker of hope sparks in my gut. "What?"

"It's not much, but it's something." Jacob looks pleased with what they have found too. He grabs a black box file off the top of the fireplace and hands it to me.

Hands shaking, I reach out to take it, then flip open the lid. Bundles of cream postcard size pieces of paper fill the box. "Premium bonds." I hold one up in wonder, looking at it as if it's a twist of destiny.

"Thousands of the fucking things." Lincoln turns around and picks up another five box of files.

"Are they all full?" I ask hopefully. This is the type of investment my grandfather would make. He was a smart man, and, unlike my father, he made wise investment choices. Buying premium bonds would have been a long-term game plan for him.

"Yup. Found them all in yet another filing cabinet in the basement in among all your grandfather's things. That place down there gives me the chills." Lincoln shivers. "We also found love letters between your grandfather and an unknown lover." He follows his words with a wink.

While my grandfather was always nice to me, he was a bit of an enigma. "I don't want to know, and that place is a dungeon, not a basement," I mutter.

"There are certificates and insurance policies with items listed from your mother's jewelry and watch collection, but we didn't find any jewelry or watch collection, either."

"Do you think my father sold it all?" I ask, airing my suspicions.

"Perhaps." Lincoln gives me a sad look. "But this is our job for today. We need to go through every one of them."

"Premium bonds are a lotto, though." I felt hopeful for all of a millisecond, but now I feel like the carpet has been pulled from under my feet. When do you ever hear of anyone winning the lotto? I've not known anyone close to me that's won.

"My grandfather bought me some when I was a younger. I still have them, but I've never won." Lincoln stares at the slips.

Jacob jumps in, "Each one has a code, right? If you get a winning code, the government has to pay out... tax free? This could be the answer to your money problems, Owen."

I look down at the box filled with hope. "Let's get started," I say, making my friends laugh and, for the first time since Richard and Gideon showed up here, I remember what happiness feels like as our laughter fills the room.

Then it dawns on me. "Christ, I have been so selfish. What about Skye?" I ask Jacob. "Go home to them. You've got a new baby." Then I point at Lincoln. "And you've got a demanding girlfriend who is on a mission to destroy your dick every minute of every day."

Lincoln throws his head back, laughing again. "She'll survive, and anyway, she's staying with Skye to help with Aurora for night feeds. She's in her element."

Jacob looks at me and nods his head quickly as he smiles kindly. "She is. We are all taking care of each other in different ways. I told her you weren't well, though, just in case Jade spoke to her or Violet." He cringes, knowing how well those three women gelled and that they have probably spoken every day since the day they met. "The sooner we find the money, the sooner I can get back to Skye. I am missing my Butterfly and my little Princess."

"Fuck, you guys are sickening,"

"Yeah, yeah, whatever, *Hotshot*." Jacob mocks me, calling me out for being a gooey mess around my woman, too.

"Oh, let's not forget about *my little Poppadom*." Lincoln fakes a high-pitched voice.

On a blush, I chastise him. "You are in no position to take the piss with all that *Sweet Petal* shit you call Violet."

"I'll have you know I also call her the dick destroyer," he says matter-of-factly.

Chuckling, Jacob says, "Fucking hell, what has happened to us? Those women have got us by the balls."

Silently, we all stare at each other and smile.

"I love you two like brothers. You know that, right?" I say, looking at my friends who I've never said that to before.

They both nod my way.

"I don't know what I would have done without either of you." They know I'm not referring to the past couple of days. They've been everything to me since we were kids.

Never one to talk about his emotions, Jacob bows his head and pushes his hands in to the pockets of his jeans. He might be built like a tank, covered in tattoos, all buzz cut and muscles, but he's a big softie underneath it all. He clears his throat. "We feel the same."

In contrast, Lincoln is one broad, Greek, smiling muscly teddy bear who overshares and could charm the pants off anyone. "Fuck man, bring it in." He holds his arms out and moves toward us, closing the invisible triangle we are standing in. Lincoln grabs my head and then Jacobs, smacks a kiss on each of our foreheads in the same way his Greek grandma does to us. "Now let's find some moola." Releasing us, he steps back and rubs his hands together.

"What if we don't raise enough and what if there is nothing in here?" I hold up the box file I'm still holding on to.

"Can you not ask your aunt for it?" Lincoln asks.

I shake my head. "I can't tell Aunt Flora about this. It will break her knowing that Dad killed her sister. That's if he did. And I'm too ashamed to tell them there is no money left. They didn't know the extent of his demise."

"But what have you got to lose now?" Lincoln asks, his

voice soft, as if he's encouraging me to shift my thinking.

I shrug. "I guess nothing, but when you've spent a lifetime putting on a front and maintaining the good name of the family, it's hard to tear that down... even if that is to family. I guess you're right. I should tell them but I will not ask them for money. This is my mess and I need to sort it."

"They hated my dad" I tell them. And they aren't like my parents. They invest in small-time entrepreneurs. There is no way they would have millions just sitting about. They are more property and equity rich than they are money rich. They weren't risk takers, but they were successful in their small business investments and kept their lives low key. Unlike my father.

"But they love you."

"I'm not asking them." I'm adamant. "I know they won't have it." I roll my neck, causing tension to flood back into my muscles. Sounding defeated, I sigh woefully. "What if he hurts her?" I can't bear to think about it.

"He could be bluffing," Jacob says, trying to sound like he believes that.

"You heard what happened to that group of women they found in one of his shipping containers, right?" I know what he's capable of. "It was all over the news."

"They all died," Lincoln whispers. "He denied he knew anything and got away with it."

Our attention returns to the box file in my hand.

"Let's find that money." We all say at the same time.

Jade

Everything feels weird.

Owen has been acting weird.

His mood is weird.

I feel weird.

One minute he's calling and texting me every minute of every day, the next, it's as if I've completely fallen out of his thoughts and haven't heard from him in days.

Before he did his Houdini act, he's asked me some seriously odd questions on the phone. I laughed at him when he asked if I noticed anyone suspicious following me or if anyone was lurking about outside the house. But the one that freaked me out the most was the question that shot straight through my heart, *can you check outside and see if someone is lurking around?*

I shrugged it off and told him he had been watching too many thriller movies since I left, but his silence told me a very different story, and I found myself closing the drapes earlier at night and peeking through them every now and again to check the surrounding area around my quarters just to make sure no one was *lurking around* like he said.

I put a stop to that silly behavior the night after, telling myself to stop being so stupid, safe in the knowledge I live inside a military base where no one gets in or out without permission.

Like I said, he was being weird, as was I.

Then Lincoln called me to let me know Owen had a stomach bug, but I don't believe him because a few days of packing up a house has now taken several and, I'm questioning if he's having doubts about moving from Scotland to England.

It's a huge ask; a big life change.

Although he assured me it's what he wants, now I'm not so sure.

I hope he would do the decent thing if he didn't want to follow through and marry me and tell me he's changed his mind.

When Lincoln called to say Owen had to stay longer because of some complications with the estate and then got a stomach flu, I don't know why, but I didn't believe him; I have no reason not to, but something's up.

I can feel it.

And I miss him so much. So does Poppy.

It's been lovely of my mom and Aunt Babs to take care of Poppy in his absence, but everything feels better when he's around. The sun shines brighter, there are fewer clouds in the sky and even the rain seems less wet when he's with us.

I wish he'd come home soon.

I'm in the restrooms at work washing my hands. As I finish up, I slide my beautiful engagement ring off my finger, pull the zipper of my flight suit down, and then hook my fingers under my tee shirt and into the cup of bra to drop it inside so he's right beside my heart.

Since Owen hasn't come back, I don't have my lucky stone to carry with me everywhere, and my ring feels like the closest thing to luck I have. Miles apart, it's the closest thing to connect us.

Doing my zipper up, I quickly gather my hair into a low ponytail and tuck some smaller loose strands of my hair behind my ears and push a breath out.

I don't have a fear of flying; what I do have is a bone deep fear of losing him and it scares me knowing he's pulling away emotionally and physically since I left Castleview Cove.

"Don't think like that." I stare at myself in the mirror and give my reflection a good talking too. "He loves you."

The hinges on the restroom door groan loudly as it's pushed open. Blake pops her head through the gap. "Ready?" she beams.

"I was born ready."

I follow Blake out and she reels off a dozen different things about the weather conditions—sun shining, beautiful afternoon—and then something about dinner with the Station Commander and meeting her tomorrow for the show. I laugh, telling her to slow down. She's the only woman I know whose brain works faster than mine.

"Go get ready." Blake waves me off and as soon as I'm suited up in my survival equipment and red display coverall, I'm in the cockpit of my red jet plane, cruising solo above the clouds to Wales to prepare for another display tomorrow.

I'm looking forward to tonight's dinner with the Station Commander and his wife. It's been a while since I put a pretty dress on. It's a pity Owen wasn't here or he could have driven and met me there. I would have loved to have introduced him as my husband-to-be.

Part of me is still in shock that he asked me to marry him, and another part of me is annoyed with him for not speaking to me over the last few days.

Chuckling to myself, I make a mental note to send him a text message with that mild threat as soon as I've landed; no sex for a month if he doesn't call me soon.

Covered in a blanket of golden sun, I'm enjoying the view of the vibrant green mountain peaks of Wales, day dreaming about Owen being home, when my jet begins to violently shake. It then stutters and then loses altitude rapidly, plummeting a thousand feet. Gripping onto the control stick to steady the plane, I manage to level out as the fuel gauge alarm starts flashing, warning me I have no fuel.

How is that possible?

Then the low altitude alert goes off as I drop another thousand feet, putting my stomach in my mouth as it falls faster than a roller coaster.

I hesitate for a millisecond.

Having trained for years and spent hours in the simulators to prepare me for something like this, I know I am losing height from engine flameout, but it's the first time I have ever had to do this in a real time emergency, "Mayday, Mayday, Mayday, Red 1."

The air traffic controller responds immediately, "Mayday, Red 1 acknowledged, send details when able."

Mind spinning yet remaining calm, I flip open my flight reference checklist to the engine seizure page and run through the procedure, while at the same time, I reply to air traffic, "Mayday Red 1, Hawk T1, engine flameout, no fuel remaining, losing altitude, three thousand feet, one person on board."

It all happens so fast; the engine sputters, then dies, and I find myself saying the words I've said so many times in training but never wanted to say in a real time emergency. "Scramble a helicopter. Will be ejecting over Mount Snowdon. Eject, eject, eject."

When I pull the ejection seat firing handle, several things happen at once. It detonates the explosive miniature cord that's embedded into the cockpit canopy above my head. The explosive cartridge under my seat ignites, then explodes, making me feel like my bones are rattling in my body. It blows off the canopy and turbulently catapults me into the air like a rocket being sent to the moon as I punch out at six hundred miles an hour. I'm momentarily hit by a wall of panic before I smash my head against something, and everything goes as black.

CHAPTER THIRTY-THREE

OWEN - 1 DAY LATER

As the sun begins to set on yet another day, since yesterday morning we have checked every serial number on over six thousand bond tickets using the online prize checker.

Losing hope, Jacob hands me the last one to check. I punch the numbers in, hit enter on the keyboard of the laptop, and wait.

"No luck." I sigh heavily.

"How much do we have?" Lincoln asks Jacob who is calculating the final tally.

"Three-point five million," he replies.

I let out a deep sigh. It's not enough. "We have two days left," I say, looking at the hundreds of disregarded tickets.

We need more time.

I tried calling Jade again later last night, but she must have been asleep. The night before a display, she likes to go to bed at a reasonable time. Hoping she would waiver her no phones ban on display days because we haven't spoken in days, I tried all day again today, praying she would pick up for me, but I still haven't been able to get hold of her. I will call her mom if I don't hear from her soon.

I need to hear her voice.

I drop her a text.

ME:

> Please call me. I miss you, Hotshot. xoxo

Nothing.

Why is she not replying?

Something feels... wrong.

"What if he's already done something to her, and that's why I can't contact her?" A violent shiver runs down my spine.

This can't be happening.

I'm drowning.

It's just a matter of time before Richard makes good on his promise and I need more time and money. Neither of which I have enough of.

Dread is consuming me, swarming like a nasty hive of hornets in my chest, making it feel like it's about to explode.

The stress of my situation is threatening to kill me, as tension runs through my tight muscles.

"Don't think stupid things." Jacob stacks the winning tickets into a neat pile.

"This is fucking bullshit." I kick a stacked pile of files and send them flying. Anger soars through my body. Unable to temper it, I flip the coffee table over, smashing it through the glass cabinet full of expensive liquor. "I never asked for any of this," I angrily spit out.

I can't save her.

"Owen." Lincoln tries calling my name to calm me down. I think the ferocity of my mood is frightening him.

Grabbing a side table, I launch it at the oversize floor

mirror, shattering it to smithereens. "He's destroyed my life." I grab the hair at the bottom of my neck and pull it in frustration. "I fucking hate you," I scream at the painting of my father above the fireplace and throw the chair I've picked up at it, tearing through the canvas.

I roar so loud it burns the back of my throat. "I wanted to break free. That's all I wanted." I fall to my knees. "I didn't ask for any of this. This is not my fault." I shake my head and punch the stone floor, splitting my knuckles open. "Why? Why would he do this to me?" Tears streaming down my face, I look at my friends for help. But I'm looking in the wrong place. They did all they could for me. We lost.

I failed her.

I can't save my beautiful Jade.
I will fucking die if anything happens to her.
I am nothing without her and Poppy.
I can't live without them.

Terror suffocates me as I wipe the streams of blood pouring from hand onto my jeans. Jacob hands me the sweatshirt from the back of the sofa and wraps it around my knuckles to stop the bleeding. "You'll need stitches in that," he whispers.

"I don't care." Emotionally bankrupt and defeated, I take one last look around the destroyed room, and briefly glance at the painting of my father.

"I have to tell Richard I can't get him the money." My voice sounds low and lifeless.

As I move, something shiny catches my attention.

Curious, I narrow my gaze to get a better look, then move toward the painting, eyeing the tear I made with the chair.

"What the fuck is that?" I ask in wonder as a sliver of silver shines through the split.

Reaching my hand that is throbbing like a bitch up to the painting, I insert a blood coated finger into the canvas and drag it down, ripping it further. I listen to the zipping noise it makes as I shred the painting, unveiling what's behind it.

"Sweet Jesus," Lincoln declares.

I look at the hidden safe that's been hiding in plain sight. "Find me a blowtorch."

CHAPTER THIRTY-FOUR

OWEN – 1 DAY LATER

I'm standing in the office of Richard Sanderson; Satan's spawn and top-shelf asshole.

Hands in my pocket, my newly stitched together flesh throbs as I nervously rub Jade's lucky poppy stone with my thumb.

"That's all I could find." I nervously stare at the devil sitting behind the desk with a heavy set bodyguard off to the side of him.

It's not enough. He knows it's not enough.

"You're one point five million short." Unimpressed, his mouth down-turned, he stares at the stacks of premium bond slips and cash I scraped together.

Not knowing the code to the safe, in the dead of night with no locksmith available, me and my two loyal friends took a blowtorch to the hinges of the cast iron safe behind the painting, where, after hours of trying, they finally popped off and after some persuasion and the help of a crowbar, the door fell away like a dead weight.

Astounded, standing in silence, we grabbed on to one

another to stop us from falling over as wads of cash, all five million of it, carefully wrapped in blue elasticated bands, came into view.

No longer convinced my father committed suicide, I found two new passports, with new identities for my mother and father.

He was running away from his problems and the backlash from his employees that no longer had jobs, some of which had worked with us for years; like me, they were left with nothing.

At the funeral, I felt the stares from the congregation burning through the back of my head as I sat at the front of the church. How I wish I could have offered them compensation and rewarded them for their years of loyalty. I had nothing to give them. I would divide the money sitting on the desk in front of me between them all if it wasn't needed to save a life.

Overflowing with prosperity, the golden age of the Brodie estate is now a thing of the past, tainted by him; my father.

Knowing a sale of the house wasn't enough, and with no payout from the insurance to settle his debt with Richard, and with only my trust fund, new passports, and airline tickets to Switzerland, it's clear that my father was planning to run away. Petrified of Richard and his evil reputation, he had first-hand knowledge of his business and what he was capable of; my father was running for his life.

My parents cared about what other people thought about them. The threat of backlash from the town and businesspeople alike would have killed their egos if a mob of disgruntled employees turned up to lynch him at his gated castle, forcing him out of the town.

He was fleeing before the news of his fraudulent claim got out.

I know for sure my father was many things, but never a murderer.

The passports and plane tickets inside that safe prove that Richard was lying.

I'm positive Camilla knows it, too.

Having not slept for hours, after I left the hospital, I showered, then as day broke, desperate to keep Jade from harm, as if the tires of my car were on fire, I pulled up outside the gated home of Richard Sanderson and demanded to see him.

The miracle I prayed for never came and with one day left, I know that I finally have to admit to him I have done everything I can.

"I have torn the house apart. I've given you the family house along with my home. You took their life insurance. I have nothing else to give you." He emptied us out.

I'm hoping he's listening to me as I explain how much effort I went to give him what he demanded.

Summoning all the strength I can, I make him a new offer. "I will work for you to pay off the rest of the debt." It fucking kills me that I have to do this, but there is no other way.

"You *want* to work for me?"

"No." I can't be anything other than honest. "But I have no other way to pay off my father's debt. I can show you how to creatively *lose* money in the business." Like a sacrificial lamb, I'm offering myself for slaughter. This is not who I am. I follow the rules and have stayed on the straight and narrow professionally since I started working in finance. I hate myself, and I hate him, for making me stoop so low. "When I save you one point five million, or make that for you in investments, then you will let me go." My words leave a bitter taste in my mouth. "And I need your guarantee you will never lay a finger on my girls. I need to know Jade and Poppy are safe."

This is the only solution I could think of. It means I will have to stay here in Castleview Cove until I pay the debt, because I don't think Richard will trust me not to run. Although I'm positive that I can pay it back quickly. One and a half million is pocket change to Richard. He probably earns that in interest in a day. Regardless, he has a point to prove; no one screws him over. If you do, there will be consequences, and if he lets one man away without paying his dues, it will make him look weak, and he can't have that.

Considering my offer, Richard rubs his forefinger back and forth across his bottom lip as he leans back in his office chair.

If he doesn't accept, then... I feel bile rising in my throat. I can't even bear to think about it.

My phone rings loudly from inside my black dress slacks. To show Richard how serious I am, I thought it was best to come dressed for negotiation, so I fully suited up. As expected, at seven o'clock in the morning, he's in full business attire, too. I swear he must sleep in a three-piece suit.

Pulling my phone out of my pocket, I frown in confusion when I see Jade's Aunt Babs' name on the screen, then double check the time; quarter past seven.

Why is she calling at this ungodly hour?

Knowing I'm dealing with an extremely dangerous man who can make people disappear, I ask him for permission to take the call. A man of few words, he nods, and I hit the accept button as I walk over to the window.

"Babs?"

With no warning or niceties, she says the words I've be fearing since I found out what Jade did for a living and the threat Richard placed on her life: "Jade's missing."

Standing in a pool of warm orange light as the sun comes up, my blood turns to ice and all I can hear is her fractured words, *accident, plane crash, eject, Welsh mountain range, major search, can't find her, rescue operation, missing since yesterday afternoon, we weren't allowed to tell you until we knew she was officially missing...*

Everything becomes a blur as every fiber of my body becomes taut with overwhelming emotion, my gut coiling and twisting, and I struggle to catch a breath.

"I'm on my way." My voice is barely a whisper, as sharp pains shoot through my temples.

"Stay where you are, Owen. The Air Force is doing all they can to keep this out of the press with the hope they can find her before they catch wind of the story." She lowers her voice as if not wanting to be overheard. "I've been sworn to secrecy but we've been ordered by the British Ministry of Defence to act like everything is okay. Jade's paperwork states that Mari is her emergency contact and next of kin, and in the eyes of the Air Force, you are just the nanny. Jade hadn't informed her chain of command of your engagement yet because of your living arrangements. As you know, they have very strict policies, Owen."

"You have got to be kidding me?" I drag my hand down my face in disbelief. "I have to come, Babs."

"They won't let you near us. A liaison officer has already arrived at Jade's house this morning." She whispers. "Listen to me, Owen. We've been ordered to stay within the safety of the base, here at the house with Poppy. Like us, there is nothing you can do. It's out of our hands. They are resuming the search by helicopter this morning. The

427

mountains are treacherous. They've told us we have to sit tight while they widen their search. You need to stay put until we know more." She goes eerily quiet.

They don't need me.

In the eyes of the military, I mean nothing to her. Or to Poppy. When, in fact, I mean everything to them.

A fucking wedding ring is all it would take to allow me to be there.

But I have no rights.

My heart feels like it's bleeding out. I rest my forehead against the cool pane of glass in front of me and ask, "How is Mari?" Fully knowing, she'll be heartbroken.

Our beautiful, talented, and vibrant woman is missing.

Gone.

"She's barely holding it together." I appreciate her honesty.

"Poppy?"

"Oblivious."

"I should be there, Babs." I need to see her, cuddle her, and protect her. "I want to leave right now!" I can't keep the rising panic out of my tone.

I should have protected Jade.

I couldn't.

I failed them.

"You're not thinking logically, Owen. There is no way you will be able to focus on the long drive to us, and what if you have an accident? We need you safe, Owen, and if you turn up here in a frantic mess, looking more upset than you should be... you are just the nanny, Owen..." She takes a deep breath in. "...You're not family. It's awful, I know."

I'm not family.

Knowing she's right, I can't get the words out to agree with her, hating how helpless I feel. And alone.

"I'm assuming Gregor and the team know?" My throat now aching with the amount of stress coursing through my body.

"Today's display was cancelled. They're distraught with worry." Her voice cracks. "Gregor hasn't called you because, well, unlike me, they all signed an Official Secrets Act when they joined up, Owen. But I didn't. I had to call. I just had to let you know."

I cover my mouth with my hand. This can't be happening. "Oh my God, Babs. I can't live without her." I have to push the shocked words out of my mouth, my legs almost giving way from under me.

"We know how much you love her. Just sit tight and I promise I'll call you as soon as I hear anything, Owen." Her voice barely audible.

Robotically, I agree with her, ask her to give Poppy a kiss from me, say goodbye, then end the call.

And my world blows apart.

Because of *him*.

Clouded in anger, I spin around on the balls of my feet, snarling at the man who destroyed my life. The need to kill the man behind the desk runs deep in my veins. "What did you do?" I scream.

Scowling at me, he shakes his head in confused. Got to hand it to him. He's a great actor.

"I still had one day left." I fly across the room, but his bodyguard leaps forward, preventing me from smashing the face of the man I despise to pieces.

Smirking, Richard casually replies, "I don't know what you are referring to, Owen."

Pushing myself against the wall of muscle to get to him, like a rabid dog, I throw myself around on a mission to kill the man who promised me ten days to find the money and keep her out of it.

And I failed.

He's punishing me for something my father did.

And now she's missing.

"Where is she?"

"I'd love to help, but I genuinely do not know." Richard slowly moves away from his desk, then confidently folds his arms across his chest.

Raging, I keep trying to get past his guard. I give him a hard shoulder push but he's as solid as a mountain, and stands firm, barely moving when I shove, scratch and punch him, launching myself with all my strength. With another foot on top of me and as wide as a house, I don't stand a chance.

"You bastard, you knew I would fail," I spit, exasperated.

Defeated, I push myself off the guard's chest and fire words of hate in his direction.

Richard smiles deviously. "Now, now, we're not in a playground, Owen. No name calling." He rubs his chin in thought. "I can't lie. You surprised me. Few men would turn up on my doorstep. You're ballsy, I'll give you that."

Frantically pacing, pulse racing, heart pounding, flesh burning, I pull, loosening my tie, then undo the top button. I'm burning up.

"Where is she?" I ask again.

He holds his hands up as if under duress. "I promise. I'm not responsible."

"Fuck this." I turn to leave.

What has he done with her?

"And you can forget my offer to work for you. You didn't keep your end of the bargain."

He easily replies, "Oh, but there was still one day left to find the rest of the money, Owen. I haven't touched your girl."

"You're a liar," I roar, pulling open the door.

His words hauntingly chase me down the stairs as I run as fast as I can out of his home. "If you renege on the offer, Owen. You are still due me one point five million," his voice echoes out behind me.

"Fuck you." I dash across the marble hallway.

"Owen." I'm startled when a faint feminine voice calls my name.

Stopping me in my tracks, I search the cavernous entryway of the house every member of the Sanderson family live in together.

Camilla.

Standing off to the side, Camilla looks as white as a sheet and ever smaller than I saw her last. Her bathrobe is pulled so tight around her, highlighting her frame that's as thin as a drainpipe.

"He didn't keep his end of the bargain," I yell at her, my voice cracking. It echoes round the bowl-shaped space. "And you know he's lying about Dad committing suicide." I move to her quickly, stepping in close to her face. "Did you know he was planning to run away?" I whisper through my clenched jaw. "Dad?"

Her face crumbles and wordlessly, she nods.

I was right.

I look up over my shoulder to the upstairs balcony. Standing wide, with hands in their pockets, Richard and Gideon watch our interaction.

Moving to the shell of her ear, I lower my voice. "They've taken everything from us. You should take your son and run. You and Sean are not safe. Do you know where Jade is?"

"I don't," she sobs, shaking her head.

"Traitor," I hiss between my lips. "You're just like them."

Glaring upward, furious with myself for believing I could trust them, I leave broken, destroyed, knowing the woman I love is missing, most likely gone.

Nothing makes sense without her.

I was too late.

I couldn't save her.

To keep her safe, I should have stayed away from her. Stayed away from everyone.

My mother was right. I am a worthless piece of shit. I don't deserve good things in my life, or happiness.

Everything I touch turns to shit.

I don't deserve her and Poppy.

Running out of the house, unable to catch my breath, I fall into the abyss of self-hatred and heartbreak.

It's like that feeling when you can't reach the bottom of the pool. I'm drowning and don't know how to stay afloat, so I do the only thing I know how to do. The thing that everyone expects of me.

I find the solution to my problems in the bottom of a bottle and drink myself to oblivion.

CHAPTER THIRTY-FIVE

OWEN – 1 DAY LATER

Instantly awake, I'm dripping in a blast of freezing water at a temperature I can only imagine you endure in the Arctic.

"What the fuck?" I gasp for air like a fish out of water and wipe my water covered face.

"Get up." The voice of a man I can't make out demands I move.

I blink several times, trying to focus on who is speaking.

A black figure stands before me.

Shit, am I dead? Is this the grim reaper coming to take me away?

Head pounding, mouth drier than sandpaper, I let out a groan.

"I said get up." Death kicks me in the shin.

It can't be death, or I wouldn't feel that, would I? Can you feel anything when you're dead?

Because the hollow pain in my chest and damaged knuckles, tell me otherwise. I am most definitely alive, and still in the hell I can't escape.

Everything hurts.

She's gone.

Desperate to make my vision focus on the tall blurry figure, I narrow them, then relax as my bleary eyes finally figure out who the man is standing in the living room of the home I no longer own.

"Knox?" I ask, confused why Lincoln's father is here.

"Pull yourself together and meet me in the kitchen." He says authoritatively, then leaves the living room.

"Shit." I push myself up off the couch and stagger. My stomach flips. I feel sick and hot, although I'm shivering from the water I'm drenched in, assuming that's what was in the black bucket now sitting empty on the floor.

I slide my phone off the coffee table and check my messages.

Still no update.

She's missing.

Presumed dead.

I fight hard to control my emotions that I tried to drown in the bottom of a bottle last night. On the brink of tears, I sway on my feet and rub my head that feels as if it's full of dust.

Having spent the last day self-medicating myself with liquor, drowning in my heartache, I realize no amount of whiskey could ever drink the ghost of her away.

She's haunted every dream, every memory. My sorrow has now transformed into bone deep despair.

My life has no meaning and I have no future.

I killed Poppy's mother and didn't deserve Jade's love.

I ruin everything.

Finally staggering into the kitchen, I find Knox, dressed head to toe in black, fitting for his last name; Black. His feet crossed at the ankles, arms folded across his chest, leaning casually against the kitchen island, he looks every bit the successful businessman he is.

Feeling numb, wishing he wasn't here, I say a sheepish, "Hi."

He holds back no punches, going for the jugular. "So, is this your new life plan, to drink yourself to death?"

"Seems like it," I mutter, scrambling about the kitchen cabinets, trying to find a clean glass to fill with water.

I stay facing the sink but can feel his eyes burning through the back of my head as I down a glass full and heave as it hits my stomach, and then I vomit it all up.

Having had nothing to eat for days, my stomach spasms over and over.

I'm running on empty. My stomach aches and groans as it disagrees with my recent life choices.

Knox throws a dish towel at my head, and I use it to clean my mouth and nose.

Tentatively standing, I hold my stomach. "Did you come here to tell me I'm a worthless son of a bitch? Because if that's the case, then get in line." I hate how pathetic and broken I sound.

"Drop the act, Owen."

Ouch, that stings. "It's fucking true."

Tutting, Knox waggles his finger at me. "Watch your tongue, son. You may still be drunk, suffering from grief, heartbreak, and losing all of this." He points to the ceiling, gesturing to the roof over my head. "But that does not mean that you forget who you are with me, so rein it in and listen." He takes a deep breath. "Lincoln and Jacob told me everything. Including that you made a deal and agreed to work for Richard." He shakes his head in disapproval.

I'm so ashamed of every aspect of my life that my face flushes with heat.

"I'm so sorry about Jade, Owen, but they will find her."

I stare at him, not believing a word he says.

"It's all over the national news now that they have finally released a press statement and they have helicopters searching. It's only a matter of hours. I have confidence."

"Richard did this," I say through clenched teeth.

"If I find out he did, he will pay, Owen." A powerful man, true to his word, I believe him.

"How much are you still due to him?" he asks.

"One point five million." Now I feel sick to my stomach for a different reason.

"Unlock your phone and give it to me." His voice demanding, I fish it out of the pocket of the dress pants I'm still wearing from yesterday morning.

He frowns, navigating around the touch screen to find what he's after. I hear a call ringing in the earpiece. He then taps the speaker phone icon and waits for the call to connect.

Who is he calling?

"Ah, Owen, so nice to hear from you." Richard's slimy voice drips down the phone.

I go to speak, but Knox holds up his finger, telling me to keep quiet.

"Not Owen, Knox Black."

There's a pause before Richard speaks, "Ah, Knox, how nice to hear from you. How is that beautiful wife and ever-growing brood of children keeping?"

"Piss off, Dick. I'm not here to make small talk. Send me your bank account details." I almost laugh at Knox's confidence and the nickname he used.

"Why?" His voice goes higher, as if he's genuinely taken aback.

"To pay off Henry's debt. Not that Owen should pay it.

It's not his debt to pay. You're a bully. Now just give me the fucking details and I'll pay it."

Oh no, he can't let him pay my father's debt for me. I'm not worth it.

I put my hand up, telling him to stop, but he ignores my refusal to let him help me.

"And if I don't?" Richard plays with Knox, as if teasing him. "That debt is not yours to pay."

"That boy is like a son to me. And may I fucking remind you who you are talking to? My father gave you the money to start Sanderson Shipping. So, fuck off with the theatrics. Text Owen the bank details and it will be paid within an hour. And I want a letter of confirmation outlining the total debt paid. He's not coming to work for you, and I if I ever hear of you harassing another member of my family again, I will have the cops all over that shipping yard of yours faster that you can say *boo*. Now, whatever you have done with Jade, either release her or let the cops know where she is. Right. Fucking. Now. It's been good doing business with you." Before Richard can respond, Knox ends the call.

Feeling my hangover mixing with a combination of gratitude and admiration, I grip onto the wooden topped island to stop me falling over. "Why would you do that for me?"

Knox sighs as if he shouldn't have to explain. "Owen, I have watched you struggle your entire life. I was so proud of you for running off to start again. You've always been a fine man. A man with good intentions, and someone I admire. You just never saw it in yourself. I hear you have new dreams, and I care about you too much to let someone take that away from you. You deserve to find love with someone who knocks your socks off. I watched you with Jade at the funeral and I knew, just from seeing you together, that she is perfect for you. And little Poppy? You know I'm not Archie and Hamish's father, but I saw how you were with Poppy down on the beach. She's stolen your heart, hasn't she? Just like those boys did to me. You're a great stepfather. A great partner. And you deserve happiness. So, sober up, clean yourself up, get your shit together, then drive to get your girl. That call is coming. They are going to find her. I know they will."

"She's been missing for almost two days," I say, my voice defeated.

"Then get on your knees and pray to the Greek god Elpis; the god of hope." He gives me a gentle smile. "That's all we have left. Hope."

I suck in a breath.

He adds, "Gather your belongings. I will have my people from the hotel come down with a moving truck to take your furniture to Jacob's. You have nice furniture. Don't let Richard take everything, Owen. And if there is anything from the house...." He points at my family home up through the trees. "Drop me a text over the next couple of days and let me know."

"I want nothing. And we ended up trashing most of the house looking for Dad's money."

A low laugh rumbles in his chest. "Lincoln told me what you guys had been up to, but I suppose it will give Richard and Gideon's monkeys something to do. From what I've heard, they are experts at cleans ups." He shakes his head. His eyes crinkle at the side with concern. "I wish you'd told me sooner. I would have made sure you got to keep your trust fund and paid the ten million for you."

"It was my responsibility."

"Keep telling yourself that, son, but it wasn't. With your parents no longer around, you're my responsibility now,

Owen. You call me anytime, day or night. No matter what." He reaches for me and pulls me into his arms, wrapping me in his gigantic frame and warmth I never received from my own father.

I struggle to hold it together when he says, "You're family, Owen. When you need me, I'll be there. Always." He slaps me on the back, twice, then, pushing me out of our embrace, he grabs my biceps. "Shower, sort your shit out, and go up to the house and take photos of anything you want to keep. Certificates and anything else that's important."

I can get rid of all the photos.

As if reading my mind, Knox says, "If you have no photos, how will your new family know your heritage or what your folks looked like? It's important. Stick them away in a box, but don't live with any regrets." He throws me a knowing wink. "And send me your bank details as well as Richard's. Lincoln told me you had to postpone your start date for your new job, but I will not have you struggling."

"I will pay back every penny," I promise.

He gently smiles. "You're ten times the man your father was, Owen. Don't let his wrong doings hold you back from the life you deserve."

I can't move forward without her.

A dinging text alert sings through my phone.

"That will be The Dick," Knox says, making me want to chuckle, but I'm unsure how I do that because I feel nothing but pain and despair.

Knox makes a note of the details. "He won't bother you anymore. You have my word." I figure Knox has information on Richard to keep him away, making me admire Knox even more than I did before.

Note to self: be more like Knox. He's a great man.

I walk him to the front door and thank him again and just as he's about to jump into his black Maclaren P1 sports car, another text comes through on my phone, making my eyes bug out of my head.

Knox clenches his jaw, making it twitch. "Tell Satan to leave you alone."

It's not him. It's a text from Mari with five words on it, and it changes everything.

"They found her. She's alive." I read them out loud.

Unable to stay upright, I clutch my chest in shock. My shoulders hit the wall and I slide down it as Knox runs back to me.

It was too much of a coincidence for them to find her, just as Knox agreed to clear my father's debt.

Richard made her disappear.

But now she's back.

He will pay for this.

Knox already has his phone by his ear. "Hunter, we need your private jet."

In no time, I'm showered, and being flown in Knox's brother in laws private plane to the nearest airfield, then driven straight to the hospital in Wales, with Jade's lucky poppy stone clutched firmly in my hand.

I have no idea what I will find when I arrive, but it doesn't matter,

She's alive.

CHAPTER THIRTY-SIX

JADE

A steady beep wakes me from what feels like the best sleep I have had in months.

So good, I can't remember going to bed last night, or if I remembered to lock the front door.

Did I?

Not fully awake yet, I don't understand the artificial smell of antiseptic I'm surrounded by.

Did I do the cleaning yesterday?

My head is fuzzy. I don't remember.

Why can't I remember?

I try to open my heavy eyelids that feel like anchors, but I struggle.

Attempting to try again, I crack them open and the fluorescent lighting so harsh it forces me to close them.

"She's waking up, again." I hear a warbled sounding voice.

"Jade, baby." I recognize that voice in an instant.

Owen.

"Sweetheart."

My mom.

I groan as I try to move, stopping when a sharp pulling pain pinches my back.

What's going on? Where am I?

Then I'm pulled under into a black inky sea.

Like a newly formed butterfly, I flutter my eyelids, hoping they take flight and open fully.

I'm so tired, and my body feels like a dead weight.

"Will she stay awake this time?" I hear a woman's voice ask.

I want to reply and ask who is waking up, but my head is pounding.

My mind focuses on the firm tone of Owen's voice. "Her body needs the rest. She's exhausted."

I don't know how long it is until I try to pull open my eyes again and when I finally do, I'm greeted by an overwhelming sight of Owen on one side of me and my mom on the other. It's only when I glance down that I realize I'm in a hospital bed.

How the hell did I get here?

"Hey, sweetheart." My mom's eyes are watery, worry lines etch deep across her forehead.

Blinking, I look around the room and a strange sense of panic riots through me.

"Do you remember anything?" my mom asks softly.

"No." I cough, my throat dry. The rasp of it muffled by the oxygen mask I'm wearing.

I reach up to remove it, but Owen does it for me. "Hey,

Hotshot." He smiles, but I can see the concern written all over his face as he lifts the mask carefully up over my head.

"What happened?" I cough again. The pain in my back and shoulders hitting me from every angle makes me moan in discomfort.

"I'll let Owen explain everything," Mom says as she leans down and kisses my cheek. "I thought I'd lost you." She pauses as if she's trying to push down her emotions. "I'm going to give you two some space, and I'll let the doctor know you are awake." She squeezes my hand before she leaves us.

"I'm so thirsty," I croak.

Always looking after me, Owen helps my stiff body to sit upright, and I groan as pain makes itself know in places I didn't know were possible. Owen then tips a cup of cold water to my lips and my mouth and tongue jump with joy as it hits them like a tidal wave. Water has never tasted so delicious.

Leaning forward, Owen kisses my forehead. "I thought I'd lost you, too. I love you so much." My body may hurt from physical pain, but Owen's voice sounds tortured, making my heart ache for him.

But wait, lost me?

"What happened? Why can't I remember how I got here? Oh my God, where is Poppy?" Panic hits me like a blazar jet as I search the private hospital room for my baby girl.

"She's fine," Owen reassures me. "She's safe with Aunt Babs."

Letting out a sigh of relief, I realize that my chest feels bruised, like I've been in a fight with a raging bull. I pull my hand to it and notice the IV in the back of my hand.

"Tell me why I am here, Owen?" I beg, already feeling exhausted and confused.

He clears his throat. "Your jet had a flameout."

"Did it?"

"You had to eject."

I punched out. "Where?"

"Over the mountains."

"What mountains?"

"The Welsh Mountains, you ejected over Snowdon. You were missing for a couple of days."

I rub my head, frowning. "Why don't I remember?" My head pounding. It feels as if it's been battered by a sledgehammer.

"They think you hit the side of your head as you ejected. Your helmet saved your life. You have a severe concussion and you've been in and out of consciousness. You are so lucky; you could have broken your neck or your back."

Owen keeps filling me in on my injuries. "Your shoulders are badly bruised from the harness straps." The violent force of ejecting can be fatal. He's right, I am very lucky.

"Are my collarbones okay?" That's one of the most common ejection injuries.

"Nothing broken. You've had an MRI, and I read your chart." He smiles cheekily. "The important muscles of your neck and lower thoracic spine, will be tender. The doctors think you could have some damage between your spinal discs, but nothing physiotherapy won't fix." That's a lot of important information I may have to ask about again as I struggle to process it.

I let the details simmer. "You said I was missing for two days?"

"Yeah." He confirms.

I feel hot and bothered by that information.

"Then they brought you here to the hospital in Wales."

"Why don't I remember being in the mountains?" I rub my head.

Owen pops an eyebrow. "You have a severe concussion, Jade. They couldn't find you because your personal locator was tampered with."

If that had been working properly, they would have found me almost immediately.

"Why would someone do that to me?" My head is a jumbled mess. I bounce to the next question. I have so many. "Who found me?"

"Mountain rescue. You've been all over the news."

I feel dizzy. "Oh God, the tabloids will love this." I rub my forehead. I'll never be able to keep them at bay now.

"Blake did a press statement outside the hospital earlier today. It's official. I'm the fiancé." He smiles widely.

"You won't be allowed to continue living in with me now." I laugh, then grimace as my body aches from the small vibrations of movement.

"We'll get married quicker then," he states confidently.

I hold my hand up. "My ring," I say, aghast. I must have lost it during the crash; the crash I remember nothing of.

"It's here." Owen fishes his dog tag out from under his tee shirt and nestled between the two tags is my ring strung from the chain. "They found it in your bra."

I have no recollection of putting it there.

Watching Owen sliding my ring off the thin gold chain, he refastens his necklace, then holds the gold and emerald gem between his fingers. "Shall we?"

I scrunch my nose up to say yes and smile.

He looks worried when he says, "But I have one

condition." The mood in the room drops a few degrees as Owen's demeanor changes.

"What's that?"

"I have to tell you something first. But I'm not sure you're ready for more information."

I worry about what he might have to say. Is something medically wrong with me? Am I paralyzed and haven't realized it? I wiggle my toes to check I can feel them. Relief overwhelms me as I feel the sensation of my toes rubbing together. "Tell me," I say boldly.

"It was my fault your plane crashed."

I scoff. "Not possible." Then he tells me the shit show his life turned into after I left Castleview Cove, and I struggle to retain all the details.

I don't remember his silent episodes or the calls from his friends telling me he was sick. In fact, I don't remember days before my apparent crash. Not one memory. The last thing I remember is driving back from Castleview Cove.

It's as if someone opened up my brain and scooped them out.

It's scary knowing my usual pin sharp intellect is like blended pea soup.

When he's finished, ignoring the ache in my shoulder when I move, I reach up and brush the scruff of his beard. "I don't blame you, Owen. For any of it. You've been through so much. I am so sorry I wasn't there to help you."

"I should be the one telling you that. You are made from titanium. You're bulletproof."

"I'm unbreakable."

The love he has for me makes me feel indestructible.

"We're unbreakable," he says with confidence. His eyes soften around the edges as his shoulders sag with relief. "I think Richard must have hired someone to tamper with your jet and personal locator beacon," he whispers. "I will never forgive myself for getting you involved in the mess."

"There will be an investigation," I reassure him. "They will find whoever did this to me, but it could also have very well been an accident, Owen." But if someone is responsible, and they find out who, then there will be a prison sentence awaiting them. "None of this is your fault," I say again, hoping he hears me this time. "When are we getting married?"

Owen laughs as I inject my lighthearted question amongst the madness.

Leaning closer, Owen kisses me gently on my lips. "As soon as you are well."

"I love you, Owen. I don't want to wait." Then I see his knuckles. "What did you do?"

"I had a fight with a stone floor."

"Shame it wasn't Richard's face." I make him chuckle.

"That might still happen."

A bright voice chimes from the doorway. "Isn't this wonderful? She's awake." Owen moves to the side and a vibrant, smiling doctor, dressed in bubblegum pink scrubs, moves cheerily into the room and then picks up my chart. "Now let's check you over."

After what feels like hours, Dr. Griffiths, who insists I call her Bethan, is satisfied with my vitals, finally says, "If you remain stable for the next day or so, then you will be discharged. I am referring you to the physio to help strengthen your back muscles and, apart from the bruising, it will be like it never happened."

According to my brain, it didn't.

"You can return to active flying duties once you pass your Air Force back to work medical." I don't want to think about getting back in a plane. My body feels battered. "But you will most likely be off work for months with your concussion." The doctor lays her hand on my shoulder. "You were very lucky. Someone was watching over you, Ms. Sommers." Her warm eyes make my body relax.

I am very lucky.

She gives my hand a gentle pat, and just as she's leaving the room, Bethan turns and adds, "And you'll be happy to hear that the baby is just fine. You have a lucky baby, too."

Owen makes a noise I've never heard before and I fix my gaze on him, worried I've missed something important. My brain is still on its own time frame, so I may have.

Owen takes my hand in his "You're pregnant, Hotshot." His voice is so soft and low that I have to ask him to repeat what he said.

"We are having a baby." His grin is wider than a mile.

"How did this happen?" I ask, in a daze.

My mom, who is sitting on the far side of the room, Bethan, who is still standing in the doorway, and Owen burst out laughing at my shock.

"Well, when a man…" the doctor begins to explain.

I wave my hand at her to stop. "I know that. I mean, I had a contraceptive shot before I went to Cyprus."

"It's not always one hundred percent effective and extra contraception is recommended for the first seven days."

"Right," I reply in a daze, as I try calculating. It takes me a minute or two to work out that it was four days after I had the shot that we had sex for the first time. Owen must have super sperm. "So, I'm about twelve weeks?" I might cry, I'm so happy. I want everything with Owen and we are going to be a little family together.

"We made our little bean in Cyprus." He winks.

I reach out to grab his hand and with the other, I lay it over my stomach. "A miracle from the Greek goddess,

Aphrodite," I whisper, then worry, asking two questions in quick succession. "And everything is okay? Are you sure?"

Owen squeezes my hand, leans down, kisses me on the lips and says, "You had a scan and everything is perfect, Hotshot."

"I've not had any morning sickness." I suffered terribly with that when I was pregnant with Poppy.

"Maybe it's a boy." Owen soothes my concerns with a soft voice and caring touch. "Girls cause chaos and mayhem," he jokes.

Emotional, hormonal, and physically drained, I burst into tears at the realization of what we both could have lost had everything gone differently.

As soon as I am out of this hospital, I'm going to celebrate the life I still have and the new life growing within me.

"I need to see my Pop-a-doodle," I say to Owen as I wipe the tears off my face.

"She'll be here in half an hour."

"Then everything will be perfect."

"And we'll be complete." Owen lays his hand over my stomach. "My family." He lifts his hand to reveal my poppy stone sitting perfectly on top of the bedsheet.

"Our lucky family," I correct him.

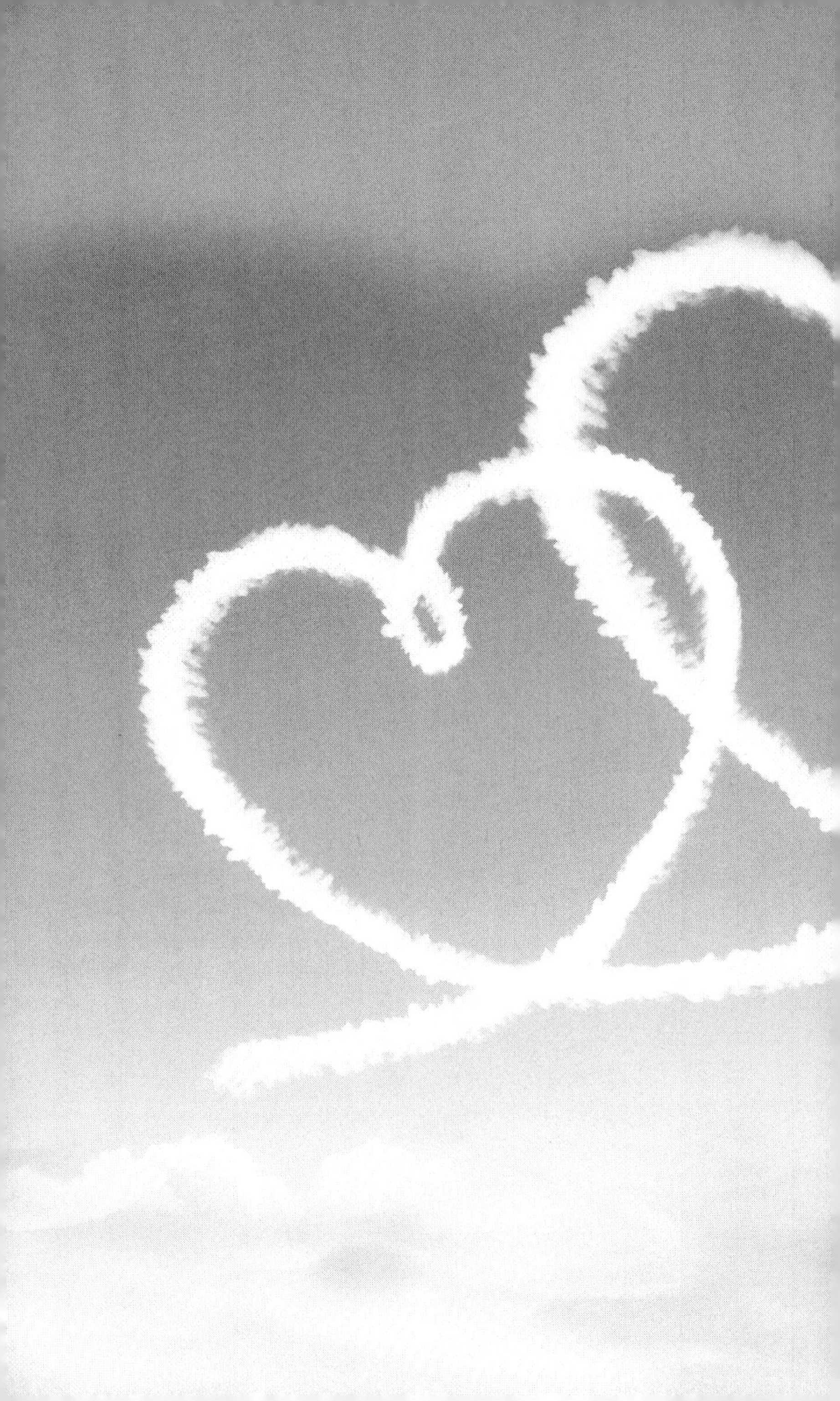

CHAPTER THIRTY-SEVEN

OWEN – FIVE WEEKS LATER

It didn't take the aviation criminal investigators long to piece together the sequence of events that led to Jade's plane crash.

The CCTV footage from the perimeter of the station and from inside the hangar revealed the most unlikely of suspects and one we hadn't even considered.

Cobra.

Using an old key to let himself through the abandoned crash gate at the far end of the base, he used his old pass to get inside the hangar, and then tampered with the fuel gauges.

He knew exactly what he was doing to show there was more fuel in the tanks than there actually was. He then entered the changing rooms to sabotage Jade's personal locator beacon.

Having worked within the squadron for years, he knew the inner workings of the fast jet and the equipment.

Mid-crime, he mindlessly pushed up his sleeves and

there was no disguising his distinguishing snake tattoo on his forearm that was easily picked up by the cameras.

On a mission to seek revenge against Jade, he blamed her for his demise and losing his job. The cruelty of his hatred toward Jade knew no bounds.

The police informed Jade that he is likely to serve a minimum of eighteen years for his attempt to murder.

The hate I feel for that man will die on the day he does, but it soothes my nerves a little, knowing he will be behind bars for a really long time.

Jade still cannot recall what happened on the days leading up to the crash, the crash itself, or the days following, although she's been listening to the Mayday recording every day on a mission to spark something hidden deep within her brain.

She's praying something will trigger her memory as she's desperate to remember.

It hasn't so far, and some days she still struggles with processing even the smallest of tasks.

Frustrated, the doctors have assured her it will take weeks, even months before her memory problems and fatigue resolve themselves.

I, on the other hand, am relieved she doesn't remember and that she's getting the time off to rest and cook our little bean to perfection.

She survived a horrific trauma. Her memory loss is a protection of sorts, and to survive in such a miraculous way, as well as protecting our baby too, is nothing short of an astonishing feat. Someone was watching over her that day.

The doctors reckon that because she was unconscious when she landed on a soft patch way up high in the mountains, her lifeless body didn't tense up like it may have done when landing under pressure, which could have led to serious injury. Then, of course, the vast expanse of parachute kept her warm for the many hours she was missing.

It's nothing short of a miracle and I couldn't be more grateful.

Jade is still signed off work for another couple of months and as the news broke of our romantic involvement, I was no longer allowed to live-in on camp, so we rented a place a mile away from base, and only a couple of houses down from Gregor's.

In hindsight, we should have hired a moving company, but Jade's entire team turned up to help us on moving day, which meant Jade didn't have to lift a finger, not that I would have let her anyway.

We know our rental is a short-term solution. In the meantime, because we have both had grief, trauma, and crazy drama happen to both of us the last few months, all we are asking for is some peace. At least until the baby comes.

Which is wild.

I'm going to be a dad.

Not that I am not one already. I cannot wait for our baby to arrive and complete our little family.

Right now, it's early in the morning and I'm going through this morning's mail, and my hand lands on a handwritten envelope addressed to me.

Curiously, I rip it open and frown as I stare down out a two-page letter.

Dear Owen,

I trust this letter finds you well and that your beautiful family is thriving in England.

I know you won't believe me when I tell you, but I'm sorry for all the pain and hurt my husband and his father put you through.

For over ten years I have lived a life I was never happy in, and you may think it was foolish of me falling pregnant with Sean when I was younger, being forced into marrying Gideon, but believe me, I have paid the price for my foolishness every day since.

I know we have never been close, and it's too late for us now, but I do wish you all the very best with your new life. With Mom and Dad leading the way, neither of us ever stood a chance.

I left him, Owen.

I couldn't take it anymore.

I have started a new life, somewhere far away from the man who has made my life a living hell.

It will have been forty-eight hours since I wrote you this letter and I will be long gone.

Please thank Lincoln for supplying me with your address and bank details.

I hope what I placed in your account is enough to jump start your new dreams that I really want you to chase. It's yours after all.

With the life insurance, I also sent checks to each one of the employees from Castleview

Printing Press to compensate them for their job losses with a letter of apology from both of us. I'm sure Gideon won't miss what I took to give our employees what they deserved.

You and I are good people. We knew what our father did was wrong. So, let's not make the same mistakes he did.

The deeds for the Castle are in a safety deposit box at the bank on the high street in Castleview Cove. I gave an envelope to Lincoln with the code to access it.

I signed it back over to you. Sell the place and use the money for you and your new family.

Good luck.

Keep dreaming and dream big.

Be happy, Owen.

Camilla & Sean

P.S. I found evidence on Gideon's laptop instructing a hit on Mom and Dad, along with many more files, correspondence, and shipping slips. Keep watching the news. You may like what you see ;)

P.P.S. In years to come, if you ever get the urge to look me up. Ask Walter Forrester, your PI. I've heard he's a master at finding people.

Not sure if I believe the letter is from my sister, I throw it down on top of the breakfast bar and dig my phone out of my pocket.

Taking care of my girls has been a full-time job, so I haven't been able to start with the finance consultancy, which means I know exactly how much money... or lack of it, I have in my bank.

"Holy fucking shit," I gasp, grabbing the edge of the breakfast bar from fear of falling over.

"Everything okay?" Jade calls from the living room as I continue to stare at the ten million pounds sitting on top of the money I already had.

I stutter, "Yeah, it's just, the, um, utility bills went up again," I lie, unable to stop looking at my screen.

I text Lincoln.

> ME:
>
> Did Camilla leave an envelope with you?

I chew on my thumbnail impatiently waiting for him to respond as the bubbles bounce across the screen, showing he's replying.

> LINCOLN:
>
> She did yeah. I planned to give it to you in two weeks when you are in Scotland for a visit. Looking forward to having a beer with you.

Holy cow.

It's true.

On unsteady feet, Poppy waddles through to the kitchen and grabs my leg, then stretches her arms over her head. "Uh, uh," she beams at me, asking me in her own language for me to pick her up. Bending at the knees, I scoop her up and rest her on my hip.

"Look what Aunt Camilla sent Owen," I whisper, then hold up the phone to show her, making a shocked-looking face and Poppy mimics me. Her eyes flaring, she makes a funny O shape with her mouth making me chuckle. She's been copy catting facial expressions for the past few weeks and it's the cutest thing to witness.

Tapping the notes app open on my phone, I pull up the list of people I borrowed money from, and at the top of it sits the man who has been the best father figure I never asked for, Knox Black.

I make a plan then work out what I have left.

"I know exactly what I want to do with the rest of the money, Poppadom."

CHAPTER THIRTY-EIGHT

JADE - TWO WEEKS LATER

"What are we doing here?" I look up at the closed air base of Licharty, situated ten miles outside of Castleview Cove.

Owen taps the side of his nose, then throws me a cheeky wink as a security guard appears from behind the locked metal gates.

Throwing him a wave, the guard opens them for us and Owen drives through.

Checking the side mirror, I find the security guard relocking the gates behind us, which has me asking about a million questions in rapid succession as Owen drives down through the hangars and out on the open stretch of the out of operation airfield.

Smiling smugly, Owen ignores every one of them.

With Poppy fast asleep in the back of the car, Owen leaps out of the driver's door and runs around to open mine.

I scowl with confusion, "I'm not getting out unless you tell me why we are here." I haven't flown in a plane since the crash, and since the news of my pregnancy, I don't intend to fly in my fast jet until I get the all clear from the doctor.

"Get out or you will spoil the surprise."

"Surprise?" I question excitedly, unbuckling my seat belt, taking his hand to help me out of my green SUV.

He pulls me slowly behind him, guiding me into the middle of the runway.

"What do you think?" He motions to the enormous space.

"I think it's a recently closed down airfield, and that makes me sad." I hate what the Air Force is doing to cut costs. Closing air bases, merging trades, and retiring squadrons. It's a very different Air Force than the one I joined two decades ago and, I've realized recently, not one I want to be part of anymore.

"It's not closed down, it will reopen soon." He bounces on his heels as if pleased with himself.

"Okay." I let go of his hand and place my hands on my hips. "Spill the tea. What has you buzzing like a queen bee?"

With open arms, he motions to the surrounding space. "Welcome to Hotshot Flying School and Outdoor Adventure Training."

"I'm sorry what?"

"Welcome to Hotshot—"

"Oh, I heard you," I interrupt him. "Are you for real?" Flabbergasted, I spin on the balls of my feet and look around, realizing the enormity of his words. "But how?" I know he gave everything to Richard.

"My trust fund turned up. With interest."

I gape at him with my mouth open. If I don't close it soon, I'll catch flies from the estuary at the end of the runway.

"So, you bought an airfield?"

"I bought *us* an airfield. A business." Like an excitable puppy, he points over to the high-low ropes area and the physical training block. Then the hangars, cabins, parking, toilet blocks, and houses. He has plans for it all. "We will run adventure weekends for schools. Run high-low rope instructor courses. Set up a flying school. A mentoring program for young people who come from less fortunate backgrounds to help them work toward apprenticeships in engineering and administration. Give them a better start in life with skills to help them along the way. We can do weekend or week-long retreats for schools and I was thinking that we could reopen the nursery that the base closed down to offer flexible sessions for moms who work unsociable hours."

His excitement bubbling over like a hot cauldron, I can't contain myself anymore as I launch myself at him and smack a kiss over his mouth. "I'm getting my own flying school?" I smile against his mouth.

"Yes. Did I do the right thing?"

"Holy shit, yes." I step back and look around. There is so much to organize and the small fire of excitement that was merely a flicker in my belly a moment ago turns into a full-on ball of energy enough to start a forest blaze. "All—"

"Five hundred hectares." Owen finished my sentence.

"Wow. All five hundred hectares of rightness." I can't stop grinning.

Speechless, I look around the area that goes on for miles. "How many family quarters are there?" I ask.

"Four hundred. I was thinking we should keep half and sell half. Plus, there are twenty blocks of single living accommodation. I think we should sell the family quarters and blocks to a developer. That will give us more money to buy you a dozen or so of those little aerobatic planes."

"A dozen?" I exclaim.

"Yeah. I've offered some of your teammates jobs."

"You are kidding me?"

"Gregor is a firm, yes." He nods, confirming he's being serious.

"They won't release him."

"By the time we are ready to open in twelve months, he'll be getting ready to retire. I'll have all the qualifications I need to instruct classes and training. It's perfect timing. Plus, we'll have our little bean by then."

"You're crazy." I'm also thinking he's an actual genius. This is an epic plan beyond anything I could ever have imagined.

He tilts his head to the side and looks at me. "About you. I'm crazy about you."

He drapes his arms over my shoulders. "This is your retirement plan. You don't have to leave the Air Force, but when you do, this place will be waiting for you. You can offer extreme acrobatic experiences. Teach people how to fly. Whatever you want."

Our new Wing Commander inferred that it's more than likely I will receive a payout to compensate me for my crash, and I would have an excellent case to submit for retiring early.

Owen made the impossible possible.

Although I can't get the cost of maintaining an airfield out of my head. "This place cost way more than your trust fund."

"You'd be surprised at how little I paid for this place, and we can charge for plane landing fees and parking overnight. Pro golfers from all over the world travel to be here for the Championship Cup. They all bring their jets when they tour. Since this place closed, the nearest airfield is over an hour away. They will park up here in their private jets. Hunter, Lincoln's uncle, who is a pro golfer, already wants his own hangar to hire all year round. The infrastructure of the place works for what you want to do and what I want to do. We have a few planes to buy and half a million should cover it. I'll go on your recommendation, though." He places a kiss on my forehead as I stare up in wonder at this magnificent man. "Camilla signed the deeds of the castle over to me. I sold it to The National Trust." He leans closer to my ear and whispers, "For twenty million. I squeezed every penny I could get out of them, knowing that it will only increase in value." He looks off to the side. "If I had thought about doing that when Richard was after my father's debt, it would have saved me a whole heap of drama." He scowls, as if mad at himself for not thinking straight while he was under pressure. "And I have an even bigger surprise."

"Yeah?"

"Get back in the car, Hotshot."

I can't sit still as Owen drives back out of the base and into Castleview Cove.

Wobbling down the cobbled streets, my wide car barely makes it through the narrow stone port leading to the beach.

In an instant, I know where he is taking me. "You didn't?"

"I did."

A glow of happiness fills me with warmth. "You bought it?" I sigh, swooning, as he parks up outside the quaint stone beach house with a white picket fence and matching shutters.

"I bought the adjoining one next door, too."

"Two?"

"Yes. One is perfect for a holiday home, two joined together is a home." He points to them.

Joy bubbles in my heart and on a laugh and a sob, I blubber like a big baby.

Still sitting in the car, he holds up the keys. "Want to take a look?"

"Hell yes, I do." I grab them out of his hand and jump out of the car.

Slamming the passenger door shut, I take a moment to check out the view I will have from the upstairs windows. "Wow. Now that's a view."

"It really is."

A glance to my left confirms he's not looking at the lapping sea, the golden beach or the cobbled harbor that leads to a pier. He's looking at me.

"I want to start the process to leave the Air Force. I think it's time for me to retire," I say confidently.

I don't want to spend time away from him, Poppy, and the baby while deployed, when I could have the best of family life and an incredible career here.

My pipe dream turned into reality.

Owen's face breaks into a face spitting grin. "I hoped you might say that."

"I told you this is what I wanted."

"I made your dreams come true?"

"You waved a magic wand," I whisper in awe at my handsome man.

"I'm Harry *fucking* Potter," he jokes.

"You are looking more like Gandalf by the day with that long beard and hair," I say, but loving how he wears it in a man bun now.

Chuckling, I look over at the house. I grab Owen's hand.

"You are an amazing man, Owen Brodie. And a hopeless romantic at heart."

"You bring out the best in me, Hotshot," he says with pride, and I can't stop staring at the man I want to spend the rest of my life with.

He lifts my hand and kisses my engagement ring before pulling me into his arms.

With his shovel sized hands, he cups my face tenderly and slants his mouth over mine, then whispers, "What did I do to deserve you?"

"Nothing, Owen."

"You like me just as I am."

"I do. Don't ever change."

Eighteen months later

The Cyprus sunset glows, coating the dark blue sea of the ocean in a blanket of warm orange hue.

Twinkling as the sun flirts with the waves, my long cream dress drags lightly over the shingle beach, making the pebbles clink softly together, creating their own tune as they sing in time with the fizzing of the water along the shore.

My body humming with blissful happiness, I hold on to my mom's hand as I walk down the beach toward my handsome husband to be as Poppy skips happily in front of us in her cream flower girl's dress embroidered in poppies.

Our little Pop-a-doodle.

"Daddy." She squeals with glee, too excited to wait, she closes the distance, running into Owen's arms; the man she idolizes and adores. Having never mentioned calling

Owen Daddy, Poppy took it upon herself to brand him as hers.

Loving us the way he does has been life changing.

Wearing a blindfold, he hand delivered possibly the best wedding present this morning; the official adoption certificate confirming he's now officially Poppy's father. Something Michael agreed to so easily it made my heart hurt and it's something I will never understand.

Owen deserves that little girl's love more than any man. She is his now and I couldn't be more happy.

Much like the stunts I performed in my aerobatic routine, moving at the speed of light, in less than two years, Owen and I turned our lives around three hundred and sixty degrees.

Calling it a whirlwind would be an understatement.

We've moved to Scotland, my mom, and Aunt Babs following shortly after. I've been a witness in a court case for my plane crash, which led to an eighteen-year prison sentence for Cobra and something I never want to speak of ever again.

My memory never did return, and I am relieved it didn't.

It's better locked away in the filing cabinet of *things I can't remember*. Completely unfazed I flew a plane without a second thought once I was given the all clear and our flying school is thriving.

Owen and I watched the news unravel of Gideon and Richard's demise following an anonymous tip off to police leading them to a trail of emails and evidence of their involvement in the death of Owen and Camilla's parents, contraband tobacco and alcohol as well as drugs and arms, and the most heinous of all, photographic evidence of their human trafficking profiteering.

Owen never revealed to me where Camilla ran off to, but he assures me she is safe, which is the most important thing of all.

Following those life changing events, I left the Air Force; we opened a flying school and outdoor adventure facility just like Owen planned. We remodeled our new home, joining the two homes to become one, and to top it all off, we welcomed a beautiful baby boy, who we named Atlas, into the world. His Greek name, meaning *to endure*, was perfectly fitting for our miracle baby, who was conceived in our special place and then survived a plane crash.

Our friends were right when they put a bet on what he would look like. Big blue eyes and strawberry blond locks. He's a picture of innocence but is a cheeky little monkey who is head-strong and hot headed.

I don't know who he takes after more, me or his daddy.

I think it's more likely to be me.

Cyprus. Our special place. The place where Owen and I began our journey.

The island of love. The birthplace of Aphrodite and the place where Owen stole my heart.

A curious twist of fate perhaps that brought us together, but I suspect, as I look at the rock of Aphrodite, she planned this all along.

We were always meant to find one another; of this, I am certain.

My smile broadens as I reach him.

Kissing my mom on her cheek, passing Blake my bouquet filled with red, gold, and green flowers, I turn to face my strong man. The man who did all he could to save me and who looks after me, Poppy and Atlas like we are the most precious gems on planet earth.

Surrounded by our closest friends and family, we recite our vows, making promises to one another that will bond us together for life.

As his eyes pierce mine, it's an easy ask. I give myself to him willingly, with or without a piece of paper to bind us together.

My heart is his and always will be.

Owen

We have everything we've ever wanted.

A beautiful beach house we call home where we watch the sun set and rise every day. And at night, as soon as the kids are asleep, we sit out on the decking at the front and watch the moon play with the sea which we've been tempted to skinny dip in several times but are too scared to brave the freezing North Sea temperatures of winter.

The business, our family, and friends, our life couldn't be more perfect.

Like now, as she twists her neck and brushes her lips against mine, she's perfection personified.

"You belong to me." From behind, I slide my cock in and out of Jade's wet pussy as I dig my fingers into her hips deep enough to leave my bruising fingerprints behind.

Love drunk, arching her neck, panting, she agrees, "I do."

Our wedding was incredible. Sunshine, friends, family, love and, of course, as it should always be, I got to wear a kilt on my wedding day. I'm a true Scotsman; no boxers.

Which was perfect for what I had planned as I pulled

her up to our honeymoon suite before the reception dinner and speeches.

Holding onto the edge of the dressing table, we lock eyes in the mirror in front of us. No words needed. I thrust my hips quicker as we chase our release, officially consummating our marriage.

Her orgasm bursts through her as I rub her clit, sending her into orbit, taking me with her.

"Fuck, Hotshot." Breathless, I kiss her bare shoulder, then lay my forehead against it as I come hard and spill my release inside of her.

I glance up to look at her. The sight of her beauty has my heart soaring in my chest.

"I hope we made another Greek baby." I slide my cock out of her and slowly turn her around to face me.

"Another one?" She pops a brow when I place my hands on her hips.

"We need a complete flying team." I'm not joking, I want a big family who love each other and tell one another daily. Where hugging is a way of life and is a crime if not carried out.

"We need a bigger house for that." She giggles, as I pull her smooth as butter, silk dress down her hips.

I lift her chin with my knuckle. "I would do anything for you."

She nods in agreement; she knows I would pull the moon out of the sky for her if I could.

Crashing her lips to mine, as if wanting to climb inside my body, because close is never close enough, she whispers, "I love you."

We have love.

So much of it.

"I love you too, Hotshot. Much more than you can ever imagine."

She smiles against my mouth. "More than all the clouds in the sky?"

"Affirmative," I answer in air traffic lingo, making her chuckle.

I kiss her again, losing myself in this incredible woman who entered my life like a speeding jet plane, sending me sky-high, and who ultimately turned out to be the luckiest charm of them all.

She's my fate.

My destiny.

My goddess.

She's more than I could have asked for and more.

My kismet.

She's my Hotshot.

My everything.

And she likes me just as I am.

THE END

EPILOGUE

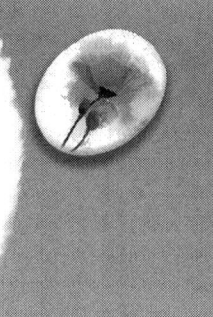

Owen – One Year Later

"Are you ready?" Jade's crackling voice sounds through my aviation headphones.

"Sure." Looking down at the beach below, my nerves get the better of me when I say, "Are you sure this is safe?"

"Absolutely." Her voice is excitable and I'm pretty fucking sure she's enjoying the torture that is yet to begin.

Since we opened the flying school, she's been desperate to get me into the two-seater stunt plane she teaches extreme aerobatics in. Students and thrill seekers travel for miles around to fly with Jade.

It draws crowds of spectators; they line the pier most days, turning up in droves at the weekend to watch her perform stunts in the sky above the waters of Castleview.

Our website uses the word *extreme* as a gauge to describe the experience. Now thinking about it, as I'm suited up, headphones and microphone in place, I want to get out as sweat soaks through my clothing and mild panic takes over my body.

Having just taken off and zooming through the skies

above Castleview Cove, I've never minded flying with Jade before, but the stunts are something that have always scared me and I have never let her perform them with me in the plane until now. She convinced me it's the best feeling in the world, telling me, *"You'll want to do it over and over again."*

In a moment of weakness, I agreed. Only now am I regretting my decision; I turn green on roller coasters so why the hell did I think this was a good idea? However, it's too late to change my mind as she says, "Here we go."

The noisy Extra 300 aircraft flips upside down and I can't control the scream that leaves my throat as the landscape I'm now viewing is upside down. I push my arms out to the side as if the edges of the plane will help me, but they won't.

Flipping us back round, I sigh with relief, but it's short lived as Jade sends the plane soaring vertically, making me scream again. "Slow down. Oh my God, you're trying to kill me," I shout, which makes Jade laugh.

"We are only pulling speeds of two hundred miles an hour. You sound like a girl when you scream."

"Two hundred? I think I'm going to be sick."

"Big baby," she mutters, her tone full of humor. "The next move is brilliant. You're going to love it," she informs me through my headset, as she keeps the plane in the vertical position.

"Hey, no name calling, Hotshot, and why the fuck are we not flying the right way up?" I shout down the microphone, still bracing myself on either side of the plane.

"Here we go again." The excitement and joy in her voice makes me feel uneasy.

Her mission in life is to go as fast as possible and to kill me, I'm sure of it.

Jade maneuvers the small plane, which sounds like an angry hive of honeybees, from its soaring position into a nosedive within milliseconds as she flips the plane, making it do a loop, then dive bombs at breakneck speed in a downward position.

Clambering in my seat, my harness and the speed we're traveling pin me in place, as I scream to the point I might lose my voice, my eyes bugging out, and I'm pretty sure my bowels might explode. My life flashes before my eyes as we hurtle to the ground, nose first, into the waves of Castleview Cove, seemingly flying faster than before.

"Holy shiittttttt," I yell as I imagine fish eating me, when we crash and I vanish forever. Then at the last minute, Jade pulls the stick controller up, shifting us from vertical to horizontal at the speed of lightning, and we are skimming the surface of the water.

"Wooooooo hooooooo," Jade whoops with joy.

Sweat dripping off my entire body, feeling like I am about to vomit, I whisper, "I think I shit myself."

From the pilot position in front of me, Jade throws her head back with laughter. "You okay?"

Mopping my brow, my stomach lurches and I have to cover my mouth to hold back the vomit that threatens to explode around us.

"Landing now," Jade says calmly.

"I hate you right now," I belch.

"Sick bags are on the left." The tires of the plane bump a few times as we land, and my stomach muscles spasm as I reach for the sick bag and spew into it, retching and coughing.

"You'll be fine in an hour," Jade says calmly as the plane stops and she unbuckles herself once she's done her safety checks.

Eventually, on shaky legs, she coaxes me out of the plane.

"You look gray." Lincoln laughs when he sees me, pointing, informing Atlas I didn't enjoy the flight.

"More like green, what do you think, Poppy?" Jacob counters, laughing with Poppy by his side.

Before I can reply, their faces become a blur, and I pass out.

"So, no more flying for you then?" Jade sticks a giant piece of halloumi into her mouth, smiling wickedly as she chews, casually leaning back in her chair.

We are having a barbecue with all our friends and family on the airfield. Something we try to do once a month.

I stomp my feet on the ground. "I'll stay here. Thank you very much." I hold my stomach from the movement. Three hours have passed, and I still can't eat anything.

"Your wife is a daredevil." Lincoln punches me on the shoulder.

"She's the devil." I narrow my eyes and stare across at where she is seated which only makes her stick her tongue out at me. "Mature of you." I nod and hide a smirk.

This woman will be the death of me.

What a way to go, death by daredevil.

My Hotshot.

Jade pulls herself out of her outdoor chair and makes her way to me. Sitting down on my lap, she cups my face. "Are you okay?" Worry lines her forehead, her lines deepening around the outer edges of her eyes.

"I'm better now." I move in for a kiss, but she covers my mouth with her hand.

"Did you brush your teeth?"

With her hand still over my mouth, I nod and her lips are on mine in seconds as she gives me a chaste kiss. "I love you." I will never grow tired of hearing her say those words.

"Are you after my life insurance money? Is that why you tried to kill me today?" I pinch her ass and throw her a wink.

She tilts her head, thinking for a moment before she answers. "Nope. I was genuinely trying to make you vomit." Her face serious, I know she's telling the truth.

Poppy appears by my side. "She did it on purpose, Daddy." She tattle tales, looking a picture of innocence today with her pig tails and rosy cheeks.

"She did." I lean down and whisper in her ear, "Do you think we should get her back for making Daddy turn the color of Shrek?"

Poppy's eyes light up and at the top of her little voice she shouts, "Water fight!"

Jade leaps off my lap as does everyone else and within minutes, Jade's mom and aunt are running about screaming and shouting with the water guns we use as part of the adventure events. As are Lincoln and Jacob, with Poppy on backup, as Violet attacks me with the biggest water soaker, the bazooka.

Pregnant with her second child, Skye disappears inside the hangar with the little ones to fetch the smaller water pistols for Aurora and Atlas.

It's complete mayhem, and I don't stand a chance against Violet when Jade teams up with her and chases me halfway down the airfield.

Running backward, I look around at my friends, my

aunt, uncle, and Gregor, as well as my newfound family and know that this is how it should always have been.

I created my own legacy; one filled with love, laughter, and my happy ever after.

IN CASE YOU HAVEN'T READ THE OTHER BOOKS IN THE BOYS OF CASTLEVIEW COVE SERIES

Lincoln's Story (Book 1): mybook.to/LincolnVHNicolson
Jacob's Story (Book 2): mybook.to/Jacob_VHNicolson

ALSO BY VH NICOLSON

The Triple Trouble Series

Hunting Eden - The Triple Trouble Series (Book 1): mybook.to/huntingeden_VHNicolson

Inevitable Ella - The Triple Trouble Series (Book 2): mybook.to/inevitableella_VHN

Unexpected Eva - The Triple Trouble Series (Book 3): mybook.to/unexpectedeva

The Boys of Castleview Cove

Lincoln - The Boys of Castleview Cove (Book 1): mybook.to/LincolnVHNicolson

Jacob - The Boys of Castleview Cove (Book 2): mybook.to/Jacob_VHNicolson

Owen - The Boys of Castleview Cove (Book 3): mybook.to/OwenVHNicolson

Frozen Flames (A Rekindled Ice Hockey Romance)
Preorder: mybook.to/FrozenFlames_VHN

ACKNOWLEDGMENTS

Can you believe it? We made it! The last book in The Boys of Castleview Cove Series. I am so sad to be leaving my beautiful boys, now men, and their beautiful, strong and funny women behind, as well as their quaint seaside town, too.

It's been a whirlwind and a half that's for sure and I really hope you loved reading Owen and Jade's love story. I took longer to write this book than any other book before, but I genuinely believe that my characters were both just waiting for the right moment to tell me their story, and for me to write it the way they wanted me to.

As an ex-military wife myself, their story took me back to Cyprus; the place my husband and I were posted for almost five years.

Those years are full of happy memories and I loved diving into that glorious country again.

This book was a labor of love for me but without the support network I find myself surrounded by, none of it would be possible.

To my husband, Paul, who continues to feed me never-ending words of encouragement, thank you. I couldn't do this without you, babes.

A huge THANK YOU to Sarah, my editor at The Word Emporium. Your sidenotes always fill me with joy and I love how much you push me to be a better writer. I'm still learning!

To Nicki, my new alpha reader... you swept me off my feet with your dedication to Owen and Jade's story. Your feedback, notes, emails and lovely messages have filled me with so much joy and there are no words to show you how grateful I am. I swear fate brought us together and you will never get rid of me now!

To Lizzy, my beautiful alpha reader from across the pond. From your incredible development suggestions to your intricate edits, your passion for my books doesn't go unnoticed. I cannot thank you enough for being in my world.

I want to say a big thank you to my military friends who helped with some of the more finer details. While I spent years in the Air Force by my husband's side, I also worked within the Air Force as a civilian for many years, and there were some aspects of military life I needed help with. Thank you Neil (thanks for answering my many MANY questions), Sally (for your air traffic control expertise), and David (for your officer training information). I am forever grateful. Especially to Sally, who was my next door neighbor in Cyprus and always made sure I ate when my hubby was deployed for months at a time and for turning up on my doorstep during yet another power cut to make sure I had enough candles - I will never forget your kindness.

To all of the book bloggers, bookstagrammers and booktokers, a huge thank you for all of your support and the beautiful graphics and videos you create, every day you blow me away.

I want to send a special heartfelt thank you to TL Swan. I can't believe this is the sixth book I have written. Without your guidance and support, I know without shadow of a doubt I would never have put fingertips to keyboard. You changed my life over lockdown. Thanks Tee.

And to you, the spicy book reader, I write because you keep me going and I can not thank you enough for taking a leap of faith on a new-ish indie author, and continuing to support my author journey. You have no idea how much that means to me, I am eternally grateful and without you, I wouldn't keep following my dream of becoming a full-time author. THANK YOU! Mwah x

ABOUT THE AUTHOR

Since writing her first contemporary romance novel over lockdown, Vicki is now completely smitten with writing love stories with happily ever afters. VH Nicolson was born and raised along the breathtaking coastline in North East Fife in Scotland. For more than two decades she's worked throughout the UK and abroad within the creative marketing and design industry, as a branding strategist and stylist, editor of a magazine and sub-editor of a newspaper. Married to her soul mate, they have one son. She has a weakness for buying too many quirky sparkly jumpers, eating Belgium buns, and walking the endless beaches that surround her beautiful Scottish hometown she's now moved back to.

Website: vhnicolsonauthor.com
Facebook Group:
bit.ly/VHNicolsonFacebookReaderGroup

Printed in Poland
by Amazon Fulfillment
Poland Sp. z o.o., Wrocław